A NOVEL OF THE ANARCHY

TOXICITY

ANDY REMIC

SOLARIS

First published 2012 by Solaris
an imprint of Rebellion Publishing Ltd,
Riverside House, Osney Mead,
Oxford, OX2 0ES, UK

www.solarisbooks.com

ISBN: 978 1 78108 004 7

10 9 8 7 6 5 4 3 2 1

A CIP catalogue record for this book is available from the
British Library.

Designed & typeset by Rebellion Publishing

Printed in the US

AUTHOR'S NOTE

There's a dirty great stinking nasty evil organisation at the core of this novel, called GREENSTAR. After researching various similarly-named organisations in a rancid effort to divert future accusations of defamation and slander, I can safely conclude that *my* GREENSTAR is *not* based on *any* of those companies sharing the same name... unless, of course, one (or several) of said companies begin to peddle in pollutants, heavy metals and toxic waste, and put their own stinking profits before the ecology of the planet – in which case, this novel *is* about them, and they can subsequently burn in Hell.

AND LO! The earth dries up, and dost wither,
the world languishes, and dost wither,
and the exalted rich posh dudes of the earth
languish!
The earth is defiled by its people dudes;
they have disobeyed the nine toxic laws,
violated the statutes and nature and
broken the everlasting covenant.

AND LO! Therefore a curse consumes the earth.
The new wine dosteth dry up, and the vine withers;
and all the merrymakers do groan from fat aching
bellies.
The gaiety of the gay tambourines is stilled,
the noise of the puking reveller dudes hast stopped,
the joyful harp is – LO! – silent.
No longer do they drinky drink wine with a merry
song;
the beer is (lo!) bitter, to its drinkers.

AND THUS! A curse dost consumeth the earth.
And its people must bear their guilt.

NEW ISAIAH 24:4-6
The Revised & Rewritten Testament
BIBLE II: THE REMIX *[Manna Edition]*

PROLOGUE

RENAZZI LODE, DIRECTOR of the Greenstar Recycling Company, stood on a barren, scorched heath and surveyed The Lirridium Store. A lake of concentrated shuttle fuel, it spread away in a glittering flat platter, still and silver like glass over mercury. Renazzi turned, and with one finger touched the comm at her ear. She surveyed the prisoners, who were cuffed and on their knees, without emotion. Behind them stood fifty Greenstar soldiers wearing olive-green uniforms and bearing the flash of gold on their berets which was the mark of The Company.

The captured, once members of a nearby village clan, had made the choice decades earlier not to leave the planet of Amaranth when Greenstar moved in to begin its new Recycling Policy. Over the years, many of these unfortunates had been *altered* by the severe toxic waste pumped into the water table, into the air and into the soil. Now, they were a sorry bunch of twisted deformations, kneeling, and drooling, and twitching.

And Company Policy?

Renazzi smiled, a narrow, tight-lipped smile. She signalled the soldiers, who drew short black swords.

They could not use bullets here; it might ignite the unrefined lirridium. What, then, would the Shamans of Manna use to fuel their starships?

"Are you sure?" she said into the comm, lips hardly moving, words little more than a murmur.

"Yes. Do it." An instruction. Hell, a *command*.

She paused a pause bordering on insubordination. "There are women. And children."

"So? They need to learn."

Renazzi gave the signal, and fifty swords cut down, followed by the dull slaps of bodies hit the ground. Renazzi watched blood soaking into the toxic soil, returning to the earth; earth to earth, ashes to ashes, dust to dust. She clicked her fingers, and a Z-chopper was there in an instant. She climbed aboard, and it soared into the smoke-stacked, pollutant-overloaded sky.

IT WAS NIGHT. A green-tinged Amaranth night.

Renazzi stood barefoot on the thick glass carpet of the Director's Office, which occupied the entire top floor of the Greenstar Factory Hub. It was a vast space, with massive plate-glass walls overlooking the subordinate factories around them. Her vision was filled with a manic bustle of activity: chimneys belching sulphur and smoke, men scurrying like ants, pipes vibrating with full lirridium payloads, shuttles loading and unloading, cranes and trucks working and roaring and churning mud, fumes spilling out, engines drooling black oil.

Behind her, a voice said, "She *will* come back to us. I know she will."

"Yes." Renazzi lit a thin cigarette and smoked. Her eyes watched the constant activity, searching for error. She was neat like that. Pedantic and anal. "But... I fear you will regret it when she does."

"Nonsense! It is ordained. You said so yourself. Those fucking psi-children predicted the event. The outcome."

"Yes. Only *their* prediction was... more than just a simple visit."

The male voice laughed, a deep rich sound. He moved forward, placed large hands on Renazzi's shoulders and gazed out over Amaranth. "You put too much faith in these toxic freaks. You know, if the Shamans heard you talking like this... Well. We'd *both* be dead."

"The Shamans are *machines,*" she snapped. "Floating like lords through Manna in their vast derelict battle ships. They seek to control us by intrigue and diplomacy. Sometimes, as today, there is a need for violence; although I do not agree with murdering children." Her voice was iron. Then she sighed, and broke. She was a woman without choice. "However. I recognise that with certain primitive peoples, it is all they understand."

"Primitive?" He raised an eyebrow, but she did not see. "So you believe in love over violence? Forgiveness over revenge?"

"No," said Renazzi carefully, watching the ten-lane freeway. It was full of digging and mining equipment. Huge machines with buckets and drills, hammers and hydraulic pistons. Many were as big as a hotel, and they lumbered down the freeway with lights blazing, lirridium engines pouring out streams of pollutant to fill the skies over Amaranth – over what the media had christened *Toxicity* – with even more filth and poison and death.

"That's a great shame," said the man, turning Renazzi around. He kissed her, then, but her face did not change. Renazzi did not have emotions; or if she did, they were buried in a deep, dark, key-locked place. Emotion was something that happened to other, weaker, people.

As he kissed her neck, she said, "The world can only take so much waste. If we continue, we *will* destabilise the environment with a toxic overload; and the Shamans would be... displeased. They like to maintain an equilibrium. We are getting too large, my love. Greenstar is becoming too powerful."

"Fuck the equilibrium," he said, pulling away, his dark, glittering eyes staring at her. "Look out there! At what we've achieved! Look at our wealth! Our power! We will go to war against the Shamans if necessary... We will bring back a natural order of chaos. We are flesh, not machines. We cannot be controlled. We cannot be defined with binary code. We don't want everything nice and cosy. We want random deaths. We want agony. We want war!" He smiled. "Because *that* is life. That is chaos. That's reality, my love."

Renazzi pulled back and gazed up into his face. "The psi-children. You recognise they are a very real danger to Greenstar? To everything we have built, or fought to destroy?"

The man turned away, waving his hand and reaching for a drink. "Go on, then. Hunt them down. Kill them all. I know this prophecy frightens you."

"I do not need to hunt them down," said Renazzi. And now it was her turn to smile. Her turn to narrow glittering, malevolent eyes. "The psi-children are a part of this place; integral to the planet of Amaranth. I will not need to hunt them down because... because *they* will come to *me*. In time. You will see."

Outside, three thousand Terraform-Class Excavators rumbled on.

ONE

ALL HE REMEMBERED was the heat. A searing inferno. And screaming. *Lots* of screaming...

ENGINES HUMMED. MACHINES whined. Against the folded velvet of deep space, where neutron stars glowed and red dwarfs died, where nebula clouds oscillated in coruscating waves of pulsating colour and fire and energy and exploded heavy metals, it slammed suddenly into existence – from nothing to something, from Cable Jump to Stationhalt, from snakehole to freedom in the blink of a blink of an eye. It hung there, solid, a mammoth ship in the shape of a bulbous, fattened donut, polished alloys and steels gleaming under the rays from a nearby green star. In discreet letters stencilled on the hull, the ship's name read: *The Literati*.

Svoolzard Koolimax XXIV, Third Earl of Apobos, lay back, naked, oiled, pleasured and fulfilled, sipping from a ruby-skin goblet of honeyed *titakya* as the mercury bed beneath his languishing, pampered shell massaged his hard, fatigued muscles, and two furry gahungas rubbed his feet with expert tentacle-pods. "Ooh," he said, closing his eyes to the rhythms of ecstasy. "Yes, just there. Between the toes. *Purrrfect.*" His head lolled to the right, mouth gaping open and slack for a moment, drooling titakya like a SLAP smuggler as he stared through the kilometre-wide portal at the glowing, throbbing words splashed green from the light of the sun:

TOXICITY WELCOMES
ALL
YOUR SHIT

"Oh!" he gurgled, managing to begin to rouse himself. There was surprise there. And a glimmer of interest. "Are we there already? I didn't hear the back-drives kick in."

"We slipped the snakehole an hour ago," crooned Lumar, reaching forward to snort kulka powder from her own flat, green belly. She, too, was naked; lizard-skinned, she was one of Svoolzard's thirteen resident mistresses on the Titan-Class Culture Cruiser, *The Literati.*

Svool held out his goblet. "Lumar. Here, girl. More wine."

"Yes, Svool, my master."

She poured him more wine, keeping her gaze averted low.

"Lumar! More nibbles!"

"Of course, silly me, more nibbles, Svool. Of course. Right away." She crossed to a fireslab table and picked up the bowl of nibbles, returned, and leant over him, popping them into his mouth one by one by one. After all, she wouldn't want his *genius* over-exerting, pointlessly expended on having to actually *stretch* for a nibble.

Svoolzard frowned, and stared at the words outside, chewing and popping the nibbles between his teeth; then he rubbed drug-weary eyes – although only after considering asking Lumar to do it.

Svool sighed. *Oh, I'm too thoughtful,* he thought, idly.

He felt suddenly and strangely exhausted – which was odd, because for the last three weeks he'd done nothing but snort drugs, drink kemog-wine and pleasure his many women, two men and this creature, Lumar, a lizard-skinned alien from Thung who was blood-sworn to serve him until she died. Or so it said in the paperwork. Very... *interesting.*

Outside the ship's portal, the three-thousand-kilometre-high hydrogen-strand fusion-sign bubble-bobbed on streams of diffusing hydrogen, against the pin-prickled twinkling velvet blanket of the Manna Galaxy. Its molecule-tether was a looping, curving, shining silver umbilical which spun away, down, down to the distant, vast lumbering spin of Amaranth far below.

Amaranth.

The waste world. The *toxic* world. Streetwise citywide slang and drug-fuelled paparazzi called it *Toxicity.* Home and bedrock to all of Manna's decadence and waste and effluence; and that didn't just include the shit they chose to dump there.

Intrigued by his new train of thought, Svool hoisted himself onto one elbow, which took a lot out of him for it was *physical effort* for sure, and Svool would rather not *do* physical effort. The action made him whimper a little, as he brushed away an errant golden curl from his forehead.

He dismissed the massaging gahungas with a lazy flap of his bejewelled fingers, his feet not completely satisfied, and the funny little creatures waddled off, trailing long brown hair. Svool sipped his drink, keeping the drugs in his veins alive and bubbling, and stared at the sweeping vista of the vast world below. "It looks..."

"Yes?" Lumar's head snapped up, short green dreadlocks swaying. Her bright green eyes narrowed, nostrils twitching at her sudden narcotic intake.

"Looks like the sort of place I should *write a poem* about."

Svoolzard Koolimax XXIV was a celebrated poet across the whole of the Manna Galaxy, that vast unity of universes which formed the Collective. In fact, he was probably the most famous and celebrated poet who had ever lived. He was certainly the wealthiest. The most talked about. The most *revered*.

"*Lo! Yonder green and pleasant star*," he began, brow furrowing a little at the effort of composition, and watched as Lumar settled back on her cushions, forked tongue licking her black lips, her hands folding over her lizard breasts as a display of rapturous ecstasy crossed her features. After all, it wasn't *every day* a lowly norm, a prole, a liz or dwat got to observe a *genius* in the act of Poetic Synergy.

"Oh, how I wonder what ye are,
Is thine lone eye all green and round,
O'erlookin' every mollusc on the ground?"

Svoolzard gave a little shiver, and opened his eyes, which had closed in this fabulous moment of rapturous ecstasy. To Svool, nothing beat the act of composition. The act of fucking *creation,* baby. *Creation.* To Svool, it was better than drugs, sex and money – all rolled into one. There could be no greater achievement. No superior satisfaction. No greater... worth.

"Magical," purred Lumar.

Svool extended one hand toward her as his chin tilted upwards, eyes closed, golden curls spreading down his chest. Lumar took his hand and kissed his fingers and their jewels.

"I *am* the Poet Master," he said, without irony.

"You are," crooned Lumar, nodding, green eyes gleaming.

"Kiss me again."

She kissed his hand again.

"Still. Despite the obvious enjoyment in this little endeavour, in these little sexual buzzes of electricity, we are here, now, at Amaranth, and it is time to deliver my speech. Do you still feel that my words – my ideas – my writing – buzzes with the electric of a billion different stars?"

"Oh, I do," said Lumar, sucking his fingers, her forked tongue a sultry and enticing thing. Her face beamed up at him. She was glowing. In awe.

"Does my monologue sparkle like starbeams from the hull of the *New Pink Titanic*? Is my wordage suitably academic in nature to please even the most nihilistic of today's gathered post-grad researchers? Hmm?"

"Svool," she mumbled, sucking his digits most erotically as her hand roved over his naked belly, stroking, and nipping, and kneading, "you are without shadow of a doubt, the most educated, the most daring, the most inspired and the most brilliantly genius writer *ever* to crawl from the womb of a human. When you enter Tennyson Hall, you will see; they will worship you as the God you are! When you enter Tennyson Hall, it will be like the perfect sexual climax of every man and woman and alien there present!"

"Yes, yes. Of course, of course." He ran a hand through his curls, leaving a V through the thick wax, as Lumar's hand strayed like a green spider across his belly and began a teasing taunting crawl towards his bulging HotShorts. Poetry always made him hard.

Lumar's eyes met his. Her tongue flickered in that teasing way he knew and loved. He imagined it, flickering over him... and shivered.

Lumar winked. "Have we time for another...?"

"No!" Suddenly, Svoolzard's eyes were hard like flint, and he gently pushed her hand away. "I am a... professional! I must prepare..." – he licked wet, panting lips, and again his eyes went distant, and hazy – "for my fans."

THE TENNYSON HALL of the *The Literati* was a truly grand affair. A kilometre-high cube, its walls were lined with tumbling gold and blood-red fabrics, the ceiling lights vast green globes in honour of the planet around which they now weighed anchor, and the floor surface had been specially constructed for this wonderful, opulent, magical occasion, tiled with specially-hardened pages taken from the self-published pamphlets of *lesser* poets. Never one to miss an opportunity to bask in the glory of his own genius, Svool was the first (and most vocal) to recognise his superiority to every other living (and, debatably, dead) novelist, playwright and poet in the long, long history of Humanity.

Gathered around the many tables on hollow stools, made of green glowing glass and filled with the finest of tolka wines (so all one had to do was dip one's Drinko-Straw™ between one's own legs to savour the fine green liquid and, as had been pointed out by Svool in his opening speech, thus precipitate a vision of near-circulatory catheterisation which required only one more tube and a little imagination, a-ha-haha) were the *crème de la crème* of Old Earth's resident academic royalty. Thousands of people were present; most of the educated and most-respected academic brilliance of Manna, the Galaxy which had first *consumed* and then *elevated* Earth to its rank as one of the Prime Planets sporting life. Earth was recognised as a Seat of Power for the Arts in Manna, and here on this Culture Cruise, the gathered Who's Who of the arts had been brought together (in fact, had paid extortionate fees from university coffers just to be included) in order to *meet* and *celebrate* Svoolzard Koolimax XXIV. The fact Svool was about to narrate for the first time his no-doubt incredibly ground-breaking paper, *On Literature*, which obviously would celebrate himself above all others, was simply an added bonus.

There was an excited buzz around Tennyson Hall. Males and females from every primary species wore their finest outfits, their most glittering of jewels, their greatest displays of wealth and culture and sophistication. Tall flutes of janga juice were sipped from jewelled kalka rat skulls, and most sophisticates gathered, nibbling on dog-da balls, whilst chatting politely (the consequence of a prescribed seating plan). The hall was alive with wonder, and as the lights suddenly dimmed, so the ruckus receded to a white noise of hushed expectation.

By the edge of the stage, visible to anybody willing to look, fluttered a small black PopBot. This was Zoot. Zoot was Svool's PR bot, agent, manager, bodyguard and, dare he say it with a digital blush, *friend*. Zoot made sure good things happened to Svool. All. The. Time.

And Zoot made sure jealous lesser poets didn't hack off his master's head with a blunt axe.

Zoot's deep, resonant voice spoke:

"And lo! To humanity was born the greatest writer of not just This Age, but of Every Age. From the delicate position of just one year old he wielded a pen like a sword, wrote his first novel at the age of four, won his first global prize aged six, and the Manna Galactic Trophy for Contributions to Galactic Literature aged *only thirteen*. No human, no gahunga, no falfa, no bozra has contributed more to the realms of literature than Svoolzard Koolimax XXIV." Zoot's voice had to pause as a roar went up, and every person in the room stood, some knocking over their glugging stools, and clapped with a thunderous round of applause – enough to raise the ceiling, in fact. "I now bring you, the Man Himself!"

Onto the stage strode Svoolzard Koolimax XXIV.

Everybody cheered and waved!

The skilfully manipulated lights picked out Svool's best features. His proud, strong, utterly handsome face. His long, golden, curled hair which bobbed all the way to his shoulders. His hands were manicured, nails painted in delicate rainbows of colour. His lips were glossy, his eyes lined with black. He looked at the same time powerful, and brooding, and sexy; he oozed charisma more than a ten-week-septic wound oozes pus. He wore an incredible glass and diamond suit that left nothing and everything to the imagination. It tinkled softly as he walked, like shell windchimes in a cool Japachinese garden by the ocean. Yes, the glass in the suit showed off his muscular ass, but this was counter-acted by the diamond shards, which diffracted light and made the sensuous bunching of muscles alluring rather than crass. Yes, the glass in the suit showed off his hairy masculine chest, whereas the diamond shards somehow *softened* the effect and showed that Svool had a delicate, feminine side open to conversation, and empathy, and understanding, and discussion rather than sheer testosterone-fuelled animal fucking. And yes, the glass laid on display for all to see Svool's hefty, well-used, but always-up-for-the-job cock, subtly diffracted by the shards to give it a more subtle and charming appearance. Or that's what the suit's manufacturers said on the tin.

Svool strode forward, waving his hands in mock humility whilst at the same time nodding in knowing approval at the recognition of the greatness of his genius. His dark brooding eyes surveyed the best of the best arraigned before him, paying worship and accolade to, hell, *him*, the best of the best, the elite of the elite. The God of Literature, no less.

"Behold," came the deep voice once again, "Svoolzard Koolimax XXIV, Third Earl of Apobos, poet, swashbuckler" – Svool placed a hand on the hilt of his dazzling jewelled sword, grinning at this introduction – "and *bon viveur*, here for your delectation and appreciation as Guest of Honour on this wonderful Masters Cruise to end all cruises. In the future, ladies and gentlemen, people will look back at this moment in history and *weep* that they were not here present. Svoolzard is, as I am sure you are aware, a legend in the hallowed halls of poetic creation, in the art of verse and alliteration, in the dazzling creation of metaphor and pun; in terms of creating 'the novel,' he has been cited as main hero and inspiration for their own works by all *thousand* New York Times-bestselling authors across the entirety of the Manna Galaxy Bubble! If that isn't enough, Steven Speilberger, himself a galaxy-wide phenomenon and director of the unparalleled movie franchise *Space Hero With A Gun* has expressed an interest in making a movie of Svoolzard's life story so far – and is in the process of commissioning scripts from the finest script writers from across Manna (including Svool himself, of course, a-ha-haha). I give you: sexual athlete, comedy chef, genius extraordinaire, Svoolzard Koolimax XXIV!"

Tennyson Hall erupted in cheers and clapping, and Svool, one hand still draped casually over his jewelled sword, flapped his other hand as if holding a lace kerchief, and smiled, and winked, and bowed, and the noise rose and rose, bouncing and echoing around the massive hall as the gathered literati showed their massive appreciation.

Svool allowed the noise to continue, then gradually subside; after all, he had an ego to massage. Then he gave a little cough, and took a few steps forward in his black high-heeled glitter boots, which clacked on the ruby-marble stage.

"Hello, darlings," he crooned, and there came whistles from many voluptuous ladies at the back, and several voluptuous gentlemen at the front. "As you are aware, I have written the paper *On Literature,* which is to be the, shall we say, main event for the evening – as long as you don't factor in the awards ceremony, a-ha-ha." The audience laughed along with him, mesmerised by his genius and charm.

"But first, I would like to begin with a piece of poetry I composed this very morn'."

Svool coughed. He made a great show of waving his hands and settling himself into comfortable posture, ready for dramatic recital. He coughed again, a double cough with an over-the-top theatrical clearing of mucus. Then he fluttered eyelashes, which sparkled with diamond dust under cleverly placed spotlights; and in lilting voice dripping gilt, began to croon:

"Barefoot, she strolls through petals green,
And though I look, no doubt it seems
My eyes do stray to her
Bosom,
And petall'd bottom cheeks.

"However, I confess. Though clit
Did poke and peep

Betwixt lacy thong and
Sweating thigh,
She caught my eye,
And I did sigh,
And 'magined what a
Night would pass if only my
Face
Was buried in her
Ass."

The roar echoed around Tennyson Hall, a violent standing ovation filled with cheers and grunts and the clapping of trotters – as Svoolzard beamed around like a village idiot, and the noise masked the first of the sounds of shell impact.

Boom.

Boom *boom*.

Then came an unmistakable, and terrifying, deafening, rending tearing of twisted wrenching steel. More screams followed – this time, suddenly, of people – and there was a *whoosh* of superheated air pumped into Tennyson Hall with such violence that Svoolzard and half the audience were picked up and tossed like socks of wet mud across the stage, where they hit the wall in quick succession with a rat-a-tat-tat of breaking bones, like machine-gun fire. Svoolzard connected with a *krump*, folded, and on his way down hit a table and stools, breaking them into glass splinters with his body weight.

"What the *fu* –"

There came a crashing, smashing, thumping sound, and the world tipped suddenly upside down as gravity generators died. The lights went out, and in the darkness, surrounded by unconscious bodies, Svoolzard lay trembling, his burst lips leaking blood into his fear-dry mouth. Then he was thrown again, and in the chaos was struck many times by tumbling bodies. He screamed, screamed like a girl, and then back-up generators kicked in and sirens screamed as emergency injecto-units buzzed and hissed. The room was slammed full of expanding foam as *The Literati* lurched into emergency mode.

Externally, the great donut was spinning. Flames gushed silently to starboard as *The Literati* spun, propelled by the missile strike which had taken out its bulbous belly. And as the ship rolled like a harpooned whale, a dark ship could be seen beyond; long, and narrow, and sleek, the black of a collapsed star, no lights, no signs of life. And even as *The Literati* did one more belly roll, the dark ship lowered more missiles, which flared suddenly, fire scorching the ship's flanks as they ejected across the arched vaults of space... hitting *The Literati* again, and again, and again.

The dying, rolling Titan-Class Culture Cruiser, trailing kilometre-high walls of fire, dropped, and staggered, and dropped again until it was caught by the massive green planet's gravitational pull. *The Literati* was tugged closer, and with more engines failing, more power lost, the fight was suddenly lost and in a trail of fire and fumes and unburnt solar fuel, *The Literati* plummeted towards the unfolding green abyss of Amaranth far far below...

A TINY OLD man sat on a beach of crushed green bottles, cross-legged, chin on his steepled fingers. The ocean lapped at his feet. His eyes were darker than a pit full of serial killing souls, and he wore nothing but rags, rags stitched together from rags, a myriad of filthy merging colours and patterns, as if his entire wardrobe had been stitched from the tattered remnants of a shredded rat nest.

Above, the sky was dark. Stars glittered, reflected in the surging, rolling ocean. A moon hung in the sky, tinged green across part of its circumference.

Then there came a *flash*, bright fire flaring like some distant orange and blue firework burst. The flare died, but something was gleaming, moving fast, and *falling...*

The old man watched, eyes stoic, and shifted a little to the sounds of grinding, crunching glass. That his legs were not spaghetti strings of meat was a miracle. He fixed on the falling object, noting tiny bursts of flame as ancillary jets tried to correct its erratic descent. Parts of the ship glowed, and the old man narrowed his eyes as he realised the donut-shaped ship was, in fact, completely missing a huge section.

More flames burst free of the arcing ship, leaving bright patterns in the sky.

A distant, beautiful whining sang across the black oil ocean like the lovesong of a Siren.

And with an almighty *CRASH,* the old man watched the ship disappear into the midst of a rearing volcanic archipelago. A mushroom of fire and smoke erupted from among the rearing black mountains, and *booms* sang across the ocean, bouncing between walls of rock, singing back and forwards like the mating calls of a school of crazed whales.

The old man sat, watching, enjoying the breeze coming in off the ocean which, at length, brought with it a stench of fire. Gradually the flames died down and the night returned to some form of serenity.

He watched the thick, rising column of smoke, one edge spookily green from the reflected light of the Toxic World's distant, drifting sun.

SVOOLZARD GROANED AND did a slow, treacle-filled internal diagnostic check. Everything hurt. *Shit.*

Everything hurt *bad*. And for Svool, the worst thing about pain was that *it usually happened to somebody else*.

What happened? What hit me?

The last time he'd felt so rough was when he'd been bottled in a bar for being *The Most Sexy Man Who'd Ever Lived*. The jealousy of others was a constant in Svool's life, and he begrudgingly supposed he couldn't blame them. You know. *Them*. Commoners. Normal people. Scrotes. Peasants.

After all, Svool was so damned *perfect*.

Barefoot, she strolls through petals green,

And though I look...

Shit. Was the party that *good?*

He coughed, and spat out a lump of foam. Then he opened his eyes and everything was black, and he panicked, and questing fingers pushed into his own mouth as he scooped out more blobs of crash foam, and choked, and coughed and spat, and then reached up and scraped wads of sticky shit from his eyes. It trailed like gooey toffee in long umbilicals, and light flooded in.

Starlight, against a pink green horizon.

It was dawn...

Svool was lying on his belly, and his feet were wet.

How odd? Is it Champagne? Vajinga Juice? Or just the sexual effluvia from a hundred thankfully satiated women?

Svool rolled to his side, groaned, and pushed himself upright, groggy, coughing up more foam and phlegm, all mixed in with lumps of vomit and drug-slag.

"Oh, man," he groaned. He held his head in his hands, and then realised the entire world was filled with a weird hissing silence; a background of white noise that was far from normal. "That was some fucking party!" His own words sounded funny,

incredibly distant, muffled, and he realised his ears
were also full of foam.

Foam?

He dug a finger into each orifice and did his best to
pull out the sticky gunk.

Foam?

The sound of ocean came to him, hissing and surging
against a black rock beach. And redoubled pain hit Svool,
pain in every limb and joint and bone and organ. He
opened his mouth in silent shock as waves of pain rushed
over him, pummelling him with fists of battering iron.

"Ow," he managed, finally, and huddled into
a crouch, coughing and choking, eyes streaming,
ears throbbing, and fighting for a moment with the
awkwardness of his sword in its scabbard.

He could see the sea, a dark ocean, and across its
rolling expanse, other islands rearing from the inky
glass waves. He frowned, brow creasing under curled
golden locks.

*What's this? Some VR simulation room in the back
of a sexy lady's boudoir? Some game instigated by
remote electron wires inserted directly into my skull?*
He reached down, fingers touching brine-slick rock.
*After all, it feels like I'm here. Smells like the ocean.
The breeze is fresh on the flesh of my cheeks... I could
write a poem about this experience, write a poem
which I can deliver during my...*

He blinked.

Crash foam. His brain did a quick rewind. He
remembered alarms. And being thrown across the
Culture Cruiser's interior like a sack of useless shit.

"Oh." He blinked. "Oh, no."

Svoolzard scrambled to his feet, wincing as broken
shards from his glass and diamond suit cut into him.
"Ouch. Ouch. Oh, you little bastards!" A fresh ocean
breeze wafted past, hot with salt and stinging his eyes,

and he stared across the vastness of the ocean platter sitting before him.

Dawn broke, green tendrils pouring across the sky. The horizon cracked open like a rotten egg.

"Where am I?" murmured Svoolzard.

"On Toxicity," came a voice from behind him, a voice he knew well, filled with familiarity and attachment; it was a voice he loved and adored, and which he knew loved him. A grin cracked his face in two, showing perfect white teeth. Svool turned, and beamed down.

"Lumar! Am I glad to see you!"

"Hmm," she said, glinting green eyes fixed on him. The sun rose behind her, making her reptilian skin glow in a most incredibly beautiful fashion. The effect was not lost on Svoolzard, who was, it had to be said, a walking erection.

"Oh, yes!" he prattled, almost forgetting his pain and discomfort, and the fact that their starship had just crashed. "I was lying here on the rocks, pin-pricked by this damn cracked glass suit – which was not my choice, I think you'll both agree and understand – and wondering just how the hell I'd been party-shelled to such an extent that I no longer remembered the drugs and the girls and, of course, your fine vagina, dear Lumar" – he chuckled, and climbed down a few jagged black rocks towards her – "and I was starting to realise that we'd crashed, and of course, the *real* problem with that sort of thing is not having, y'know, your loyal and faithful *staff* around to take up the slack, to do the shit, you know, to perform those all-important *little things* that make life so worthwhile." He stopped, and started panting a little. The sun was rising fast, and the heat climbing, especially when magnified through a glass and diamond three-piece suit.

Smiling, he held out his hand to Lumar, palm down, fingers quivering.

She looked down at the long, tapered fingers, the nails painted with magnificent scenes. Not so long ago, Lumar had sucked those fingers and made murmuring sounds of pleasure. Now, she stared at them, and then, very slowly, lifted her green lizard eyes to stare unblinking at Svoolzard.

"Yes?" she said, voice made modestly sibilant by her forked tongue.

"You may kiss the hand of your master," he said regally, lifting his chin a little and, for the first time, noticing the jungle beyond. It twittered and warbled, now the sun was up, and steam was rising from dense foliage. But there was something *not quite right* with the vision across the green rocky beach.

"Really?" She raised an eyebrow, stepped in close, and delivered a beautifully well-balanced right hook that rattled loose three teeth and dropped Svool to his rump as if poleaxed.

"Gnk," said Svool, as Lumar loomed over him.

"*That* is for being a *cunt!*" she snarled, and Svoolzard recoiled from the pure animal hatred in her eyes, in her face, in her spittle, and then he watched her whirl about and head off across the green pebbles, which crunched in a strangely musical way.

Svool sat, rubbing his jaw, a billion stars of confusion fluttering like escaped butterflies in his mind. *What? Why? Where? Who? What? I... I just don't understand.* And truly, he did not.

Wincing as shards from his suit dug into buttocks and thighs and biceps – the suit was getting worse; more fractured by the minute – he pushed himself to his feet and spat blood on the rocks.

"Wow," he said, frowning. He watched Lumar clamber up more distant rocks and stare off across the ocean, shading her eyes with her hand.

Svool looked around himself. There was nobody else visible. No people. No animals. No servants. No wine. No cunnizinga liquor. No SLAP-snort. No ship. *Oh shit, no ship.*

Svool climbed down from his rock and started off after Lumar, hobbling a little in his glossy high-heeled boots, hand on the hilt of his jewelled sword. All the while he was shaking his head, and wondering what the hell had swayed his Mistress and turned her Massive Love against him. *It must be a serious concussion,* he rationalised. *That's it! A massive blow to the head during our recent crash, despite the crash foam. It's left her unknowing, and stupid – an idiot, in fact.* He nodded to himself at this train of deduction. *Of course. She's now an idiot. What else could there be?*

He crunched to a stop on the glinting beach, and stared up at Lumar. "Lumar?" he crooned. "Lumar, my darling. Come down here for a moment, my sweet, ripe little butterfly peach."

"Fuck off."

Svool frowned. "Hey, baby, now listen to me, I understand you may have taken a rather nasty bump to the head..."

"Bump to the head?" she shrieked, and her rage and hatred were real animal things as she bounded across the rocks like some lithe, supple leopard, for a moment *all humanity* lost as she proudly displayed her alien physiology and utter physical power. She landed on all fours before Svool with a crunch, and uncoiled like a striking serpent. She leaned close, until her mouth was just inches from Svool's tender battered red lips, and he could see a raging green fire burning like a supernova inside her eyes.

"Er?" he ventured.

"What am I?" she hissed, forked tongue flickering out and tickling Svool.

"Er, my Mistress, a creature of great physical pleasure, a female kroona who has shared my bed for many months now and brought me squealing and moaning to massive multiple orgasms, a sexy alien SLAP-snorting culacoca-licking bitch of the highest degree." He nodded, getting into the flow of it. "And appointed by my management company to cater for my every flippant whim... and I *know* you were very happy to comply, because a) you signed the contract, and b) you were so naturally *happy* to comply to the whims of a natural genius of my truly natural awesome reputation and ability and genius!"

Lumar was shaking her head, and she took a step back. "You truly don't understand, do you?"

"Understand what?" He was wearing a look of injured pride. As if she should *dare* question him on the finer points of their contract.

"I am your *slave*, Svool. Your fucking *slave*. The kroona are persecuted across Manna; we are the lowest of the low. On my planet, my sister was taken hostage by the kroon ganga gangs. I was sold into slavery in order to earn big fat wages for the Men in Power, and to stop my sister, my own flesh and blood, from being murdered."

Svool opened his mouth to speak, saw the fire in her eyes, and closed it again with a *clack*.

"You have abused me for five months, Svoolzard. You have used me for drugs and sex and sport. And I have taken it. I know my position in the galaxy. And I know the kroon ganga gangs are the most dangerous of bastards to cross. For once in your life, I want you to *use* your brain and think about what I've just said. Really *think* about it."

Svool frowned even harder. He thought about it. Finally, he licked his wet lips. "So, you faked your orgasms?" he managed.

Lumar hissed, and tossed back her green dreadlocks, moving away from Svool and walking in a tight circle before returning to him. She thrust her angry face close, and Svool shivered, not used to seeing such primal expressions on the face of a lover he had so much adored.

"You are an idiot," she snarled.

"I don't get it!"

"You *owned* me. Well, your management company owned me. I had to play ball and they paid the gangs. And my sister would live. Surely you can understand the simple concept of trade?"

"But... but why didn't you go to the police?"

"The PUF? Ha! Do me a favour, you docile lump of tard."

"Now listen, I've had just about enough of your insults, young lady. If you're not careful, I'll..."

She came even closer, oozing malevolence. Svool stepped back, stumbling on one high-heeled boot.

"You'll what?" she asked, eyes narrowed. And he saw her claws had emerged. *Wow. She has claws. Like a cat! If only I'd known that during our sex games, I could have used them...*

"I'll, er, I'll..." The claws were glinting in the green sunlight, each one an inch of razor-sharp wickedness.

"You could write a fucking poem about it," she mocked, and the barb flew straight to his heart, sharper and more deadly than any intrusion of serrated steel.

Svool deflated. "That's a little... unfair. Okay. Okay. You win. I won't do anything. I just... find it hard to understand, hard to comprehend this sudden change." He realised his voice had emerged as a squeak. He felt tears at the corners of his eyes. He would have dabbed at them theatrically, only his cuffs were made of chipped glass-shard.

"Your company bought me. And I played their game. But now? Now we're on our own." She gave a nasty little smile. "*You* are on your own."

"Er," said Svoolzard.

Lumar retracted her claws and looked around, and then at the jungle that was swaying... *oddly*. She pointed. "That way is north. If I'm right, this place is Jusko, the largest island of the archipelago into which we have plunged. It has a trading port, which means people and ships. But there are bad things out in the jungle, Svool. *Real* bad things. So be careful, yeah, mate?" She winked. "Be careful, lover."

"Be careful?" he echoed, stricken with horror as her words sunk into his detoxing brain.

"And goodbye."

She started crunching up the green pebble beach and suddenly, as if lurching onto this side of reality, Svool realised the beach wasn't *green pebbles* but *green bottles* and many still had part-faded jagged plasti-labels, which read things like *Arthur's Piss Whiskey Gin* and *Puke Puke Tonic* and *Raw Sewage Alky – Great For All You Cheap & Nasty Drunkers*.

What? What the hell is this? He stared at the ground as if it had betrayed him. *I don't get it.* And distant words drifted to him, words spoken by a machine in a soft lilting female voice. *The planet of Amaranth in the Zynaps System is run by The Greenstar Recycling Company, sometimes referred to planetside simply as The Company. The Greenstar Recycling Company recycles the majority of Manna's waste, leaving the rest of the galaxy free to pursue its Heavenly Pursuits.*

Svool stared at the quite obviously *non-recycled waste* under his glossy boots. Then up towards the jungle, and the athletically disappearing figure of Lumar. Within the blink of an eye she had vanished, and Svool realised he was alone. Alone, with no bodyguards, on an uncultured world fondly referred to by the locals as *Toxic World*. Tox World. Toxicity. Or even just *Shit City*.

"Great," he muttered, and drawing his jewelled sword, more for his own morale than as any real form of protection, he started awkwardly up the bottle beach, his glass suit prickling him all over and his heels playing havoc with the slippery glass underfoot.

What I'd give for some fresh drugs, he sulked.

SVOOLZARD HUNG UPSIDE-DOWN from a tree, twine cutting into his ankles and giving him a particularly intense new type of agony, as he watched the collection of short, waddling, hairy men and short, waddling, bare-breasted hairy women with weary, cold-turkey eyes. He wondered how his life had gone from *damn-near-perfect-with-a-thousand-whores-on-tap* to *sucking-on-the-lollipop-of-imminent-death* in such a short period of time.

"Shit," he said. He coughed, and spat, which is harder than it sounds if you're upside down.

"Ug!" said one hairy beastman, and waved a stick at Svool. Svool paled, noting the stripped human skull adorning the top of the stick like some grotesque totem. It still had a small patch of scalp and hair attached, as if the face and head had been peeled like a fruit leaving a hairy summit, then shrunken, then stuck on a pointy stick, then waved at *him*.

It did not fill Svool with confidence and hope.

After all, he was used to more... *sophistication* than this. He was a respected academic, dammit!

He was... a Poet.

"Er, excuse me? Excuse me! Do you know who I am? Do you realise *who* I am? Do you actually comprehend the magnitude of your error? *I*" – he puffed out his chest, which was quite a feat when all the blood was in his skull – "am Svoolzard Koolimax XXIV, Third Earl of Apobos, son of Svoolzard Koolimax XXIII, grandson of the *great* Svoolzard Koolimax XXII, and seventh in line to the Throne of Apobos. I'm practically royalty, I am!"

"Ug." Another wave. Another flash of the quite terrifying shrunk-head totem.

"Oh. I assume I don't get a phone call, then?"

"UG!" The stick swished past his nose.

"Ahh. I'll be quiet then, shall I?"

And that's another thing, thought Svool morbidly as he swung by the tight twine digging through and *ruining* the fine gloss leather of his boots and now threatening to cut off the blood supply to his toes. *These trees. They're not right.* As he swung around aimlessly, observing the trees, he tried to work out what was wrong with them. What *exactly*. The colouring was nearly right, but the trunks were made from a kind of ribbed rubber. *Like... like... like a stack of old tyres?* he thought. *Gods!* And the massive, breeze-wafted fronds and leaves, although green as Nature had intended, seemed to be made from...

Green plastic bags.

Like supermarket bags, folded into leaf shapes.

Is this for real?

And then the beast-man wearing naught but a loincloth poked Svool with the sharp end of his skull stick, and grunted, "AG AG KAK!" and Svool realised it was definitely bloody real, and he'd been caught as easy as a chicken in a sack, a fly in a web, a sexy starlet in *his own bed*... and now he was to be...

Well. *Well?*

He eyed the fire they were stoking in a circle of rocks, rocks that looked, to his untrained eye, suspiciously like rectangular lumps of lead or some other heavy metal, and he wondered uneasily exactly *why* they needed a fire. For warmth, maybe? But it was already warm. Warm enough to make him sweat like a cooking pig.

"I say," he said.

The hairy men and women, many of whom, he now noticed, seemed to be wearing bones on strings around their necks and – horror – pierced through their very flesh, continued to ignore him. As if he was a chicken. Or a captured pig. Or throat-slit cattle hung up to bleed.

More uneasy prickles ran up and down his spine.

Why do I feel like a chicken on a spit?

Why do I feel like a lamb joint in the oven?

Why do I feel like a beef carcass in a warehouse?

Svool had an unusual relationship with food, indeed, as with sex. With sex, he'd fuck anything that couldn't crawl out of his bed. And with food, he'd spear and eat anything that couldn't make the leap from his plate.

And here, and now, he suddenly began to feel like food.

It was a new one on him.

A sarcastic part of his inner psyche snarled, *Write a poem about that, you fucker.*

He suppressed the urge to giggle.

Svool swung gently, and watched the fire being built higher and higher. Then he watched as some of the – savages? indigenous peoples? *cannibals?* – erected a kind of *spit* with good solid sturdy timber. The spit was a little over six feet long. Svool anticipated it would take both his length, and his weight.

"Er. Excuse me? Can you listen to me for a moment, good peoples?"

"Ug."

"Ag."

"Kak."

"Wok."

"Snuk."

"Snog."

"Dek."

"Fak."

"I say, I say, I am a *very* famous poet, about to become a *very* famous film star, and I do believe I have lots of money in a ggg Galactic Account which I could access for you if you were to escort me, for example, to the nearest cash dispenser."

He looked on, hopefully. The hairy bone-clad stick-waving peoples ignored him.

"I could also offer to include a little stanza about our meeting in a future poem? A *published* poem, I might add."

Nothing. Nada. Zip.

"Indeed, being a leading member of the Culture Ministry I could perhaps bring some kind of foreign aid to your plight? Make the people in power and with money and influence aware of your terrible afflictions, your lack of funky clothing, your horrible predilection for rendering your own bodies with bone piercings. How's that sound? We could maybe supply you with razors to get rid of all that ghastly body hair. Especially for the women; indeed, if you are women. Lots of people in corduroys would trot along, become involved, and start getting you medical treatment and building schools for your children. How's about that for a slice of fried gold?"

He beamed, pleased with his proposition.

The cannibals, for now he was sure they *were* cannibals on account of a toddling toddler who'd just wobbled into view sucking on a small human skull, ignored him.

Svoolzard felt his lower lip start to emerge; a prima donna pout. What a cheek! First, his thesis performance was interrupted. Second, the indignity of a crashing starship! Third, Lumar, that sexiest of sexy pliant bendable mistresses, goes all weird and strange on him, no doubt because of a savage bump to the head, he was surer than sure, and stalked off into the jungle in a huff like they'd had some kind of teenage lover's tiff! *Then* he was hit from behind by some kind of sleeping dart, and awoke to find funny little hairy people refusing to speak to him.

It was just... *not on*.

Svoolzard felt his temper flare, aided and abetted by his cold-turkey situation from at least fifteen different types of narcotic. One of them, SLAP, had a cold-turkey come-down period of seven *years*. Now *that's* what you call an addiction.

Right, he thought. *RIGHT!*

"OKAY," he suddenly bellowed, swinging frantically as he really punched from his diaphragm, "THIS IS A BLOODY DISGRACE AND I'M JUST NOT HAVING IT! NOT HAVING IT AT ALL! THIS IS A RIDICULOUS SITUATION AND YOU FAIL TO UNDERSTAND THAT YOU HAVE HERE, TIED TO THIS TREE, A BONAFIDE BLOODY *GENIUS*! I AM A POET! I AM A SWASHBUCKLER! I AM A GENIUS! I AM REVERED THROUGHOUT THE GALAXY OF MANNA! I AM WORSHIPPED BY ALL WOMEN! I AM WORSHIPPED BY MOST BLOODY MEN, ACTUALLY! I AM A HELL-RAISER, A DRUG-WORSHIPPER, A LOVER AND A HIPSTER, AND YOU HAVE NO RIGHT TO HOLD ME LIKE THIS! NO RIGHT TO TIE ME TO A TREE AND SHOUT 'UG' AND 'KAK' AND WAVE YOUR POINTY STICKS AT ME, YOU SHITTY LITTLE HAIRY HEATHEN SAVAGES! I WANT THE AMBASSADOR FOR EARTH CONTACTING RIGHT NOW! I WANT A COMM CALL! I WANT MY RIGHTS! GET IT?"

There was a long, long pause.

In his passion at his oratory, Svoolzard had closed his eyes, as well as drooling down his own forehead. Passion-spittle, he called it. He knew his many lovers found it extremely sexy.

As he opened his eyes, a "shitty little hairy heathen savage" was crouched before him, skirt of grasses parted, long pierced penis unrolled to touch the ground. The shitty little hairy heathen savage grinned up at Svoolzard, showing teeth filed to points and inset with rusted twin razor blades rescued from old disposable razors.

"Yes?" said Svoolzard, hopefully.

The shitty little hairy heathen savage held up a knife and fork, his grin getting wider at the same time as his bulbous eyes.

"Time for supper, fancy man," he grinned.

TWO

"SHE'S PRETTY HARD."

"Not as hard as my cock."

Smoke swirled. Glasses clinked. Chips clattered.

"No, really, mate, I've heard she's as tough as an iron bar."

"Heh, I'll give her my iron bar up every single orifice, I can tell you. Hear her sing like a canary." Laughter.

"Come on, Jones; don't talk about the lady like that."

"Fuck you, Zanzibar. All I'm saying is, no matter how hard she is, my cock is harder. And bigger. And man, would I give her a good time long time. I'd ride her like a fucking donkey. I'd fuck her like a fucking donkey. She's lean, and mean, and if I got my hands on those little titties she'd be moaning and creaming in my hand before you could squeal '*Give it to me, Big Boy.*'"

The group of squaddies laughed, many uneasily and casting nervous glances about, and Jones threw down his cards and cracked open another beer. It was hot, and he was bare-chested, his upper physique criss-crossed with scars from downtown knife-fights. His dark eyes burned with a fever as he pictured in his mind's eye the tight hard little body of his Squad Leader, Jenny Xi.

"Well, that's an interesting point of view," came a soft voice from the shadows, and the squad – all except Jones – jumped. "But then, there's always one in the crew who has his brain hard-wired to his cock. In the middle of a firefight, BAM! There he goes again, ruining his pants."

Jones half-turned, a sneer on his face. "Little lady, I knew you was there all the time."

Jenny Xi stepped forward, and coolly lit a narrow, evil-looking cigarette. She had long auburn hair, lightly curled, now tied back. Her face was narrow, pretty, tanned, her body tall and lithe, powerful and athletic. She wore dark combat fatigues and a khaki shirt, open at the neck and showing her dog-tags. Although this little unit weren't strictly military – or at least, not employed by Amaranth's resident standing army, navy or air force – they were mostly *ex*-forces; all disgraced one way or another. And somehow, they had found their way here, crawled their way into the welcoming arms of the anti-Toxicity movement known as *Impurity*. "Good people putting a bad world right." That was one of the many anti-Greenstar slogans. Anti-Company slogans. *ECO terrorist slogans*...

"I wondered why you had a hard-on," she said, blowing out smoke.

Jones scowled. "That ain't for you, bitch. That's for the killing."

"Interesting," muttered Jenny, rubbing her chin, watching the group. They were all hard-nuts, with polished guns and combat boots. Some had SMKKs, some D4 shotguns. They were a battered, scarred, hardened butch. She'd seen it all before. But *now* she was their new Squad Leader and she couldn't let the slur stand; and besides, sometimes she just liked a fight.

Jenny moved to Jones, who refused to turn and acknowledge her. As if, by continuing to present his broad, heavily-muscled back, he was showing a lack of fear; as if tilting his lifted chin and grinning was a fuck-you middle finger to authority. But there *was* no authority. Cut the shit. They were a terrorist squad intent on bringing down the twisted government of the Greenstar Recycling Company. Intent on restoring their once-peaceful green and pleasant land *back* to being a green and pleasant land. Although with every million tonnes of shit dumped in the sea, every million tonnes of toxic sludge poured down mines drilled for this very purpose, for every million tonnes of old tyres, smashed bottles, crap and shit and heavy metal landfill...

Well. In her heart, Jenny Xi knew that the day would never come.

No matter what Old Tom had once dreamed...

Toxicity was the dumping ground for the civilised galaxy of Manna.

And Manna, despite the claim of being a perfect utopia... well.

It would always need a toilet.

Jenny moved close behind Jones, noting the many scars on his back. She moved close, and leant, blowing smoke in his ear. "You know what they say about a man with scars on his back?" She grinned, voice barely above a whisper but suddenly the card games, the drinking, the back-slapping boasts were all forgotten; now *Jenny* and *Jones* were the centre of attention. The night's amusement. A game for bored soldiers on stag.

"Go on," growled Jones, voice dangerous, eyes narrowed.

"Well, they say that man's done *a lot* of running away."

There was some laughter, a couple of gasps, a general feeling of shock; for despite Jones having a loud mouth and dubious views on the integrity of the female of the species, he was without doubt a tough, bone-headed motherfucker.

"They say that, do they?" said Jones, rising slowly and turning to face Jenny Xi. He looked down at her with a sneer on his face. Jenny was tall, a touch over six feet. But Jones was nearly a head taller, a rippling, stocky, powerful example of an arrogant male in his prime.

"Jones..." said Zanzibar, his voice filled with warning.

"Hey, fuck you, Zanz. Keep your nose out of this."

"Hey, I can see you're saving your hard-on for your boyfriends here." Jenny winked, taking a few steps back, smoking, eyes glittering with humour. "You wouldn't want to give it to a real woman like me now, would you? I bet you'd need a strap-on, you pathetic piece of shit."

Jones rolled his neck. "Oh, I'm going to give it to you, all right," he said, taking a menacing step closer.

Jenny lifted her fists and tightened her jaw. "You see, all *I'm* bothered about is a modicum of respect. And seeing as *I'm* the new Squad Leader, I see respect is something that's got to be earned."

"I'll show you some respect," growled Jones, moving forward, his own fists raised.

"Come on, let's see it, fat boy," said Jenny.

Jones came at her fast, and despite his weight of muscle, he moved quickly. Right straight, right hook, left jab, left hook. Jenny swayed, ducking the blows, then shifted back a few steps to give herself room.

"You're slow," she said, and took a puff on her cigarette, flicking the butt away.

"I'm going to kick your ass, bitch."

"Yeah? Less talking, more fighting."

Jones growled, and charged. Jenny ducked a swipe and rammed a fist into Jones's ribs. There came a *crack* and he staggered past, wheezing, gripping his side, and whirled on her, face flushed, hate filling his eyes.

"I'm going to fucking kill you," he snarled.

"Come on, then."

He charged again, fists flailing, and for a moment they were both moving in a blur, a punch-up of staggering skill, dodging, weaving, straights and hooks and jabs smashing and connecting. Jones hit Jenny with a straight to the chin and she took a step back, amazingly keeping her feet, avoided a follow-up punch, and delivered a right hook so powerful it lifted Jones from his feet and deposited him on his rump with a slap. Stunned for a moment, Jones rolled to avoid Jenny's boot, which cracked the earth. He slammed an elbow into her knee, folding her leg, but on the way down her own elbow came over in a sideways blow like a bone knife, splitting the flesh under Jones's eye and sending him rolling away, growling like a dog.

Jenny leapt up, and there was a sheen of sweat on her skin. Slowly, she lifted her fists once more and lowered her head.

Jones stood, and in his own fist was a knife.

"Don't be silly," said Jenny, head still lowered, eyes glittering dark and dangerous.

"You fucking bitch," he spat through saliva and blood.

"Jones, don't be a dickhead," came the warning rumble of Zanzibar.

"Yeah, you fucking idiot. Put the knife down," came another voice.

"I'll kill her!" Jones slurred, lurching forward a step.

Jenny held up a hand, palm out. "Stop."

"You scared, motherfucker?"

"You're raising the stakes, Jones. Don't make me put you down. I need you in the squad. This has gone too far..."

"Fucking whore!"

He charged her, and Jenny lowered her hands, eyes dark, mouth a grim line, and the rest of the squad watched in hushed silence as the knife glittered through the gloom and at the last moment Jenny took Jones's wrist, twisting the knife away, side-stepping, ramming his arm up his back. Jones's momentum carried him on forward, as Jenny leapt, still holding onto his twisted arm, her knee connecting with his spine as she rode him to the ground. Jones's face planted the soil and he grunted, spittle exploding from his lips. Jenny took the knife from his fingers, lifted it in the air, and stabbed Jones in the back of the shoulder. Blood bubbled and pumped. Jones howled and squirmed, but Jenny held him there, her body hard and taut, her face and eyes grim.

"Lie still," she said.

Jones struggled.

"Lie fucking still!" she hissed.

Growling and snarling, Jones was finally still. Jenny leant forward, and into his ear, said, "You're lucky this time, boy. Don't fuck with me. Next time I push it through your ribs and cut out your heart. Do you understand?"

Jones mumbled.

"Do you fucking understand?" She grabbed the hilt of the knife and twisted.

"Yes!" he screamed. "Yes, I fucking understand!"

Jenny stood, and turned on the rest of the squad. They were deathly quiet. Her eyes were flashing mad and dangerous, and she held up the bloodied knife. "Anybody else want to be Top Dog? Do I have to prove myself to any other cunt? Or are you all happy?"

"You *know* we don't all think like him," said Zanzibar, his incredibly deep, dark, brown eyes fixed on Jenny. The large, dark-skinned soldier stood and moved forward, and gently took the knife from Jenny's hand. "Calm down, Xi. Calm down, my friend. Come on, we go a long way back. You know you can trust me."

Jenny took several deep breaths, and Zanzibar turned and made a hand gesture. Somebody left to get a medic. Jones was unconscious; nobody moved to help him.

Zanzibar guided Jenny to a seat, and somebody put a glass of whiskey in front of her. She decked it in one.

"I'm sorry," she said, lifting her head then, looking round at the gathered faces of the squad. "I shouldn't have..."

"Don't apologise," rumbled Zanzibar. "Prick had it coming, right?" There was a muttering of agreement.

Medics arrived, and Jones was rolled onto a stretcher and carried out. Jenny toyed with the knife. "You know what? I know he isn't a bad man. I know Jones has done... *good* things in his time. He's a good soldier. A good fighter. Good for the cause. But I..."

"Hey, when your blood's up, it's up," said Zanzibar, and patted her arm. "Don't worry about it. Now come on. Pick up the cards. Let me relieve you of some of that hard-earned pay you carry in your fat purse." He winked.

"Is that fighting talk?" smiled Jenny, breathing deep.

"Always," smiled back Zanzibar.

FROM BEHIND HER cards, through the smoke, fuelled by whiskey, Jenny surveyed her squad. Many were new to each other, these men and women, and new to her – except Zanz. But she felt like she already knew them. She was also *sure* they had been informed about her previous squad; killed to a man on an assassination mission. It happened. What looked mildly suspicious was that *she* was the only one who'd survived, and she didn't like that. Made her look like she was either a coward, or on the inside spitting out. And she was neither. Jenny licked her lips, rubbed her eyes, and rolled a fresh cigarette. Sometimes, it was better to die with your men.

"Your hand, girlfriend," said Randy, in his effeminate voice, and Jenny grinned over at him. She'd seen Randy's profile. Randy was tall and slim, with masses of long curly black hair. He had designer stubble and a designer uniform. Even his boots were decorated with glitter. It had led to a lot of misunderstandings, and a lot of agony – for other people. Just because Randy sounded like a squeaky girl didn't mean he fought like one; he was an expert in martial arts and street fighting, and a dab hand with a machine gun. Maybe not a man to have in your bed, but certainly a man to have behind you in a firefight.

"Thanks."

Randy winked at her. "Don't let Jones worry you. He likes a bit of rough and tumble, but then don't we all?"

"I know I do," said Jenny.

"Ooh, saucy."

"Why don't you shut your hole," growled Bull. Bull was a short stocky man with angry eyes, an angry face and so many facial tattoos they often squirmed together to form new ones, depending on the expression he pulled.

"You can fill one, if you like," winked Randy.

Bull went red. Well, the few remaining bits of untattooed skin went red. "What have I told you, eh? What did I say about making suggestive comments? Bull doesn't like it. Bull likes his women quiet and chunky. Bull doesn't want an amorous relationship with a fop."

"Oh, fop now, is it?"

"Guys," said Zanzibar, ever the voice of reason, and Jenny realised she was actually *enjoying* herself. Yes, her knuckles hurt like a bitch, but Flizz, the glamorous assassin, tall and slender and beautiful, and as deadly as a striking cobra, had been down to the kitchens and brought her back two bags of frozen haranga. Flizz was quiet, shy, and with her glossy long hair and perfect make-up made Jenny feel quite dull, in her stained combat clothing and facial bruising. Still, she'd met Flizz a few years back; they'd been on the same squad for a short period.

Jenny sighed. Anyway. She'd not made a brilliant first impression on this new squad, by any stretch of the imagination.

"Right," said Zanz. "I'm upping the stakes. Twenty."

"Shit, I'm out," crooned Randy, and tossed down his cards.

With a grin, Jenny laid out her own cards. "I'm out as well." She rolled her neck, feeling tendons like steel threatening to strangle her. Randy stood and came round the table.

"Here, girlfriend, let me help you with that." He started a slow massage, and Bull scowled at him.

"Leave her alone, you big girl."

"You *wish* I was a big girl," said Randy with a wink.

Bull snorted. "The only day I'd shag you is on the day you died," snapped Bull.

"Ooh, Bull, don't tempt me." Then down to Jenny, "Ignore him. He's a bullish brute. I, and the rest of my colleagues, are far more sophisticated. Just look around you – you never could hope for such a group of efficient military effluvia to back you up in bringing down the Bad Guys."

Jenny usually hated to be touched by people she did not know, but the fight, and her realisation that her gung-ho approach had perhaps not been the best of early introductions, had left her wired tighter than a junkie on peppered koona jock-strap. She let Randy ease her tension. And realised, suddenly, that she missed the basics of human touch. It had been a long time. Far, far too long.

"Just don't get any ideas," she growled, long and low.

"All my ideas are my own," Randy whispered in her ear.

Jenny relaxed more thanks to Randy's questing, nudging, teasing fingers, and she found herself smoking, and drinking whiskey, and looking around the table at the other squad members. They were all at ease with each other, and seemed unconcerned that Jones had been removed from the action. Unconcerned, in fact, that Jones had not just had his head kicked in, but a knife put through his shoulder blade.

Mentally, Jenny re-scanned the metal leaves for each of her squad members. Their cell, Impurity5, was part of what the government liked to call "an illegal and violent radical *terrorist* cell," "under the enfolding embrace of the greater umbrella, The Impurity Movement". Yes, sure, Impurity had an official, legal, political and positive face to their actions; the face that went on TV and cubes and ggg, smiled for the cameras, condemned The Company for its constant illegal and repressive underhand recycling techniques, ran for government and tried – vainly, it would seem – to achieve votes. But when Impurity's members started being randomly picked off – assassinated – and those assassinations were rumoured to be carried out by the highly illegal and dangerous *Anarchy Androids*, Impurity had decided to fight back with the creation of a covert paramilitary wing: cells, squads that used underhand methods – as did The Company – in its fight not for freedom, but for an end to pollution.

Impurity fought to highlight the toxic poisoning of their world; something so obvious it was in front of every member of the Manna Galaxy daily. Unfortunately, it would seem humans and aliens alike enjoyed their happy utopia so much they would cheerily condemn Amaranth to its Toxic World status without the blink of an eye, without a thought for the dropped hot-dog carton, the frothing psycho-sud suds, and – as with everything – a constant eye on the fucking bank balance. At the end of the day, Jenny, and every other member of the Impurity Movement, *knew* the whole shitty corrupt process was about money. No... Money, with a capital fucking M. And that was what was so galling. If Greenstar, if *The Company*, did what it said it would do – recycle *everything* in a completely non-toxic, ethical, positive, life-affirming manner – well, then everybody would be happy. But they didn't. They cut corners. Saved money. Pumped shit into the soil and the water. And as a result, people died.

And, Jenny knew, there was a hard core who wouldn't stand for it.

She wouldn't stand for it.

Which is why it pained her so much, truly, to fight somebody like Jones.

Hell. They shouldn't be fighting each other.

They should be disintegrating The Company and its lack of ethics.

People, animals, fauna; everything on Toxicity was dying or dead. T-Day was coming. Total toxicity. Then there would be no going back; then, there would be no more time to stand up and fight and be counted. On that day, Jenny knew, it would be a good day to die.

Out of the game, Jenny shooed Randy away, who skipped off, his pointed boots with skull buckles clacking, his cuff lace fluffing; she smiled wearily, tested her bruised jaw, and lit another cigarette.

Meat Cleaver was also out of the game, and she watched him carefully. Stocky and powerful, even at a game of cards he must have been carrying... what? Ten or twelve sheathed knives about his person. And of course, down the middle of his back like some *Conan*-wannabe, a massive, slightly curved meat cleaver which, he claimed, was more accurate in combat than any petty trinket samurai sword. "What happens when you meet a man with a machine gun?" had been Jenny's first question on hearing that Cleaver refused to carry a projectile weapon of any sort. He'd grinned toothily at her, looked up to the sky, and said, "God works in mysterious ways. And you'd be surprised what seeing my meat cleaver does to a man's aim."

Jenny's eyes moved further round the group, past the dazzling gorgeousness of Flizz (gorgeousness she'd used, predictably, to ensnare many a border or gate guard, dazzling him with beauty and smiles and lip gloss, then rendering him unconscious with a kick to the nads and karate chop to the neck).

Beside her was Nanny, the oldest member of the group. Female, hair in a crew cut, face harsh and haggard and brutal and square. She'd be the first to admit she was the complete antithesis of Flizz; where Flizz dazzled, Nanny groggled, where Flizz beamed smiles, Nanny cracked sour cynicism, where Flizz laughed and skipped and bounced, Nanny moaned and plodded and waddled. Nanny was stocky, muscular, heavy-set, big-boned, wearing size 12 boots and with fists like shovels. She carried several pistols and was the resident detonations expert, having once worked the infamous DemolSquads of Old London. Often the others would poke fun at Nanny, and her nickname was not, as Jenny had first suspected, because of her age; but because of her supposed resemblance to a goat.

Finally, there was Sick Note. A small, skinny, gangly-looking man, completely bald, with thick veins crossing his polished dome. He was never to be seen without either a cigarette or a quarter bottle of whiskey. He constantly moaned (he was moaning now, about losing his hand in the game) and was a hypochondriac. Jenny had questioned this fact when she'd first read it, only to be told, with a wide grin, "Wait till you meet him!" They had, of course, been correct; Sick Note earned his name for good reason. Not a day went by without him developing some new cancer, deadly virus, genetic mutation or terminal illness.

More drinks were drunk, and a feeling of euphoria washed over Jenny. The group were completely at ease with one another. They oozed not just confidence, but... the ability to mesh. Like gear cogs interlocking. They were a team, a unit. And that was good...

Except for Jones.

Had she misjudged?

Zanzibar gestured to her, and she stood, and stretched, and followed him outside into the cool night air. A light rain was falling. It tasted bad on Jenny's tongue, like ash. Like toxic rainfall. Which, surely, it was.

"Don't worry," said Zanzibar.

"About?"

"So coy, mistress," he grinned. "About Jones. I know how the human mind works. You can see us all as a unit, and you're wondering if you fucked up. Trust me, you didn't. What you're witnessing in our behaviour is the absence of Jones. He is a fly in our butter. A maggot in our collective sweet, juicy apple pie. There is a deep prejudice in him, a deep bad strand. Nobody here thinks less of you."

Jenny shrugged. "It's good of you to say, Zanz." She clasped his hand, wrist to wrist. "Internal bitching and fighting is a pointless excursion; we have a common enemy. A common enemy we need to bring down and fuck up with extreme prejudice."

"You've come to the right place," smiled Zanzibar.

Jenny nodded. "Well. We're going to make a difference. I promise you that."

JENNY SAT ON her bunk, in a tiny 8x6 bunker, and checked over her weapons. She had a Browning 13mm, an SMKK standard-issue machine gun, and a variety of weird and ingenious grenades, everything from smoke and white phos, to DetX and Detox pills.

Happy everything was in order, she kicked off her boots (in need of a polish) and lay back with a creak of springs. She wriggled around for a few moments, trying to get comfy, but resigned herself, as a bad-bed professional experienced in the art of shitty military springs, *never* to get comfy. She closed her eyes anyway and grasped for strands of sleep, but it wouldn't come. As was usual when she drank enough to mess with her mindset, she thought about the drink, the alcohol, and drifted back through time.

Sleep tugged at her like a dying man on a rope, and she drifted in and out of consciousness. She felt bad about the fight earlier; in an ideal world, a true world where only good things happened, the fight wouldn't have happened. But the problem was, there were too many arseholes with too big an ego floating around. Yes. Ha. Even in *her* unit. Her eyes flickered, and she licked dry lips, and for some reason she was thinking about her dad, Old Tom. She smiled grimly, for although there were many, many nice thoughts of Old Tom – snippets of early childhood, of laughing, being carried high on strong broad shoulders, of wallowing in warm oceans, of building castles in the sand – there were also other memories, more recent memories. Bad memories.

Jenny blinked, and for a moment he was standing there, long hair tangled and unkempt, a bottle in one hand filled with colourless piss, swaying, staring at her with that vacant stare he always had when hammered.

"Please stop, Daddy."

"Ach, don't be silly, little Jen. I've only had a few."

"You drink too much, Daddy."

"Just keeping the winter chills away."

Always a line, always an excuse. She scrunched up tighter in her bed, eyes narrowing. She had been too young, too frightened, too weak. But her older brother, Saul, he should have known better. But no. He had one cruel eye turned on the piggy bank, the other holding onto the self-destruct lever and ratcheting it down one notch at a time.

"Saul, do something!" she would hiss, with bright eyes.

"He's okay, he's a grown man. He can look after himself." But she caught Saul checking out bank statements, taking Old Tom's bank cube when the old man was too frazzled on cheap liquor to even know his own children's faces, never mind how many credits he had in his account. And with a gradual, cold, slippery descent into understanding, Jenny had come to realise what her own brother was *really* like. He didn't care about Old Tom. Didn't want to get her father help. Oh, no. He was *waiting* for him to die. Waiting for the bastard to drink himself into an early grave, thus funding Saul's lazy, drugsmoke, groundcar-obsessive lifestyle.

Years later, they'd head-butted it out. But not now... Not now.

"Why didn't you help him, Saul?" she murmured, as she fell into a well of sleep.

WHY DO YOU hate your father?

Oh well, that's a long story. A complicated story.

Well, why do you hate your brother?

Longer. Even more complex. And much more savage.

And your mother?

Poor, dead mother. Don't cry for me, my darling.

And... your sister?

Nixa? Sweet dead Nixa. I'll cry for you, honey. We'll all cry for you.

OLD TOM. TOMAS to his friends. A likeable man. Big, jolly, funny, intelligent, friendly. Not a bad bone in his good bone body. Shaggy hair, shaggy beard, the kids called him "Chewbacca" and he laughed alongside them, laughed with their jokes as his hand touched the cold glass of the bottle in his pocket.

Tom liked to walk, and would head into the hills around Kavusco, long strides in his sturdy shoes. He wore thick molecule-tweed and smoked a pipe. A lot of the locals chuckled, and nudged one another: "There's Old Tom off on another walk. A simple man. An honest man."

But what they didn't know about this loveable, amiable friendly giant was that he was on a *mission*; he had his orders, orders so important the Quad-Gal Military could have issued them from top Army Brass. The order was: to drink. And the mission was: to drink. And the secondary briefing was: not to get caught. And a sub-mission was: to hide it from his family. Old Tom's own mother, Jenny's grandmother, was on a slippery descent into death; she was ancient, frail, withered, skin like dry paper, eyes losing the light of life. Her batteries were discharged. Almost empty. Almost gone.

That's why I drink, Tom told himself, believing it as he believed all the other lies. *I can take it or leave it. And I don't drink too much. I know I don't drink too much. I can stop anytime, you see. But the wife doesn't*

*like it, always squawking and moaning, and the kids
don't like it, always asking, "Why are you so happy,
Daddy?" and, "Why are you falling over, Daddy?"
and, "Why are you being sick, Daddy?" People say to
me, it's an illness. People say to me, I don't understand.
Why do you drink until you're sick? And then start all
over again? Vodka for breakfast? Brandy for lunch?
Whiskey for dinner? You're a sick man! Better believe
it.*

Tom stopped, and breathed in the cold crisp winter
air. He looked up towards the Kavusco Hills, with
their peppering of snow. Behind him, far behind, a Tox
Tipper droned through the sky and Tom found himself
pausing, waiting for the "dump". It came a few seconds
later than he'd anticipated, the banging clattering
rattle of junk being tipped into an open landfill. Tom's
nostrils twitched, trying to catch the scent of methane,
of rot, of shit and crap; but nothing came. Tom's sense
of smell had been killed decades earlier.

"Damn you, brother," he muttered, and glanced
around before pulling out the bottle and taking a
hefty swig. He felt the cold behind his eyeballs, and
lowered the bottle, spluttering, piss whiskey warm on
his lips and burning in his gullet. His ulcer stung, but he
ignored the pain. It would soon leave him, along with
his sobriety.

Once, Tom would have said, "I'm just popping out
for a walk, honey."

"Sure, no problem. I've put a beef casserole in the
oven. Be back by five."

Now, he knew, she knew, they all knew, "just popping
for a walk" was a prelude to "just nipping out to drink
until I puke," and he didn't say the words, and by not
saying the words he knew he wouldn't get into another
argument.

She'll leave you.

No, she won't.

She will. She's sick of your drinking, falling on your face, bloodying your nose, not coming home at night, leaving her worrying and shivering in a cold bed alone, looking after Jenny and Saul alone, going through her life... alone.

No. *She understands me. She supports me. She loves me. Everything will be okay.* But it wasn't okay. And Tom knew his mother was dying. He looked into those eyes which had once sparkled so brightly, but now were dimmed, like failing, tumbling stars. Brittle and broken, she was. Eaten inside. Too far gone to help.

My poor mother. I can't take it!

I'll just have another drink...

And that's what this was, a walk in the hills, a drink in the hills, to get over the knowledge that his mother was dying. Had mere days left. And he knew, *knew* he should be by her side, holding her hand, telling her he loved her just like his brother was. But he didn't. He wasn't. He needed a drink. Just a couple. To get over the knowledge that she was leaving this mortal realm...

"Be a man," his brother would say.

"Fuck you, Kaylo!" he would snarl.

"Don't blame me for what we did," his brother would say.

"Go back to your evil," Old Tom would snarl.

"Tom. Tom. We started this together, Tom."

"Go to Hell."

And Kaylo would smile, and his eyes shone like tiny candle lights, and his face was rugged and strong and handsome and Tom reached for his bottle, and downed another drink.

TOM'S BOOTS CRUNCHED ON the gravel path as he moved further up into the hills, through forests of twisted old trees, diseased from the junk in the ground and sporting weird and wonderful corrugated bark, a testament to some ancient pollutant. *The whole world is poisoned,* he thought. And laughed. *My whole mind is poisoned!*

He stopped after a few more minutes, panting, sweating, and had another drink. He spluttered, piss whiskey burning his lips, and turned. Lights glittered through the fast-falling darkness and the valley spread out before him: the valley of his childhood, the valley of his adolescence, the valley of his adulthood. Kavusco. The town of his life. He'd been born there, he lived there, and he would die there.

And there'd been so many changes. From Beauty to Desecration.

Old Tom lowered his head and wept...

I LIVE IN a fucking soap-opera, thought Jenny as her eyes flared open. She lay there, staring at the ghost. It was a white apparition. Shimmering. Ethereal. It reached out a hand to her, and smiled. And, like she did every other morning, Jenny reached out a hand to her sister. Her dead sister.

"You are sad," said the ghost.

"Yes," said Jenny, clutching the covers that little bit more tightly.

"Bad dream?"

"I always have bad dreams," said Jenny, face neutral.

"You still full of hate?"

Slowly, Jenny's lip curled into a snarl and the reality of her situation and the reality of the world came tumbling back into focus.

"Oh, yes," she said.

The ghost of Nixa smiled.

"Then it's time to go to work," she said.

*   *   *

IMPURITY5 HAD BEEN watching the Reprocessing Plant for a month, and it was quite obvious The Company, as usual, were not doing their job. Greenstar promised 100% recycling of alien tox. It was policy. It was what not only got them votes, and kept them in power, but earned them a lot of money and a number of God Award certificates from various planets, governments, and monarchies from around Manna – and indeed, the entire Quad-Gal. As far as the members of Impurity5 could work out, the reprocessing ratio was as little as 5%. Which meant 95% of waste being dumped direct into the ecosystem, or what *remained* of Amaranth's ecosystem.

In reality, it was a huge shit pie. Quite literally. And the people of Toxicity were forced to take a very big bite in more ways than one.

"So what happens to the other ninety-five percent?" said Randy, running a hand through his flowing locks. "They can't just dump it. That would be... immoral." His dazzling, beautiful face was fixed on Jenny. She smiled. Damn, he looked so out of place squatting in a hole in the ground.

"They can, and they do," said Jenny, and they sat in their covert hole, peering through Long Lenses as a convoy of Super Tankers arrived, perhaps a hundred in total, like huge black slugs buoyed on hover jets, each one as big as a thousand HG Truks. Jenny took photographs.

"I don't get it." Randy was frowning. "Those tankers, they could just be delivering more crap. What makes you so sure they're taking it away for illegal tipping?"

"Watch," said Jenny. "And learn."

They watched, as slowly the Super Tankers rolled through high spiked iron gates, one by one.

"I think this is bullshit," said Randy, pouting. "There's nothing to see here. We're on a wild goose chase." As the newest member of Impurity5, Randy was prone to what the others considered *ill-thought-out comments*. Randy was the sort of dandy who truly did *not* know when to keep his mouth shut.

"You have to watch, and trust Jenny," rumbled Zanzibar. "All will be revealed."

"Well, I know what I'd *like* to be revealed."

Randy was staring at Jenny, head tilted to one side, a curious look on his face.

"Oh, no," said Jenny. She held up a hand. "Not here. Not now. It's neither the time nor the place."

"It's always the time and the place," smiled Randy. He tossed back his head, and his curls bounced.

Jenny looked sideways at Zanzibar. His dark-skinned face had gone pale.

"You vouched for him," she said.

"What can I say?" Zanzibar gave a narrow, straight smile, although his eyes were dark. "He came highly recommended. You know it yourself. *You* fucking helped recruit him!"

"Hey!" snapped Randy. "Don't talk about me like that."

"Like what?" rumbled Zanzibar, turning his full attention on Randy.

"Like I'm not here, you big oaf! All this *he came highly recommended* bullshit. As if I'm not here. As if I'm a prat, a joker, an idiot."

"Maybe you are?" said Jenny.

"Oh, you spear my heart, dearest one; dearest girlfriend. We are both part of the same universe, it can be seen nestling in our eyes, and yet your lack of poetry is anathema to my very being."

Jenny sighed. After all, Randy *was* the newest member of the team. Yes, he looked like a popinjay, but his bomb circuit-building was unbelievably brilliant. His bomb-making was... just perfect. And this was to be the test. To see if they could justify it – and him – to Cell Commander McGowan.

"Why the photos?" said Randy.

"I'll explain later."

When the shit hit the fan, they had to have evidence for the media: that way, they weren't seen as terrorists picking soft targets, but as freedom fighters attempting to save the planet. Which, Jenny knew in all their hearts, was what they were. It's just sometimes certain radical idiots got in the way. Sometimes, real bad people used "The Fight" as a personal vendetta and things got out of hand. Innocent people died. That wasn't the way Impurity5 operated.

"Go on, tell me now."

"Be quiet, dickhead, and focus on the job in hand."

Randy opened his mouth, but Zanzibar gave him a stern look, and Randy closed it again. The huge Asian had a reputation. No. He had *A Reputation*. You didn't mess with Zanzibar. Not if you wanted to keep a hold of your kneecaps. Or your face.

Zanzibar threw Jenny a smile and a shrug. Jenny replied with a nod, and got back behind her Long Lens. The tankers were almost in, now. Behind her, there came a steady *shring shring* as Meat Cleaver started sharpening his knives.

"What now?" said Randy. He was impatient, full of energy. Sexual energy, from where Jenny was sitting.

"We wait," said Jenny, settling back. She looked around, and smiled. These were the moments she liked, revered. The quiet times. Reflective. With her squad, her unit. The people in the world she *knew* she could trust; but more, who were fighting alongside her to achieve a common goal...

And what's the goal, girl? came the voice of Nixa.

Jenny froze for a moment, as she always did. Her eyes flickered around the group, wondering if any of

them had heard the words, or even seen her stiffen at
the ghostly interruption. Meat Cleaver was sharpening.
Sick Note was smoking endlessly, a tiny smoke-
extractor on a ring on his index finger making sure
no fumes escaped and gave even a hint of their hide-
hole. Flizz was seated in a corner, silent, watching, as
she always was. Randy had tried it on with Flizz first;
Flizz was stunningly beautiful, it had to be said, but
when Randy persisted Flizz put a knife to his groin
and got in close and whispered, "I'll cut it off, wide
boy," and Randy got the message. To Randy, having
a penisectomy was worse than death itself. Randy was
the sort of man who wore a Kevlar codpiece rather
than a helmet. Or, as he wittily put it, a helmet over his
helmet. Nobody laughed.

The goal is to close down Greenstar. To show them up
as the liars they are. We want the toxicity gone from our
planet. We want our world back. No longer a tipping
ground for the crap of Manna. We want freedom. A
clean planet. Clean air for our children. Clean water to
drink. We want the politicians to stop lying to us. We
want The Company to fuck off. We never asked for it,
and the people of this world don't want it!

A noble goal, mocked Nixa. *Every world wants the
same.*

"Uh?" said Jenny.

Randy was staring at her, a quizzical expression on
his face. "I *said,* gorgeous girlfriend, what games can
we play whilst we wait?"

"We hired you to make bombs, not to dick around,"
said Jenny harshly. She was unsettled by Nixa. Nixa
usually only came at the time of sleep. Why was she
here now? Haunting her during her waking moments,
and more importantly, when she was out on a mission?

"I know that," said Randy, smoothly, and Jenny
looked into his eyes and for the first time she *understood*

him. He was there, genuinely, out of support for their clean world ideology. He was there to help. But... a leopard never changes its spots. What Randy said and did; that was just the way he was. And Jenny would have to get used to it, or kick him from the squad. And they were down Jones now; they needed all the manpower they could get.

Jones. Gone, after his beating. That had been four weeks ago...

Vanished! Self-discharged from the hospital, he'd taken his kit and fucked off. Now, the whole incident sat uneasy with Jenny. Something was *wrong*. Out of kilter. Jenny had a funny feeling she hadn't seen the last of him...

Still, the rest of the cell were happy Jones was gone. He was like a maggot at the core of a fresh apple, nibbling away from the inside out until all the goodness was gone; or he over-gorged himself and died in the process.

"Shit."

"What's the matter?" rumbled Zanz.

"Just thinking about Jones."

"Don't mention that bastard to me. We should have dealt with him sooner. We shouldn't have let him run."

Jenny nodded. She understood. He *knew* too much. And Jones was the sort of man likely to wage a vendetta against their unit. She corrected herself. Against *her*. She knew his type.

They watched the Reprocessing Plant, and Jenny studied its lines for the thousandth time. She had the plans stored in her head; every corridor, every level, every staircase, every vat, every press, every blast chamber. All of it. As a team they'd gone over the maps time and time again until they knew it like their own bedchambers. They'd built a model in a rented cellar, and sat around drinking coffee and smoking and playing out scenarios with tiny holographic figures. TommyTom™ holographic action figures, in 7D! The most played with TommyTom™ toy in the Quad-Galaxy! TommyTom™ was guaranteed to give your little Tom *decades* of endless fun. Some of the guys in Impurity5 thought it was highly amusing to be using TommyTom™ to plan out their destruction of a fake reprocessing plant; a factory that was an integral player in the *pollution* of the world known as Toxicity.

Jenny didn't find the TommyTom™ so funny. The name Tom always reminded her of her dad.

And that was a bad place to be.

"They're coming out," said Randy, and Jenny got behind her Long Lens. The iron gates opened smoothly and the first of the Super Tankers, bobbing on air suspension, poked its long black snout from the factory and began to emerge – as Sick Note so inelegantly put it – like a turd from a pipe.

They watched the tankers. Jenny took more pics on her cube.

Evidence. Right there before her.

"See it?" she said, turning to Randy.

"I just see a whole load of tankers rolling out after delivering their loads for reprocessing. What's there to see? We can't justify this det, Jenny. They'll crucify us in the papes and on ggg!"

Jenny and Zanzibar exchanged glances. "Do you want to tell him, or shall I?"

"You do it," rumbled Zanzibar, and gave a broad grin showing yellow teeth.

"Look at the ride height," said Jenny.

Randy squinted. "Looks the same to me."

"Compare the images." She showed him on the Long Lens cam monitor. Randy licked his lips.

"They're lower on their suspension coming out."

"Which means?"

"They entered empty, filled up, and now they're going somewhere to dump the shit."

"Good boy."

Randy shrugged. "My skills lie in, shall we say, other areas." He gave her a wink, and she laughed.

"You have tenacity, my friend."

"Better believe it. So what now?"

Zanzibar stood, and stretched his mighty shoulders. "It's time for action," he said.

IMPURITY5 HAD SPLIT into two groups. Jenny, alongside Randy, Sick Note and Flizz, would hit the Reprocessing Plant; and Zanzibar, with Meat Cleaver, Bull and Nanny, would attack the Super Tankers. They would co-ordinate attacks to detonate at the same time, whilst making sure the print and ggg media found out *real* fast so they could get reporters on the job and to the gig and putting down Greenstar's lying ways for good.

The two groups spent the next twenty-four hours planning infil, det and exfil, and cross-referencing plans and data, checking weapons, and analysing Randy's incredibly brilliant new bombs. Both Jenny and Zanzibar had never seen anything quite like the tiny machines. Randy said they were based on alien tech, but more than that he would not say. He'd tap his nose with his finger, smile, and try and get a kiss from Jenny.

Finally, they were ready. One of the scouts had sent a comm; the Super Tankers were loading up. It was evening. The sun was falling fast from the sky. It was time to get the job done.

Zanzibar stood and embraced Jenny.

"For freedom," he said.

"For freedom," she echoed.

And hoisting packs and weapons, they headed out into the night.

Last to leave was Randy. He gave a look behind him, a smile, and pulling a small button from his pocket he gave it a tiny *click* and dropped it on the floor, where it glowed blue, briefly, before returning to the disguise of a normal button.

"For freedom," he muttered, and vanished into the falling gloom.

SICK NOTE LOOMED from the darkness, pale and pasty and looking like shit. He crouched in the hole beside Jenny and gave a single nod.

"All three?"

"Out for the count, mate."

Jenny gave a single nod. The Reprocessing Factories had originally been easy meat; pretty much unguarded targets. Until Jenny, her crew, Impurity5, and the Impurity Movement as a whole started detonating them. Subsequently, security had been increased, but was nothing somebody with the military background of Sick Note could not easily overcome.

Jenny watched Sick Note move. A hypochondriac he might be, constantly moaning about his knees, back, elbows, headaches, flu, and a million other minor ailments that either inspired roaring laughter or complete frustration. "How are you going, mate?" he'd always ask; not as a genuine inquiry into your health, but as a prelude to a litany of his own woes. It was a question most of the unit had learned to neatly side-step. But despite his moans and groans, he was a dab hand at stealthily rendering guards unconscious. Formerly special forces, Sick Note was a damn sight more deadly than he looked. Especially when not in bed whining with Man Flu.

"Let's do it."

Jenny, Sick Note and Flizz climbed and slithered up

the muddy slope, boots kicking in, closely followed by Randy, who was focused on Flizz's fantastically shaped behind. She glanced back at him with a deep scowl, gloved hands muddy, hair tight back and face dark with camo cream. "Don't get any ideas, motherfucker," she snapped.

Randy held his arms wide with a smile, as if to say, *I wouldn't dream of it, angel.*

They crawled under cover of twisted, leafless trees, one of The Company's toxic gifts to the flora and fauna of the planet. It was rare to find anything organic on Toxicity *not* affected by the pollution of the past thirty years. Toxicity was a horticulturist's idea of *Hell.* And a perfect model for people's idea of a poisoned world.

They stopped at the edge of the trees and surveyed the comically named Reprocessing Plant. Even though Jenny had memorised the plans, the layout, the wiring and ducting schematics, now – here, up close – the place was not only *huge,* but dark, brooding and intimidating. Jenny didn't know if The Company had set out to build a factory which oozed malice, but they had certainly succeeded. Its vast matt-black walls, lack of windows, and massive array of cooling towers, vats, pipes and open engines, all black, all without lights; well. Jenny smiled. They wouldn't be throwing any children's parties there, that was for sure.

Randy had pulled out a sniper scope and was surveying the plant. Up close, the place wasn't just dark and foreboding, it was *loud.* A constant buzz and smash and thump and grind, as if the place lived. It was loud on the ears, and the thumping pounded a person to the pit of his stomach. The constant onslaught made Jenny feel physically sick.

"How does it look?"

"Deserted," said Randy. "Night shift. Skeleton staff.

As we expected. The last loading of the Super Tankers have just gone. It's like taking pie from a kiddie, darling."

"We'll see," said Jenny. "Okay. We all know what to do. Comm silence unless it's an emergency. We clear?"

"Clear."

"Clear."

"Clear, girlfriend."

Jenny gave a tight dry smile. "Let's move."

They ran through the darkness in crouches, boots churning mud and long grass. The Plant was surrounded by a high spiked fence. Dropping at the base, Jenny pulled out an ECube and activated the laser, which cut through five bars in as many seconds. Smoke drifted from the glowing steel, and they crawled through the narrow gap and silently split up, Jenny and Sick Note to one corner of the Reprocessing Plant, Randy and Flizz to another. They would work their way around, covertly placing charges, then meet back at this hole in the fence to co-ordinate with Zanzibar for the simultaneous detonation.

Jenny ran, and a million emotions pumped through her like a narcotic. Fear was there, of course, harnessed and used to keep her on edge. Joy was also a factor, mingled in with exultation at what they were about to do; not just a thorn in Greenstar's side, they were a vicious multi-pronged spike right up its arse. They would make Quad-Gal's governments sit up and take note. They *would* force a change. The people on the planet of Toxicity had had enough of the lies, enough of the political bullshit, enough of the poison. They wanted their world back, and the Impurity Movement were there to give the people what they so desired.

Jenny crouched by a corner, and Sick Note was close, his unhealthy, pock-marked face pale in the gloom. This was the one time you'd find him without a cigarette and a bottle of whiskey. The one and only time you'd find him focused, and realise his underrated professionalism.

"We good?"

"Yeah."

They drew silenced Sig72 pistols and moved towards a blank metal door, checking behind them, then towards the perimeter sirens and emergency lights they knew were awaiting them. They'd seen the wiring diagrams.

"Can you talk?" came Zanzibar over the net.

"Yes. Be quick."

"There's something wrong."

A cool chill blew over Jenny's soul.

"What is it?"

"I'm not sure." Zanzibar's voice was low, slow, controlled, but something had twitched him. Jenny cursed. "Let's call it a hunch. Some tiny element is out of place. Out of alignment. I feel like we're being watched. Set up. How is it there?"

"All good," said Jenny. "Go with your instincts, Zanz. If you want to withdraw, withdraw. Even one hit on this shit-hole will send a middle-finger message to the bastards at Greenstar. We don't need the double-det." But inside, she was seething. Cold and annoyed. They both knew the double detonation would have a much larger impact.

"No. I'm good, Jen. Jumping at shadows. Will keep you updated."

"Good lad."

Jenny signalled Sick Note, who took out the lock using a tiny sliver of what looked like silver, but was in fact a controllable fluid pick. It took him half a minute, and then he opened the blank metal door and they slid inside.

They were in.

*   *   *

A COOL DARKNESS greeted Jenny, along with an undercurrent of stench that made her flinch. Living on the planet of Toxicity, the constant aroma of rotting crap was ever-present. For all who lived there, all those who called it home, olfactory senses became eventually dulled, and from childhood to adulthood, as Greenstar gradually wasted the planet of her kin, Jenny had come to see this gradual stripping of her senses as a sensory theft. Olfactory rape and murder. Another reason to curse Greenstar. Another reason to hate The Company.

But this. *This* was real bad.

Even Sick Note coughed, grip tightening on his Sig72.

Jenny signalled, and they moved down a narrow corridor. Through the walls, the thumping and grinding was louder now; more harsh. Like bricks in a grinder. It set Jen's teeth on edge, like a steel claw being dragged across a blackboard, and she fought to control herself. Focus. Job in hand. Plant charges.

Swiftly, they moved through the gloom of the Reprocessing Plant. Reaching several camera points they followed the same slick routine: Jenny would halt, Sick Note would come forward, and release his tiny silver worm, which would crawl its way up the wall, enter the camera and destroy its internal digital structure. One by one the cameras were shut down, and Sick Note grinned his sick grin. "No challenge for this technological master," he muttered, and winked at Jen. She patted his arm and they continued through the gloom.

Randy had been right. Skeleton night staff. But then, that's what they'd expected. What they'd seen during the days and weeks of monitoring. The Greenstar Company were methodical and predictable, if nothing else.

They reached a large chamber filled with bubbling vats of blue tox. They paused for a while, surveying the area, watching, waiting. A worker passed to their right and they let him go, hearts hard. They didn't want to kill people. But if they had to, they had to. These people were torturing the planet. These people were killing Jenny's world...

"Look at the stars, little lady. Look how they sparkle! How they light up the night sky!"

She stood with Old Tom, her dad, her father, her love, her hero, the Biggest Man in the World, the Greatest Man in the Galaxy, on top of the hill. Ice was under their boots, a wind snapping at them like wolf jaws; but she was snuggled and warm inside her fleece and hats and scarf and gloves and boots... and snuggled up to him, with his huge arm around her shoulders, holding her tight, protecting her. But more, she was warm inside. Warm like honey. Warm like angels. She was with her dad. And his love and strength were bright, real things.

"Aren't they tiny?" she said.

"No, they are massive, so big they would swallow our whole world if they wanted to."

"Wow. Is that true, daddy? Really true?"

"As true as their beauty. Look out, Jenny. Look out on our planet, our world, our incredible, fabulous planet. Amaranth. Deep in the heart of the Zynaps System. Wonderful, and fabulous, a million years of history deep under our very boots."

"It's so beautiful, daddy. I love the world. And I love you."

He gazed down into her big baby blue eyes, and ruffled her hair through her thick bobble hat. "I love you too, munchkin. Love you till the stars go out."

A month later, Greenstar bought the planet and signed the paperwork. The Company made their signed-in-blood agreements with corrupt Quad-Gal politicians, and the Titan-Class Space Freighters moved in. Orbiting Dump Pipes were set in place; vast, armoured, mech-

laser-protected itanio tubes which freighters could lock to above orbit and dump trillions of litres of crap to the surface through without having to land. Of course, the global population of Amaranth were offered generous payouts to pack up and ship out. Whole villages and towns, even cities, were abandoned overnight. Bus Shuttles shuttled millions from the condemned planet's surface. But, as was human nature, millions more *chose* to stay. This was their planet. Their world. Their home. Their history. Their *soul*.

Old Tom chose to stay. Three months later, his wife, Jenny's mother, had died from a rare allergic reaction to some of the new pollutants introduced to Amaranth – now being commonly touted by the media as *Toxic City*, or simply *Toxicity*. Oh, how *The Daily Shite* mocked and harangued those people who chose to stay. Funny cartoons depicted the remaining populace growing three heads and extra legs, and spouting comedy penis growths and jocular new diseases. They laughed and laughed and laughed. The day of Jenny's mother's funeral, Old Tom started to drink *real bad*. And he never stopped.

The Daily Shite ran comedy sketches, columns, cartoons and features... right up to the day when Jenny and three newly recruited Impurity Movement activists had bombed their HQ on Earth. That had been the beginning...

And although Jenny knew it was wrong; well, fuck it. It was also *right*.

Jenny and Sick Note waited until the worker left the chamber. They moved across the big space, slowly, confidently, in control. Their target was close, now. One of the main Reprocessing Decks that also formed a structural connection point for the whole plant. The Plant had four, one in each corner; foundation stones holding up the roof and the towers. Blow the Decks, where the toxic crap was supposedly "reprocessed," and the whole factory would come tumbling down upon itself...

As they drew near, Jenny stopped. "Listen."

"I don't hear anything," said Sick Note.

"Exactly. The Reprocessing Decks should be running 24/7. They're not even operating. Which is incredible, seeing as a hundred Super Tankers have just supposedly dumped their loads here for reprocessing."

"Jen," said Sick Note, softly. "You don't need to convince me. I'm on your side."

She gave him a dark look. "Sometimes, I think they think I'm mad," she said.

Sick Note touched her arm, tenderly for such a skinny little psychopathic madman. "Not me," he said.

Zanzibar came through on the net. "You copy?"

"Yeah. We're on target. You?"

"In position. The convoy is eleven minutes away; we'll hit it with so many bombs they'll think it's fucking Detonation Day!"

"Roger that. Will connect. Out."

"We on?" said Sick Note.

"We're on," said Jenny, and pulled a small, brown charge from her pack. "Let's do it."

They moved towards the massive Deck, which squatted in the gloom like a warship tipped on its nose. It veered off, upwards, a curiously angled skyscraper. Sick Note looked around, not nervous, but manically cautious. His weapon tracked different arcs. If they were spotted now, they were fucked.

Jenny knelt, and slowly spun out thin loops of gold wire. There was a *clack* as the charge connected with the metal, and tiny teeth chewed their rapid way into the alloy surface.

Satisfied, Jenny rocked back on her heels and glanced up at Sick Note. "We good?"

"We're good," he said.

Suddenly, both Jenny and Sick Note's comms burst into life. There was rattling gunfire and explosions. The pitter-patter of falling debris. "It's a set-up!" screamed Zanzibar. There came several *krumps*. "They were fucking waiting for us! Get out! Get out now!"

The comm went dead.

Jenny felt her heart drop into darkness. Hackles rose on the back of her neck and across her arms. Her jaw clamped tight, and she gave a sideways glance at Sick Note. "Come on. Let's finish it."

"But..."

"We've gone too far. We fucking finish it."

They ran through the gloom, unchallenged, heads low, SMKKs at the ready. Sick Note watched Jenny powering forward, a woman possessed, and made sure they weren't followed. Or watched. He grinned manically. Hell, how would they even *know?* This place could be rigged tighter than any high security bank. Just because it looked scummy from the outside, what was basically a glorified *tip,* didn't mean they didn't have access to all manner of high-grade observation technology. They could afford it.

They reached the second Deck in just under four minutes, and SickNote was streaming with sweat, wheezing, and wondering if it was time to finally give up the weed. Annoyingly, Jenny was not even out of breath. She knelt, priming the charge, as Sick Note tried to raise Zanzibar, Meat Cleaver, Bull or Nanny on their comms; nothing. They were either down and out of the game, or their tech had been compromised.

"Shit."

"Nothing?"

"No. Let's get the shit out of here, Jen. This is turning real sour and I don't trust this place."

"Let's go."

They made their exit with care, and it was with incredible relief they ran to the fence and their rendezvous with Randy and Flizz. The two hadn't yet arrived, and Jenny waited impatiently, crouched by the wire, eyes focused on the direction from which she thought they would emerge. A cold wind blew across her, and it felt strange; like somebody crawling over her grave. Amazing, as she wasn't dead yet. Not yet.

"Still can't raise Zanzibar. What do you think is going down?"

"Bad shit. Zanzibar wouldn't have cut in on our mission like that for fun. It sounded like an all-out warzone."

"They're here."

Jenny glanced left, a tiny frown creasing her pale skin. Randy had emerged from a narrow alleyway, looked left and right, then cautiously approached in a crouched run. "Shit, did you hear Zanzibar on the comm?" he hissed, dropping to his knees before Jen.

"Where's Flizz?"

Randy stared at Jenny. "She's just finishing up. Laying spool decoy, or something. Don't panic. Have you got the det?"

"Yes," said Jen, showing him her left hand where the digital detonator squatted like an oval bug.

"Good," said Randy, and placed the muzzle of his pistol against Jenny's head. "Then you'll be handing that over to me," he said. He smiled.

Sick Note spun, eyes filled with rage, body tense for combat.

"I wouldn't, motherfucker. This baby has a hairline trigger and could go off with the slightest squeeze. And by that, I don't mean Jenny's clit."

"How much did they pay you, Randy?"

"Not enough," he said, voice charming now as he stood and Jenny rose with him. Her guns and bombs; so close and yet so far. If she could just...

"Do not be fooled by my apparel, nor my nonchalant charm," said Randy, leaning in close to her. "I'd kill you as readily as swatting a fly. I *will* spread your brains across the wall."

"What did you do with Flizz?"

"Let's just say some big men in big coats with a big black van took her away. Somewhere nice. She can, oooh, perhaps have a snooze, with a nice meal; then a spot of torture for dessert? I think that may be on the menu."

"Blow it," said Sick Note, eyes and gun fixed on Randy.

"She'll have a job," said Randy, smiling easily. "I swapped the trigger lines. Now, give me the det."

Suddenly, there was a deafening clatter of three choppers, slick and glossy, which zoomed across the sky, searchlights painting massive circles of light against the ground. Jenny sensed, more than saw or heard, the special ops soldiers behind her; creeping through grass, drifting like ghosts between the trees with weapons primed and hearts hard. They really had been set up. The enemy. The Company. Aided and abetted by a back-stabbing Randy. The bastard.

Jenny turned and looked at him. "Why?" she said, eyes haunted, lost, hurt. Then she spat in his face and watched the dandy in him leave, like a soul drifting upwards from a corpse. *Was it just a persona? A created character for our benefit; to get inside Impurity? To get inside us? To break us?*

"Give me the detonator, bitch," he said.

The special ops soldiers were through the fence now, a ring of weapons around Jenny and Sick Note. Slowly, Sick Note bent and placed his weapon on the ground, hands in the air, game over. Jenny, however, seemed locked in battle with Randy. As if some great contest of wills was taking place, and he really *didn't* have a gun to her head.

"When I detonate," said Jenny, slowly, enunciating every word with care, her eyes locked to Randy's, "you know as well as I the whole fucking place is going to come smashing down. This close, it's a toss-up between whether we live" – she licked her lips, and smiled – "or die. I believe in my cause, and I'm willing to die with honour, Randy. Are you in the same place? In your heart? In your soul?"

"I explained," barked Randy, annoyed now. "I swapped the trigger lines." He gave his own dark smile then; it was almost as dark as his hooded, glassy eyes.

"And I'm explaining now," said Jenny, dipping her head a little and lifting the detonator in her gloved fist, "that I bypassed them altogether. I didn't trust your alien shit. I wanted the job done."

Her hand was high in the air, now. Her eyes shifted and met Sick Note's. He knew what to do.

"So – it's live?" he asked.

Jenny could see a pulse beating at Randy's temple. It was flickering wildly.

"Oh, yes," she said, and squeezed the detonator like a lover... and in a dream, watched the world come tumbling down.

THREE

NEVER LOSE YOUR temper.

Horace was bald. Horace liked being bald. He especially liked it when somebody shouted, "Oi! You! Bald bastard!" Then, Horace would have to remove a few teeth. Horace had removed lots of teeth in his career, but that wasn't why they called him The Dentist.

"Never lose your temper."

Horace stood cupped in the shadows of the gloomy, low-rent, drag-strip neon-tattooed bar, arms limp by his sides, face neutral, and stared at the three large, hairy, overly-angry men before him. Glass lay shattered on the whiskey-stained boards. A woman in a leopard-skin mini-skirt sat, stunned, blood trickling from her smashed lip.

One man growled something incomprehensible, and snapped a pool cue over one knee. Horace gave a long, slow, reptilian blink. The length of splintered wood whistled as it slammed through the air, and the modest-looking, mild-mannered Horace twitched and swayed to the side by just enough, eyes cool, face serene, breathing calmly.

The second strike was avoided with equal ease, and screaming in frustration, the large, heavily muscled wife-beater leapt at Horace, who simply turned sideways, allowing the huge man to cannon past, charge uncontrollably into a stack of tables, and send the whole tower tumbling down with a noise like a fat man falling down the stairs.

With neat little movements, Horace turned his back on the group and walked towards the exit. On his way out from the darkened, seedy bar he pocketed a photo cube in his expensive neat black suit pocket. A glass flew past him, shattering on the wall, and then Horace was outside, breathing cool, snow-laced air, neon party-lights flickering above him with promises of SEX SEX SEX and CUNT CUNT CUNT. Digital echoes played across Horace's alabaster skin.

He started down the sidewalk, filtering out the noise of the partying nightlife all around. He sensed the three men emerge from the bar behind him. A door cracked shut.

"Oi, you! I said YOU! Bald fucker!"

Horace stopped dead.

A tiny muscle twitched in his jaw.

Horace sighed. And turned. He watched the three men charging towards him, and waited until the last moment before twitching sideways to the right, right fist driving upwards under the middle man's jaw and lifting him clean off his feet. In a reversal of the same movement, his elbow drove backwards into another man's eye socket – disintegrating the bone – and as the third man stood suddenly still, shock registering through alcohol and hate, Horace stepped in close and leant towards him.

"Do you know what they call me?" he said, quite placidly.

The man tried to take a backward step, but realised Horace had hold of his belt. He stared down at the neat white features, the polished dome of the bald head, and he felt a tremor of terror ripple down his spine.

"No," he managed, gusting sour whiskey fumes and spittle.

"They call me The Dentist," said Horace, gently, words little more than an exhalation of calm air. "Have you heard my name?"

The half-drunken thug nodded, eyes growing wide. Everybody had heard of The Dentist. Everybody had heard *bad things* about The Dentist. Growing up in Callister Town, the wild frontier for partying nutcases, the rumours were always exaggerated; but always, as these things were, based on a grain of truth. *He's as big as five men, son,* the bullshitters would bullshit. *He can punch through plate steel, and has balls the size of watermelons!*

But... why do they call him The Dentist?

Only he knows that, son. But one thing I can tell you is that if you hear that name, you'd better run, 'cause your meat is deader 'n dead meat.

Jonboy had heard the rumours, of course he had, everybody had, and the stories, and seen the pictures (artist's impressions) in papes and newscubes. The scenes of destruction. Of torture and murder. The wanted posters containing blurry images and colossal reward sums for information leading to the capture and execution of the killer known as The Dentist.

Nobody would invoke that name without having some serious backup, or serious hardware. Jonboy looked frantically for a gun, but could see none. No stick, no knife, no 'dusters.

Shit, he realised. This greasy little pasty-face bastard was taking the *piss!*

Jonboy let out a snort, partly fuelled by alcohol, partly fuelled by the realisation that only a skinny little bastard without *real muscle* was gripping his belt. A little bastard who was about to get the kicking of his life.

"You don't fucking *say*," Jonboy snarled, bravado returning on a surfboard of adrenaline and whiskey.

"Yes." Horace smiled. "Actually, I do." His hand came up swiftly, formed a fist, and drove into Jonboy's mouth like a pile driver. Fingers opened like grappling hook irons, and Horace gave a violent twist of the wrist, like he was unscrewing a lightbulb, breaking both lower and upper jaws with one swift *crack*, and extracting both gleaming teeth and yellow jaw from the suddenly gaping cavity of the skull. The bone trailed ripped tendons on a torrent of torn muscle and gushing blood.

Jonboy gawped for a moment. He had little option.

Horace surveyed the excised jawbone in his fist, and slowly analysed each tooth sequentially. He gave a little smile, as if acknowledging some internal diatribe. He then dropped the jaw to the ground with a clatter and strode away, watched by Jonboy who slowly folded to his knees, hands pawing his missing lower face.

Within moments, Horace was lost in the crowds.

HORACE LIVED IN a big white house on a hill. The house overlooked a vast surrounding countryside, which constituted flowing, waving keeka grasses and red-leaf woodland. The expansive grounds of the house were marked by a clear boundary, a high stone wall topped with black iron spikes. The drive was guarded by high iron gates which could be controlled remotely from the house, and on the stone pillars there was a marked absence of an intercom. Horace did not welcome visitors. Horace did not like visitors. Horace did not welcome *anybody*.

The house, which went by the name of the *Nadir,* was a good hundred kilometres from the nearest village, and nearer two hundred from the nearest city. The only access to the imposing white-walled residence was up a narrow dirt track guarded on either side by dangerous lakes and overhanging, sharp-thorned trees. The land surrounding Horace's home was not a welcoming place. It was the sort of location chosen by a dedicated recluse.

The seasons had shifted, an almost imperceptible slide from autumn to winter. On this cold, crisp morning, the lawns were peppered with ice crystals and a cold pastel sun hung low against a sky as broad as infinity.

Horace stepped from the side entrance, and shivered. Silka, his pet shifta, slunk over to him and wrapped herself between his legs, much the same way as an affectionate cat would. Her long tail tickled his calves and he smiled, bending down, picking her up in one hand. She purred, wide orange eyes watching him as her almost serpentine body curled around his hand, six legs with their little hands gripping him lightly.

"You catch anything?"

"Of course," said Silka.

"So the hunting's good?"

"At this time of year, the hunting is always good." She smiled, and her face was almost human. *Almost.*

"Come on, climb down. I have work to do."

"The shed?"

"Yes, the shed."

Silka leapt from her master's fist and slunk off into the auburn autumn grass. She disappeared immediately, engaging her chameleonic colour-shifting abilities and, as usual, Horace spent a good minute searching for her, without success. Despite Silka's size – about that of a ferret – Horace knew she was one of the most deadly hunters on the planet. Her sharp teeth could easily rip out a man's windpipe, and coupled with her near invisibility and human intelligence, she would make a deadly adversary for any organism. Luckily, she was mostly interested in hunting small rodents. Well, today, anyway.

Horace walked across the gravelled drive, boots crunching, breath smoking, and stopped to look at his shed. It was a large, rough-timbered affair which Horace had built himself. He stared at it proudly, analysing its odd angles and imperfect planking. Silka had constantly derided him for his limited carpentry skills, but Horace simply nodded, watching his shed grow and expand and become... complete. If truth be known, he revelled in the fact that it was imperfect. It had to be imperfect. He *wanted* it to be imperfect. Every angle was slightly different. The frame was not square. The roof slope was a different elevation on each side. Most of the frame and indeed the covering boards were of modest, unequal length.

It has to be uneven, distorted, warped. Because that's the way I am. Deep down inside.

Horace worked hard in the cold morning air, sawing fresh planks to line the back wall, and nailing them in place. Sweat dropped down his face and he stripped off his heavy shirt, the top half of his naked, wiry body showing a heavy slew of twisting, swirling tattoos. There were no distinct images; just patterns, almost random swirls and arcs and spikes.

Horace was just completing the rear wall, covered in a second skin of fine sawdust and sweat, when he heard the heavy drone of a large engine. He knocked up the last plank with three accurate, hefty swipes of the hammer, removed several nails from between his lips and moved to his shirt, pulling it on and deftly fixing the buttons. Only then did he turn and look out from his hilltop vantage.

It was a large black 4x4, sweeping along the narrow track at a dangerous rate of knots. Horace moved to the shade of the large white house, leant with his back to the wall and placed his hands in his pockets.

The car halted, and waited, engine running, exhaust fumes pluming. After a few moments Horace asked, voice quiet, "Who is it?"

"The Fat Man," said Silka, materialising; drifting into view as if phased into reality by a gradual analogue dial.

"He has a new car."

"Yes."

"Let him in."

Horace ignored the gates swinging open, and set about tidying his tools into a large black toolbox. The car growled up the long gravel drive, tyres crunching, blackened windows showing the reflection of the white house. It stopped to one side, and the engine cut out. The door opened, and the Fat Man stepped out, his huge frame almost too much even for the vast 4X4.

"Horace!" boomed the Fat Man, and strode mightily forwards, hands outstretched, a big smile on his big face. His hair was black and shaggy, his shoulders broad, his belly huge, his legs like sturdy tree trunks.

"Fat Man," smiled Horace, encompassed by the embrace, and not for the first time he acknowledged Fat Man's prodigious strength. Yes, he was fat; but it was a layer of fat over a rock-hard, iron-ridged, muscle core. He had been underestimated many times by lesser men.

"It's been a while," said Fat Man. "The Company has missed you!"

"Yeah, well. I work when there is work to be done. You changed your car. That's a shame. I liked your old car. It had... character."

"Ach, she met with a large accident. Unfortunately, there were two bad men in the boot as she went over a cliff. You know how it is."

"Yes," said Horace, face registering no emotion.

"A drink?" suggested Fat Man.

"Of course. Come in. I'll get Jemima to rustle up something to eat."

Fat Man grinned and rubbed his hands together. "Good," he said.

THEY SAT ACROSS from one another. Horace's house was decorated with sparse but expensive taste. He had white pash ornaments placed strategically on puf-watch puf-stands. The carpets were seaweed and edible. The furniture was bombool crack coca cane, and glittered orange.

The Fat Man finished his third piece of black slab cake, and licked his fingers noisily, dusting crumbs off himself and smiling at Horace. "The Company has a job for you."

"I am ready," he said.

Fat Man reached inside his suit, and pulled out a sheaf of metal leaves. He laid them out on the table, shifting the cake plate with a scraping sound, and brushing aside a few more crumbs from his expensive trousers.

"Greenstar Agency is having a few... problems."

Horace gave a little shrug. "They're always experiencing a few problems." He gave a tight smile. "That's the nature of your business. That's why you employ me. It's why I exist."

"The Company thinks you're a little too... *high profile,* at the moment. Here on Earth. So we have another option for you."

"Go on."

"On Amaranth, which you know is our principal recycling facility, there has been 'an escalation of violence.' An increased number of bombings and attempted sabotage of various facilities."

"I know. I saw reports in the papes and on ggg. The whole of Manna knows this."

"What's not being reported is the success rate of these bastards. You know what The Company is like; even if the bastard ECO terrorists wiped out our entire HQ with a Q Bomb, we'd put it down to rats in the cabling, a glitch in the matrix, and weather it out until our repair squads got us at least superficially up and running. You know how it is."

"I do," said Horace, and broke off a corner of cake. At the same time, he touched the metal leaves before him, eyes scanning the data, the pictures, the statistics, the gathered intel.

"These ECO terrorists have five operational squads," he observed.

"Yes. And because of the poor living conditions on Amaranth, they're recruiting more and more to their 'cause' all the time."

"Why don't they leave?"

"You know what these freaks are like. It's their homeland, ancestors buried under the ground, blah blah. The fact is, until Greenstar arrived, the planet was a backwater shit-hole, a no-place for hillbilly redbollock rednecks. The Company brought jobs and education."

"And toxicity," said Horace, showing a rare smile.

"Don't you fucking start. Everybody knew the deal when they signed."

Horace held up a hand. "Hey. I don't care. You pay me, I do the job. I leave the politics to the... politicians."

"So. That's where you come in."

"Oh? I thought I'd be going after the ECO terrorists."

"No. There has been a leak from the Green House. One of The Company's own *directors* is pissing out intel to the ECO nuts, giving them access codes, handing out military-grade weapons and explosives like it's candy at a little girl's party. It's a fucking political *nightmare*. We need you in there. Fast. A clean kill. No witnesses. You know the score. We don't know which director – yet. But we have a location of leaked and uploaded files. Rather than send in the pigs – well, we thought we'd send in you."

"When do I leave?"

"We've got you booked on a Shuttle. As a tourist."

"A tourist? *Tourists* go to the Toxic Planet? What are they hoping to see?"

"You tell me, pal," said Fat Man. "How long do you need to sort your shit?"

"Ten minutes." Horace stood, lifting the metal leaves with him. "You go and warm the car. I'll get my case."

"Good. The Company will owe you one if you pull this off."

"I'll pull it off," said The Dentist, face straight, eyes staring straight ahead. "I always do."

NEVER LOSE YOUR temper.

Horace was sat on the Shuttle in a casual suit with black shiny shoes, listening to the argument behind him. Two half-drunk shebangs wearing spotted shirts and too-tight shorts had been sneaking cheap voddie into plastic cups and fumbling with each other under the blankets. They were caught by a Shuttle stewardess, who tried to confiscate the voddie, and an argument ensued:

"You're not having it!" the male shebang said, facial tentacles waving.

"Sir, it's company policy that you do not bring liquor aboard Greenstar Shuttles. We have an adequate drinks trolley where you can buy the beverage of your choice."

"Yeah, at your over-inflated prices!"

"That's not the point," said the stewardess. "Rules are rules. Now... *give* me the bottle."

There were sounds of a scuffle.

The male shebang was growling something incomprehensible, and as Horace stood up and turned, the female lurched upwards, eyes on him. She pointed in his face. "Don't get involved, shitbag!"

Horace hit her with a right straight on the feeding tube, so hard it would have dropped a horse. It certainly dropped the female shebang, whose alien head folded in on itself for protection, leaving nothing but a tennis-ball-sized mini-head.

Horace turned to the male. "Are you going to give up the voddie, you cheap little shit? Or shall I pop your inflatable head as well?"

"Bastard!" he shrieked. "Bastard, bastard, bastard!" and leapt at Horace, who dodged a slapping tentacle with ease, dropped his shoulder, then cracked him with a right hook that could have felled an elephant. As the shebang hit the ground, there was a hissing sound and fluid pissed out, and his head deflated into a miniature head.

"Oh, thank you, sir! Security are just arriving now! But thank you, thank you for stepping in!"

Horace, who was still staring at the shrivel-headed aliens, shrugged. "What a strange defence mechanism," he said, frowning, then looked at the stewardess. He gave her a nod. "My pleasure, ma'am," he smiled, and knew by the look in her eyes that he was going to be *very* well looked after on the Shuttle voyage.

*   *   *

IT WAS RAINING at the Shuttleport in Bacillus Port City, Toxicity's capital. They flew in low through heavy rainclouds which sounded like thunder on the Shuttle's hull. Horace watched the vast sprawl of the grim, dark, polluted city hove into view. It was like an architect's nightmare, a vision of Hell and a toxic wasteland, all rolled into one. It was rumoured to be the most poisoned city on the planet, but Horace doubted it. He'd read the files. However, it wasn't called Bacillus for nothing and he welcomed the fine antibacterial spray which constantly emanated from the Shuttle's CleanBeing WishYouWell ConstaDecontaminate System.

As the spacecraft touched down, stubby legs groaning and creaking into suspension housings, the rain eased off. Horace made his way into the connection umbilicals and along endless corridors filled with... space. Lots of space. As if Amaranth had once had a booming tourist industry, but now only catered for a dribble of curious visitors. Which was probably a good analogy, thought Horace, as he collected his single case and stepped through immigration. A toxic dribble. Pus from the overflow pipe.

He showed his Quad-Gal passport, several other papers, and walked across gleaming tiles, his boots clicking, until he stepped out into the fresh air of Bacillus Port – although the air wasn't very fresh. It stank like a rancid corpse.

"Hmm," said Horace, and moved to a nearby taxi rank. All the taxis were hover models, as if by refraining from the use of wheels they might somehow halt the spread of contagion across the planet. Doubtful, when they welcomed it in by the billion-tonne tanker-full.

As he relaxed back in the hover taxi, the driver growled, "Where to, Mister?"

"Bacillus Hilton, good sir."

The taxi moved from the rank and the rain started again, hammering down, gushing black through crap-filled gutters. A thick snake of commuters hurried down pavements, their silver shining umbrellas up-spraying black tox water at one another. There came many curses, and several fist fights on the pavement as people pushed and shoved, jostled and hassled. It made for grim watching.

Lights flickered across Horace's pale white face, as they sped through the narrow streets of Amaranth's capital.

HORACE WALKED THROUGH the night, his suit drenched through with toxic rain, his gloved hands carrying a slick wet briefcase. Horace liked the rain. In the rain, the majority of people became invisible, heads down, scurrying, thinking only of getting *out* of the rain; of keeping dry and getting home for that hot mug of cocoa or dram of whiskey juice. Horace gave a brief smile; a flicker across his lips. Yes. The rain was good. It distracted people. Made his job easier to carry out. Much, much easier.

His boots waded through mud as he walked up the edge of the road. He was on the outskirts of Bacillus Port now, and the dark night sky, lit only by a few green stars, contained a corrugated horizon, a serrated skyline of a thousand factories, towers, cooling humps and reprocessing plants. Many were privately owned, companies having jumped on the "recycling" bandwagon trailblazed by Greenstar, and indeed, fed down crap by Greenstar in their capacity of appointing sub-contractors. But Greenstar were the Masters. This was their planet of crap, and they would never let go their stranglehold and monopoly.

The Fat Man had misled Horace a tad. Horace found this annoying, but he internalised the situation and dealt with it. The Fat Man had said *a director of*

Greenstar was feeding information and pass codes to the ECO terrorists; he'd never said which one, but they were "on it." Well, no new intel had come through. And the problem with *that* was that there were a lot of directors. Greenstar had turned the *entire* planet of Amaranth into a waste zone, a dead zone, a planet of rubble and tox and broken glass. There were whole cities that were factories dedicated to reprocessing; nearly the entire population worked the factories. This was an industry based on waste. A hive of shit, the leftovers from a hundred thousand planets all brought here to be reformed into something *positive*. Or so the advertising spiel went.

Lirridium.

A New Fuel for a New Space Age! Created Entirely From Your Waste!

Yeah. Right.

Greenstar had no less than nine-hundred-and-ninety-nine directors. So Horace's task was a little more difficult than first envisioned. The directors were organised into a tier which shuffled up and down due to performance – presumably, financial performance. Greenstar was one of the most financially buoyant companies in the entire Four Galaxies.

There were five tiers. Horace would start in the middle. Horace liked the middle. The bottom tier or two would contain the slackers and the useless. The top two tiers, admittedly, would contain the best; but also the complacent, the wealthiest, the most heavily protected. But the middle tier! Ahh, the middle tier would have the fighters, the scrappers, those with the most knowledge and data; for knowledge and data were key in screwing and clawing and biting your way to the top.

And Horace had a trump card.

He knew from whence the intel was leaked...

Horace walked, through rain and mud. Occasionally a truck would pass him on the road, a great lumbering beast, gears crunching, engine labouring, tyres grinding through mud and sludge on its way to or from a rendezvous with waste. Horace tended to step back from the road when such a vehicle passed, lowering his head. No need in advertising his whereabouts unnecessarily, he reasoned. And he knew he was invisible to these people; these drivers and workers and wastemongers. He was a ghost.

The lights on the hill twinkled like a beacon, and Horace stopped in the mud by a road sign warning "NO TIPPING." Ahh, that would be Greenstar's amazingly surreal sense of humour, would it? *No tipping? On the Toxic World? Boom*-tisch. Comedy at its most sophisticated. Horace stood for a while, watching those distant lights, then his eyes traced the winding road back down the steep hillside, twisting like a snake to his present position.

He continued to walk, trudging along, his pace never faltering. Behind him, even through the darkness, a green smog hung over Bacillus Port like a bad toupee. Horace pushed on, legs working hard, his bald head slick with dark rain. But no matter. Soon he would have his answers, and head back to the Hilton, and dry off, and freshen up...

The gradient increased, and Horace had to work hard, but still showed no signs of fatigue. After all, he'd climbed a thousand mountains in his life; both physical and metaphorical. None of them caused him problems. *Not one*. Horace didn't get tired. And he never got angry. *Never get angry...*

Because.

Well, because *bad things* happened when he was angry.

It took him a half hour, and closing on the house – which wasn't so much a house, as a vast mansion of the über-wealthy – Horace slowed and observed. There were high iron gates and a high chain-link fence. Horace's experienced eyes picked out surveillance cameras. There was also a sign. For attack dogs. Horace moved off the road, swift now, sure-footed on the drenched, hardy heather of the hillside. He crept around the edges of the perimeter fence until he found a suitable spot, distant enough from the imposing white house, and situated on a rear corner of the property. He moved to the chain links, scanned them, witnessed the anti-intrusion wires. He placed his briefcase on the heather, finding a nice flat spot, and listened to the rain drumming on its cheap leather for a moment before opening it and taking out several pieces of filament silver. These, he wove into the fence, and watched them ripple and then *merge*. He removed cutters, and starting at hip-height, cut downwards to create his entry point. He could hear the tiny *snicks* as the filament wire intercepted digital signals, blended them, and soothed the system so that there was no alarm.

Through the fence, dragging his case after him, Horace settled into the darkness and surveyed the surveyors. There were twelve cameras he could detect from this position; and until he could get to a master hub, he would have to do it the hard way. The Secker P5K fired a narrow-range atomic pellet. Horace took out the cameras one by one. He knew if there was somebody *physically* monitoring the cameras, it would be a dead giveaway to intrusion; but then, that mattered little at this point. This was mostly to prevent leaving any evidence. Horace was in. And the police, guards, army – they were at least five minutes away. That was enough. That was always enough.

Horace moved forward in a commando crawl, which must have looked ridiculous to any onlooker; a bald man in a suit with a briefcase, commando crawling across lawns and gravel drives. But it worked for him. Horace had little use for comedy.

He reached the wall, a mixture of stone and rendering. The windows were old and made from steel. Glancing left and right, Horace heard the attack dogs coming from the darkness, with a *pitter patter* of promised violence. The lead dog snarled from the darkness, a huge black and tan beast baring its fangs, saliva drooling at the thrill of a fight and a feast. It leapt for Horace, and was easily half his size, rippling with muscle and a coiled spring of aggression.

Horace moved fast, stepping forward, left hand grabbing its long snout in mid-air, right hand cutting under, between the dog's legs, and grabbing its cock and balls in one great handful. The dog, surprised at this sudden turn of events, grunted and Horace... *folded it in half,* with a terrible cracking of breaking spine and neck and jaw. The dog hit the ground limply, as its four brethren emerged from the darkness like demons. They were growling, eyes fixed and focused, long strings of saliva pooling from twisted fangs.

Horace held both hands wide, almost in pleading, in supplication, in a posture begging forgiveness.

"Here, doggy doggy," he said, and the dogs leapt...

The night was soon filled with snapping, cracking and breaking sounds.

HAVING REMOVED HIS shoes, Horace padded silently through the house. The place oozed opulence, but in bad taste. The sort of opulence *learned* by a poor person who'd made it good and rich, as opposed to opulence instilled by decades of breeding and education. It mattered little to Horace. Because Horace was The Dentist, and he was here to do his job.

He'd found the central console for the alarm

system, and with deft fingers, had twisted, removed components, and isolated the entire camera and alarm system to external alert. It was almost with disappointment that he realised there were no armed guards to kill. Obviously, this particular politician-slash-Greenstar-company-director hadn't quite upset enough people *just yet*. But it would come, Horace knew. It always did.

The stairs were broad, sweeping in a generous curve to a wide balcony overhead. Horace moved at a leisurely pace. There was no hurry. His target wasn't going anywhere, he would be asleep and fat and snoring, with his snoring fat wife beside him, both of them pumped and slumped on rich food and red wine and bad perfume and drunk sex. After all, it *was* Saturday night.

He searched through various rooms before finding the master bedroom. The door opened softly on well-oiled hinges, the work of a master craftsman; ironic to find one operating on a planet filled with junk. Still, Horace was wise enough to understand the entire planet of Amaranth would hold these pockets of perfection every once in a while. Power and wealth bought quality no matter on what shit-hole one decided to exist. Horace chose the word *exist* as opposed to *live*. For Horace didn't believe that people such as this, with planetary atrocity on their tox-smeared hands, could ever truly *live*. Living was what the noble of heart did. Existing... well. He smiled. That was left to the rest of the trash.

The bed was large and vulgar, as befitted a director of Greenstar. Two blubber mounds were tunnelled under the blankets like fattened, hibernating pigs. One was snoring like bubbles blown through a mouthful of marbles. Horace gave a narrow, straight smile. *Oh, the comedy of the situation! It will be a pleasure cutting the slabs of fat from your distended bellies...*

Horace's nostrils twitched and his eyes flared and he knew in an instant something was wrong. A metallic scent. The scent of...

A boot hit his head, slamming him backwards to the ground, where he rolled fast, savagely, into a crouch. The figure, highlighted by weak starlight, landed, whirled, and Horace caught the flash of silver. A knife. The attacker came at him again, knife slashing down left, right, left. Horace shifted from each stroke, then grabbed the wrist, ducked under a right hook, spinning behind the attacker, and dragged the knife back into the attacker's own chest. Horace let go and front-kicked the attacker away, and an almost sixth sense alerted him and he twitched, as a second attacker flew by him. He grabbed the figure from the air by the ankles, swinging it around and launching it at the wall, where there came a crash and the smash of a large mirror, and assailant, mirror shards and broken frame all landed on the bed, revealing the dummies within.

A set-up.

Horace smiled grimly. A fucking *set-up*?

That normally happened to *other* people.

The two attackers were on their feet, a knife in the chest not even slowing the first figure. Clouds had shifted outside, and by green starlight Horace saw the two attackers were – women. This didn't matter. He'd killed women. Children. Priests on the job. Politicians on the toilet. It was all the same kettle of mashed-up organic pulp from where he was standing.

And yet it made it *interesting*.

Horace moved his head left, then right, releasing cracks of tension, and lifted his fists. His T5 9mm was in his pocket; not enough time for that.

"Who sent you?"

No answer. They launched at him, silent, professional. He dodged various punches and over-athletic high kicks, then dropped and slammed sideways, sweeping the feet of the first attacker. She hit the carpet with an "umph" and Horace grabbed the knife in her chest and wrenched it sideways. There came a flush of blood, and the woman seemed to deflate. She sighed. Horace rammed the knife into her eyeball with such power it drove through eye, brain and skull, and pinned her head to the floorboards beneath. She lay, body spasming and twitching, head pinned in place.

Horace rolled, came up, and looked down the twin barrels of a D4 shotgun. He slammed left as the *boom* deafened him, making his ear ring, and something cut a searing hot line over his right shoulder. He dived into his pocket, T5 in his hand, and was shooting through the fabric even as he rolled and hit the wall with a slap. Bullets fizzed and whined, ruining the cut of his mud-splattered suit. Another shadow passed the doorway.

A third attacker.

Horace clenched his jaw, pulled out the T5, and put ten rounds through the wall. There came a *thump*. He smiled. Horace had been conned like that before.

He scanned the sudden bleak darkness; an awesome, deafening silence.

Rain battered against the windows. Gun smoke hung heavy in the air, shimmering in twisting slow-mo coils

Horace eased himself upright, T5 tracking the gloom. He knew his bald head shone under any form of light, and it was moments like this he cursed his baldness with a wry irony. *Oh, to be killed by his bald head!* That would be a great line for the stand-ups.

Lowering himself to the carpet again, on his belly, Horace scanned the room. There. At the head of the bed. Slowly, he extended his T5 and aimed, waiting, breath held, body rigid. And then the feet were gone, and Horace rolled as a D4 *boom* spat fire and ferocity at the point where he'd lain. The T5 gave a *crack* and he heard the splatter of blood on wallpaper. Still tracking, he fired again, blind but precise. Another *crack*. Another splatter. There was a thud as the shotgun hit the carpet, and Horace stood. He moved through the gloom to the shotgun, picked it up, checked it was still loaded. Then he stepped backwards and to the side, poking his head out into the hall. Another woman, lying on the patterned carpet, face screwed in silent agony, clutching three bullet holes in her belly. Horace gave a nod, and moved back in. The attacker who'd taken two rounds was crawling towards the wall – and God only knew what. There was no escape there. But maybe... were they here to protect the Greenstar director, or to kill him? It was unlikely both were true. So which was it?

Horace walked forward, wary of more attackers leaping on him from the dark. He hated that. Hated it with a *vengeance*. Horace liked to be in control. Horace liked to be calling the winning shots. Horace liked to be the one behind the pistol. Like... now.

He knelt on the shot woman, feeling blood pump from her wounds as he did so. She groaned, and Horace put the T5 against her lips.

"Who sent you?"

"Fuck off."

"You're an android, right?"

"Fuck you."

"So this isn't murder, my beautiful little sweetie pie. When I merge your teeth with your brain with the carpet, it's just a retirement, as the old cops used to say. A put down. A meat wrap. And, I might add from a personal viewpoint, a fucking *pleasure*."

"Go. To. Hell."

"I doubt it," said Horace, and grabbed her hair, dragging her kicking and groaning across the carpet and out into the hall. The second attacker was still clutching her stomach, and Horace's eyes narrowed as he made a shrewd judgement. Which one would last the longest? Which would talk the most? The prettier one would probably have more self confidence, but then with these fucking androids it was all a sham anyway. He smiled at the irony. To think like the killer. To hunt like the predator. To retire an android with complete understanding.

Horace *did* so like his work.

"Who talks first? The one who talks, lives."

The two women, side by side now, glanced at one another uneasily. "Don't tell him *anything*," snarled the T5-wounded android. Horace knelt on her, his knees compressing her small, pert breasts. Again, he put the gun against her lips and glanced to the android with triple stomach wounds.

"Talk, or I kill her."

"No."

"Talk."

"Fuck you."

Horace shot the android through the mouth; through her clenched teeth. Broken teeth and the bullet mashed into her brain, pulping the innards, before exiting into the floorboards. The android went limp, slack, dead. Blood flooded out in a large black pool.

"You next," said Horace, T5 turned on her. And he knew; deep in his heart he *knew* she wouldn't speak, wouldn't blab, wouldn't sing like a canary. Because *that* was the way she was created. Engineered. Unless... unless she had the dreams, the visions, the longing for humanity that so many androids seemed to capture like a particularly nasty virus. The plague of the engineered human. A need to *be* human.

Horace spat to the side.

"There's no heaven for you, bitch. You're a created thing. A fucking machine. When you die, you'll fade into dust. Your memory will be as nothing when the valves stop working."

"What's your name?" she whispered.

Horace tilted his head. *Interesting.*

"They call me The Dentist," he said.

"I have heard of you."

Ah! So, not here to eliminate him. Or rather, if they were, they had no idea who they were dealing with.

"Were you sent to kill me? Or were you just here to protect the Greenstar director?"

"To kill you," she whispered, and tears filled her eyes, bubbling up, spilling down her blood-speckled cheeks.

"Good girl," he said, and eased himself up from the dead meat on which he knelt.

"What's your name?" asked the crying android.

"The Dentist."

"No. *No.* Your real name."

Horace stepped over her, and lowered himself to crouch above her. He stared down into her frightened eyes. And that wasn't right. There shouldn't be fear there. After all, she wasn't human, and she knew it.

"Horace," he said. "And you?"

"I am Michelle. Listen, Horace. I don't want to die, Horace." Her hands clasped his legs, then. Clasped the fine material of his suit, splattered with mud. He noted her hair was tied back in a pony-tail. She was quite pretty, when her face wasn't scrunched up in agony.

"Michelle, my sweet. *Nobody* wants to die," he smiled, and placed his T5 in his pocket.

"So you won't kill me?"

Horace considered this, then reached forward, took hold of her jaw with one hand, and with a wrench, pulled her front tooth free with the other. Blood spurted and drooled down her shirt. Michelle writhed. Horace's eyes gleamed.

"Not yet," he breathed, and strange wild thoughts were flickering through his brain. "I have some more questions."

"I'll talk!" hissed Michelle through a mouthful of blood, spraying him with a fine mist. "You don't need to torture me! I will talk!"

"I know you will," said Horace, and pulling out a small, black pack from his inner suit pocket, he unrolled it on the ground. It was full of gleaming silver instruments.

"Please don't torture me," wailed Michelle.

"I must," said Horace, with the calmness of a surgeon.

"But why?"

Horace gave a comforting smile to his patient, and the corner of his eye twitched. "Because I must," he said.

IT WAS OVER. Perhaps an hour had passed; maybe less. Horace sat with his back to the wall, exhausted and fulfilled. Some people said alcoholic drink was the best intoxication in the world. Others, a wild plethora of drugs which could stimulate any variety of wild experience. Yet others voted for virtual battlefields to get their milporn juices going, and others a rabid addiction to sex and all its various deviations. But in Horace's heart, in his soul, he knew nothing touched perfection like the creation of true art.

Horace looked over at his true art. She was dead now, of course. Her arms and legs were all broken and twisted at savage, irregular angles. Well, he'd had to, hadn't he? To stop her fighting like that. He looked at her face, at the ring of her blood-sodden skull; her beautiful, wounded, scalpel- and needle-destroyed face. She was no longer Michelle, of course. No. Horace had taken that away from her, starting with her teeth, one by one, each removal an exquisite pleasure, each snap and crack of bone a shiver of ultimate arousing ecstasy. On one side, he had piled up the teeth in a neat little pile, as Michelle fought and battled, struck at him, cursed him and begged him, weeping and screaming in equal measures. That's when he broke her arms like brittle twigs. After all, he didn't want her to tear his suit.

The pile of teeth were perfect, but Horace's perfection, his dentistry, went further. He'd pulled out a micro-filament titanium saw, eyes gleaming with a light of – not insanity, but something deeper, something dark; a chord in perfect tune with a demon's soul.

"I'll talk, I'll tell you every fucking thing!" screamed Michelle, her words deformed by her lack of teeth, her mouth full of blood and saliva and vomit.

Horace held up a finger, as if conducting an orchestra. This was the soundtrack of the doomed.

"Too late," he said with wet lips, and the saw went to work on Michelle's jaw. Not to silence her, but to complete the final pieces of The Dentist's puzzle. A key opening a lock with a *snick*. A perfect symbiosis: of victim, and killer.

Now, he sat back. Exhausted. Fulfilled. And his mind, his twisted, drifting mind, came back to the present with a gentle *bump*.

His mission was unfulfilled. But more than that: *they* knew he was here.

They were trying to kill him. He had competition. He had a fight.

Horace smiled, and placed his tool roll in his pocket. Outside, dawn was daring to stroke the horizon.

Sirens drifted through the haze.

It was time to leave.

FOUR

WHEN THEY CUT you down, you know what you have to do. You must fight, fight for your life, fight with every tooth and claw and fang and fist and finger and boot, kick and stomp and punch and slap and bite and elbow and knee and head-butt until you're free of these heathen peasant tribal bastards who seek to cook you over the fire! You get it? You'd better fucking get it, because if you don't, then you're gonna end up as pate in their bellies, as meat on their sticks, as arse slabs of gristle on their little bark plates. They'll use your eyeballs as delicacies, your belly-fat as candle wax, your dried-out skin as clothing, and your fucking scalp as a stick totem to wave at other captured unfortunates. Understand, Svoolzard? This is it. Time to fight. Fight or die, like never before!

Svoolzard tried hard not to cry, to whimper, to pout, or to sulk. He didn't want to fight. Yes, he had a jewelled sword, but it wasn't for fighting with, it was for showmanship! Fighting was what other, uncouth, uneducated, primal-tattooed stinking scabby arseholes did. Svoolzard was *above* that, intellectually, socially and academically. Svoolzard was a *lover*, not a *fighter*, man. But here, and now, he'd have to fight or he'd be...

Cooked.

He didn't see the tribesman scale the tree behind him, so when the twine was snipped he hit the ground on his face – and, more importantly, *his nose* – with a thud. Stars flooded his mind like some cheap special effect in a movie, and when consciousness deigned to make a return, they'd already cut away his fine clothing, tied his wrists and feet to a long pole, and were carrying him towards the flames.

"Hey, hey! What are you doing?" he screamed.

"Hey, oy! Why am I *naked?*" he wailed.

"Hey, that's a fire, that is, you really don't want to be putting me over that! No! No! Aieeeeee!"

The "Aieeeeee!" came as they indeed lodged the pole into the two upright Y-sections of the primitively-hacked frame. And no matter how primitively-hacked the frame was, the end results were the same. It supported the pole, which in turn supported Svoolzard Koolimax XXIV.

The flames licked his back and backside, scorching the flesh. Svool lifted himself up as high as the pole would allow, muscles bunching, his whole body writhing as it suddenly got *very* hot and the tribespeople, who had all gathered to watch the spectacle of The Cooking, starting chanting and giggling and running circles around him.

"Nooooooooooo!" wailed Svoolzard. "Don't coooooooook meeeee!"

Tears streamed down his cheeks, but tears didn't matter to the cannibals. What mattered were Svool's generous belly and his generous arse cheeks. Not for them the ethical dilemma of murder. Svool was food, simple as simple is.

A cough echoed across the bizarre, night-time scene.

Orange light from the flames flickered from black rubbery trees. There, at the edge of the clearing, stood a figure, tall and powerful, and sporting short green dreadlocks.

She held a sturdy staff, sharpened at both ends. She gazed across the scene with shining green eyes.

"Cut the poet down," she said.

There came cries and howls, and the tribespeople shook their weapons at Lumar L'anarr. She took this as an aggressive act, and as a refusal to her command. In response, she leapt to the attack...

From his suspended perch over the fire, Svoolzard watched with mouth open, in total awe, as Lumar danced and leapt amongst the hairy little village people. The stick swept left and right, knocking heads, slashing bellies, then rising in great overhead sweeps ending with the dull *cracks* of fractured skulls. Bodies toppled all around, brains leaking through ears, and Lumar moved like lightning, a savage cat, easily avoiding the tribespeople's sticks and arrows. She moved so fast she was a green blur, until – only a minute after the battle had begun, and with at least twenty of the tribe dead or dying – the rest suddenly turned tail and fled out into the jungle, howling.

Suddenly, the area was still.

The only sound was the crackling of flames.

And then, "Ow, ow, ouch! I'm burning, Holy Mother of Manna, I'm burning! Cut me down, please please cut me down! My *arse is on fire!*"

Warily, Lumar strode across the camp, stooping to grab a knife from a dead enemy. She slashed the bonds holding Svool's legs, and his feet dropped into the fire. He stood for a moment, then started doing a crazy little dance and shuffle, wailing, until Lumar cut free his hands and he *leapt* from the fire, stomping on the ground, his feet and skin smoking.

"Ow, ow, ow, oh, the indignity, oh, the agony, I will never live this down in the Court of Professors, oh, what am I going to do, how will I ever recover, how will I ever be Svool again?"

He stopped, and watched Lumar watching him.

"You came back," he said, and his face broke into a broad grin.

"Yeah, well, don't get any fucking ideas."

"No, no, you came back, you saved me, you rescued me, and although I have indeed incurred terrible burn injuries to my feet and bottom, I am sure you can summon up some pain-killing narcotics and some kind of unguent to make all the pain and nastiness go away."

Lumar considered this, her eyes scanning the edges of the clearing. "First," she said, "I didn't come back for you. I was passing nearby and saw the fire. I've scouted the jungle, I know where we are, and I was heading back to the beach to see if anything else useful from the crashed ship was available for scavenging before the long trek ahead of me."

"Oh. But you *did* save me."

"Hmm. Yes. I wonder how long it'll be before I regret it?"

"So you have painkillers? And unguent? For my burns? Preferably something that doesn't smell too bad?"

Lumar looked at him with pity in her eyes. "No."

"But... but... but you must have!"

"Why must I have?"

"Because... you simply *must*."

Lumar sighed. "Svool. I'm in this shit, just the same as you. You really need to get your head switched on to this plane of reality. You need to tune in, mate. If you don't, then you will *die*."

Svool stared at her, tears running down his cheeks.

"Okay." He coughed. He puffed out his chest. He manned up. "Okay. I hear what you're saying. "There!" He ran over to some rocks, yelping and limping on his burnt feet, and grabbed his jewelled sword. He waved it triumphantly. "See? See! I can do this! I can be of help! We will adventure our way out of this place!"

Lumar watched him, and suddenly a smile cracked her face. "Fucking hell, Svool. You really were brought up like a pampered idiot, weren't you? I thought most of it was just for effect, for the benefit of your effete arsehole friends. But you're real, aren't you? Really a... *dick*."

"Harsh," said Svool, frowning.

"Not as harsh as this fucking jungle," said Lumar. "Now grab your clothes and boots, we need to get going."

Svool scanned for his clothes, painfully aware of his nakedness, and the cold of the night when he strayed too far from the fire. Then, with a yelp of horror, he scrambled on hands and knees to the edge of the cooking flames and, using his jewelled sword, fished out the half-burnt remains of one of his glitter boots.

"Oh, woe!" he wailed.

"Oh, woe?" said Lumar.

"Do you *know* how much these cost? They are Prince Gok von Gok IIIs, you can only get them in London, and by that, I mean fucking London, *Earth*, baby. Most Space Platoon Generals couldn't afford a pair of these glossy high-heeled beauties!"

"Or would want them, being that they're combat soldiers," growled Lumar.

Svool stood up, ramrod straight, his small penis dangling in the firelight. He fixed Lumar with a steely look. "They burned my clothes," he said. "Well. Melted them, at least. I always *knew* Gok von Gok made stuff from cheap plastic baubles, the cheap bastard! And my high-heeled boots! Those cannibal fellows, they've massacred them! Annihilated them! Oh, woe!" He still held the remains of one at arm's length. It smoked, gently.

"Oh," said Lumar, face impassive.

"What can I wear?" said Svool.

"I don't know," said Lumar.

"And my boots? What can I wear on my feet? I can't traipse through the jungle, all naked, with nothing on my feet!"

"I'm, er, sorry. I think you're going to have to."

"Can't you rustle me up some leaf clothing and footwear? You look like you're that kind of handy sort," he said.

"No," said Lumar with a tight smile. "I don't believe that I can."

"And why the hell not?" A snort of annoyance.

"Because," said Lumar, pointing to the edges of the clearing, where a curious widespread glittering had accumulated, "I believe our little hairy tribespeople are back. And I think they've brought their friends."

There came a guttural rumbling, very much like that of a Big Cat.

"Advice?" said Svool, eyeing the glittering luminescent eyes in the darkness of the tangled foliage.

"I think it's time we made ourselves scarce," said Lumar, softly, and began to back from the camp, her eyes focused on the edges, her movements smooth and careful. Now, more rumbling sounds joined the first. She could make out three, maybe four discrete *voices*.

Svool stumbled after her, and they reached the edge of the camp. There was a narrow trail leading away through the jungle, which was alive with the sounds of buzzing, gnawing, flitting insects.

"What now?" Svool said, peering down the organic corridor as if it led straight down to Hell; which, maybe, it did.

"We run," said Lumar, quietly.

"In bare burned feet?"

"Run or die," she said.

"Okay," said Svool, and ran.

Lumar followed him, and behind them, a snarl cut across the jungle clearing like a blade.

SVOOL RAN LIKE his life depended on it, which it did. His arms pumped, his legs pumped, and his poor sore feet burned and chafed and were scratched and pronged and poked. Branches and ferns and vines slapped and whipped at him, and it was all most uncomfortable and undignified. He felt naked without his vast array of glass and diamond plastic bauble clothing arrangements; in fact, he *was* naked without them. His bare skin was whipped and chilled by the sudden night-time jungle air. It all added up to the most uncomfortable race for his life he'd ever had. Yes, it was the *only* race for his life he'd ever had, but he was sure that in a more civilised society, on a more *civilised world*, it would have been somehow more... convenient. All the time he was muttering and whimpering, whining and dribbling. He could hear Lumar crashing after him, but it was easy for her, she was more animal than he was; more *primitive*. An educated man – dammit, a fucking *poet!* – shouldn't have to run for his life, naked, with burnt feet and ass; oh, no, that should be solely the preserve of the comedy Japachinese Torture TV modules blasted across the Quad-Gal by those deviant gangers and orgs! It shouldn't have *anything* to do with civilised society...

There came a bang, a thud, a snarl and then a roar so loud Svool felt hackles rise in places he didn't realise he had hackles. His arms pumped harder than they had ever pumped, and for a few short moments all discomfort ceased to exist as he pounded on, ploughed on, through the alien jungle of Tox World.

There came a sudden scrabbling sound, then a *whine*, and something hit Svool in the back and he went down hard on his face, outstretched hands ploughing a furrow in rotting jungle detritus. There were more thumps, and something sailed over him. Svool opened his eyes, pushed his golden curls out of the way, and saw Lumar in a tight crouch in the middle of the trail, pointed stick held before her. There came a bowel-loosening scream from behind him, and a dark object flew over Svool's head, snarling and with teeth gnashing. Lumar steadied herself, and the creature flew straight at her, impaling itself on the sharpened staff. A wooden point emerged from the beast's shoulder in an explosion of blood, and Lumar scrambled back as the big, maroon, yellow-spotted cat kicked and thrashed, claws swiping, huge distended head biting and snapping at thin air... until, finally, slowly, it died.

Lumar approached the beast, rolled it to the side, put her boot on its torso and jerked free her spear. She gazed down at the creature; it was *almost* like any normal jungle cat, except its maroon fur looked unnatural, as if it had been glued on in segments. Its head was too large, with eyes at different levels and long yellow fangs, crooked and bent, in a mouth that didn't close properly. It was a truly terrifying sight.

"What the fuck is that?" squawked Svool.

"No idea," said Lumar, her voice cracked. "But there's more of them. And they're coming."

Svool scrambled to his feet, and started running again.

He realised, then, it was going to be a very long night...

*   *   *

DAWN WAS BREAKING as they emerged onto a beach. This was a different beach from the one on which they were washed ashore after the crash. The surface was a huge stretch of grey sand, the sweep broken in parts by violent upthrustings of black square rocks at regular intervals. Svool was unbelievably grateful for the softness and coolness of that sand under his scorched feet.

They padded across the sweep of grey, away from the jungle now, and Lumar guided them to a large section of rocks, rounded and squared, which sat in staggered sizes like a disjointed cluster of scattered dominoes.

Reaching the rocks, Lumar stopped and surveyed their back-trail. The jungle was silent; unmoving, except from some huge fronds that wavered in the gentle breeze skimming in off the sea.

Svoolzard Koolimax XXIV sank gratefully to his knees, and pressed his forearms against a great grey slab, and sighed into his arms as his head rested down and he seemed to almost deflate.

"Thank Mother Manna," he wept, kissing his own arms, his feet burning, his back burning, his arse burning, and all the while a cool breeze chilling the rest of him so that he felt almost like a vessel filled with fire and ice.

"Don't get too comfortable," growled Lumar, crouching beside him, her eyes still on the jungle.

"What do you mean?"

"They're still coming."

"What are?"

"Those fucking spotted cats, you dickweed."

"But... no, surely, we lost them! In the jungle!"

Lumar started laughing, a sound of genuine humour pealing across the grey sand. "What? On a straight trail? Don't be a moron. They're just playing with us. Tailing us. I killed one, and that made them wary. Now

they're being careful. They know we're not muppets."
She stared at Svool. "Well, they know *I'm* not a
muppet."

Svool didn't care for her insults. It no longer mattered.
He was so exhausted it was untrue; a feeling he had
never, ever before experienced; well, not like this! He
thought, when he'd had all-night sexual relations with
the Saucy Sally Sluts, all eighteen of them – that had
been true exhaustion. But that held little to what he
now suffered, and was still suffering. Every muscle was
a cramp. Every blood-vessel was filled with horror.
Pain was his mistress, agony his mother, mockery his
father. His feet were stumps of severance. His fire-
raw back and bottom felt as if they'd been grated by a
particularly vigorous foul-mouthed chef. Surely, his life
couldn't possibly get any worse?

"Don't get too close to the sand," said Lumar.

"Eh?"

"The sand," she said, glancing down, where it was
smeared over Svool's legs, and arms, and damn, he
even had it on his face. How had he done that? "Don't
get it on you."

"You can't say that!" he snapped, fuelled by pain.
"You can't let me fucking roll naked in it, then
nonchalantly enunciate, *oh, don't touch it*. Why ever
the hell not?"

"I worked out where we are," said Lumar, voice
level, eyes still scanning the expanse of jungle fringe.
Behind her, the sea rolled and sloshed up the sand. The
sun had started creeping up the sky, bringing with it
welcome green light and warmth and hope.

"So? Where are we?"

"That, in which we crashed," said Lumar, pointing
out over the rolling waters, "is The Sea of Heavy Metal.
Polluted to the fucking gills, Svool. I don't know how
much of that toxic shit we swallowed when we crashed,

but I'm pretty sure we'll be on the toilet for a month. Shitting out our internal organs, if we're lucky."

"Polluted? With what?"

"Hah! Everything from magnesium, potassium, strontium, cerium, barium, neodymium, promethium – those have what is considered *low* toxicity; but then we get onto the real *gems*. Beryllium, cadmium, cobalt, copper, palladium, polonium, radium, niobium, osmium, tantalum, uranium... shit, it's a toxic cocktail, a radioactive soup. I'm surprised it even looks like water!"

"Er. Are all those things bad?"

"Pretty bad, and in the quantities found in *that* sea, I'm only surprised we can't walk on the waves."

"How do you know all this?" said Svool, frowning, and tenderly touching his feet.

"I'm a chemist. I have degrees in biological chemistry, pure maths and environmental chemistry," said Lumar, staring at Svool with her cool green eyes.

"So... so you're *educated?*"

"Yes."

"I never knew that."

"You never asked. You were too busy groping my tits."

"But... but... where were you educated?"

"Quad-Gal Royal University."

"I am... stunned!" said Svool, who really was.

Lumar smiled. "Don't worry. Events and reality rather ran away from me. When they took my sister. When the ganga gangs fucked up my life. But then, that's what it is to be a kroona. We're ranked lower than the fucking androids."

"That is disgraceful," said Svool. Then, suddenly looking up, "So... what's wrong with the sand?"

"It's sand made from toxic heavy metal particles. As I said, cadmium, cobalt, polonium, niobium, uranium, lead. And you're smearing it all over your skin like mascara."

"Is it dangerous?"

Lumar snorted. "Of course it's fucking dangerous! Heavy metals are much more dense than water, and your body cannot metabolise the constituent particles; thus, the toxic shit accumulates inside you. It affects your lungs, kidneys, nervous system, mental functions. Just don't fucking put it in your mouth, okay?"

"What about these rocks?" wailed Svool.

"Look like weathered lead slabs to me," said Lumar, gaze sliding back to the jungle. Her green eyes narrowed, and she took a tight hold on her sharpened staff. From the edges of the jungle had stepped three of the maroon cats, with their odd fur slabs and yellow spots. The wild cats stopped at the openness; at the daylight. Lumar saw their eyes fall, as one, on her and Svool.

"I just don't believe it," moaned Svool, "you let me walk across this, this, this *toxicity,* smear it all over me like the sexual juices of the Humphammaraha Twins, then cry my tears onto slabs of lead or *whatever the shit the shitty toxic shit really is,* and then you calmly stand there telling me you're a toxic chemist or whatever you are, and you reel off all these bloody names and you *still* let me roll around in the crap. Only at the end do you spill the beans that this can affect my kidneys and spleen and mental conditions! You need to get your priorities right, Lumar. Right, girl? Right? *I said...*"

"Get up."

"But what about my mental faculties?"

"You won't *have* any mental faculties if you don't haul your arse out of that toxic sand, lover boy..."

Svool turned. And watched with rising horror as the three huge cats, each one as big as a lion, made a decision and, with disjointed heads swinging to glance up and down the beach, started towards them with long, loping strides...

"Get up!" screamed Lumar. "I can't kill all three on my own!"

Svool scrambled up, wincing at his burns, and then scrabbled at his jewelled sword. Lumar was already moving away from him, putting distance between the two in order to split up the huge cats.

"What shall I do?" bubbled Svool.

Lumar gave him a nasty glance. "I sure hope you can use that pretty little fucking sword."

"But! It was a present! From the Galactic Council's Chief Royal Emerald President, Googall von Suckerberger, after I performed a particularly fine evening of poetry, music and dance at the Galactic Palaces of Suckerberger and Suckerberger." He fumbled again with the weapon, until, finally, he was holding it the right way round.

The cats accelerated, leaving deep pawprints in the sand.

Svool felt suddenly numb. Numb, and lost, and very, very frightened.

"Is there nobody to help us?" he wailed, swishing his sword from side to side.

"We have to help ourselves," growled Lumar, eyes narrowed, taut body tensed as the cats separated, two peeling away to focus on Lumar – whilst the third, the largest and most ferocious looking, swung its massive shaggy disjointed head, with maroon ears and square patches of tufted fur, towards Svool.

The creature advanced.

Svool urinated on the sand, and waved his glittering, jewelled sword. As the beast approached, the weapon looked suddenly ridiculous, even to his own eyes. Like a golden toothpick. Or a diamond knitting needle. It didn't appear as the sort of weapon that could take down five hundred kilograms of rancid jungle cat...

"Oooooh," said Svool.

The cat roared, and a fetid stink of rotting meat blasted over Svool as, drawing closer, its charge accelerated with massive power and a bunching of steel muscles...

With a roar the great cat leapt.

Svool stumbled back, squealing like a pig on a stick, his bare feet pedalling in the grey sand, his arms frantically waving his glittering sword bauble at the mammoth beast rearing over him.

Lumar had her own problems as the two large cats split, circling her, and she knew with dreaded certainty that she could maybe pull off her trick where the animal leapt onto her spear and impaled itself; but it would only work once. If she was *lucky*.

Son of a bitch! Why did I have to get lumbered on this stinking shit-hole with a useless poetry-reciting narcissist? Why couldn't he have been some kind of military action hero with a machine gun? Then I wouldn't be having this problem!

The cats rumbled, circling her. They were more intelligent than she gave them credit for. They had seen her handiwork on the cat back on the trail; and they wouldn't let such a simple trick work again.

One cat feinted, and Lumar jabbed out with the stick. The other was behind her now, and it, also, darted forward. With a howl Lumar spun, the sharpened stick catching the beast across the muzzle with a whack and knocking free a long, curved silver fang.

The cat took a step back and fixed her with a cool, levelled gaze that sent a chill through her soul. The intelligence glittering in those feral eyes reminded her of a human opponent...

"Svool!" she shrieked.

There was no answer.

As the cat leapt at Svool, he screamed like a girl, wailed like a massacred nun, caterwauled like a fighting feline, brayed like a horse in a mincer; he closed his eyes, the sword slashing and swishing before him as he stumbled frantically backwards and tripped, just as the cat landed above him and the sword carved a long groove above the beast's eyes. Blood flushed from it as if Svool had yanked a toilet chain. The cat, in turn, screeched and back-pedalled as Svool continued to waggle his tool.

"Uh," he panted, as Lumar risked a glance towards him. The big cat was now standing before him, blood dripping to the sand, its charge halted. A huge disjointed paw was scratching at the wound as if trying to stop the flow of blood.

"Kill it!" she screamed. "Fucking kill it!"

"Uh?"

Svool scrambled to his knees, then his feet. The cat was blind before him, and it lay down now, both paws over its eyes, worrying at the wound. Svool glanced across at Lumar, who whacked a beast with her stick, but went down under a tangle of fur as the second cat leapt across her back. She vanished under a flying furball. Svool felt very, very sick.

He charged at the cat, then pulled back at the last minute, but the beast ignored him. This fuelled his rage. How dare it! *How dare it ignore his charge! The... the damned furry critter! The mewling sack of bullying shit! The... the big stupid pussy cat!*

Svool moved forward, and stuck his sword straight through the cat's eyeball, which popped in a flurry of milky fluid; he pushed hard, leaning all his body weight into the strike, and skewered the brain within. The cat screeched, then flopped to its side, all four legs kicking as its bowels loosened. Then it lay still.

Svool stood up, staggered, then waved his sword in the air. Yay! He was triumphant!

He was, goddammit, a Hero!

"Hey, Lumar!" he cried, but both enemy cats were stood over her, and he caught just glimpses of her green flesh. A terror grabbed his heart in its fist, and his eyes widened, and *oh, my God of Manna, they'd killed Lumar! They were eating Lumar! And next they'd turn their attention on him and see that he'd killed their friend and they'd come for him and eat him as well! What to do? See if Lumar was all right, but of course she wasn't all right, look at her, surrounded by fur and teeth and claws and she'd be all dead and eaten up by now. So the only thing to do is*

Run.

Svool ran, arms pumping hard, his blood-encrusted, jewelled sword in one fist, glittering in the light of the green sun, but forgotten for the moment as terror took over and cowardice became his brother; he pumped hard, sprinted, burnt feet forgotten and ignored as he padded across the sand. He could hear cracking sounds behind him. *Oh no. They're eating her! They're breaking her bones! I don't believe it! Now, the horror, I am truly all alone and now more of those horrible cannibals can take me into the jungle and eat the meat off my genius bones...*

Oy! Idiot! What are you doing?

Excuse me?

I said what are you doing, fuckwit?

I'm sure I don't understand what you mean?

You fucking back-stabber, Lumar saved you, saved your stinking worthless carcass, and here you are hot-footing it away when you've got a fucking sword in one hand and she's in trouble.

I'm sure she's already dead, and I can certainly be of no service to the young lady...

Oh, yeah, that's convenient, I'm sure! Convenient that you didn't check and didn't even try and help, and now you're sprinting across the sand like your arse is on fire and she's back there fighting off two huge mauling lion-cats!

Well it has to be said, I am a rare talent in the Galaxy of Manna, I am a genius, no doubt, a poet prodigal, and soon to be the finest film star the Quad-Galaxy has ever seen! I do not desire to die here and now! I desire to be rescued!

Oh, you back-stabbing, turn-coat, cowardly bastard...

A *whine* cracked across the sand.

Svool slowed his sprint, but did not dare turn back. *Oh, my! What could possibly have happened now?*

There came twin *thuds* and the sounds of sprinkling. Followed by a low growl.

"Oh, no, oh, no, oh, no," muttered Svool, reaching the edge of the jungle and leaping full length into its protective undergrowth. He hit the soft ground in the cool shade, glad to be out of the baking sun and toxic sand. He lay for a while, panting, wondering what to do, and how to get himself out of this fix. Then he crawled around on a carpet of bent ferns and knobbly creepers and crept back to the edge of the jungle to see what was occurring.

Confusion met his confused gaze.

There was a small cloud of black smoke on the beach, funnelling upwards as if some ancient diesel engine had slammed a valve open and was busy burning oil. The cloud perfectly eclipsed the area where Lumar and the cats had been.

"Uh?"

Various concepts vied for precedence in Svool's mind. Missile strike? Spontaneous combustion? Hidden land mine? None of them seemed probable, although the land mine could be a possibility...

The sea sighed against the beach, rolling and, to the naked eye, beautiful despite the hidden loaded toxins within.

Svool wondered what to do.

A cool breeze blew, and the smoke started to disperse. Svool was just wondering whether to run for it again, or to hide under the ferns, when he saw Lumar step from the smoke and stand, hands on hips, staring across the beach at his hidden location.

"Oh," said Svool, and stood up. He gave a wave. Lumar did not wave back.

Then, from the smoke eased the gliding matt-black tennis-ball body of Zoot, Svoolzard's PR PopBot, manager, bodyguard, agent, manager and all round *good egg*.

"Now I understand!" He beamed. *Somehow* Zoot had also survived the crash, and eventually had come looking for them when his circuits came back online, and he'd seen the battle on the beach and zipped along and zapped the bad cats. Wahey! Well done that PR PopBot!

Feeling buoyed and triumphant, Svool strode out onto the sand in all his nakedness, and watched as Lumar and Zoot approached him. Lumar had a long slash from her temple to her jaw, and another set of triple gashes across both arms, and one very sexy thigh.

"Zoot! You survived! And came back to help us!" beamed Svool, placing both his hands on his hips and standing there, tackle out, free and proud and brave now his bodyguard had arrived.

"I did indeed," said Zoot, smoothly, bobbing to a halt on a cushion of ions.

"And Lumar! I'm so glad you've not been gobbled up by those nasty cat beasts!"

"You are?"

"Yes!"

"Why?"

"What do you mean?"

"Well," said Lumar, her eyes narrowed, "I saw you stab that cat through the eye, and stagger around drunk on combat glory; and as the beasts reared above me, my wooden spear the only barrier between me and gaping gnashing maws, I thought *Svool will save me, just like I saved him!* Yet through the legs of the attacking, mauling creatures all I saw was your cherry-red arse fucking off up the beach."

"Er," said Svool.

"You left her?" said Zoot. "Left her to be eaten?"

"No, actually, no, it wasn't like that..."

"But you did run off?" said Zoot.

"Er, yes, but I thought she was already dead!"

"I don't know how you came to that conclusion," snapped Lumar. "You were too busy running the fuck away."

"Wait, wait," said Svool, "now, don't be like that." He held out his hands, smiling broadly with friendship and love and charm. "Come on, you know I would have helped you if I could..."

"Yeah, right, back-stabber."

Zoot bobbed. "We need to get out of the sun. We need to get away from all this toxicity; the beach is a chemical hotspot. My scanners are... *stunned* by the level of pollution. I had to run three tests. I thought my scanners were faulty at first! This is not a safe place for two organic meat-sacks."

"Okay. Which way?" Svool was still beaming, almost oblivious to the seething rage emanating from Lumar's eyes and body-language and snarling lips. She still held her spear, bloodied and chipped and claw-scarred. She did *not* look like a happy bunny.

"I have detected a settlement of some kind, twenty kilometres northeast through the jungle. We should be able to rent passage there to the nearest city – which, according to my database, would be Organophosphate City. A place less cheery than its name, I assure you."

"What about my clothes? And boots?" beamed Svool. He seemed unfeasibly chirpy. As if Zoot's arrival was the sudden end to all his problems.

Lumar and Zoot turned to face Svool. Or at least, Zoot rotated until the flickering lights on his matt-black casing were pointing in the direction of Svoolzard Koolimax XXIV.

"You could make some?" suggested Zoot. Then, to Lumar, "Come, my dear, let's get you into the cool of the jungle; I need to sterilise and seal your wounds."

"What a good idea!" beamed Svool.

Lumar and Zoot ignored him, and moved away under the wavering rubbery palm fronds. Svool followed, beaming like a happy pup.

IT WAS EVENING and progress had been slow, mainly due to Svool's injured feet. Under Zoot's instruction, Svool had fashioned wide shoes made of fronds and twine, but they were still far from comfortable and Svool complained with *every single fucking footstep*.

Zoot suggested making camp for the night, and as Lumar built a shelter and laid out sleeping mats, Svool was sent off into the darkening jungle to collect "dried combustible material."

Svool wandered alone, in the gloom and lengthening shadows, mumbling and cursing and tripping. He carried an armful of dead creepers and branches, which although they were definitely *not* wood, were at least something he was sure would burn.

"Not bloody fair, this, a genius poet of my incredible standing and reputation collecting shitty firewood in the shitty jungle." He tossed back his golden curls, which were no longer gleaming and oiled and beautiful, but instead matted and stained and stuck with twigs and bits of creeper. The rings on his fingers glittered, but seemed somehow tarnished under the light of the sinking green sun; like cheap fairground baubles.

"What happened to the honeyed wine? The endless succulent women willing to wrap their vaginas around my suckling face? What happened to the drugs – oh, the drugs, I miss the drugs, hey, I wonder, wonder-wonder if Zoot has some stash stashed away in his little black casing. Hmm?"

He halted. There had been a sound, registering on the fringes of his acuity; but he'd missed it, missed its solidity, like waking from a dream and trying to grasp the wispy tail-end before it struggled away.

Svool stood, his nakedness covered by a simple leaf in the shape of a V, his bottom still exposed and red-raw from the kiss of the cannibals' fire. He wondered what the noise had been. A stealthy pawfall of another beastcat tigercat? Or maybe the creepy figure of a hunting cannibal, ready to shoot him with another sleep dart and drag him off into the jungle to cook and chomp before the others even realised he was gone...

Svool shivered, and looked around, and was frightened.

He dropped his collected kindling and ran, leaf-shoes flapping, back in the direction of their makeshift camp.

He emerged into the clearing. A small fire was burning, and Lumar, her perfect shelter already complete, had cut several plates of bark and was cooking some kind of basic nut broth from ingredients sourced by Zoot.

Svool stumbled forward.

"Got the firewood, I see," snorted Lumar.

"Where's Zoot?"

"Not sure. He scanned this food, said it was safe to eat, then hummed off into the jungle. Looking for your sorry ass, I'd wager."

Svool frowned.

"I can't help but notice a negative vibe emanating from you," he said, flapping forward and sitting on a fallen log next to the fire. He held out his hands to the warmth, and acknowledged there was something deeply primeval and satisfying and *morale-boosting* about the simple honest beauty of a roaring camp fire.

Lumar laughed, and he realised she was sharpening another piece of wood with a small, silver knife. Beside her were a pile of... stakes? Spears? There was certainly a collection of sharpened wooden spiky implements. "You think so, do you, back-stabber?"

"I am *not* a back-stabber," said Svool, eyes wide, pouting.

"You left me to die, motherfucker."

"I... I... I thought you were already dead!"

"Bullshit. You were looking after your own sorry carcass. You saw those beasts dive on me, you shit your pretty little jewelled panties and hot-tailed it off across the sand like somebody had lit a fuse under your testicles. You're a sorry fucking excuse for a human being, Svoolzard Koolimax XXIV. You have no honour, no nobility, and no fucking friends. So shut up, before I stick one of these sticks up your nose."

Svool flapped his lips for a moment, then closed his mouth with a clack. He sat, stewing, staring into the fire. *How did it come to this? How did it end up like this? How had his beautiful vixen mistress, so supple and willing with hand and tongue and orifice, how had she turned into this vile-tongued, bitchy, nasty Svool-hater? And that was something else, the way she said his name. Her eyes shone with mockery, and she spoke it with such emphasis as to make it sound ridiculous; like he was a breakfast cereal, or a sexual lubricant, or something.*

Svool sat, stewing, as night fell over the jungle.

Eventually, the broth or soup or whatever it was was ready, and Lumar poured a little into a cleverly fashioned bowl of wrapped leaves. Svool took it from her in silence, and started eating, then looked up at Lumar again.

"Yes?" she snapped.

"Thank you," he said.

Lumar's eyes widened, and she bit her tongue. She gave a nod, and lowered her head, green dreadlocks brushed to one side as she delicately drank from her bowl. Svool, also, drank his soup.

"It tastes like shit," he added, "but thanks all the same."

Lumar snorted into her soup, and it took a moment for Svool to realise she was laughing. She looked up, and her face had softened, and she took a great, deep breath and let out a great, deep sigh.

"You know something?" she said.

"Hmm?"

"That's the first time, ever, that I've heard you say 'thank you' for *anything*."

"Maybe I'm a changed man," said Svool, grinning at her.

"Your new, ahem, attire is certainly a changed fashion statement; better than that peacock shit you used to wear, though."

"I am particularly proud of my shoes," said Svool, holding out a foot and wiggling it for Lumar to see. She let out another laugh, and Svool realised something very, very important. Lumar laughing was a truly beautiful thing to hear.

"Maybe you should write a poem about it?" said Lumar.

The smile fell from Svool's face, and he looked away. Lumar stood, more of an uncoiling than a human movement, and she moved to him and touched his arm. "That wasn't a dig, Svool. It was a genuine suggestion."

He looked up, like a little lost boy through his golden curls. Here was a man who had truly had the rug pulled not just from beneath his feet, but from under his world. He was a spoiled, pampered brat, an individual to whom every pleasure imaginable was just a click of his fingers away. Drugs, sex, appearing on the cover of GGG TIME magazine, all were there in an instant. And now he was half-naked and lost in the jungle of a toxic world with burnt feet and empty veins. Lumar could see, his eyes were haunted but also... clearer. More pure.

"You hate my poetry," he said, voice thick. "I see it in your eyes. Hear it in your snide comments."

"I confess," said Lumar, voice level, "that to me, poetry is a pointless thing. I understand a good book, a story, getting involved with the characters and the narrative; but in your world of poetry, Svoolzard, all I see is bickering egotistical wordsmiths trying to be clever, trying to outdo one another, clawing their way up the literature ladder with no real thought of *content* or of *entertainment*. The focus, for you, is on a manipulation of words to satisfy your ego and narcissistic tendencies – whereas *I* am kroona, we're tribal clans, and we value the content of story above all else. Maybe it's a feature of my species, but when you look at it in the cold light of day, you have to admit, your entire world of poetry and poets looks like one big pissing contest."

Svool considered this, for quite a long time.

Eventually, he said, "I cannot agree. I have written poems with narrative strands. Poems that tell a story. Admittedly, they are often stories of my sexual conquests, but by your definition it is not whether the subject matter is tasteful or distasteful – after all, that's a subjective viewpoint – what matters is the fact that the poetry *told* a story."

"Tell me this, Svool. Do you spend more time on the story, the content, or on the structure? The wordplay? Do you clap your hands in glee when you come up with a clever little word construct? Are you pleased with yourself when you get a particular rhyme to work, or dream up some intelligent new metaphor? And most of all – when you look at your own poetry, at your collected work, do you think of yourself as a genius?"

"Yes, I spend more time on wordplay. And I see where you are going with that. And yes, I do think of myself as a genius; but only because my poetry has brought me galactic fame and fortune, and so many other people *say* my work is that of a genius." He grinned at her, then. "I admit. I have too much self-love. But that was put there by others; they passed me the baton, and now I run with it, Lumar. If that makes me a bad person, if having six naked concubines suck Nutella from my belly button makes me a bad man, then you'll have to kill me right now."

"I don't need to kill you," said Lumar, gently, sitting down and staring into the fire. She shivered, as if she'd seen a ghost. "There's plenty of things on Toxic World that'll happily do that for you."

"If you like, I *could* write you a poem..."

Lumar held up a hand, and smiled. "Not now, Svool. I need some sleep. It's been a harrowing day. The poet in you might have thought today adventurous, a rapturous joy of manly pursuits, o'erthrown by the love of a good strong woman, a strangely succulent sojourn into the misty mists of mythical majesty; but me? Personally? I thought today was a shovelful of pigshit, and I want my bed and oblivion dreams."

She crawled into her shelter. Her voice echoed out.

"And when Zoot gets back, tell the little sod he forgot to bring me the mushrooms he promised."

"Okay," smiled Svool, and despite being tired, weary, and filled with pain from a hundred different areas, he sat there and looked around – *really* looked around himself – and realised that this, here, now, this was *living*. And with a sour feeling, as if he'd just bitten a bitter pill, cracked it open to allow reality to flood his mouth and brain, he realised his life up to this point had been... a sham. Pampered. Shielded. Sheltered. Protected. A spoilt only child on a truly galactic scale.

A cool wind whispered over him, and he listened to the sounds of the jungle. The whisper of ferns, the creak of the rubber-tyre palm trees, the chatter of insects. *What is this place?* he found himself thinking, and could almost be lulled into the sense that he was in some magical wonderful mystery world, instead of a once-beautiful place poisoned beyond recognition.

Somebody had ruined Toxic World. Somebody *bad*.

SVOOL DREAMED. HE was in his palace on Taj, the one built from pure gold ingots, and in every single room hung enormous portraits of his own face on the covers of various Manna Galactic Publications. In fact, Svoolzard's image was everywhere: the statues were carved in his likeness, the ruby busts chiselled to show his strong jawline and golden curls; the tapestries were woven with the most incredible fine detail, each one showing a scene in which Svoolzard triumphed. The fountains trickled and spurted with his own brand of Champagne – *Zardpagne,* they called it, completely missing the point of what Champagne actually *was* and where it was created. Svoolzard's own poetry recitals, the albums which had sold hundreds of millions of copies all over the Quad-Gal, played in continuous rotation. Softly, just at the level of hearing; he wasn't so crass as to have them blaring out, oh, no! And in his dream, as Svool wandered naked from golden chamber to golden chamber, seeing his own image in every room, hearing his own voice in every orifice, he smiled, for this was luxury, this was happiness, this was perfection. Surely?

He padded over carpets made of SoftGlass™ and SquishDiamond™ and ToothFibre™, revelling in the feeling of his toes sinking deep into the massaging strands.

He passed through dangling organotubes and tickletickles, shivering and giggling as they caressed him *all over,* and onwards into the dimly lit bedroom chamber, where not just the bed was fluid and alive, but so were the floors, ceiling and walls. Somebody was there, in the gloom, all naked and oiled and crooning. Svool slipped from his gossamer robes and squelched his way across the floor, slopping onto the bed and reaching out to touch warm flesh. She moaned, a low "ooooh," and wriggled seductively, and he kissed her feet, sucking her toes which wiggled and squirmed in his mouth. He got harder and harder and harder. His need and lust and need rose and rose and rose. He wriggled upwards, his tongue tracing a line up her firm calves and across her quivering thighs. Both her hands were wound in his long golden curls now, and he was crooning himself as she squirmed and thrust against him. He found the warm wet honey place, and his tongue darted in, and he tasted her, and smelt her, and was filled by her, and her hands caressed his head and tugged gently at his hair as he cunnied her cunnilingus. She was so warm and wet and willing and hot and sweet and honeyed. And that was it. Heaven. Right there between her squirming thighs. Nothing, nothing on Earth or in the whole of Manna could cum close to this...

*   *   *

LUMAR, EXHAUSTED, SLEPT like a zombie. Slept like the
dead. But something intruded in her dreams. It was a
dog. A huge, golden dog with flopping golden ears and
curly golden hair. It was a beautiful dog. It licked her
toes, and she giggled, and squirmed in her sleep, and
then it licked her legs and she started to get annoyed,
for she knew dogs licked their own testicles and a dog's
tongue on her flesh wasn't exactly what she wanted,
and then, in the dream, the dirty dog went further...

She swam up through mists and glittering oils,
surfacing into the realm of dozy consciousness with
her mind fluttering and brain filled with smoke. She
groaned, and then, suddenly, like a striking cobra,
she was awake. Fully awake. One instant asleep, the
next, ten-coffees-caffeine-injection-awake, sat up in the
sleeping shelter.

"Oy!" she screeched, noting in the gloom that
somebody – *bloody Svoolzard* – had his head between
her legs and was sliming her with his slimy tongue. She
whacked him across the head with such force he flipped
and rolled across the shelter, whining and whimpering
and clawing at his battered skull.

"What the *fuck* are you doing, you sexual fucking
deviant?" she snarled.

"Urh, erh, what's going on?" Svoolzard sat up.
He rubbed at his eyes. He coughed. He clutched his
whacked skull.

"You, you bastard molesting dirty fucking pervert;
what do you think you're doing?"

"Ahh, ahh, ah! I see! I was dreaming, Lumar, and,
obviously, you were the delight in my dream..."

"Well you were a *dog* in mine, you disgusting bastard
pervert."

"Will you *stop* calling me a pervert!"

"Well only a *pervert* attacks a girl in her sleep…"

"I didn't *attack* you, I was giving you some special Svoolzard loving…"

She stared at him. Stared at him hard.

He sensed her total and absolute *RAGE*.

"If I wanted some Svoolzard personal loving," she said, coldly, "I'd fucking ask for it. Now, I suggest you sleep outside. In the jungle. With the other insects. Because next time, my sweet, I'm going to cave your pervert head right in."

"But, but Lumar! After all we've been through! We were lovers…"

"No, you bought me."

"That wasn't the way it felt at the time. I could see the love in your eyes…"

"That was the reflection of yours, Svool. And it wasn't love."

Svool crawled onto his knees, scowling. "You know something, Lumar? When we were together, back on *The Literati*, I truly believed we had something there. Of all the thousands of girls who've shared my bed, and my drugs, I thought of you as something special. Yes, you were appointed by the PR company, to no-doubt help keep my manic needs in check; but, well, if ever I was going to marry one of my many ladies, it was going to be you."

Lumar stared at him, in silence, for long, long moments.

"Get out," she said.

"What, into the jungle?"

"Yes, into the jungle."

"But it's cold out there."

"Not as cold as in here."

"There's ants and things. They'll bite me."

Lumar loomed close. "Trust me, Svool, whatever awaits you *out there* is nothing – I repeat, *nothing* –

compared to the hell I'm going to give you in here. Get out now, before I crack open your skull and fist-fuck your rancid brain."

THE DAWN LIGHT was creeping through the jungle like twisting snakes in the air. A stench of putrefaction from rotting vegetation and... *something else*... filled their nostrils. The jungle was filled with pockets of cold air, which chilled their skin, and then they'd rise from a seemingly random area into heat. Svoolzard wondered, with a strange shiver, what caused these odd temperature fluctuations; because it wasn't the sun, which kind of pointed the finger at some kind of weird pollution. Temperamental temperature toxicity. *Great.*

"It's up ahead," said Zoot.

"The deserted village?"

"Yes."

"Is it safe?" said Svool, frowning.

"As safe as anywhere else in this jungle," said Zoot, voice neutral.

"That doesn't answer the question," said Svool.

"It's not terminal," said Zoot.

"Good."

"Well, not short-term, anyway."

"You're not filling me with confidence!"

Zoot gave a machine *buzz*. A kind of digital sigh.

"Shh," said Lumar, who had moved up ahead and crouched behind a fallen tree. She parted sap-sticky fronds and gazed at the village ahead.

She could make out three buildings and part of a deserted roadway. The buildings were small, rough-built from some kind of amber stone filled with tiny, glittering minerals that caught the early sunshine and sparkled. The roadway was dust and still contained tracks and ruts.

"It's not been deserted long," said Lumar.

"Why do you say that?"

"The jungle would have reclaimed it by now. The jungle needs to be kept at bay; cut back." She looked at him. "The jungle invades like an unwanted pervert. It has to be fought off. Slapped down. Put out of its misery. Time and time again."

Svool averted his gaze, instead watching the deserted village.

"Zoot. Do you detect anything?"

"No movement. No life."

"So it's safe?"

"Ye-*eees*, but I'd still err on the side of caution, Svoolzard. This world is alien to me, also. Potentially, there are factors I could never comprehend. You must be careful."

"But no big pussy cats?"

"No big pussy cats," said Zoot.

They crept through the thinning jungle, and Lumar had been right. There was still evidence that the jungle was being cut back using blades. Trees and vines still showed scars.

They walked out onto the roadway, looking around themselves as they turned slowly in the dust, surveying the angular stone buildings. Windows and doorways were bare, black holes. Each building had a gently sloping roof made from... Svool frowned.

"What is that? Up there?"

"You mean the roofing tiles?"

"Yeah."

They all stared.

"That one," said Lumar, slowly, pointing, "is made from pan lids."

"Cooking pans?"

"That's how they appear. Look, you can see the plastic handles on the lids."

They stared again. "That's fucking weird," said Svool. "Who makes a roof out of pan lids? And anyway, they wouldn't interlock. They wouldn't form a protective barrier against the rain. It just... it just *wouldn't* work."

Svool turned. "Look at that, there."

"The walls?"

"Yeah. They're made from... glass bottles. Kind of fused together."

Sunlight glinted on different colours of glass. "And the roof is, well, it's made of interlocking panels this time. Only each panel is a TV screen. Bolted together with straps made from old belts."

They stared some more.

Svool moved to the house with the pan-lid roof. Stooping, and wrinkling his nose at some incredible stench, he peered inside. Glancing up, he saw chinks of light glinting through the badly fitting roof tiles. And yes, it was confirmed, pan lids made possibly *the worst* ever roofing slates imaginable to man.

"It would appear these buildings have been repaired," said Zoot, as Svool emerged from the building. He was carrying a pair of pants and boots, a shirt, and an old, tattered felt hat.

"What you got there, soldier?" grinned Lumar.

"Some clothes."

"What's the matter? Tired of being a stick-naked savage?"

"Let's just say I'm tired of you staring at my ass," he snapped.

"Touchy, touchy. Go on, then, dress up in your curious alien clothing."

And Lumar was indeed right. The pants, although only down to Svool's knees, had thigh panels reinforced with suede. The boots were black and battered, with spurs on the heels which jangled as Svool pulled them on. He threw his battered, homemade palm-frond

sandals away into the jungle in disgust. He struggled
into the shirt, which was too small for him, and coarse
against the burns – fire- and sun- – that covered his
shoulders and back. But at least it was protection from
the sun. And finally, he pulled on the broad-rimmed
felt hat. He felt foolish, standing there in his new,
worn, oddly-stained clobber; but it beat being naked.

"How do I look?"

"Like an idiot?" suggested Lumar, with a giggle. She
composed herself. "Sorry. Sorry."

"Fuck off."

"What's that?"

"What?"

"That badge, there."

Svool looked down. There was a silver badge with
five points attached to the shirt. It read: SHERIFF.

"Whoo har, Sheriff Svoolzard," cackled Lumar.

"Fuck off!"

"Hey, Law Maker, don't be using offensive language
like that!"

"Well, you're just taking the piss."

"You're giving it away, mate."

"Listen, I need protection from the sun! Another
day like this and I'll have no damn skin left on my
shoulders; understand?"

"Just our luck to stumble into a weird jungle tribal
village." Lumar grinned. She glanced at Zoot. "What
do you think has been going on here, Zoot? Hmm?"

"This is an old village. The construction style and
materials – *original* materials – date back several
hundred years. But the buildings have been patched-
up, repaired by an incompetent using whatever junk
they could find to facilitate such repairs. Or indeed,
in their eyes, probably enhance the quality of the
buildings."

"Is it junk they've found in the jungle?"

"Possibly. It is common knowledge that occasionally junk containers crash, be they airborne or land- and sea-based. I believe the philosophy of the Greenstar Company in these situations is to leave any crashed vessel where they lie. Effectively, the vehicle becomes just another dot on the chart of waste recycling."

"Recycling?"

"Yes," said Zoot. "Recycled from working vehicle to non-working vehicle, and left there until such passing strangers see fit to recycle it further."

"That would explain that, then," said Svool, stopping in the dust and pointing at another building which had been repaired with car body panels. It looked like a third-rate Transformer. Wings and doors had been patched onto random sections of the house, and several buckled car bonnets made up the roof. Headlights were mounted above the door. The windows had been filled with old tyres, then concreted around, so that the house had round rubber portals.

"That is depraved," said Lumar, knuckles tightening on her sharpened stick.

"Yeah, let's hope nobody's home, eh?" said Svool, grinning weakly.

"That's not even funny."

"What makes you think I was joking?"

"Come on, sheriff, let's check it out. See if your pardners are here."

Svool stared at Lumar. "Any more jokes and you can sign in for a stand-up slot at the Pig & Perkin."

"Well, you certainly provide me with enough raw material," she said, giving him such a dazzling smile and a toss of her green dreadlocks that his heart fluttered. She strode towards the door of the car/house and peered inside. She turned back to Svool and Zoot. "It's been inhabited. Recently. *Very* recently."

"How do you know that?"

Lumar pointed with her sharpened staff. "The bubbling pan on the stove."

"You call that a stove?"

"I call it a radiator grille, but hey, who am I to criticise a mad car-gobbling lunatic?"

They moved into the house. "Hello?" called Lumar. "Anybody home? We were just passing through; any help with directions would be most helpful."

Svool sniggered, and Lumar gave him a sharp look. "What?" she hissed.

"Any help with directions would be most helpful."

"And?"

"Your lack of poetry stabs me through the heart."

"It'll be my sharpened staff that stabs you through the heart in a minute."

"I bet you say that to all the boys."

Lumar stopped, and glanced around, and then stared at Svool. "You really are a dick. The minute you get within spitting distance of a bed, you start flirting again. There are possible *hostiles* in here, and you're making jokes about sex."

"Ahh, that's because all life is a joke..."

"And all sex is a joke?"

"That isn't what I was going to say."

"Svool, shut the fuck up, will you?"

Lumar stalked off, checking the other rooms were clear, whilst Svool poked around the chamber containing the stove. There was a bed in the corner, covered with thin blankets, all of them the kind of muddy brown of once-were colours, used and washed and soiled for decades. There were lots of holes, some of which had been carefully repaired. A single wooden chair, one leg shorter than the other three, so it wobbled when Svool leant against it, stood next to a table made from... Svool squinted. Beaten-flat food tins which had been flattened and pop-riveted together. It looked like something that had been through a crusher. Still, mused Svool, at least I suppose it's functional.

He moved to the stove, where the pan bubbled, and traced rubber hosing to a gas canister. He turned the canister off, and stared into the pan. It was full of beans and... eyeballs.

"Urgh!" Svool leapt backwards as if shot, and he brandished his jewelled sword and looked around the room, carefully, searching every corner, as if some hidden dwarf might leap out at any moment.

"Lumar, I think we should go. I don't like it here."

"Just wait a minute..."

"No, Lumar, whoever was here was cooking beans and *eyeballs.*"

"*What?*"

"I have to say, I am accustomed to far more civility than this!"

Lumar emerged, and she was pushing something into the inside pocket of her shirt.

"What you got there?"

"Nothing."

"Doesn't look like nothing."

"It's something. Feminine. Private."

Svool looked at her aghast. "You found something feminine and private – in *this* shithole?"

"Just leave it!"

Lumar stalked from the building, and Svool followed, still checking for the occupant, still shivering at the thought of beans and eyes.

As they stepped out, Zoot spun into view. "There's something over here I think you should see."

They followed the PopBot, around another corner of weirdly-repaired houses, many containing plates and bowls, old bottles and flapping trashbags as part of their building construction. Zoot led them down a narrow street, then turned right onto another. Here,

the buildings were leaning at crazy angles; some had
actually collapsed, leaving nothing but piles of rubble.
There was a fetid, stale aroma in the air, like something
had died under the stones.

"Down here," said Zoot.

They followed him, noses wrinkled, even by the
standards of Toxic World. Then they came to a clearing,
and they stopped, and they stared.

"What, exactly, am I looking at?" said Lumar.

"It's cars, obviously," said Svoolzard.

"Ye-*ees*, I can *see* that. But *what* am I looking at?"

There was a large clearing, leading off into broken
jungle. And arranged at the edge of the village from
which they had emerged was a horseshoe of broken,
bent, smashed, damaged, rusted, battered cars and
vans. Their panels were buckled and dented, broken and
sheared. The car arc numbered perhaps sixty or seventy
vehicles in total. All the headlamps were smashed, as
were all the windscreens, except for a couple which
were simply holed and webbed with cracks. They had
been peppered with gunfire. They had obviously been
here for some time, because the jungle had, to some
extent, taken over in patches, vines and creepers and
ferns winding their way up through battered, crumpled
bodywork.

"Is it a salvage yard?" said Svool eventually, for many
of the cars were stacked two high. Some had obviously
started out that way, but in places the top vehicle had
fallen to the ground, leaving a gap like a missing tooth.

"No," said Lumar, slowly, looking behind herself,
then around. For some reason she'd got the creeps.
"No. This is something different."

"It appears to be a protective shield," said Zoot, his
digital voice soothing; the voice of reason in a world
of chaos.

"Like a wall?" said Svool.

"Yes. A barricade."

"A barricade against what?" said Svool, unease growing.

Lumar had moved forward, and was fingering several of the holes. "These are bullet holes. 8mm. Whatever was firing them, and there's a hell of a lot of holes, was coming from the jungle."

"So an attack, then?" said Svool as the scene clicked neatly into place. Attackers from the jungle; a barricade to protect the village from attackers. But who was attacking who? And more importantly, where had they gone?

"You tell me, sheriff," said Lumar.

"No longer funny."

"Was it ever?"

"I am beginning to seriously miss my academic comrades aboard the Titan-Class Culture Cruiser, *The Literati*. I miss their wit and comradeship. I miss the poetry, song, literature and sculpture. But most of all, I miss the..."

"Drugs?" said Lumar.

"Actually, I was going to say *security*. Security in which to work, in which to create, in which to *be* creative. I recognise now that I was in a bubble, and that my bubble burst during the crash – quite literally. I had forgotten what the real world was like. A world of hardship and pettiness and pointlessness. I have been a pampered – although deserving and much loved – literary genius. I have so many fans I need to please; and I can't do that whilst I'm crashed on this shithole!"

"Come back down to Earth, Captain Kirk, we're talking about this place, this shit, these bullet holes. We're talking about what could have happened *here*, and the possible proximity of possible bad dudes. You know, ones with guns?"

"Ach, tsch and nibble," snapped Svoolzard, his eyes clouded, his face hard, and Lumar clenched her jaw muscles as she watched his arrogance return with a vengeance. He was away, in his mind, away in another place; a place of dreams and memories, a reservoir of self-love and narcissistic extravagance. How quickly he had forgotten being punched and smacked and clawed at; how swiftly the cannibals and feral jungle cats had slipped his mind, along with the bottom burns and wearing of fern flip-flops. It was a terrible and saddening thing for Lumar to watch; for it did indeed mean Svoolzard had a brain like runny butter dripping from his ear holes. "That's a lot of idiot talk. Look at the cars! Rusted to bugger and buggery. And with the grass and weeds growing between the alloy wheels. Look. Just look. You're being paranoid, woman! You're being a total flapping histrionic psychedelic love-honey."

"*What?*"

"Hey!" Svool hummed a few bars. And sang:

"You're a flapping, histrionic, psychedelic love honey,
Hmmmm, mmm,
Flying on her way to Mars,
Hmmmm, mmm,
I know you really want my money,
Ooooh, ooh,
And a slice of all my superstar cars,
Yeeeah, yeah."

He stopped. Looked at Lumar. She was staring at him. Hard.

"What?" he said, reddening a little.

"Fuckwit," she said.

"Hey! Come on, stop being a prize turkey idiot at a village gala for idiot turkeys. There *are* no mysterious attacking gun-toting enemies bearing hot an' blazing six-shooters! There are no hordes of ravenous jungle attackers intent on our current demise! Just relax! Chill! Chillax, bitch! Stop being a parsnip!"

THERE CAME THE creak of leather, and boots hit the dust hard as a heavy rider dismounted. There came a hawk, a gurgling of phlegm, then a spit.

There was a metallic screech, then a ratcheting sound; then another curious sound, of spinning, and grating metal, like a heavy flywheel; then a soft *clang*.

There came a patting sound, like a heavy hand in a leather glove whacking the flanks of something big; big and made from metal. There was a snort. Steam ejected from nostrils like a kettle boiling oil.

"Whoa boy," came a low, gravelly voice, a voice so low and gravelly you wouldn't believe it was real.

There came another snort, then a stomp of a metal hoof, then a whinny. And a tiny, tiny sound. Like a *ticka ticka ticka*. Then a *clonk*.

The sun was high in the sky, now, casting its eerie green light across the jungle. The street was deserted, except for the one rider and his mount, which creaked and groaned, and made strange metal sounds. It could only be described as a horse because it occupied the same physical wireframe. It appeared to be made from old, rusted metal panels, hand-beaten to a tube trellis frame. The creature had a gangly look, like most of its legs weren't put on quite straight, or were indeed even sturdy enough to support the bulbous bulk of the metal creature's rotund body. Rivets lined flanks like bullet holes. The mane was made from a mad tangle of razor wire. The equine head was long and brutal and sharp, ending in fangs like knives and watched over by eyes like boiling blood oil.

The metal horse snorted again, and turned as more hoofbeats drummed down the street. There were six more riders, all clinging to their savage metal animals and wearing a collection of thick pants and shirts, and long leather coats. They wore wide-brimmed hats to shield their eyes from the sun. They carried guns at their hips, and each man had dark eyes, a hard face, narrow lips and a ten-day beard.

They reined in around the first, who was broad shouldered and cruel, with a scar from eye to chin. He was chewing on a fat cigar, and he watched the other six riders dismount, and spit, and rub at stubble. They all appeared weary, but they watched their leader with bright intelligent eyes.

"Are you right?"

"Yes," said the man with the scar, and spat again. "Somebody *has* been here." His nostrils seemed to twitch, as if scenting the air. "Somebody has entered the Sheriff's Office. Somebody has claimed the sheriff's uniform and badge. So you know what that means, boys?"

The seven men grinned, and drew their pistols, long, dark, gleaming weapons; six-shooters, battered and old, but well maintained. Well-used.

"What's it mean, General?"

General Bronson chewed his cigar, and grinned at his men. "It means we have a new Law Maker in town," he said. "And new Law Makers are not *wanted* in this town! So we have to gun him down, boys. Kill him right dead here in the street. No prisoners. No mercy."

FIVE

THE FIRE RAGED, an inferno of thundering and screeching and wild detonation. Chaos lived. It walked the world on jagged legs of razors, breathing fire and gas, its eyes pits into hell, its soul a tarry mess of compressed evil. Both Jenny and Sick Note were picked up by the blast, and flung like rag-dolls away from the Greenstar Reprocessing Plant. They were joined by the other special ops soldiers, many of them burning. The hovering choppers, their bright piercing searchlights fixated on the captured ECO terrorists, were slammed skywards out of control in hissing, fizzing arcs, engines screaming and stalling, until they plummeted to the earth a kilometre away to explode in roaring balls of flame. Randy had been facing the factory as the explosion kicked in and the world erupted. He, too, was picked up and thrown away like a plastic toy, but not before the detonation blast had ripped most of his face off.

The Reprocessing Plant roared like a dying monster as the fire tore up and outwards, and inside it a million pieces of combustible rubbish ignited and detonated, and the whole messy fireball raged and fought itself,

purples and blues scything the heavens and cutting the
sky in half.

Jenny landed hard in a ditch, and lay for a while,
wheezing, all wind, all life kicked from her. She looked
to her left, and saw Randy lying in the mud with most
of his face missing, his blood-red features like melted
wax, his nose gone, his face stripped very nearly to the
skull. Jenny coughed, and grinned, and realised she
was on fire herself. "Serves you right, motherfucker,"
she managed, as she heard the screams and the shouts.
And then a squaddie cracked her with a rifle butt, put
a knee in her back, and after that, it was all stars and
blackness and the eternity pit.

IT HAD TAKEN a lot of effort, money and time to infiltrate
the Impurity Movement; and even more effort, money,
time and *cunning* to get accepted into the Impurity5
ECO terrorist cell, as they liked to be known. Randy
Zaglax, however, simply thought of them as cunts.
Terrorist cunts, if pushed for more detail; but cunts all
the same.

Randy had started his infiltration a year previously
when a tip-off led his surveillance team to one of the
minor runners working for the Impurity Movement.
Technically, this should have been a police or military
job, but Randy, as Governor of Internal Affairs at
Greenstar Company, had been taking the recent
bombing and hellfire destruction of fifteen of the
facilities under his direct jurisdiction *personally*. Also,
with a background in covert ops himself, Randy felt
more than qualified to take on this little responsibility;
after all, you couldn't trust nobody in this world, in this
life, and he knew if the order had come from above,
from Director Renazzi Lode or Assistant Greenstar
Director Sowerby Trent, then somewhere along the

myriad of connecting information streams there would have been a *leak*. And, no matter how small, it would have compromised his position; indeed, his very life.

And so Randy had set up his own intelligence and observation systems and teams, which had been running on and off for three years now. When the snippet of information about the runner, a lowlife dregscum SLAP peddler called Caleb, had been confirmed as an Impurity lead by his own people, Randy had sat down alone one night, naked on his jelly couch, with a bottle of finest Isle5 HoneyWhiskey, and come up with The Plan. And it had been a Good Plan. In fact, it had been The Best Plan.

Randy, as Governor of Internal Affairs, had always kept a very low public profile within the company. After all, he investigated the investigators, and a certain lack of familiarity with staff and the public helped him no end in the kidnapping, torture and interrogation of suspects. As such, he was well-placed to infiltrate the Impurity ECO terrorist movement *himself*. A high risk, yes, but not as high-risk as the wound he had taken to his pride, his ego, his self-esteem. Impurity5, their Cell Commander and the Squad Leader he knew simply as "Jenny" were fucking him over and pissing on the grave of his career. And Randy would not stand for it. Randy would not stand for *anything*.

With Caleb tagged, they'd watched him for three months, building up a database of his movements and contacts and rhythms. He was a SLAP dealer, and a SLAP user, which made him unreliable, violent, unpredictable; but he did have certain routines which panned out over a five-week period. Randy admitted he was amazed Caleb could *remember* the sequence over a five-week period, but it later emerged he was fitted with an in-brain electro-zap stimulator which would *painfully* guide him in the right direction if he went off course.

Impurity5 were careful, and used Caleb to courier messages between other message couriers. It was in this careful set-up, one evening in November, that Randy had introduced himself. Caleb was delivering his message to his superior, and they found themselves surrounded by five PUF – Police Urban Force. Very nasty, very tough, very aggressive. Screaming. Weapons cocked. *Get down on the ground, motherfuckers, or we'll shoot your fucking skulls in.*

From a dark side-alley Randy stepped out, and calmly put five bullets in five skulls. The PUF wore helmets, but if you shot just below the visor then a round would smash through cheekbone and into the brain beyond it. Instant kill. Headshot. Just like a game. Bam, bam, bam, bam, bam, then Randy was helping Caleb and his superior up off the ground.

"Wow, man," groaned Caleb, in the throes of a SLAP high. But the other runner, the superior, was switched on and panting hard. "Why did you do that, brother?" he asked.

Randy shrugged. "I hate the fucking system, man. Hate those Greenstar maggots. They killed my father, right? So now it's time for me to fuck them over in any way I can."

"Where do you live?"

Randy told them, giving a shitty downtown dreg address.

"We'll be in touch."

Randy went off the grid, then. For *five weeks*. Five weeks living in a slum, eating from the gutter, fucking only the warped and diseased meat that walked the toxic streets of the downtown shithole. But playing his part well, and looking as good as Randy did, it would have been foolish and out of character to not play the game. So he went to bars and picked up hot chicks with tight sweating bodies and an eagerness to show him how good they were. He fucked them all. He ate in the shitty slumscale burger joints, forcing down tepid slimy meat which could only be called meat because it came off some kind of animal; although he suspected it was rotten, raw fish. And the beer! Don't get him started on the beer, from shit-filled kegs and tox-filled pipes, each glass afloat with scum like open sewage, each mouthful a burning of his pride and body temple and purity. Yeah, purity. Oh, the irony.

They were watching him, obviously. So he threw in the odd hint. Beat up a PUF policeman outside a bar one night; gave him a kicking so severe he'd be paralysed and pensioned off from work; no doubt his family would descend into the slime like all the other scumdreg who worked Toxside. But hey, you makes your choices, right? And Randy was after bigger fish.

After five weeks of slumming it, of casting aside his favourite lacquers and unguents, creams and potions, oils and shampoos, waxes and aromas, of getting his long dark curls full of toxic *shite*, dirt under his nails, shit in his pores, effluvia in his bed; well.

She came to him.

Jenny. Jenny Xi.

Thus started the recruitment process, and at least then Randy could drop some of the forced bad habits, because he was now being "professional" for the sake of the unit, for the sake of impressing his new employers. And they watched him, always watched him. At this point, he reported back to Renazzi Lode, for the Director of Greenstar Company, he knew, was the one person he could trust. She allowed him maximum freedom and it had come as no shock to the petite, meticulous brunette when Randy had disappeared. After all, he was either dead, or on a special mission. He had a reputation for *doing* this kind of thing. Always for the benefit of Greenstar. Always for the benefit of The Company.

The Impurity Movement gave him tests, sucked him slowly deeper and deeper into their organisation. They were in no rush, and despite anger and loathing burning Randy like a red-hot brand to his scrotum, he paced himself, and played the game, and infiltrated the ECO terrorists... all culminating in the attack on the factory, and the detonation which had gone so very, very wrong.

Jenny Xi had clocked him, at the last picosecond.

How had she done that?

How had she *realised* at the last moment that he didn't have the interests of the ECO terrorists at heart?

Maybe it had just been a hunch. Listening to her weird, twisted sixth sense. Maybe she was just being extra-super-cautious; after all, Jenny had a reputation for being a bitch's bitch. Harder than hard. A radio-controlled psychopath.

And then... the bomb.

The blast. Destruction. *Another* factory destroyed...

Along with his face.

RANDY ZAGLAX WAS a vain man. He was a *beautiful* man, for sure, but he accentuated God's fabulous gifts with an excess of effort. Every morning, he would step from the soft cotton/silk sheets of his vast bed into a specially directed stream of cool air, where he would languish for three or four minutes, cooling off his night-sweat. Then he would walk, naked of course, for one as fine as he should be *proud* of his body, to his gym, where he would spend precisely thirty minutes in a hard workout, usually press-ups and sit-ups, or bag work, or a thirty-minute sprint. Something to get the old cardio-vascular system pumping, something to bring a red blush to his dashingly handsome cheeks. Then it was to his vast porcelain bathroom, white and pure, so pure, where he would begin with clipping his toenails, gently scouring the dead flesh from his feet, then rubbing a thick lavender unguent between his toes and around his heels, followed by electro-shocksocks which gave an electric-shock foot massage for the duration of his pampering. Then into the shower with tweezers, and as the hot water soothed his shoulders and spine, he'd generally tidy up his leg hair, moving gradually up to the pubic mound.

Oh, how Randy loved his pubic mound, the carefully cultivated bush of which he was so proud. He acknowledged that *usually* it was the female of the species who took excessive pride in her pubic smash of straggling garnish, because – let us be frank – a man gives pride of place to his cock, and what a superb and magnificent cock Randy did have stashed in his pants. Not thinking of the mass of scar-tissue beneath it, no; but his cock, that was a thing of beauty. But, not to be outdone by so many bush bashers he'd met in his career as Gigolo – after all, it would not be done to drop one's pants in the company of six or seven voluptuous Valkyries just to have them mock and chortle at your barbed-wire tangle – Randy went to great pains to trim and pluck and groom and condition and *pamper* his poodle. Yes, it came secondary to his throbbing penis, but only an uncouth barbarian would so overlook the quality of the silk matting behind such a prominent rod. It was at this point that he obviously became hard, rock hard, so hard it was harder than hard. Viagra? Fuck that. Viagra was for *other* men. Men who weren't hard. Or at least, not as hard as Randy.

So Randy would have his morning masturbation, sometimes a slow sensual thing, his head buzzing with images of all the fine ladies he'd known, for although at times Randy could be effeminate and wear perfume and silks and lace and ruffs, thus confusing the odd homosexual into thinking *he* was similarly inclined, in all reality Randy was hot damn bona fide straight. *Straighter* than straight. Occasionally, his wank would be a hard fast one, almost as if to get it over and done with; a necessity of habit, rather than something sensual and romantic. Either way, job complete and necessary satisfaction taken care of, Randy would continue his grooming. Shampooing and conditioning first his pubic hair, then his brown curls, washing behind the ears, and then stepping down to dry off with fluffy towels... then the *real* cream and potion pampering began...

RANDY STARED IN the mirror. Normally, at this time, he would be applying a thick pink ointment to his face in order to "iron out those little creases of accelerated decrepitude" and "banish those nasty wrinkles which creep up on a man as he progresses through life" and "moisturise your male skin with our Male Man's Man Moisturiser™, we fight the TOX! so you don't have to!!" He'd put Moose's Magical Mousse into his hair and scrunch it with the ends of his fingertips. He'd apply a light touch of kohl around his eyes to give them that deep, brooding, menacing, meaningful air. And finally, Randy would apply a delicate gloss lip balm to accentuate the natural curve and pout of his full, generous lips. Lips which, many ladies had told him, were very fine for kissing.

Randy stared into the mirror.

He couldn't do *that* anymore. Because he had no lips.

No lips, no cheeks, no eyelids.

Hell. No fucking *face*.

The surgeons had performed an emergency medical rush job in order to save his life. A kind of Fast Food Face Surgery for the Needy. The blast that ripped off Randy's face with sheer unadulterated *force* had also popped three fingers from their sockets. He'd been holding a gun, which had wrenched his hand apart. And his fingers had been lost in the mud, despite the best efforts of the search team. What had they called *that*, he wondered, hysterical giggles rising in his throat as he studied his destroyed visage. The *Find Randy's Lost Fingers Search Party?* "Here sir, I've found one! / Which one is it, son? / It's Randy's middle finger, raised just for you..."

Yes, the surgeons had done the best they could in the short time available. And the problem was, here on Amaranth – on the Toxic World – the medical profession was incredibly and suitably *awesome* when it came to skin diseases, toxic poisoning cases, radiation poisoning, mutating genetics – any and every condition relating to the excess of toxic shit pumped into land, air and sea by The Company and its affiliates. What it *did not* specialise in was *plastic surgery*.

Randy stared at a face created by Frankenstein. A monster stared back.

What once were lips were now bulging flaps of skin which did not quite connect properly to the rest of his face, but that was irrelevant because the rest of his face looked like a patchwork quilt of sewed-together skin panels with, it had to be said, some very untidy stitching. Skin had been grafted from his thighs, arse and back, and they'd rebuilt his face with all the expertise of a DIY motorcycle mechanic. He still had no eyelids, and his eyes were wide and bulbous, as if he was in a permanent state of shock. His nose was a flat blob of a thing, twisted and constantly leaking blood and snot. His lips did not fit his face properly, and he permanently showed his teeth. The blast had knocked quite a few teeth out, and for reasons unknown to Randy as he lay in a pit of pain and incomprehension, they had fitted new steel teeth straight into his jawbone. When he smiled, which was not often now, they'd made him look like some torture-victim doll; he looked like an advert for plate steel. He had burnt tufts for eyebrows, and annoyingly, random tufts of beard seemed to grow in tiny patches all over his face, thick wiry spider hair like nothing he'd ever cultivated before. And his curls! His glorious curls! Burnt, gone, massacred. Now, random knots of hair sprouted from his head like the leafy stalks of a carrot; the rest of his head was bald, and scarred, and blackened by fire and pressure into coal-black blotches that would not come off. The fire had tattooed him with its permanence.

In total, Randy was a fucking mess.

He stared at himself in the mirror, because he had to stare, he could not close his eyes. *Ironic, isn't it, that now I don't want to fucking look at myself and yet am forced to do so, constantly. In every puddle of water, every plate glass window, every piece of polished silverware, every passing mirror. And all for what? All so Jenny and her ECO scum friends could blow up another fucking factory and save the fucking planet. Oh, well, my heart bleeds for them, and their impending pain. But not much.*

I have suffered, and they will suffer. Jenny will suffer. She will tell me everything. Everything I need to know. And then I will continue, I will torture her until there's nothing left. For she has taken my face away. She has created a monster. And I'd like to repay her the fucking favour...

Randy smiled, but it hurt him too much. So he satisfied himself with imagining what he would do to Jenny, and the other captured members of Impurity5. He imagined their pain, with the pleasure of knowing it would soon become reality.

She's going to sing for me, he thought.

Sing like a pop star.

*   *   *

JENNY XI FLOATED on waves of pleasure. Not sexual ecstasy, no, for that would be too intense; that would have been an overloading of joy; no. This was a gentle lulling, like a babe being smothered by love in a mother's arms; like a half-sleep of post-hedonistic satisfaction; like soft warm bed covers after total exhaustion. Jenny floated, and her fingers and toes tingled, and everything in the world was *good* and it was *right*.

Eventually, she awoke. Sunlight beamed bright behind gauze curtains, which rippled gently in a summer breeze. She climbed from the bed wearing nothing but soft, silk pyjamas. In bare feet, she padded across a wooden floor, pushed aside the gauze, and stared out into paradise. A turquoise ocean lapped against white sand beaches that curved off around a distant archipelago. White foam breakers eased up the beach, and palm trees stood, scattered in random phalanxes, their fronds waving and dipping. Jenny breathed deep the smell of the ocean, and she could smell salt, and the sea, and it was pure, and natural, and perfect.

Jenny sighed, at peace at last. It had been a long, hard fight. It had taken decades to clean the evil from Amaranth. But her fight, and the fight of her brothers and sisters in the Impurity Movement, had been strong, from heart and soul; and they had been the victors.

Jenny looked down at her wrinkled hands, and welcomed old age. It was no great loss to her, for she had achieved her life's ambition – to rid Amaranth of the Greenstar Company, to cast out the cancer which had infested the planet for decades, and to restore her world, her family's world, to its former glory. The clean-up operations had been like nothing before ever seen; and the whole of Manna, hell, the whole of the *Quad-Galaxy* had got involved, such was the uproar at the scale of deviation carried out by Greenstar Company...

And now.

Now.

Amaranth was returned to its former glory. Through their acts of violence, Jenny and her comrades had brought about a better world, a cleaner world, a world free of pollution and filth and depravity and inhumanity.

"Save our world," her father had said, as they stood on the hilltop.

And she had.

JENNY AWOKE, DISORIENTATED and happy, knowing she had *done the right thing*. Amaranth was pure again. Amaranth was whole again. No longer the dumping ground for a thousand human and alien civilisations; no. They had thrown off the shackles of oppression, stood together and fought for freedom and justice and purity They had saved the world.

Her eyes flicked open.

Gradually, as if awakening from a drunken stupor, the pleasure and happiness fizzled and faded away, to be replaced by a gradual awareness of reality and an internal pounding of body, of flesh. Like she'd done ten rounds in a boxing ring. Twenty, even.

No, she thought to herself, and tears welled in her eyes. *No!* Because the dream had seemed so real, so true; so solid she could reach out and touch it. It had been a dream not just of belief, but of certainty. A vision of the future. Savagely, Jenny pushed back her tears and focused and sat up.

She frowned.

Her body assailed her with aches and a dull, throbbing agony.

She was seated on a bench like a slab of obsidian, almost tomb-like in its structure. She turned, allowing her legs to swing down. The room was reasonably large, and all four walls were fashioned from glass. With a blink, Jenny realised she was under the sea. Light came from far above, and the water shimmered a deep blue, sometimes green. It was mostly murky, but occasionally light broke through. Jenny had a sudden sense, an impression, of massive pressure, the weight of an ocean pressing down on her. She shivered. If one of those glass walls gave way, Jenny would be crushed quicker than the time it took to scream.

Jenny eased herself down from the slab, and looked around, frowning. If this was a prison cell, it was the oddest she'd ever encountered. In one corner there was a very narrow black door; she padded over to it, looking down, realising she was dressed in a single white cotton slip and soft white cotton slippers. Like a patient. *Odd.* She crossed to the door and touched it, then recoiled with a yelp, leaving a patch of skin. The alloy, whatever it was, was way, *way* below freezing. Jenny gave an involuntary shiver, noting there was no door handle, then she moved back to the centre of the chamber. She stopped, and calmed her breathing, and *listened*.

Silence. But more, deeper than silence, a sense of great *weight* and great *mass*. And a kind of deep, bass *booming*. Like the ocean was talking to her in her glass cube.

She moved to one of the glass walls and touched it. It was quite obviously massively thick in order to combat the incredible pressures of the ocean. Just then, a shaft of sunlight broke from far above and Jenny realised how deep she was. Light flashed through the water, sparkling, dazzling, and seemed to light her face and give her warmth and hope and promise...

She gasped.

"Don't get too excited," came a voice. Feminine, husky.

Jenny turned and stared at a petite woman, dressed all in black, with bright blonde hair tied back in a ponytail. The woman smiled in a friendly manner, but Jenny could read her blue eyes. They were hard; harder than flint. This woman was a killer. Jenny could smell the stench of death a thousand miles away; the blood on her hands. The souls on her conscience.

"Where am I?"

"You are a guest of Greenstar Company."

"If I am a guest, then I am permitted to leave."

"Not... yet. Let us say you are here to help us with our enquiries."

"Fuck you, sweetie," said Jenny, smiling and moving around the room, keeping an equal distance between herself and this small, blonde woman. "What's your name, then? I'm assuming you know all about me?"

The woman gave a narrow smile. "I am Vasta, Head of Security. And yes, we do know something of you, Jenny Xi. Some of your history. And we know a lot about your ECO terrorist exploits and your destruction of twenty-eight Greenstar facilities. We have much video evidence, and of course, Randy Zaglax has been gathering intelligence for over a year now..."

"So that's his name? That back-stabbing motherfucker." Jenny's eyes were angry now and she stopped her pacing. "Let me out of this room."

"You will help us with our enquiries."

Jenny was weighing the woman up. Even if she attacked and beat the woman, which she knew she could, there was no guarantee she could get out of the freezing door. Unless... she took her hostage. But that was supposing Greenstar Company didn't think of her as expendable. And Jenny doubted that.

So... what to do?

Her immediate quandary was answered by the black door opening and a figure stepping through. Again dressed all in black, he was tall and slim and... and he had the face of a monster. A patchwork quilt of bad surgery. He strode across the chamber and stood beside the woman. He carried a pistol. Jenny felt her heart chill. Her lips compressed and she relaxed herself, despite her many aches and pains. She made herself ready for combat...

"Jenny," said the monster through mashed lips and steel teeth. His face wobbled as he spoke, as if the rough-sewn skin panels weren't properly attached to the subframe and might go tumbling to the floor at any minute with a sodden squelch.

Jenny opened her mouth in question, then closed it again. Distant recognition filtered into her brain, but she was tired, deathly tired, and lethargic, and aching herself from, from... from the *bomb* blast. The world came tumbling back, upside down and in reverse. Her mouth was suddenly dry and a million images from the previous year flickered like a black and white horror movie through her spasming mind. The stance. The tilt of the head. The angle of the arms. It was...

"*Randy?*" she said, frowning, voice soft, Vasta forgotten.

"Ahh! You recognise me! Thank god. I thought maybe I'd changed a little *too much*."

Jenny stared hard at the disfigured horror before her. *Holy fuck, what's happened to his face?* screamed her brain, but of course she knew. The pressure blast from the bomb, *her* bomb, hell, *his* bomb, had quite literally ripped his face clean off.

"You betrayed us," said Jenny, eyes going hard.

"You betrayed yourself!" snapped Randy, moving forward and placing both hands on the bed slab. The gun went *clack*. Jenny noted Randy had three fingers missing, and was holding the gun in his left hand. Which meant... he wouldn't fire too straight.

Jenny shifted forward, subtly, as she spoke. "We trusted you, we embraced you into our organisation, and at the last minute you turned out to be a traitor to our cause."

"That's the problem, *Jenny Xi*, it's *your* cause. You have your fucking focus set straight, thinking only of yourself. *Look what your fucking bomb did to me!* I didn't deserve this, woman. You're a fucking terrorist, there's no other way to describe you. Yeah, we all have our causes, all have our own personal honour; but at the end of the day you pick soft fucking targets to make your point. You call yourself soldiers, but I'd like to see you go up against the real military. They'd chew you up and spit you out like the fucking detritus you are. The *shit* you are."

"We only attack installations," hissed Jenny, eyes angry now. She moved yet closer to Randy. "Never people."

"Yeah, but look at the collateral damage," snapped Randy. His eyes, one weeping more than the other, were hard and unforgiving and riddled with pain and angst. He was hurting, not just in the flesh, but deep inside. Jenny could see that, and a tiny part of her heart went out to Randy; no person deserved to have his face ripped free. But then, this was business. Business was business.

"There are always casualties in war," said Jenny, voice hard.

"So I deserved this? *FUCKING LOOK AT ME! YOU TOOK AWAY MY FUCKING FACE!*"

Jenny stared at the monster before her. She had never seen something so ugly and badly put together. It was as if the surgeons, knowing how incredibly handsome Randy had been before the detonation, had addressed the imbalance and made him hideous now. Behind cackling fingers they'd brought forward scalpels and scissors and knitting needles, and put together a shock-horror black-comedy B-movie horror face from a low-budget indie production. Randy looked like a bad special effect.

"I'm sorry about that," said Jenny, softer now, stepping even closer to Randy. She could see the agony in his eyes. In his stance. The gun on the slab was pushed to one side, in his fury, in his torture, and it was a few tantalising inches away. Jenny could sense Vasta shifting, maybe realising the danger, maybe reacting to Jenny's proximity to the gun. She only had seconds. She would have to move fast, make this count...

Jenny surged forward, slamming a right straight to Randy's ruined nose and scooping up the pistol in her left hand. With a cry, the mutilated dandy staggered back, one whole hand, one mangled hand coming up to his face as tears streamed down his stitched, swollen, jagged cheeks.

Jenny pointed the gun at him. Behind Randy, Vasta had relaxed into a combat stance. She was special, Jenny could see that. She *was* the real danger in the room.

"You bitch," hissed Randy, cradling his face. A line of stitches had broken open and blood ran down his cheek. It dripped to the floor with a slow, steady rhythm.

"I'm sorry, Randy," said Jenny, gun pointing at his head, and then, with a subtle shift, transferring to Vasta over his shoulder. "You. Fucker. Open the door."

"No."

"One last chance. Open the door."

"She can't open the door," snapped Randy. "It's externally controlled."

The gun cracked, and Randy staggered back with a bullet in his shoulder. "You hear me?" shouted Jenny. "Next bullet goes in his head, and then I start on the pretty little daddy's girl. What do you say you simply open the door?"

Randy, holding his shoulder, holding the bullet wound, said, "Yes. She's ready."

Jenny frowned, and was suddenly struck. It was like a lightning bolt, only made from water. It came from above, hitting Jenny in the chest, flinging her to the ground, vibrating in shock. The gun clattered off across the cold stone floor. And Vasta was above her, kneeling on her arms, and Jenny was trembling with a taste of copper in her mouth and none of her limbs working properly. Her fingers were shaking and twitching uncontrollably. A smell rose to her nose and she realised she'd pissed herself.

She stared up into Vasta's face, and the petite blonde woman was smiling. "Perfect," she said, and pulled back her fist.

Then the lights went out.

SIX

HORACE STOPPED BY the open door and smelled the breeze. It smelled bad. It smelled of... toxicity. He gazed down the hill, the sweep of Bacillus Port City before him like some crazy electric network. Sirens howled through the rain, and the city shimmered with a low-level haze of pollution. Blue and green stroboscopic lights glittered against mist and rain and toxic clouds, and Horace's eyes narrowed in anticipation.

Why do I feel like I've been set up? A pawn in another man's game? And if there's something I despise, it's being a tool when I haven't given permission. Haven't given the nod. Haven't given my android seal of approval. He smiled. Most androids felt inferior to the humans that created them, but he *knew* he was superior in every way.

He stepped out onto the gravel, rolling his neck and shoulders. The T5 was in his hand, a cold, dark brother. *No point running now. They know I'm here. Probably knew I was here before I got here, but wanted to give enough time for me to be exterminated... then I'm just another homicide, and when they find I'm an android, I'm not even a murder. Just the death of a machine, a tool, to be swept under the carpet at the Halls of Justice. Industrial accident, that's what they'll call it.*

Horace crunched out onto the gravel drive and waited. There were five police cars. Their sirens bounced up the long lane above the roar of engines. Horace's nostrils twitched at the smell of a distant fire. Rubber was burning, thick and black against the darkened horizon. His keen eyes – far more keen than any merely augmented human could ever hope to possess – picked out two passengers, two *Police Urban Force officers* – per car. He could see their broad flat faces, some stubbled, their eyes dark and serious. Their body language suggested they were carrying long weapons, machine guns or, more probably, shotguns. Horace approved. A shotgun was a good weapon to take down an android; the wide blast to knock it from its feet, then twin or quad barrels in its mouth – and it was game over, baby. But what they didn't know (or maybe they did, whispered a thrilling chill in his soul), and this made Horace smile for a moment, baring perfect white teeth, was that he was an *Anarchy* model. If they did know, they should have brought specialised capture and destroy equipment. If not...

You could run...

No.

Stubborn.

A perfectionist in search of the truth.

Do you want to know the truth?

I always want to know the truth.

The first car crunched to a halt on gravel twenty metres away, and Horace smiled as the T5 came up. He shot the first PUF officer through the windshield, a hard *crack* and the body slammed back, shards of nose protruding through the skin, tongue slack in lolling jaws. His comrade was faster, rolling from the car with a D4 shotgun in both hands, blood speckles of his friend and comrade on his cheek, a look of shock raping his features. He hadn't expected *that*. Not so fast. Not so clean.

So they haven't been told, then.

Yes.

Do you feel no remorse?

Never.

The others cars screeched to a halt in an arc of blaring lights and flashing stroboscopes which momentarily blinded him. He smiled. That was the idea, surely? Doors were slamming open, PUF officers disgorging, and someone screamed through a megaphone "Get down on the ground and put your hands over your head!"

And then Horace was moving, and when Horace moved, Horace moved *fast*.

He ran at the first car, flinching left even before the D4 shotgun made a low, heavy *boom*. He leapt onto the bonnet, T5 dropping low to punch a bullet through the officer's face. His hands twitched on the D4 as if playing the flute. Now Horace was on the roof, leaping as guns rattled and cracked, knowing they were focused on his last position. He landed in the mud and stones on his knees, rolling low and shooting under the next car. Five bullets ripped out, killing two PUF officers, who flopped back, still staring up towards the house and its haunting darkness. Horace saw tongues loll out. Saw blood in eyes.

A *boom* crashed behind him and stone rattled against his flank. *Clever. Swift. Almost good enough to be an Anarchy Android*. Horace calculated the location by sound and the scatter of stones, and the T5 fired backwards, blind, and punched a man through the throat. Horace rolled onto his back and looked up through the rain and bright lights. The man had dropped his shotgun and was clutching his windpipe.

His eyes were wide and pleading and filled with disbelief and despair. But that didn't matter to Horace. None of it mattered to Horace. He fired another shot, and the officer's brains mushroomed from the top of his skull. Then he crawled forward and took the shotgun. It felt good in his hands. Cool and slick and perfect.

Scattered images. Sounds. Memories.

Guns cracking.

Lights flashing.

BACKUP, WE NEED BACKUP!

The boom of a shotgun.

The rattle of automatic fire.

The explosion of a car tyre, and the car slumping down on one sagging corner.

The rain, falling, pattering in puddles.

Bullets whining through the air like insects.

The *wham-wham-wham* of shells punching holes in car bodywork.

The splash of Horace's boots through the mud.

He strode the world like a colossus, untouchable, bullets tearing into faces, the D4 shotgun booming in his hands and sparking through the darkness, through the rain. One PUF officer cowered behind the door of his squad car, and Horace shot him through the metal, then leaping onto the roof of the car, shot him through the top of the head.

A bullet whizzed along Horace's cheek, a hair's breadth from opening his face like a zip. Horace moved his head accordingly, and even as the PUF officer was screaming in anger – hatred – disbelief – a sound of violence and rage – so the shotgun came up and blasted him backwards against the squad car, where his blood left a long smear down the glass and panels. Horace hopped down from his perch and put two shotgun shells in the officer's face, effectively destroying most of the man's head. The body flipped and twitched and

Horace knelt by the corpse, hand reaching out to rest on the deceased man's belly. "Shh," he told the corpse. "Shh. It will be all right now."

He scanned the area as the policeman loosened his dead bowels and a stench rose around Horace. Horace did not mind. It masked his own aroma of sweat and metal – whether real or imagined. Although an android was totally organic, Horace almost fancied that he was a robot, a created thing of gears and cogs and pistons. He did not mind that he was not human. He revelled in the fact, for humans were weak and shallow and petty and pointless. Androids were strong and merciless. It was always the strong and merciless that survived the horrors of Fate.

There.

Horace moved fast, leaping, connecting with the final PUF officer as the man tried to make a swift covert exit. The man hit the ground on his face, shotgun flying from slick slippery fingers. He sprawled in the mud, whimpering, and very slowly rolled over onto his back and stared up at Horace.

"D-d-don't kill me. Please!" He held up both hands, pleading, tears running down his face. "I have a young wife, we've only been married a year, and a baby girl. She's a beautiful creature, something we've always dreamed about... she's just started to walk, and talk, and it's the most incredible thing I've ever been part of – don't take me away from her, please, please, sir, don't take away her daddy."

Horace shot the officer through the shoulder with his T5, and the man screamed, flailing back in the mud. Horace looked left and right, bald head gleaming under the rainfall, and strode forward to kneel beside the stricken PUF officer. Shards of bone poked from the shell's exit wound, and the officer was whimpering, crying, tears mixed with rain. His hands clawed at Horace's arm.

"Don't do it. Don't kill me, man. Please. My baby girl..."

"I'm not going to kill you," said Horace, and gave a little smile.

"Thank God!"

"I'm going to torture you." Horace's finger extended, and pushed into the officer's eye. The man screamed, grabbing Horace's arm, legs kicking as he fought with what seemed an impossible strength. Horace pushed, and felt the eyeball squish and squirm, then pop. Then he was through, and into the mucous jelly. "I want to know," said Horace calmly, removing the eyeball with a little *pop*, "who set me up."

"I don't know, I don't know!" screamed the officer, thrashing, fighting, striking out.

"You really need to think harder," said Horace smoothly, "if you want the pain to go away."

There came a flash and a *crack* from the darkness. A bullet slashed the arm of Horace's suit, cut through the flesh beneath to open it like a knife. Ignoring the sudden stab of bright pain, Horace put a T5 bullet in the tortured officer's eyesocket and leapt, clearing the road, to plummet into the toxic underbrush...

Branches and grass whipped at him, and he powered down a slope and skidded to a halt. The woodland was very tightly knitted together, with hardly space between trunks and thorny bushes. Horace knelt for a moment, observing the ridgeline of land above him. He waited patiently, watching. Who had come? Backup? Support? Or had they dropped snipers down the road a little earlier on to cover them? If that was the case, they'd done a fucking poor job. Horace had killed ten cops. He spat on the ground. Ten was not enough.

Shadows shifted, highlighted by the flashing police lights. Horace had picked his spot well, as he knew. There were three men. Special ops. Snipers. Whatever.

They were being careful. Very careful. Horace observed their movements, watched them split, saw the flicker of their hand signals. They were spreading out, moving down the gradient, through thick woodland. They were going to hunt him like an animal – or so they thought.

Horace got down on his belly and moved through the dense vegetation, slowly, a snake on its belly, picking each inch with the utmost care. And then he waited. Waited, in the cold and the dark, rain pattering on the treetop roof canopy, irregular thick drops dripping all around. It was cold. Very cold. Only now did Horace realise just how cold it was, and he realised his breath was smoking. He stopped breathing.

Without breath, Horace's heart beat sounded louder in his ears. Bu-bum, bu-bum, *bu-bum*. He eased himself to his knees as the first armoured police sniper came past, drifting like a ghost; professional, yes, but unaware of *what* he hunted. Well, that answered *that* question. So. A simple response unit, then? Yes. But they knew he was fucking dangerous, or why send so many men?

The man was shifting softly, each footfall a gentle rolled depression. Horace eased himself up as the man glided past, and his hands snapped out, taking the weapon. The man made a startled "Ah!" taken completely by surprise, and drew a knife, but the machine gun cracked against his jaw, breaking it with a brittle *SNAP*, and he hit the ground squirming. Horace worked swiftly, stripping off the man's clothing, taking his own dagger, then cutting long grooves down both his arms, around his chest and waist. He dropped the gun and with bloody dagger between teeth, Horace grabbed the flapping sections of skin and – skinned the man. First he tore off the arms, then the chest and back. The sniper screamed then, writhing in the mud. He screamed and screamed and screamed, and his comrades came crashing through the trees, voices bellowing, guns weaving frantically. They let off random shots, but Horace was on his belly, waiting. As they arrived, and mouths dropped open in horror and surprise, so the dagger went through the first man's boot, pinning him to the ground. He fell back, machine gun rattling, bullets cutting up his comrade who dropped, spewing blood, to the woodland floor. Horace stood amidst the three, covered in blood, eyes gleaming.

"Now, boys, it's time to talk," he said.

And with that, Horace went to work.

HORACE WALKED DOWN the road and found the aircar "Chris" had told him about. It had a SlickCloak covering it; a electronic light diffraction fabric. They weren't perfect, but unless you were actively looking for the hidden, or "cloaked," object, especially at night, they could be hard to spot. Horace pulled the SlickCloak from the aircar, noting the BMW badges, the gleaming panels, the stowed miniguns. Powerful. *Expensive*. Not normal PUF funded kit, of that Horace was certain. This whole thing stunk like a dead donkey of Greenstar involvement. Their own private fucking urban police force. Their own *army*.

It had taken every inch of Horace's skill as an Anarchy Android torture model to extract the information he'd wanted. He had tied all three PUF snipers together by their ankles, stripped their skin, put out their eyes, castrated them, played Russian Roulette. The officer accidentally shot by his friend had – unfortunately for him – not died under the stray discharge of bullets. And so had begun his ordeal. It had only taken ten minutes. But Horace was sure it was the worst ten minutes of their lives... leading right up to their swift, brutal deaths.

Now, he sat in comfort in the BMW aircar. It bobbed as he got in, and plush hydraulics closed the wide arched door. His suit was completely drenched in blood – sodden, in fact – and the car registered he was wet. Small hot-air fans hummed into existence and began to dry him, wrongly assuming he was simply wet from the downpour. Horace pulled out the control deck and fitted the headset. A HUD flickered onto the windscreen internals and with several key presses, Horace ignited the near-silent engines and lifted vertically from the covert parking spot, up fast with streamers of rainwater cascading from the BMW's gleaming hull.

Horace hit MANUAL OVERRIDE and killed the lights.

"Warning," came a gentle, female voice. "You now have no lights and may present a hazard to other aircar users."

Horace gazed down, at the large white house with its sweeping gravel drive and three dead androids, at the skewed Police Urban Force cars with their still-flickering stroboscopic lights, and at the scatter of corpses. Nothing passed through his mind, other than perhaps the concept that it was a job well done. The Dentist had carried out his work with skill and precision, and, yes, maybe he had indulged himself a little bit in the pastime of

(torture)

but, hell, an android was still skin and flesh and bone, still had thoughts and feelings and emotions. Or so it was claimed. Horace smiled at that. *So it was claimed. But maybe I'm different? Maybe they made me different? Maybe I was intended for a different market, a military market, or the assassination market?* Horace frowned, and stared down at the distant corpses of the police officers. And that's all they were. Old meat. Dead meat. They meant nothing. Were as nothing. Yes, they had wives and children and mothers that loved them. But so what? So. Fucking. What? So did every other species on this planet and a million others. And when a rabbit ran out into the road, was squashed by a groundcar into a bloody pulp of split skin and bulging bowels, its squashed skull and brain painting a portrait of fresh meat on the concrete roadway, didn't that creature have parents, and children, and another rabbit it had mated with? Did the human stop and get out and weep and wail for the loss of a rabbit? When a wasp crawled on a human's arm, and was squashed by a heavy hard blow – guilty and murdered before committing the crime – didn't that wasp have the good of the hive, the good of the fucking *Queen* at heart? What made humans so much better? So much more important? Life was life was life. And if you live by the sword, then you should fucking well die by the sword. Horace lived by the sword, and when he eventually got a machete through the neck, sending his head rolling down the road – then so be it. That was the way it went. But if you left the house with a fucking gun or a knife, for whatever reason, or even if it was just your fists and an intention to do harm – then you were guilty. And so many were guilty.

Horace noticed he'd clenched his fists. Anger was raging through his mind.

He calmed himself. Forced himself to be calm.

He looked at himself in the smoked-glass rear-view mirror. *Really* looked at himself. *Why so angry, Horace? What's the matter now?*

But he could not place his finger on it. Could not identify the deviant feeling inside.

Never lose your temper.

"The fuckers."

He slammed the aircar into gear and powered off, away from the murder scene. He swept away, through chundering rain, away from the lights and the city, away from the people and toxic pollution. Over slag-piles of abandoned crap the aircar hummed, until he was gone from Bacillus Port and was out in the wastes, out in the rocky wasteland where few wandered and few dared to explore.

After all, who knew what presents Greenstar had left for the unwary traveller?

Now, HE HAD a name. A focus. A *target*. Juliette JohNagle. Horace confessed to being surprised when he found out his new target was actually a man-i-woman. Not that it mattered. Man, woman or child, he truly did not care who he annihilated. Men-i-women were neither and both; not just a "chick with a dick," as some politically incorrectibles would deem them (usually in a pub after nine pints of Japachinese lager), a man-i-woman was actually a full *merging*, a full *blend* of two separate individuals. Sometimes a married couple would do it – become one. Sometimes, it was strangers who had met through the small ads of the ggg or cube, become bored with life, or felt that something important was missing, something deep down at root level; a sliver of necessity missing from their very existence. Whatever the reason, men-i-women tended to be a strange breed of creature – mainly because there were two minds intertwined, a schizophrenic made real, made flesh. And as the process was a one-way process, there was a possibility of the two minds becoming sick of one another. On many occasions, a man-i-woman had gone quite literally insane and hacked itself (herself/himself/themselves) apart with a cleaver or other sharp implement in a mad, brutal attempt to get away from each other. Juliette JohNagle, on the other hand, was a successful director of Greenstar – and a successful politician peddling the success of Greenstar Company across the Manna and the other galaxies.

Horace shrugged. It was irrelevant, unless it made the target harder to kill. And in this case, and flicking through the news papes on the aircar media channel, Juliette JohNagle would hardly be hard to miss...

Now, also thanks to his torture victim, Chris, who had overheard a damn sight more than he should have done back in that police boardroom, Horace had a location for his target. Not some wild stab in the dark, like was offered by the Fat Man. This was Meltflesh City. A beach hotel on the slick oil beaches of the Biohazard Ocean, where Juliette JohNagle, no doubt, was fucking and snorting his/her/its way into an oblivion heaven of powder puff whores and beyond. If the papes were anything to go by.

So, target and location secured.

Another set-up? Maybe. But this time, Horace would be ready.

He brought the aircar around in a massive thirty-mile loop in order to avoid any follow-up PUF traffic. He'd disabled the craft's onboard trackers, and flew without lights, low, returning to a slumfest back-alley a few streets away from the Bacillus Hilton. This time, he needed the big guns. And this time, he needed backup.

Horace moved slowly through dark and steaming alleyways, nostrils wrinkling occasionally at the toxic vapours that emerged from the sewers. *What's the point?* he thought. *What's the point of sewers, when the whole damn city stinks like this?*

He made it back to his hotel room without incident, and as he slowly closed the door – and not exactly relaxed, but at least stepped down from his highest level of tension – he left the light off and moved around in the darkness.

Fresh clothing. A fresh suit. After all, one must always present a professional image at all times.

"That went badly," said Silka, her young, smooth voice penetrating the room with a crisp clarity.

"I fear it was a set-up."

Silka considered this. He saw her outline on the bedside table. She was preening her fur, and making a tiny purring sound. So, she had chosen her non-chameleonic phase. It must be that time of the month.

"You should have taken me with you," said Silka.

"No. I wanted to check it out alone."

"Ha! And nearly get killed, foolish android."

"Don't be ridiculous," said Horace.

"And the wound to your bicep?" Horace had used the BMW aircar's emergency staplegun to punch the wound shut. It had hurt. A lot. But it *was* the most effective fast way of closing an open flesh wound and getting on with the job, which was why the PUF carried them. A shame none of the wounded officers were repairable... "You bit off more than you could chew."

"No. There were three androids, then ten officers, then three special forces snipers. I'd say I did pretty well okay to take that lot out and only suffer a single cut to the arm."

Silka jumped down from the bedside table and bounded across to him, tail swishing. She leapt onto the bed, tiny muzzle and whiskers twitching, and stared at the wound as Horace removed his jacket with a wince. "Made by a bullet, foolish android. One inch to the right and you'd have lost the use of your arm. Then it *would* have been game over."

"I'm getting old," said Horace, and sat on the bed.

"We all get old," said Silka, and rubbed herself against him in the manner of a cat.

Horace picked her up – and if this had been anybody other than Horace, they would have immediately lost three fingers. Silka may have looked like a cross between a ferret and a domestic cat, but her bite was worse than her bark. In fact, she had been known to bite off entire heads. Yes, it took her a while to gnaw through the spine, but it was doable when she put her mind to it.

"Take me with you," she said. "On your next target."

"No. It'll be dangerous."

"You know I love danger," purred Silka.

"Too dangerous." And yet he knew he needed her, and that he was playing a charade. Why play? "Okay," he said. "Your offer is much appreciated. I do need the backup, and I think this game is bigger than both of us realise."

"You think Greenstar have finally grown tired of you?"

"I think I've done so much dirty work for them, one day that eventuality must be inevitable. I just didn't think it would come... now. Not with so much still to do." Horace stood, and stripped off his ruined suit. He moved to his case and pulled free a small plastic ball – an example of the Ultimo™ Packing System. He pressed a button and tossed the ball on the bed, where it made a *zwang* noise and opened up into a full suit. Horace had a quick shower, dressed, checked his T5, then picked Silka up in one hand. She scurried up his arm and sat on his shoulder for a moment.

"What will you do?"

"Fulfil my mission."

"Even thought the mission may be compromised?"

"We'll find that out soon enough."

"Will you share your thoughts?"

"Yes."

Silka pushed her nose into Horace's ear, and he closed his eyes for a moment as she rifled his memories. It tickled. Horace smiled. Horace liked smiling, but recognised there was very little for him to smile about.

Finally, she emerged. "Ahh. I see. A man-i-woman. Juliette JohNagle. Interesting."

"Meaning?"

"I have seen this person. On the media. They have also been on the news many times, and stood trial for crimes against Amaranth."

Horace shrugged. "About that, I do not care. They can poison the whole fucking Quad Galaxy for all I care. All I care about is life..."

"...and death," whispered Silka, little more than an exhalation caressing his face. She kissed his cheek. "Let's go."

DAWN HAD ARRIVED, and with it, huge bruised skies filled with towering rainclouds. Rain clattered against the aircar's panels and windshield, and Horace kept the BMW low and away from civilisation. They headed east out of Bacillus Port, moving on past millions of simple block adobes and then past a kind of shanty town, where hovels had been constructed from... waste. That was the only way to describe it. Scavengers had obviously taken advantage of the open dumping policies of Greenstar, and created their own city on the outskirts of the city. Nothing had been *wasted*. Houses were built from stacks of old TVs, planks of corrugated asbestos, wood and metal off-cuts, car panels and old tyres; old propane cylinders formed the corner supports holding up asbestos roofs. Oil tanks had been upended and turned into sleeping chambers. Walls had been constructed from bright yellow bags of medical waste, piled up like sandbags. Need a used needle in the middle of the night? *Just rummage through the wall*. Old garage doors had been leant against one another, forming vague rusted wigwams of second-hand mild steel. The variation and creativity was intense; and went on and on and on.

"You have to admire them," said Silka after a while.

"Admire them?"

"The Scavs. Down there. Rummaging through their short lives, existing amongst all this shit."

"It's amazing the lengths a human being will go to in order to survive. I have seen it. Many times."

"Yes, you've seen it on the end of a scalpel or drill-bit. I'm talking about their *ingenuity*. Look down there! A house built from old fish tanks, the weight of water giving the walls stability, and the top one – where the water is freshest – feeding drinking tubes down into the chamber. Simple, yes. Basic, yes. But effective."

"Did I really hear you use the word 'fresh' about *this place*?"

"You know what I mean."

They left the slums behind, and turned northeast. Before long the huge, towering Yellow Virus Peaks to the north could be seen. There were five mountains, each towering to thirty-five thousand feet. The summits were crusted with ice and snow; yellow ice and snow. The joke on the underground streetslam was that Greenstar had dumped a trillion tonnes of horse piss which had immediately frozen, giving the mountain range its colour and its name. In reality, it was a rare mineral found in the rock that turned the snow yellow. But what *was* true was the highly toxic nature of the mountains – the Yellow Virus Peaks were a serious no-go area. Not unless you wanted to contract something biologically devastating and end up shitting your stomach out of your arsehole. And yet, every year, a hundred or so "mountain adventurers" would arrive from other planets, drawn in like moths to a candle with the promise of adventure, danger, and being the *very first* to conquer this hazardous mountain range.

Their survival rate was 0%, and as a statistic, this should have been warning enough.

They flew for most of the morning, and eventually the toxic storms abated and green sunshine sparkled from above, making the barren land, stripped of all vegetation, at least *seem* a little more hospitable. Horace had seen some dreary, inhospitable places in his life, but this wasteland took the cherry from the top of the cake. Deserts had vegetation, or at least the noble sculptures of dunes. Even arctic wastelands could be stunning, with a savage beauty created from snow and ice and wind. But this... this *desecration,* this was the pinnacle in an exercise of poisoning. There was no joy here. No pleasure could be found. Only pain. And desolation. And death.

They crossed the River Tox, which ran from the Yellow Virus Peaks and down for a thousand miles, from north to south, a vast winding tributary that eventually flowed past the port cities of Encephalitis Dance and Shitdump, then out into The Sea of Heavy Metal.

"Sunshine," murmured Silka.

"Yeah. That's probably why they call this holiday complex *Meltflesh* City."

"That, or the chemicals in the ocean," said Silka, and Horace could hear the laughter in her voice. She was the one thing that stopped him descending into a perpetual morbid depression. She was like a breath of fresh air over a corpse. Like a kiss from a virgin. A sigh from a satisfied lover...

"I often wish you were human. Or even better, android."

"It would never work," said Silka.

"Why?"

"You think you know me. You do not know me. Our minds work... so very differently."

"But you appear so..."

"Appear, yes," said Silka, and her eyes gleamed in the weak light of the aircar's cockpit.

After another hour, they saw the distant cityscape of Meltflesh City. Vast towers ranged like teeth along the shores of Biohazard Ocean. Even from this distance, a shimmering light seemed to hover above the vast expanse of houses and towerblocks, cubescrapers and skyscrapers. It was vast. As big as Bacillus Port, Amaranth's capital, surely; and home to the most select. The wealthy, the privileged, and the fucking *insane*.

Horace laughed. "What a fucked-up place this is."

"Better believe it," said Silka, shifting to sit on his arm. "Why are you landing?"

"I want to approach under the cover of darkness."

"Yes. Let us wait, then."

THE HOTEL WAS a huge complex, with ten swimming pools, swim-up bars, children's areas, entertainers, and fake plastic palm trees. The main difference between any normal hotel in the Manna Galaxy Bubbles and this one was the regular *detox points,* see-through plastic cubicles where you could pop in your toxic kids and let them have a happy chemical wash down before they melted. Lovely.

Horace had parked up on the outskirts of the city and headed in on foot. The city – and indeed, the resort – was only a kilometre wide, a stretch of tourist-based hotels and restaurants that flanked the Biohazard Ocean like a bad case of genital herpes. As Horace approached, despite the late hour, the streets were serpents of hedonistic flesh. He shook his head in wonder. "Who in the name of hell comes to Amaranth for a holiday?"

Silka, tucked inside Horace's suit jacket, said, "It takes all sorts, Horace my dear. I would expect many are inhabitants of the planet, possibly Greenstar employees who feel their chemical and biological protection tablets give them enough immunity to brave the air and soil and waters. Others are probably alien-based life-forms with a natural resistance to toxicity. And yet others are lunatic humans drawn to what they consider a danger-holiday; an adventure-fest."

"Hmm," said Horace.

He walked along the pavement, ignored by the partying revellers. As Silka had predicted, there were a wide range of humans and aliens alike, everything from single-sex stag parties to tentacled couples with children. It boggled Horace's mind. Assassination was a much simpler concept. Life and death. A monetary transaction. No emotion. No empathy. But this... this *wanton self-destruction* was much harder to comprehend.

At least I am built this way.

At least I understand.

At least I have a singular function.

Horace walked. To his right, lit by a million fluorescent tubes, the ocean crashed on the sandy shore. The beach was a jungle of scrap, as was to be expected for a junk world. Everything from half-submerged, rusting motorbikes, to old tyres, boxes, plastic bags and bottles, and even an old half-beached nuclear submarine, its vast, matt-black hull pitted and corroded in blotches as if it had been subjected to the world's largest acid bath – which, in fact, it probably had.

"A nuke sub," said Horace, shaking his head.

"You're beginning to sound like a grumpy old man," chided Silka.

"Sometimes, I'm fucking glad I'm an android. Life is much simpler this way. Humans are so... damaged."

The incessant party noise pounded and thumped, screamed and chattered. Music spilled from ten thousand bars. The ocean crashed, a rhythmical percussion of poison. Horace located the hotel and bought himself a hot-dog (With Cheeze and Chillees!!!) from a shop-front vendor he'd normally execute rather than look at. However, trying to remain inconspicuous, he held the hot-dog (With Cheeze and Chillees!!!) and nibbled at it without enthusiasm as his eyes took in the cubescraper where Juliette JohNagle was supposedly a guest. Horace even had a room number, gibbered on a stream of phlegm and blood by Chris the Helpful Special Forces Victim, in an attempt to not be brutally executed. Unfortunately, Horace did not take prisoners.

"Looks good to me," said Silka.

"We'll hang back. Wait awhile. See what happens."

Horace followed his unwanted hot-dog (With Cheeze and Chillees!!!) with a coffee, then a sugary donut. A PUF car pulled up and two fat cops waddled over, buying a bucket of donuts each. "Go easy on the sugar, darling," one said through his rolls of fat, six chins wobbling, "I'm on a diet" – before making eye contact with Horace.

For a long thrilling second Horace thought he'd been bubbled, and would have to fight his way free of Meltflesh City, the worst holiday resort he'd ever encountered. But then the fat cop waddled back to his groundcar, squeezed his bulk through the door, setting the suspension rocking wildly, and cruised off, face crusted in sugar.

"Close," said Silka.

"Lucky for them," said Horace.

After an hour, Horace could take the party atmosphere no longer, with the drunks and the vomiting (was that down to alcohol, or toxic kidney poisoning?), and muttering to himself that if he died, then he fucking died, he strode down the pavement, Silka warm against his chest, hearing one another's heartbeats and sharing the pleasure, and he approached the steps and foyer of the Grand Meltflesh Hotel.

The front of the hotel, a massive blocky cubescraper with fancy plastic graphics, overlooked the Biohazard Ocean from a raised platform and had its own section of private beach, patrolled by guards with hefty wooden peacemakers.

Horace strode confidently up the steps and into a foyer with low-level lighting. Plastic shrubs littered the space like tumbleweed, and leather sofas in a hundred different styles lay seemingly at random; Horace wondered if they were actually junk salvage put to an interesting new life.

Horace moved across thick sticky carpets, boots pressing softly, and smiled at the two girls behind reception, who returned his smile in a pleasant fashion, then lowered their heads back to work. Horace crossed to the lifts and pressed the CALL button, listening to a grinding of gears, then stepped inside the compartment. One wall had a window overlooking the Biohazard Ocean, and as the lift climbed he got a brilliant bird's eye view of the ocean in all its terrible poisonous monstrosity. At least twenty ships lay wrecked in what must have been a modestly shallow bay, some of them on their sides, all rotted and holed by the acidic ocean. They formed a jagged set of teeth on the horizon, giving the ocean jaws. A wind whipped yellow and purple froth across the waves, and the puke-coloured ocean lapped at beaches where even now, at this late hour, people were happily paddling and swimming under the onslaught of so many powerful beach lights.

"What a shit-hole," murmured Horace.

"Your people made it this way," said Silka.

"Well, they should be exterminated for the sacrilege," said Horace.

"You're hardly honouring your employers," laughed Silka.

"Honour? What's that?"

Suddenly, the lift stopped with a grinding clang. Horace frowned. They were between floors: a ridge crossed the window at eye level. Horace pulled out his T5 and, with a punch, destroyed the in-lift camera.

"Trouble?"

"Always," said The Dentist.

Horace punched the keys on the console, but it had gone dead. No power. He moved to the doors and started to lever them open, his powerful fingers hacking into the gap and exerting a force far greater than any human could ever administer. There came a screeching sound, a grinding of gears, a tearing of steel bolts. Horace gritted his teeth and pulled harder. The doors opened several inches, along with more sounds of tearing steel.

There came a *click*.

Horace's head snapped up, his eyes searching the roof. There were holes. Lots of holes. Horace frowned. From the holes spat a sudden spaghetti of long white worms, but these weren't normal white worms, these were something far more terrible and dangerous and *alien*...

They landed on Horace's shoulders and head, each one about ten inches long and slightly metallic. They were silent, and squirming, and Horace caught a sight of their tiny metal jaws, chomping, chewing, searching for flesh. He brushed frantically at his shoulders, felt a piercing pain at the top of his skull and he grabbed its tail as it began to burrow into his flesh. He pulled it free, feeling it slither from his own skin, and crushed his hand into a fist, destroying the worm. But more fell. And more. It was snowing worms... killer worms...

Trapped, Horace stamped on the worms on the floor, crushing their bodies into pulpy white paste. But still more poured from the ceiling holes and he felt one go down his shirt collar, and tried to grab it but missed. It started to burrow between his shoulder blades and Silka was there in an instant, chewing a path through his shirt and suit and biting through the worm.

"You have to get out of here!" cried Silka, crawling up onto his shoulder. Her jaws snapped left and right, pulping the wriggling worm creatures, which, Horace suspected, once inside him would make a swift burrowing towards his internal organs. And God only knew what damage they would cause when they arrived.

With Silka's jaws chewing and biting and spitting, Horace leant into the lift doors with a growl, and feeling his fingers ready to snap under the intense pressure, he slowly, inch by inch, dragged the doors open, to a soundtrack of singing, screaming steel...

"Get out," growled Silka, and leapt, landing in the mass of writhing white worms. Their teeth snapped at her now, trying to burrow into her flesh. Horace jumped, caught the lips of the floor and heaved himself out onto a foul-smelling carpet. He lay there for a moment, then felt wriggling inside his clothing and began to roll, hands thumping at himself, tearing at his clothes, as in at least five places he felt tiny jaws burrow into his skin, eat under his flesh and begin to worm through the muscle...

Horace grunted. It was rare for pain to bring out any sound from him, so high were his tolerances, but this was *more* than pain; this was an invasion. A rape of the flesh.

Horace caught a worm by the tail and pulled it out, a long quivering worm turned pink by his flesh and supped blood. It squirmed under his fingers, jaws snapping at him, and savagely he put it in his mouth and tore it in two. He grabbed another, but a sudden wave of weakness struck him. He felt like he'd been hit by a sledgehammer, but it was something different, something internal. As if he'd been...

drugged.

They'd poisoned him.

Horace tried to crawl down the corridor, but within a few short seconds his hands lost their strength and he slumped to the carpet on his face. He felt the four remaining worms burrowing inside him, eating his flesh, gnawing their way to victory and a horrible, bubbling, impending death.

Arrogance, he thought.

Arrogance has brought you to his.

And as his eyes flickered and the lights started to dim, a door opened and a pair of feet walked towards him. They wore red high-heels. Red high-heels, containing fat, hairy feet.

"Bring him this way," said a gruff voice, and for Horace, it was a short hard blow to oblivion.

SEVEN

"THERE ARE SOME riders approaching," said Lumar softly. She was stroking the green scaled skin of her arm. Her tongue flickered as her green eyes fixed on distant figures.

"Eh?" Svool looked up from where he'd been polishing the silver star sheriff's badge. "It's kinda pretty, don't you think? The way it catches the green sunlight and sparkles like that. One of the prettiest baubles I ever did see. I know you will probably laugh, but I feel like it's an inspiration for *another new poem*."

Lumar said, "I think you should put it away." She had already moved, picking up her sharpened stick from where it leant against one of the battered, bullet-holed cars.

Svool stared at her. "What?"

"These dudes look like mean dudes."

"What dudes?"

Now, the hoofbeats from their horses rattled from the stone buildings. Svool whirled about, and his mouth dropped open. For there were seven riders, mounted atop tall metal horses. Each rider wore thick cotton and tweed, and long leather coats. Each face was a barrage of stubble and scars and mean eyes and ugliness. They all wore wide-brimmed hats, and high boots, with spurs that jangled.

"They're..." he said.

"They're cowboys," said Zoot, spinning slowly, black lights glittering. The PopBot hovered to a halt before Lumar and Svoolzard. "Or they think they are. Their mounts are homebuilt metal horses, built on a ripped-out chassis subframe from a DumbMutt special robotic friend. They've been twisted beyond all recognition – not that that's a bad thing if you've ever met a DumbMutt before."

"What's a cowboy?" said Svool, uneasily.

"Many, many years ago there was a place called The Wildy Wild Wicked West. It was very wild. And wicked, I presume. There were lots of horses and men who ate beans out of pans. They would dance around fires showing their bare behinds and whoop and holler and make love to their sisters. Sometimes, they would fight injuns."

"Injuns?" said Lumar, eyes narrowing sceptically.

"Yes. Injuns."

"What's an injun?"

"I haven't got a clue," admitted Zoot.

"Hey, well, that doesn't sound too bad," said Svool, breaking into a grin. "Because *we're not injuns!*" He pushed past Zoot, waving both his arms in the air, a wide smile on his open face, his golden curls tumbling behind him. "Hey there, friends, are we so very very glad to see you! You see, our starship – that's a big floaty thing in the sky –" he made a shape with his hand and mimed a big floaty thing in the sky, "it crashed in the sea with a *SPLOOSH!* and we were stranded here, on this heap of toxic shi... on this lovely world of yours."

The horses had slowed, their hooves stomping dry dust, and Lumar noted they had formed into a semicircle, with the biggest rider at the centre. He had a cruel scar running from temple to jaw; it looked angry and purple, like it had only recently healed. The man rubbed it absently, his eyes fixed on Svool, his mouth narrowed into a cruel bloodless line.

The horses stopped, a couple of them pawing the dirt.

Svool was still jabbering. "...so as you can see, we're here in this fine village, a-ha-ha-ha, and I suppose it's *your* village, anyway we was wondering if you could see it in your hearts to be kind, and generous, and give us a comfy place to sleep for tonight, preferably with a double bed for me and the little green lady here, nudge-nudge, you never know your luck, and then you could maybe pack us up some generous supplies and maybe supply some transport, a groundcar or groundvan would be just perfect, and we'll make our way to the nearest city, which I believe is called Organophosphate City, which is a very strange name if I may be so bold."

There was a long, curious silence.

The seven mean mounted riders looked down on Svool. The biggest man, with the scar, glanced up and his eyes passed expertly over Lumar, and she would have reddened if her skin hadn't been green, for his eyes mentally undressed her, then moved on to Zoot. With the PopBot, he showed no surprise. Lumar had reckoned him to be a heathen, brainless, backward local on an idiot metal horse; now, she revised her impression. He was dangerous. Very dangerous. They all were. And her eyes picked out the guns.

"How do, Sheriff," said the big man, his voice a slow long drawl. "I'm General Bronson, but you can just call me General Bronson."

There was an undercurrent of laughter from the men, and this wasn't the laughter of a few guys having a bit of fun; these people were killers. Yes, they were dressed in outlandish clothes and were misplaced in this jungle environment; but they were killers all right. Lumar's hands tightened on the staff.

"Hi there, General Bronson!" beamed Svoolzard, grinning like the village fool and flapping his hands around like they were chicken wings. Lumar recognised his danger immediately. Svool did not see their menace; he heard the laughter, and being the egotistical maniac he was, immediately thought they were laughing *with him*. It did not occur to Svool that somebody could laugh *at him*. "So then, what I believe I need to do at this juncture is point out that, tush, I am *a little bit famous,* I know, I know, my name is Svoolzard Koolimax XXIV, Third Earl of Apobos, and yes, it's me, I've been on the cover of *GGG Time Magazine*, and my books have been best sellers across the entire Quad-Galaxy, and you may recognise me from the many vidbox recordings I've done, everything from my own poetry, which of course is my personal favourite, to several famous reimaginings of some of the *Great Classics*, as they are humorously known. It was indeed *I*, gentlemen, who rewrote Shakespeare's entire collection of Sonnets, I know, I know, I don't need thanking for that little gem; I reworked T. S. Eliot's *The Wasteland* so that it, you know, made some sense, and I have also been instrumental in the redrafting and modifying of Tennyson's *The Lotus-Eaters*." He coughed, stepped his legs apart, and thrust one hand out before him as must any great orator, and before Lumar could stop him, Svoolzard boomed in a loud crooning voice:

"Branches they bore of that enchanted stem,
   With quite a bit of flower and fruit, which they gave
   To each, and whoever received those bits of flower
and fruit,
   Tried to eat them,

And tasted the gushing of the waves, as if drinking
water,
    And far, far away they did seem to dance and jiggle
    On alien shores; and if a friend did speak,
    His voice was thin, like voices from a very long way
away,
    And they looked like they were asleep, yet awake!
    And lo!
    Music in my ears like a beating heart, there was.
Hurrah."

So lost was he in his recital, in his brutal murdering
of Tennyson, that Svoolzard failed to see General
Bronson slowly draw his hefty black pistol and point it
straight at him.

Awaiting his applause with rapturous expression,
Svool *finally* opened his eyes and his mouth dropped
open.

"Say another word," drawled General Bronson from
around his cigar, "and I'll shoot yer fucking teeth out
the back of yer head." He hawked and spat on the
ground, and sighted down the pistol.

"Ah..." began Svool, and Lumar hurried up and
kicked him in the back of the shin. Her eyes shifted
right to Zoot.

"I'll handle this," said the PopBot quietly, and drifted
forward on a stream of ions so that he was directly
between Bronson's gun and Svoolzard's head. The
PopBot surveyed the large man on the large metal
horse.

"I suggest you put down your weapon," said Zoot.

"Get out of the way, you little bastard."

"I'm warning you; if you continue to pursue this
course of action, I assure you, you will regret it."

"*I'm warning you; if you continue to pursue this
course of action, I assure you, you will regret it,*"

squeaked one of Bronson's men in a high falsetto, and they all sniggered.

"Right," said Zoot, but before he could do anything, Bronson *fired*. There was a WHAMP sound, but no bullet, and Zoot dropped from the air and spun a few rotations in the dirt, before lying still.

The band of cowboys burst out laughing, and Bronson levelled the gun at Svool once more. Reaching forward, he adjusted a tiny switch on its body. "Throw down the pretty sword, boy, and I won't switch this beast to metal bullets and, as they say, *fill yer full of lead*." General Bronson stared down his long nose and longer pistol at Svoolzard and Lumar. He looked extremely mean, and like he meant business, which he probably did.

"I'd better do as he says," muttered Svool.

"Coward," muttered Lumar.

"Hey, he has a gun!"

"Yeah, well, I have a –" she turned with awesome speed, as if to hurl the sharpened stick like a spear. There came a *crack* and a whip caught the top of the staff, dragging it from Lumar's stunned hands. A second crack of the whip caught her cheek, slicing through green skin and sending blood trickling down her face. A cigar-chomping, narrow, evil face grinned at her, and the man with the whip jumped down off his horse.

"She looks like she needs a horse-whippin' to me, Bronson," said the man, and spat a glob of brown glob onto the dirt. "And then, yee har! We'll have some fun with this pretty little green lady!"

"The only fun you'll have with me is when I shove my fist down your throat!" She snarled. But the whip cracked, even as Lumar leapt with cat-like speed and grace. The whip was faster. It curled and snapped round like her like a live electric snake, *humming*. The whip plucked Lumar from the air and deposited her at the man's feet, trussed up and hissing.

He knelt. Leant forward. And kissed her.

Lumar struggled, kicking in the dirt, and Bronson strode over and kicked his man in the head, so that he tumbled sideways with a grunt, lying alongside the seething figure of Lumar and staring up at the General with angry eyes.

"What you do that for?" snapped the fallen cowboy.

"Leave her be," said General Bronson, and gestured to Svool. "We have this one to deal with first. And he's a dangerous bastard, I can tell." He hawked and spat, then chewed down on his cigar.

Now all seven riders had dismounted from their curious metal horses. The man in the dirt climbed back to his feet. Lumar was hissing and snarling on the ground, but Bronson kicked her in the face, and she was quiet.

All seven riders pulled out their pistols and pointed them at Svoolzard, who visibly paled, and lifted his hands, and took a step back. "Whoa," he said, "what are you guys doing? Do you know who I am? Do you *know* how famous I am? Do you *know* the kinds of poetry I write? The wonderful novels I have created? I have *film deals* in the pipeline! I am going to *act* in my own movie! I am... I am a *genius!*"

"That may be so," said Bronson, coolly, looking down his levelled pistol, "but you took up the position of Sheriff in this here town, and we don't want no Law Makers coming and taking away our business."

"What? Sheriff? Eh?"

"You put on the badge, son," snorted Bronson. "Now, you represent the Law. Now, you *are* the Law."

"I am the Law?" squeaked Svoolzard. "Trust me, my friend, trust me when I say this: I am *not* the Law. Or even the law. I have no interest in the police. Or sheriffs. I have no interest in criminals, you can go on and about and do whatever the hell you like, I won't arrest you, I can't arrest you, how could I arrest you? I have no gun."

There was a *thud* as the gun landed at his feet.

"Pick it up," said Bronson, drawing a second pistol.

"What?"

"Pick up the shooter, son," said General Bronson, and his cigar chomped from one side of his mouth to the other.

"Ha-ha," said Svool.

"If you think this is a laughing matter, Law Man, I'll shoot your fucking nose through the middle of your face."

The manic grin fell from Svool's features as if dragged by a charging horse. At last, the severity of the situation kicking him in the balls, he stared at Bronson, then at the other six riders in their dust-stained ancient clothing. *What madness is this? What craziness? Who are these bloody lunatics? Where did they come from? What's going on? What do they bloody well want from me? All I want is sex and drugs and gorgeous-girlfriend-sex-honey. I didn't want none of this shit; I still don't want none of this shit; I'm a lover, not a fighter! I'm a genius poet, not a gun-toting wildy wicked wild west sheriff. Oh, God. Oh, hell. By the Holy Mother of Manna, how do I get out of this crap?*

"Pick up the gun."

"No."

"Be careful, Law Maker, or you'll make me angry."

"Will you *stop* calling me 'Law Maker,'" snapped Svool, his eyes flashing angry. "I am *not* a sheriff! I was captured by some little pygmy cannibal things, and they burnt all my clothes, and I came into this damn village or town or shithole or whatever the tox it is, and I was wearing fucking *leaves*, man. You understand that? *Leaves* over my nuptials. And the first damn house I went into had these clothes, right, so I put them on rather than be naked. But I'm telling you this, I didn't want to take on no responsibility for being the sheriff of this here town, and I'm not *going* to take on the responsibility of this here town! So there." He practically stomped his foot in indignation.

General Bronson sighed, and rubbed at his whiskers with a scratchy sound, and strode forward, spurs jangling. Svool went pale. Bronson pressed the barrel of his pistol against Svool's forehead.

"You took up the badge, son. And if you wear the badge, you are a symbol. And if you're a symbol, you have responsibility. And if you have responsibility, then you stand up for that responsibility. If not, well then, you're nothing worse than a worm in the soil and I might as well exterminate you here and now." He looked back at the other guys, and there came a low rumble of gurgling laughter.

"But if I pick up the gun you'll shoot me," squeaked Svoolzard.

"I'll shoot you if you don't," said Bronson.

"But... but... but..."

"That's an awful lot of butts," grinned Bronson, showing blackened teeth, and half-turning to his men, who gave another low rumble of gurgling chortling. It was like watching a particularly bad comedy routine by a low-grade university comedy club.

Taking his opportunity whilst Bronson was turned, Svool suddenly brought his knee up between Bronson's legs with as much force as he could muster. There came a *thud*, and Svool felt the considerable impact, the connection, the squash of some dangling soft tackle being heartily compressed, and the sour grunt that burst like corpse-breath from Bronson's mouth.

General Bronson took a staggering step back, then righted himself, and took a deep breath. His pistol never once wavered.

"That's a good cheap trick, son. Do it again, and I'll beat you to death with my fists. Now, that ain't a man's way to go. That ain't a warrior's way to go. Not when he's chickenshit like you." He cocked his pistol. The sound was deafening. The whole world seemed to be paused, and deathly silent. The sounds of the jungle and the chomping horses had faded away into soothing infinity. The cock of the pistol was a screeching metal intrusion and Svool swallowed. Hard. This was it. He was dead! He wanted to cry. He wanted to scream. He wanted his mummy.

"Last chance," said Bronson.

"Pick up the fucking gun, you idiot," hissed Lumar from her trussed-up position on the ground.

"They'll shoot me!" squeaked back Svool.

"Pick it up!"

Slowly, Svool bent down like a woman in a short skirt bends down, a lowering of haunches, a feminine curtsy, and at the end of it the long black pistol made its way into his paw and he lifted it as if holding a rearing rattlesnake.

"Good boy," breathed Bronson.

"Is it loaded?"

Everybody laughed at that.

"Now point it at me," said General Bronson.

"I'm quite sure that I can't," said Svool, face drooping, lower lip quivering.

"Shoot me," said Bronson.

"*Shoot the motherfucker!*" snarled Lumar.

"This is a joke, isn't it? The gun isn't loaded? I'll pull the trigger, and it'll go *click*, and you'll all laugh at me, and then we'll head back to the saloon or whatever and eat a pan of beans."

General Bronson regarded Svool with narrowed eyes.

"You taking the piss?"

"Er, what?"

"You think all we ever do is eat beans and fart around a fire? Is that what you're saying?"

"Er, no, it's just I saw a pan of beans back at the sheriff's place, I thought, I thought you all, I thought maybe..."

"*Yes?*"

The single word was like the closing of a lead coffin lid; like the boom of the ocean against terrible cliffs; the solemn chime of a solitary funeral bell.

"Oh, nothing," squeaked Svoolzard Koolimax.

Lumar took that opportunity to attack. Yes, she was trussed up at her whip-wielding captor's feet like a turkey waiting to be stuffed for the festive season, with her arms pinned tightly by her sides and the man's flesh too many inches from her gnashing teeth to allow the rending and tearing she would have desired. But her legs were free, nearly from the hips down, and she was supple, and massively agile, and slowly, *so-slowly-it-was-a-painful-crawl,* she lifted her legs around, crawled around a bit, bent herself almost in two until her captor's knee was *right there* –

She stomped out, like a horse stomps out, and the man's leg folded neatly back the wrong way at the knee joint. The *crack* was like dry tinder snapping. There was a pause, then a scream like an animal in pain and *sudden chaos...*

Lumar scrambled up, onto her knees, face wild and teeth bared, and the man with the broken leg was writhing on the ground; all attention was on Lumar, and she struggled to be free of the whip. Bronson strode forward and pistol-whipped her savagely against the side of the head. Lumar hit the ground, tasting copper, stars fluttering in her mind. And as she lay there, on the ground, disjointedly feeling the men tying her ankles together, listening to the blubbering of the man with the broken leg, she could see the dwindling sheriff's uniform of Svoolzard Koolimax XIV as he disappeared through the rusted car horseshoe...

"Goddammit!" snarled Bronson, and fired off a shot. There came a metal *zip* sound as the bullet ricocheted; but Svool was gone.

"Shall us boys go after him, General?" said one man.

"No," said Bronson, kneeling in the dirt beside Lumar. "Let's take this pretty green lady back to the saloon. I know his sort. He won't let his friend die. He'll come back for her. And when he does, then we'll have our sport."

Lumar heard the words through her spinning brain, and she wanted to say *You're fucking joking, right? Svool is a bastard, a spoilt child, and a massive coward. He's hot-tailed it away thinking only of his own arse, he'll throw his toys out of the pram because he's now alone, and his bravest course of action will actually be to run away from here as fast as he can whilst convincing himself he's doing the right thing... going for help or some other such nonsense...* but instead, she managed only a gentle deflating sigh before unconsciousness claimed her.

SVOOL FLED INTO a twisted mess of trees and tangled foliage, his arms pumping, his knees lifting high, doing perhaps the fastest three-hundred-metre sprint of his entire life. Bronson's pistol was heavy in his hand, but it didn't exist during his sprint, didn't register as being part of the fabric of reality. Svool's singular simple focus was to *escape*. To *run away*. To *get away from the bad men*. He ran and ran and ran, waiting with an itching feeling between his shoulder blades, *waiting* for a soft *thump* and the *crack* of a pistol. Waiting to be shot. The run seemed to take a million years. His legs moved through the thickest of treacle. His arms were punching through water and the whole process was one of humiliation and despair and agony and terror. He waited for that bullet. Waited damn hard. It became an obsession as the picoseconds ticked by. The *bang*. The *thump*. The feeling of hard steel wading through cloth, then biting into flesh, and pushing right through to his heart to kill him dead...

When the bang came, it *did* make him jump. Made him leap into the air like a comedy cartoon character being zapped up the bottom by an electric cattle prod, and it was an age between the pistol discharge and the *ping* as the bullet glanced from a knackered old car. In that time, in that slice of life, Svool lived his whole life again. In that split shard of infinity, he waded out into his past like a fisherman getting into trouble in a very deep pond, and he looked at himself, looked at his sexual conquests, looked at his poetical creations, looked at his writing and performance and recitals and academic writings and his speeches and his *adoration*, dammit, his fucking *adoration*. He was loved. The people loved him, And his PR and management and agents and publishers and marketing department and his *brand* kept him locked in a cocoon, a cocoon of warmth and comfort and safety and lies. Lies. It was all false, all fake, and here and now, without those safety nets, some hairy, stinking cowboy bastard was trying to kill him.

When Svool crashed into the shattered stand of trees, a section of jungle that had been destroyed by some kind of storm, he staggered, sprint turning into long loping strides as if he really *had* been shot, then the loping strides turned into a tumble and he fell to the floor on a platter of wood shavings. He leant on a fallen trunk stripped of bark, as if something had been eating it, and reclined like a Victorian lady who'd become overheated in the sunshine and was now lolling with a fan and a glass of lemon-infused water.

"Oh, woe is me!" exclaimed Svool, theatrically, and then remembered the big men with guns had shot at him, and he looked fearfully at his back-trail as his chest heaved and sweat stung his eyes and he panted, panted, panted, his sheriff badge gleaming in the sunlight filtering through the high forest canopy.

When his puff had returned, Svool stood up on jelly legs and tottered to the edge of the jungle. He hid behind a tree and peered out. He'd covered a good five hundred metres. He squinted, marking the place where the jungle took over from the town, then following the line of buildings back to the horseshoe of battered, rusted cars.

Nothing.

He could see nobody and nothing.

But then, on the upside, there was *no pursuit! Hurrah!*

Unless... they were circling behind him? Damn.

His head snapped round, his pistol lifting, and he blinked rapidly. No. Nobody behind him, creeping through the jungle to strangle him or horse-whip him. Svool looked down at the pistol. It was long and sleek and black and heavy. It hurt his hand just to hold it, and he held it in a way a man might hold a scorpion; or a woman might hold a herpes-infused cock.

Ha! Bloody stupid thing. It was all a tricksy, a set-up, a wind-up. Damn and bloody thing isn't even loaded!

Svool pulled the trigger. The *BANG* was so loud it made his ears ring for ten minutes. Smoke spat from the gun like it was on fire and the bullet *pinged* from a tree trunk and embedded in the soil with a *whump*. The recoil slapped Svool's arm nearly a hundred and eighty degrees around, and the whole process made him feel like an idiot. Hot damn. It *was* loaded. Loaded with bullets. Loaded with bullets that could kill somebody!

"Hot buggery," he said, and his cheeks flushed red as he realised... realised he *could* have killed General Bronson, and rescued Lumar, and they could have bush-whacked those darned cowboys and stolen horses and hot-tailed it away out of there shouting "Yeeeee-har!"

The flush in his cheeks went redder.

General Bronson. Well. He must be an idiot... or insane. To have Svool point a loaded pistol at him? Why would he do that? Why would he put his own neck on the line for the sake of... what?

Sport, whispered an inner voice. *He was playing with you. He saw you. He knew you. He understood you. He knew you didn't have the bollocks to do what a real man should do. You're a fucking spineless jelly of a man, Svoolzard Koolimax. You talk the talk but tip-toe and wobble and ballet-dance the walk, mate. You're not a man; you are an amoeba, all soft and jelly and without any real wedding tackle.*

So.

What to do?

What to do *now*?

Well, it's obvious really, innit?

Is it?

Oh, yes! I have escaped simply to put myself in a position where I can go and get help. I will travel to the next town and rouse the Law Makers of this toxic world, and then we will come back in force and rescue Lumar! Hurrah!

She might be dead by then.

No, they wouldn't kill her...

How do you know?

I just know!

How?

I fucking know, I'm telling you, so shut up and let me get on with the rescue!

(yeah, a rescue from a distance in two weeks' time, you coward)

I am not a coward!

Oh, yes, you are.

Not!

Are.

Not!

Fucking are, you spineless, jelly-brain, weak-kneed, yellow-belly turd.

I have done brave things!

Like what?

Like when I stood up on stage at the Spingo University Academic Conference for Academics. That took a lot of guts, a lot of bravery; there were five hundred of my peers there! It was most traumatic!

And if you had done something wrong, what was the worst that could happen?

I could have been... discredited!

(oooooh)

Laughed at!

(oh, dear, oh, dear)

Mocked! Mocked and berated!

(oh, you sad pathetic little fizzle)

They might have stopped publishing my work, stopped attending my lectures and poetry readings! I might have lost my chance at being a movie star and rock star and poetry star all rolled into one!

(ha and ha and fucking ho-ha)

Will you stop muttering in the background, you fucking insane and separate part of my self-mocking brain? What are you, anyway? Where did you come from?

I'll tell you where I came from. I came from the part of you that knows. *I came from the part of you that* understands. *Inside every single one of us is a mechanism for comprehension; no matter how hard it gets, no matter how bad it gets, no matter how fucked up you become, you fucking know, deep down inside yourself, what you really are; you fucking* know *deep in your heart whether you do the right or the wrong thing; and you fucking better know in your soul whether you are worthy of that gift called life. When some scumbag hits an old woman with an iron bar to steal her purse, that cunt knows in his soul he's done the wrong thing; the weak thing. He might blank it out for a time, but trust me, it comes back to haunt a person. When that shitbag coward fucking serial killer beats another woman with a hammer and buries her out on the soothing singing sighing moors, the fucking weasel might have his twisted reasoning, be able to quantify his actions in his own deviation soup; but trust me, deep down in his soul, in his darkest place, in the fucking core of his being, in the distillation of his humanity, he knows. He knows better. There may be a Hell, Svool. There may be a place of Eternal Torture for those who cannot bring themselves to do the Right Thing. Maybe not. Maybe that's just a bucket of pigshit. But what I'm telling you now is you have a choice. Not everybody out there chooses the right path. But you need to, buddy, or I'll break your spine over my knee like kiln-dry tinder and cast you out to wriggle with all the other maggots.*

Svool sat there, mouth opening and closing silently. The feeling, and the words, drifted away like smoke in his brain. *So that's what it's come to? Being threatened by my own rambling psychosis?*

He stood up. The sun tickled him with strands from the high canopy. His panting had stopped, and he lifted one hand to his breast, and spread his fingers, and looked down at the dirt, and the tears, and the snot.

He took a deep breath, and lifted his head. His eyes focussed.

How could he leave Lumar?

How could he run away?

Easy... whispered a soothing nag at the back of his brain.

No.

I must go back for her.

I must save her.

Svool looked down at the pistol. It had a thick barrel, with chambers holding the bullets. Svool played with the weapon for a few moments, found the switch, and there was a *click*. The barrel swung out and with tinkling sounds seven bullets fell to the ground. Svool dropped to his knees, cursing, and found the bullets – well, found six of them – and he was cursing even louder. How could one have gone missing? They were gold and bright and sparkling. How could he have *lost one already?*

That left him with six. Shit. There were seven of those bad cowboy men.

Svool breathed deeply and took his time, sliding the bullets back into the pistol and closing the barrel. He spun it, and it went *clicka-clicka-clicka*. Svool grinned, and a kind of light-headed feeling rushed over him.

Goddammit! He *was* going to rescue Lumar!

For the first time in his life, for the *first time* was going to do something completely selfless.

He was going to rescue her.

Or die trying.

And it felt *good*.

SVOOL CREPT FROM the broken jungle an *inch* at a time. He held the pistol in both hands before him, and he was shaking, and the gun was shaking, and he crept forward, imagining at any moment a gunshot would crash towards him from some unseen location and he would be punched backwards off his feet, broken and bloody and bleeding, and die right there in the dirt.

Finally free of his cover, he stood there for a while, and when no murderous death came at him, he started to walk back towards the scene of Lumar's capture. Back in the jungle cover, when he'd come to the realisation he would do the *right thing*, it had felt good; better than any orgasm he'd ever experienced. But now doubts started to creep through him, and obviously, because he was a genius with a genius imagination, his inner TV screen started to air a thousand eventualities, where in every single one he got shot and died and ended his budding silver screen career.

"Bugger," he muttered, and as he started to get close to the horseshoe of cars, he slowed his pace even more, if that was possible. Svool wasn't conscious he was taking shuffling, one-inch footsteps, and if somebody had pointed it out to him he would have commented on how ridiculous he was; but that's what he was doing. Jungle snails were overtaking him.

The cars were close now, close enough for Svool to see whether the cowboys, or whatever the hell they were, had gone.

Crawling into view, he realised there was no sign of them.

Suddenly, he spotted Zoot on the ground and stumbled forward towards the PopBot.

"Zoot!" he hissed. "Zoot, buddy, are you okay?" But obviously the little PopBot was far from okay. Svool touched the black casing and it was cool under his fingers. He scooped both hands under the PopBot, obviously with the intention of lifting the tiny machine, but to his very great surprise Zoot was too heavy to lift. He grunted and heaved and strained for a moment, again with the curious sensation somebody was having a laugh at his expense and would jump out with a full film crew, shove a boom mic in his face and shout, "Svoolzard Koolimax, you've been *FUCKED! Ha-ha-ha!*" But that didn't happen and Svool found himself kneeling next to Zoot, and staring around with nagging fear, and then eventually tapping the PopBot with his knuckle.

"Zoot? Zoot! Wake up!" But the machine continued to lie still, unmoving, without life. "Shit and buggery."

Then, from the corner of his peripheral vision, Svool caught a movement. Feeling the need for urgent survival creep up over him, he made an effort to show no outward emotion or indication that he'd noticed. He coughed, and rubbed his chin, and tossed back his golden curls, and then at the very last moment – as he felt his nerves jangling like runaway church bells – he leapt up and around with pistol outstretched and shaking in both hands.

"A-ha!"

The metal horse was grazing just off from the rusted car horseshoe. It lifted its big, sad, disjointed head and stared at Svool and his shaking pistol, then lowered its head once again and continued to crop at grass and ferns and indeed branches and stones, crunching them to a pulverised dust between its metal teeth.

"Stand still!" commanded Svool.

The horse obeyed, for it was already standing still.

"Don't move!" he instructed.

And indeed, the horse obeyed, since it took very little jaw movement to chew on grass.

Svool edged closer, finding new bravery in this obedient metal beast doing what it was told even though he knew deep down in his heart it was doing it anyway.

As he edged closer, he actually looked properly at the horse. It was made from what appeared to be hand-beaten panels of different kinds of metal. Some were silver and shining, but most panels were a bronze or copper colour, and some showed streaks of rust. Each panel was a different size and shape, and whereas a skilled engineer could have made the horse look like a well-oiled, well-engineered, kickass fighting machine, in this instance it looked more like it had been bolted and riveted together in somebody's garden shed.

"Look at you," muttered Svool, edging yet closer. His gun wavered, and he lowered it, for the horse was obviously just a dumb beast, and not an enemy, and something which had been left behind. Probably by the man whose leg Lumar had broken. Could you ride a horse with a snapped kneecap? Probably not.

The horse lifted its head again and regarded Svool.

Inside it, something went *clonk*.

Svool looked around, to make sure this whole thing wasn't a set-up, to make sure he wasn't about to get a bullet in the back of the skull. Then he shuffled closer. The ugly metal horse lowered its multi-panelled head, the head that looked as if a circus strongman had taken a large sledgehammer to it for a good three or four hours. It was bent and twisted and battered and dented, pitted and corrugated and welded and rusted.

"Well, look at you," said Svool, and shuffled yet closer.

The horse lifted its head again.

"Neigh," it said, in a gurgling, gravelled voice, although the word was spoken as a human would speak it, not as a horse would actually neigh. It wasn't an animal sound; it was a word.

"Who's a pretty boy, then?" said Svool, for want of something better to say, and patted the metal horse's neck. There was a hollow reverberating sound, as if he was patting an empty oil tank.

Inside it, something went *clank*. Then there was a buzzing sound. Then a farting noise.

"They left you behind, have they, boy? Hmm? Poor little old you." Svool patted the horse's neck some more, and its head lowered and it chewed its way through a lump of granite with *cracks* and *bangs*, showering the dirt with ground stone dust.

In fascination, Svool walked along the beast, trailing his hand over its high shoulder, along its flank, and across its bottom. There was a tail there, made from rusted barbed wire. It swished and flicked. Svool observed the huge, plate-sized hooves, then walked up the other side of the horse, and patted its neck again.

"You're a fine beast, that's for sure. It's a crime they left you behind!" Then a wonderful concept sidled into his brain. "Hey, what do you think of me maybe riding you?"

The horse was chewing a log now. Wood splintered and crackled.

Svool eyed the simple saddle, and, cocking his leg up, got one foot in a stirrup and hoisted himself into the seat.

Svool had never ridden a horse before. In fact, he had never ridden any sort of creature, unless you counted his many, many willing lovers. He recognised that would make a good line for a poem, and filed it away in a mental drawer entitled: *Possible Future Poetry Material.*

He sat atop the beast, which still placidly chewed on wood, and he bounced in the saddle a couple of times. "Hey, this ain't so bad! Moderately comfortable. Not so tight on the happy sacks. I'm feeling pretty much in total control, at this rate we can gallop into town and save Lumar! Hurrah!"

There came a very, very soft *clunk*.

With a whirring sound, the horse's head lifted up and its legs straightened. Then, with a clicking ratchet sound, the head rotated one hundred and eighty degrees so the creature was staring straight at Svool, with a back-to-front head.

"Neigh," said the horse.

"Er," said Svool, licking his lips nervously.

And then, speaking in the voice of a human – possibly the engineer who had created or programmed the metal beast – the horse said, "*Congratulations! on your purchase of the DumbMutt v0.3 [MUCH IMPROVED!] special robotic friend. This little special friend will be your friend. A friend for life!! Please find enclosed the instruction manual and ownership deed in a variety of Manna languages, Braille dot, PSI and scent-sensorship.*"

"Hey, hold on a minute. The purchase of a *what*? I didn't purchase an anything! For a start, I haven't got any money on me, and even if I did I'm pretty sure I wouldn't be buying a battered, er, bashed, er, hammered-out old rusted..."

The horse stared at him. Svool rolled to a halt. The horse continued.

"*As you listen to this, a genetic sample is being taken from your buttock area by a saddle prick and relayed digitally to the DumbMutt's brain. He is now yours. He will never, ever leave your side. He is forthwith electronically registered to your individual and personal DNA coding and as such will follow you FOREVER and TO THE ENDS OF [whatever planet you inhabit [insert here]]. If you lose or misplace or become detached from your DumbMutt v0.3 [MUCH IMPROVED!] special robotic friend, do not fret, do not cry, do not panic, because HE will eventually find YOU. If you vacate the planet, your DumbMutt v0.3 [MUCH IMPROVED!] special robotic friend has emergency funds to book* passage on a Shuttle to anywhere within the Quad-Gal [Manna] Bubble. In effect, your DumbMutt special friend will follow you to the ends of the Galaxy. Well done in this, your Smart Choice."

"Now hold on a bloody minute!" snapped Svool, staring in horror at the metal horse's head in front of him. The jaws were working spasmodically as if trying to mimic a human's lips whilst reciting the words of the *contract*, but in reality it was doing a very bad job of synching to the sounds, and simply looked as if it had gone badly insane. "Now, now, now, *I* didn't give you no permission to give me a saddle prick, in the buttock area, and what's all this about DNA and stuff and you following me to the ends of the planet, eh? I didn't agree to none of that, so stop it right now, I don't need a horse, or want a special robotic friend, I certainly didn't buy you and I never made no smart choice!"

At that point, something sharp injected his bottom. "Ow!" he cried, predictably, and nearly fired the heavy black pistol into the face of the horse. Cursing, and reaching under himself to rub his arse, Svool gave a very severe frown. "That's a bloody intrusion, that is!" he snapped.

"Thank you, Svoolzard Koolimax, Manna resident DNA number 6764783643 3896653652 3653652732 5347645 376457532 999994652. We do hope you enjoy your DumbMutt v0.3 [MUCH IMPROVED!] special robotic friend. He will be a very special robotic friend. For life. Your special friend DumbMutt v0.3 [MUCH IMPROVED!] special robotic friend comes with many exciting innovations and technical upgrades over the previous DumbMutt v0.2 [A BIT IMPROVED!] special robotic friend, which tended to accidentally activate its inbuilt hydrogen cell auto-destruct initiation sequence and destroy both DumbMutt Unit and Rider Unit in one massive blast.

Don't worry! That doesn't happen anymore! Not often, anyway [please read legal addendum]."

"Argh!" gargled Svool.

"Your friendly special friend DumbMutt v0.3 [MUCH IMPROVED!] special robotic friend is called [HERBERT]. Please be kind to it. And remember. A robot horse is for *life* not just for [insert applicable religious festival]. ©qv2907 Metal Mongrels Inc. QGSMA Quad-Gal Safety Mark Assured (pending). MSMA Manna Safety Mark Assured (pending). Registered with the Federation For Safety With Metal Mongrels, Inc."

There came a *ticka ticka ticka* sound. Herbert opened his mouth, and a long stream of punched foil paper ejected. Svool took the paper, and read in letters made up of pin-prick holes:

Please take good care of your DumbMutt v0.3 [MUCH IMPROVED!] special robotic friend [HERBERT]-model. Your DNA has now been registered with the MMI central core database. Your deed will last: 999 years. Thank you for your custom. ©qv2907 Metal Mongrels Inc. QGSMA Quad-Gal Safety Mark Assured (pending). MSMA Manna Safety Mark Assured (pending). Registered with the Federation For Safety With Metal Mongrels, Inc.

"Ahh," said Svool. "What's this?"

"It's a deed of ownership, buster," said the horse, in a much more normal but still quite alarming voice. Svool stared at the twisted-round head, with its flared metal nostrils reeking of hot oil, its beaten face plates, and its big brown marble eyes.

"I don't understand."

"You own me."

"No, I don't."

"Yes, you do. Your DNA has been accepted. Neigh."

"That isn't even a real sound."

"What?"

"That neigh."

"That's what horses do. And I am a horse, therefore, I neigh."

"Yeah, but they *make* a neigh sound. They don't say the word."

"Listen, buster, I yam what I yam."

Svool sighed. "Listen, I'm going to get off you now..." – all ideas of some heroic horse-bound rescue had flown off into the jungle, along with Svool's dignity – "so just put your head back where it should be and I'll get off and we can both go about our merry ways."

"No," said the horse.

Svool's smile remained fixed in place. "Excuse me?"

"No. You're going to rescue Lumar."

"What... *how* could you possibly know that?"

"It's a process of 'limination, innit? Neigh."

"No it isn't. This has NOTHING to do with you. So I'm getting off. And you're *fucking* off."

Svool tried to move his legs, and realised in horror that narrow clips had ejected from the horse, wound about his ankles, and pinned them in place. Slowly, the horse's head returned to a "normal" position, with a *click-click-click-click-click*.

"How do you want to do it, buster?"

"Wait! Let me off!"

"Time for the rescue. Innit."

"Get OFF me, you fucking insane robot beast!"

"Ha. Hold on! The West is about to get much Wilder! Even though we're, y'know, technically in the south. Innit. Neigh."

With a complicated series of movements, the horse's legs began to flap and flop all over the place, and there were clanging and clanking noises, and slowly, it managed to turn around.

"Have you got your pistol?"

"Er, yeah...."

"And your sword?"

"Er..."

"And your sheriff badge?"

"Just wait a...."

"Then you're a fully tooled up sheriff! Yeeeeeee Har!" With that, Herbert reared, shouting "Neigh, neigh, neeeee*ighhhghhghhghghh*," and galloped between the rusted metal cars.

And towards the saloon.

"HE'S COMING, BOSS."

The sun was high in the sky and baking the boards of the saloon's porch. Bronson lowered his boots from the table, and cast a look back to where Lumar lay on her side, trussed up like a trussed-up turkey. Her narrow green eyes bored into him with unadulterated hatred, but Bronson's deviant men had a certain expertise with knots, and despite Lumar's incredible agility, she was now stuck.

She spat at Bronson.

The large man ignored her, and tipped the brim of his wide cowboy hat back a little.

"Showdown, boss," said one of the men.

Bronson hawked and spat, and with a chinking of spurs, strode out to the centre of the street. He stood, hands hanging loose by his sides, twin pistols holstered – how many pistols did this man *have?* – legs apart, in a classic gunfighter stance.

He waited, patiently, the sun behind him.

"What are you going to *do?*" wailed Lumar.

Bronson didn't look at her. He was focused on the figure that had just stopped at the end of the street. Again, he hawked and spat, and simply stood there, waiting.

Somewhere distant, a jingly little tune began to play.

The sort of tune which sometimes came from a pocket watch. It played a sad slow hymn. On the porch, one of Bronson's men got out a harmonica and began to strangle it. The wails cut across the dry dusty street.

"What do you think he'll do, boss?" asked one man.

General Bronson grinned, and patted his holstered pistol. "Why, I think the sheriff is going to do some dying."

"Yes!"

"No!"

"Yes!"

"No!"

"Yes!"

"I am *not* having a fucking gun battle with that fucking lunatic! I've never aimed a pistol in my life, and I've certainly never aimed it at a person, and I have no intention of killing *anybody!*"

"Well?" snapped Herbert, "Why have you just ridden into town on the back of a horse wearing the sheriff's outfit and carrying a Law Maker's pistol then, if you weren't looking for trouble?"

"That's *because* you locked my legs to your ribs and forced me to come here, *idiot*. Of course I'm not looking for trouble. I couldn't shoot an elephant that was trying to sit on me! *I* was going to sneak in the back way, wait for it to go dark, then cut Lumar's bonds and we could have all snuck away without any hassle, but oh, no, clever-arse metal mongrel horse shithead here had to go charging in, didn't you?"

"Well, you should have said," sulked Herbert.

"I should have said? Right, turn around, get us the hell out of here, *now*."

"Can't do that," said Herbert.

"What? *Why?*"

"Can't do that. Oh, no. Traditional gunslinger showdown, this is. You've, er, laid down the gauntlet, buster. Given him the challenge. Innit?"

"What, by riding my horse here?"

"Yes, to rescue your good lady woman from the evil banditos, sort of thing."

"She's *not* my good lady woman."

"Your bitch, then?"

"Listen," growled Svool, close to the horse's twitching metal ear, "you need to release my ankles, turn around, and walk slowly away."

"So you're fleeing, then, are you?"

The sounds of a harmonica floated up the street. Svool thought it was a cat being slowly massacred.

"No! I mean, well, I can't possibly face him..."

Herbert started trotting down the street towards General Bronson, whose fingers were flexing slowly. Svool struggled like mad to free his ankles, cursing and thumping the hollow body of the metal horse.

He gave up, and lifted up the pistol. He squinted towards General Bronson, but the sun was in his eyes and he realised with alarm his error. Bronson had picked the battleground and the position. Now, not only was Svool disabled by his complete lack of usefulness with his pistol; he was also effectively blinded.

"Drat," he said.

"Good luck!" Herbert grinned optimistically.

Herbert stopped in the middle of the street. Awkwardly, the harmonica music faltered, and all was quiet, except for the sad sound of the tinkling watch.

"Er," said Svool.

"Congratulations, son," growled Bronson, switching his cigar from the left side of his mouth to the right. "You did the right thing coming here to rescue this young green lass."

"Fuck you," snarled Lumar.

"She's a feisty one, all right, but once us boys have killed you dead, we'll all be having our wicked way with her and then probably cutting her throat. Sorry. That's just the way it is out here in the West. Well, south. You know what I mean."

Svool glanced across at Lumar. Fear filled his face.

"Why didn't you run and fetch help, you idiot?" she snapped.

"That's what I was *trying* to do!" wailed Svool. "And then I felt all guilty and stupid and like a cowardly idiot, and I knew I had to do *the right thing* so we could both escape!"

"So facing down seven gunslingers is the right thing?"

"Shut that bitch up," growled Bronson, and there was a thud.

Svool's teeth clacked shut. His eyes narrowed. From nowhere surfaced the words, "You're going to regret hurting the little lady."

What? mouthed Lumar silently.

"That may be so, or it may not be so," growled Bronson. "But – you hear the music?"

"The tinkly, jangly, crappy, cheap elevator music?"

"Yeah, son. When the music stops, then draw and fire. I'll do the same. Whoever is left standing, well, he gets the fun with the little lady."

"Will you *all stop calling me a little lady!*" hissed Lumar, struggling on the rough-planked porch.

"Er, Mr Bronson?"

"Yes, son?"

The watch tinkled away, the tune getting slower, and slower, and slower...

"I have a question?"

"Yes, son?"

"About this music, about when it stops..."

But it was too late.

The music stopped.

EIGHT

SLOWLY CONSCIOUSNESS DAWNED, and with it a bright, brittle fear. Jenny Xi was still in the glass-walled cube beneath the ocean. It was dark now, the ocean a gloomy, murky black.

Night.

The real fear came when she tried to move. Her arms were strapped by her sides, wrists and ankles tightly manacled to the cold black obsidian slab. A steel band across her brow pinned her head. The steel dug into the flesh of her forehead, biting her like teeth.

She wanted to cry out, to thrash, to scream, but she controlled herself. No. Why give them the satisfaction?

Jenny had been tied up before, of course. As part of kinky sex games, or even when she'd been arrested in her younger days; but never like this, never with such cold callousness, and with the stakes so high.

There came a cough, signalling that she wasn't alone. Jenny was itching to turn her head, to focus on the sound, but she could not. She had to wait for the figure to come to her.

It was Vasta. The blonde woman was smiling. Jenny couldn't help but note she was wearing thin leather gloves.

"How are you feeling, Jenny?"

"Like I was hit in the face by a train."

Vasta pulled out her lower lip, as if sulking. "Oh, dear me. Well unfortunately, that's as good as it's going to get. From here, it all goes downhill. Very, very quickly."

"Fuck you."

"Not me, my little sweetie. But I am sure *fucking* will feature high in our priority list when we get down to the real... torture."

She left the word lingering in the air like a bad smell. The effect was not lost on Jenny.

Jenny, her squad, and the entirety of the Impurity Movement had been through "torture training." How to react in these situations, the do's and don'ts for when they start stripping skin from your bones... of course, it was all well and good in theory, and even in the role-play exercises they did, very much in the manner of military special forces. But Jenny knew, deep down inside – as she was sure most human beings knew – that when it came down to it, when it *really* came down to it, everyone had a breaking point, everyone had a trigger. Jenny always said she would rather kill herself than be tortured. She cursed herself now. She'd had the gun, and put a fucking bullet in Randy, when she should have been putting a bullet in her mouth.

"Let me explain your situation very, very carefully," said Vasta. "By attacking and shooting Randy, you have condemned yourself to our care. We were, of course, filming the meeting, and by attacking the recently *seriously* wounded and highly honourable and decorated Greenstar Company Governor of Internal Affairs, you highlighted your guilt within the eyes of the law on this planet. Under Quad-Gal Military Policy, to protect the rights of Greenstar against further terrorist attack, we are allowed to detain you for questioning for six months." She let that sink in. "*Six* months, Jenny Xi."

Jenny said nothing. Her lips compressed harder.

Vasta came close then, looming into view. Jenny would have twisted her head away, but the steel strap held her tight, pinned like a butterfly awaiting scrutiny on a lepidopterist's examination board. And, no doubt, impending dissection.

"You obviously do not know my name," said the pretty blonde woman, and it just didn't fit with Jenny. This beautiful little lady, and the words that poured from her mouth like filth. "I am the chief torturer for Greenstar Company. Obviously this is not a position they broadcast or acknowledge; I am simply referred to as Head of Security. But let me assure you, I have thus far tortured nearly two hundred prisoners for The Company. Some of them even lived."

Vasta's face disappeared, and Jenny realised she was panting softly. She forced her breathing to calm. The woman appeared again, and her face was a perfect mask of concern. Her eyes seemed to soften, and she leant forward, intimate, until her lips were only an inch from Jenny's. So close Jenny that could smell her sweet breath, the musk of her skin. So close, so intimate, and yet so far.

Vasta said, "We are going to grow very close, you and I. It will be a relationship of love; my love for you. I do not want to do the things I am going to do to you. I want only that you tell me the information I seek. If you do not speak to me, Jenny, then I cannot help you with your pain." She kissed Jenny then, a long, lingering, passionate kiss. There came a dart of her tongue, and then she pulled away, and Vasta's hand came to rest on Jenny's belly. With a start Jenny realised she was naked. Idly, Vasta started to stroke Jenny's skin with long, gentle strokes.

"What are you going to do?" snapped Jenny. "Torture me or fuck me?"

Vasta smiled, a genuine look of humour. "Probably both. Now lie back and relax. Sleep if you like. But consider my words. I will give you an hour before I begin. If you choose to co-operate, then there will be no pain. If you choose *not* to tell me everything concerning your friends in Impurity5, the Impurity Movement as a whole, your Cell Commander McGowan, and his contact with the higher echelons of Impurity, Mr Candle; well, then we will not be friends. If you co-operate fully, who knows, maybe Greenstar will be thankful and allow you to live."

"Get fucked," said Jenny.

Vasta tutted, and held a finger against her lips. "Spoken like a terrorist," she said. "Now don't go anywhere, my sweet. When I return, I will bring my tools. Then, we will dance together. You shall see."

IT WAS PERHAPS the longest hour of Jenny Xi's life. It was up there with the death of her father and the subsequent funeral in terms of sheer enjoyment. She lay still on the obsidian bench, the dark ocean above her, all around her, shifting and dancing and coalescing. Cramps gradually wormed into her muscles, into her calves and thighs, into the intercostal muscles between her ribs, into her forearms and shoulders and neck, every single cramp making her want to writhe in agony as her muscles rebelled, turned against her own physiology, and she spasmed, rigid, in agony, unable to move, unable to break free. The pain was incredible, but one by one her muscles eventually relaxed, leaving just a dull throbbing and her own panting loud in her ears.

How long has it been? How long before the *real* fun begins?

As part of her anti-torture training, they had been lectured by a man, a broken man, a bent and hammered and twisted individual who had been the unfortunate victim of the heartless *junks*, the scourge of the galaxy, during the long-distant, half-forgotten Helix War. The man, Jabez, had been the victim of an interrogation he could not answer – simply because he did not have the answers. As a result, he had been permanently crippled. All fingers and toes that still remained were bent and broken, deformed, bones allowed to fuse at odd twisted angles during the length of his incarceration and sustained agony. His legs, also, had been broken and forced to set at odd angles. His knees had been smashed with sledgehammers, he told the group.

They had sat in a chilled silence, in awe at this broken wreck presented before them in a tiered, sterile lecture theatre, like some circus freak on a stage for their pure entertainment. Jabez showed them scars from where his skin had been stripped from his body. He showed them scars in his legs, where whole veins had been teased free like strings of spaghetti. His fingernails had been torn off, each knuckle cracked with pliers, his testicles ripped free with tongs of steel, the end of his penis slit with a scalpel over and over and over again; they'd let it heal, and scar, then slice it again. He joked with the recruits, said it gave him extra holes to piss out of. Said that when he peed, it was like a sprinkler for his hosepipe. Nobody had laughed. How could they? This man before them was destroyed. They'd put out one of his eyes, shaved his ears with a cut-throat razor, striped his neck and his wrists, allowing him to bleed like a pig. They'd cut off his lips, smashed out his teeth, cut off half his tongue – not all of it, you understand, because they still expected him to talk. But he couldn't talk, he said to his horrified watchers. How could he tell them what they wanted to know, when he did not have the answers?

"Did you tell them what you did know?" asked one young man with wide, horrified eyes.

Jabez explained, then, how he had told his diseased, decadent tormentors *everything*. He had screamed answers, told them anything and everything whether he thought it was relevant or not. When he realised they would not stop, and he did not have their answers, he had made up things... but this was worse, for they went away, and checked his lies, and came back with triple the fury, triple the ingenuity.

Exhausted, of answers, of energy, of strength, and tip-toeing along a razor-edge of sanity, he had finally thought they had finished with him. Left him broken and massacred. But that had just been the start... that was when they began to remove his internal organs before his very eyes, replacing them with artificial units and force-feeding him his own liver, and kidneys, and spleen, and heart...

Now, every word Jabez had spoken came back to Jenny with chilling clarity. *But that had been the junks, right? The most despised and evil race in the whole of the Four Galaxies. They hated all life, hated all love, and simply existed to spread their toxic existence, their organic pestilence, their festering disease to every other living organism in totality. What they didn't infect, they sought to destroy. Surely, surely a human being couldn't do that sort of thing to another human being? Surely this Vasta was simply boasting of her talents in order to crack Jenny before the real pain began... hence the hour in which to make her decision. Psychological torture. Present you with some facts and leave you for the longest hour of your life to make a decision.* But a streak of stubbornness ran through Jenny Xi a mile wide, a lodestone of strength born of her father, broken and destroyed by the destruction of the planet he loved; and a belief, a true, pure belief, that what she did was right. Not just for herself, or her family, or the human beings on the planet; but for the planet itself. For the good of the World.

TIME CRAWLED BY. Jenny tried not to think about her future. Instead, she regressed, and thought about the happy moments in her childhood. Eventually, through exhaustion and fear, she drifted off into sleep. She slept lightly, dreaming about meadows filled with flowers back when Amaranth was a place of joy and warmth. Before Greenstar moved in. Before the pollution began.

She awoke to a tiny *click* and saw a table had been erected, just at the periphery of her vision. On the table was a small black case, like a briefcase, matt in finish, terrible in its sinister implications.

"Welcome back to reality," said Vasta, smiling in a friendly manner as she moved into Jenny's view. "You've had your hour, my sweetie. Have you decided whether you will answer my questions?"

Jenny considered this. "I'd rather fuck myself with a chainsaw," she said.

Vasta's smile widened. "That can be arranged," she said. "Okay, then. So be it. You have made your decision and now we must play the game. I apologise in advance for the agony I'm going to put you through. But, hell, I just work here, right? And somebody has to do the job I do – to make the world a safer place."

"TELL ME ABOUT your family," she said.

"No."

"Tell me about your family, Jenny. What have you got to lose? I don't want to hurt you. I don't want to take this gently heating needle and push it through your eyeball. But I will."

It wasn't fear of pain or torture or death that started Jenny talking. It was a regression, from this bad place into *that* bad place. A stepping back through time to *remember.*

"I had a brother. Called Saul. We grew up together, had a happy family time together... until Dad died, of course. I suppose there were cracks in Saul's character even back then, for father had become a very heavy drinker and these things always rub off. We're influenced by our parents, right?" Jenny gave a small laugh. "But as time went on, he showed his true colours. The true nature of the beast. Always small, petty things that took away from the nobility of his humanity."

"Such as?"

"Saul would never help people. Not even with the smallest thing. He'd sit by and watch somebody struggle, or suffer, and never lift a finger to help. At the time I told myself it was because he didn't notice these things; he was just being vague, you know, being Saul. After a while you accept him for that, accept the lack of a present or card, accept the lack of a thank you, accept his miserly nature. 'Oh, that's okay, it's just Saul.' But in truth he was a tight motherfucker, not just in monetary terms, but in human terms. He didn't have it in him to *give.* He didn't have it in him to *share.* Most people enjoy watching other people have pleasure; so by giving, you also receive. Not my brother. His mind mechanics were wrong. Fucked up. He was not a very nice person."

"Is he part of the Impurity Movement?" Vasta's words were a soft winter chill.

Information. That's all this game is about. Information on Impurity. Well, tell the fuckers nothing... because to tell them anything is to betray the cause, betray your friends, betray your brothers – your real brothers, not the fake fucking water-for-blood decrepit family flesh that should be buried six feet under...

But what if I crack under the pressure? The pain?

You must not tell them anything... they are The Company! If they close down Impurity, then Amaranth is doomed...

I don't know enough, realised Jenny. A kind of horror took hold of her then, freezing a rictus grin to her face. Even if she'd wanted to talk, what did she *truly* know? She was a cog deep in the machine. She was simply a tool used to do a specific job. Yes, she came up with ideas, came up with targets; but those above her were the ones truly in control...

Jenny felt her eyes narrow, then she relaxed. There came a gentle *hissing* sound which she suspected was the heating of the needle.

"No. We argued. He left. He was a... spineless man."

"Where did he go?"

Jenny shrugged. Something glowing flickered past her vision, and she caught just a momentary glimpse of the red-hot needle. Then it was gone, leaving bright after-images burned into her retina; for a little while. She smiled. Just a tease. A prick-tease. Lest she forget...

"Like I said, he was a weak, spineless creature. After our father died, he met a woman. Chelle. They seemed good together, for a long time. I always found her cold, distant; she'd brought up two children on her own and managed to turn them into criminals. Bank robbers, they were, although she absolved herself of all blame. She called it *bad blood* from the father's side, ha, anything but take some parental responsibility. Anyway, Chelle cheated on my brother, repeatedly, fucking other men whenever she got the opportunity. Not only that, but she started to clean him out financially as well, holding back money, squirreling it away. He knew it was going on; hell, he told me about it often, about his snooping around after her, checking her underwear for guilty signs, following her car, checking her mobile when she was on the toilet. Chelle had got rid of all his friends, forced them away, one way or another." Jenny laughed. "There was a time, they were out with his best friend, Kramien, and Kramien's wife. They all got drunk, had a great time. But afterwards Chelle said Kramien had made a pass at her, and persuaded Saul to dump his mate... and Saul, being a spineless fuck, never said anything. Just cut Kramien out of his life like a cancerous growth. Cut out his best mate like a loop of necrotic bowel. Chelle got what she wanted – an ever-tightening stranglehold. Saul got good sex. It was as open a trade as prostitution."

Vasta came into view, then. She held no implements of torture, but she did not have to. Jenny was talking, rambling, her mind in a different place, a different world. Jenny suddenly came into focus, like a manual camera lens being adjusted. She coughed, almost self-consciously.

"How would you feel if I told you that Saul Xi is a member of the Impurity Movement?"

Jenny stared at Vasta for a long time, their gazes locked.

"I'd say you were a liar," she said, eventually.

"Nevertheless, it is true. A Squad Leader. Just like you."

"Impossible."

"Why?"

"He doesn't have it in him, the shitty, spineless little gimp. He let Chelle walk all over him. She was sucking dick like it was going out of fashion, and he stood there and looked on and took it up the arse as if he was enjoying it. When the private investigator he hired finally got video proof of Chelle down in the woods, fucking Smark E. Smarks in the back of his

Land Rover Psycho, Saul decided to *do the right thing* and forgive her; you know, take her back, gloss over all her indiscretions – both financial and otherwise – and you know who he turned his anger and and frustration and drug-paranoia on then? *Me*. It became *my* fucking fault, because he had Chelle's poison tongue whispering and plotting in his spineless ear, just like she'd always done before, and now, to her, *I* was the enemy because I knew everything. Her halo had slipped. She was no longer the angel but the comedy humping bike of Kookash-ka. I knew everything, and would forget nothing, and she knew it. She said so herself. She said she could never, ever face me again. Because of her shame, and her horror, and her gutless, poisonous back-stabbing nature. So she had my pathetic, useless, weak, spineless, gutless, jellyfish of a brother cut me off. His own sister. After all we'd been through with my father. After all we'd been through together – in *life*. Well, it was a fucking disgrace, he was a fucking snake, and he hasn't got the bottle to lift a rifle, never mind command a terrorist cell!"

Vasta perched on the edge of the bed. She was smiling, and her hands were empty. "We have him here. We captured him after he tried to detonate a Greenstar Shuttle bringing nuclear waste from Praxa 6. His three comrades were fried by an AnkleWire, and Saul Xi was brought down with a StubGun bullet to the back of the head from a Greenstar ProtectSniper."

Jenny shook her head. "Impossible."

"But true," said Vasta.

"I don't believe you."

"You'll believe this."

There came the sound of a trolley, and Randy Zaglax appeared with his destroyed face and weeping scars, the pain in his eyes an ever-present testament to the horror he was enduring. Randy was pushing an alloy trolley like Jenny had seen in a million anonymous hospitals. One wheel squeaked. On the trolley lay a figure, strapped down like her. Randy spun the trolley around, with its *squeak-squeak-squeak*, and then Jenny was able to make eye contact with...

"I don't believe it," she said.

"Hello, Jen," said Saul Xi.

"How's Chelle?" Jenny's smile was narrow, bloodless, frosty.

"Dead," said Saul, softly.

"Good. The dead bitch. Did you kill her like you said you would, in one of your drug-fuelled rants? I believe you told me you'd slit her throat, but then you welcomed her back into your groping arms with her pussy full of another's man's juice."

"Let it go," said Saul, voice grim, eyes haunted. "Yeah, I blamed you. Yeah, she was bad for me. But now she's dead. Let her rest in peace."

"Fuck her," snarled Jenny. "Everyone else did."

"There's more important things at stake here," said Saul, eyes angry, and she saw that petty anger and hatred rise rise rise so fast within him; he'd always had a bad temper. Jenny remembered his fists.

"They say you're part of Impurity. How come I didn't know?"

"You're a baby terrorist," said Saul, smiling then. "Let's say you're not far enough up the cell chain to have that kind of information. We call them cells for a reason, you know."

"So you've been watching me?"

Saul nodded.

"And now you're going to watch him," said Randy, stepping forward suddenly with a click and stamp of boots. "Isn't that right, Saul, my friend? We're going to torture you in front of your sister. And if you don't talk, we're going to torture *her* in front of you. And if she doesn't talk... well, it's going to be a long fucking night for both of you. It's too fucking convenient that you both work for Impurity and yet Jenny claims ignorance of you. There's so much shit here it's blurring the lens. What I need from both of you is focus. I need clarity. I need truth. But most of all, I need *information*."

Jenny and Saul allowed their eyes to meet. Both were hard and narrowed; filled with steel. But Randy was grinning, and Vasta, the Head of Security, looked sad.

"Last chance for you both to talk," said Vasta. Then, almost as a whisper, "*Last chance.*"

Randy appeared again, and he was carrying a set of steel pliers. "Let's loosen their tongues," he said.

JENNY FELT SICK. Another *crack* echoed through the chamber and Saul screamed, and gurgled. In the periphery of her vision she saw him arch his back and then slump again. Blood dripped from the trolley with a steady *pit-pat-pit-pat* sound. There came a rattle as Randy dropped a tooth into a steel bowl.

"It's as easy as pulling teeth," he cackled, and Jenny caught a glimpse of steel soaked with blood.

"You're a despicable human being," said Jenny through clenched teeth.

"You just keep showing me those lovely perfect ivories, my darling," said Randy, and loomed close, face a horrorshow mask, making her jump. "You're just prick-teasing me to pull them out, aren't you? You want me to take them, one by one, just like with Saul."

Saul groaned on his own trolley. There had been seven *cracks* so far, each accompanied by a straining against steel bands. In the movies, Saul would have broken free, knocked Randy to the ground, released Jenny and they would have fled their imprisonment killing the guards en route. But this wasn't the movies. The steel bands held. Saul strained. He screamed. He bled.

Randy whirled on him. "Will you talk?" he beamed through his lipless hole. At least Jenny took it to be a smile; it was difficult to tell with so many tatters of flapping skin.

"Fuck you," mumbled Saul, and spat blood at Randy.

Randy turned back to Jenny, and he was obviously enjoying himself. He gestured to her with blood-stained steel pliers. "Are you ready to talk, my little sweet? First I want to know the names of your team. I want their names, ages, serial numbers, waist sizes, favourite soup and how many times they wank in the morning."

Jenny said nothing.

Randy shifted close, and Jenny shivered. He moved the steel pliers to her face, held them just under her nose. She could smell the coppery stench of her brother's blood. Randy moved his mouth hole closer to Jenny's ear. When he whispered, the air tickled her. "Go on. You can talk, girlfriend. You can tell old Randy *everything*. And I know what you're thinking, because, believe it or not, I've been there, been where you've been. I was tortured, many years ago. They were saving my face until last because they knew what it meant to me; so they cut off my testicles with blunt shears. Ironic, yes? I spoke then, Jenny Xi; I sang like a fucking songbird. Don't fool yourself that I'll get myself a conscience and stop the hurt. Once I start, Jenny, I never stop. So do yourself a favour and start singing for me now." He kissed her then, on the cheek, then on the lips, the ragged hole of his smashed mouth caressing her lips, and she squirmed in absolute horror. His tongue slipped into her mouth, his bomb-blasted tongue, and she could feel its lumpy, tattered meat. She gagged, and Randy pulled back. "Sing for me," he crooned, and in his eyes Jenny saw the light of madness.

"I always knew you had no bollocks," she said.

He smiled; well, she *thought* it was a smile through the twisted flesh of his face. He came in at her, fast, and her muscles strained as she tried to deflect the blow. Something cold and hard and steel forced into her mouth, clamping it open, and she swallowed back the urge to scream, for she was stronger than that, tougher than that, she'd been through enough bad stuff and pain in her life to get past this. The cold metal felt alien in her mouth. It was slick and smooth, chromed. It glittered with reflected lights and was frustratingly out of focus. She felt as though she was in a dentist's chair as a child, and wild giggles rose through her belly but were savagely quelled. This was no dentist chair. This was no childhood escapade. This was real and this was bad.

Randy was close to her, she could feel his proximity, his warmth, hear his panting, smell his sweat. She flexed her fingers, trying to grab him in some way, but she could not. And then he was looming over her, his face in hers, his blasted features leering at her, and she was sweating now, panic bubbling inside her, and Randy grabbed the steel pliers, forced them into her mouth and she wanted to shout "No!" but only a garbled mess of words tumbled free. She felt the serrated pincers of the tool fasten over one of her back teeth, sliding and grating against bone. She could taste saliva, and oil, and steel, and fear. She tried to swallow, she tried to wriggle her head, she tried to wrench the pliers from Randy's grasp. And then he was squeezing, leaning his weight on the lever, and pain ripped through her. But instead of abating, the pain grew as the pressure rose, building like a rising torrent behind a pressure valve until she believed she could take no more – and there was a *crack,* and blood flooded her mouth, so much blood she thought she would drown, and she choked.

There was a moment of relief, and then the pain came back tenfold.

But the worst part was Randy, swinging on the pliers, wrenching at her head, at her jaw, at her tooth, tugging at it, twisting at it, until it finally broke free of the root and came away in a sudden rush. Jenny gave a guttural moan, mouth full of blood, fists clenched, urine pushing through her pants. But even through the pain and the disbelief (*are they really doing this to me, who can do this to another person, what kind of sick fuck? It must be a dream, it has to be a dream, and I'll wake up and be back at the blasted factory site, detonator in one hand, Randy's severed head in the other...*) Randy came back at her, bludgeoning into her view, and the pliers dived into her mouth again, cutting her lips and tongue, and she chomped her teeth, trying to fend off the long cold steel pliers, her head twitching within the confines of the restrictive steel band, and the pliers fastened on another tooth, and again she felt the pressure, only this time it was accompanied by a pressure in her *skull* that built and built as the pain built and built, and when the *crack* and the rush of exploding damn blood came it vomited from her mouth, into Randy's face, and flowed down her throat and the blackness was there, punctuated by glittering lights, and she fell into the galaxy, spun away into infinity, and was lost forever down an eternity well.

"You know I love you," he was saying, softly, whispering the words into her ear. "You know I love you, I've watched you, every subtle movement, every tender footstep, every twist and tilt of your hips, every hand gesture with those long, beautiful fingers, every toss of that head, that luscious brown hair. I've watched you, and I've coveted you, and one day I was sure we would be together. But then you blew the factory and you took my face. When you look at me, do you see a monster? Do you see a deviant strain? Do you see somebody who you could love?" Soft laughter. "I doubt it. You never loved me. You could sense my decadent nature, but more, I fear; you could sense my loyalty to The Company, and that was something you would never forgive." She felt his hands then, on her belly, touching her skin. The pressure was gentle, searching, and his fingers slid across her belly to the tops of her thighs. They paused, and she sensed him watching her, then looking down, and his fingers stroked down her thighs and pushed between her legs...

She coughed, and the pain battered her like a hammer, and her mouth tasted bad. Like a rat had died in there. Like dried blood had formed a solid dental cast, a toad in her mouth. How many teeth had he taken? Which teeth? Her tongue probed around her mouth and a chilling cool settled on her brow. He had removed four. So, even after she had passed out, he had continued working on her throughout unconsciousness. That was not even torture. What was that? It was a simple satisfaction of *his* needs. *The cunt*.

She opened her eyes. For some reason, the pain seemed to get worse. It was like a fist pounding at her lower jaw, beating against her temple. There was a soft white light. She was no longer under the sea. She was...

She moved her head, was amazed that she could. She turned to the side, and saw large stone block walls. Randy continued to explore her but she shut off her mind to his intrusion, filing it away for revenge. He was turning her into a different creature, she knew, and her eyes narrowed because surely this alteration of her mind was worse than any physical brutality he could inflict.

It was then, with certainty, she knew she would kill Randy Zaglax. One way or another.

He was back to whispering in her ear, and kissing her hair, and touching her breasts. She was still tied down; she tested her bonds gently, trying not to give away the fact that she was awake. It was incredible what one could learn when others thought you weren't listening. But the pain, that was the problem, the pain in her skull and her jaw and her mouth. Randy had invaded her face, and for a while forgotten about the act of torture, of asking her questions, of seeking answers. It had been a simple act of sadism, that was all. A personal achievement. A satisfaction.

Oh, I'm going to fuck you up, she whispered to herself in the dark halls of her mind as her tongue probed the huge gaps where her teeth had been. Huge gaping wounds in her skull that felt bigger than was humanly possible.

Silently, tears rolled down her cheeks.

"You are awake," said Randy, suddenly, jumping a little. He stood, fingers withdrawing from her. He stood, erect, and stared down. Jenny sighed. "Are you ready to talk?"

"I will talk." Her voice sounded funny to her own ears. By removing her teeth, Randy had removed her voice. Changed her. Changed her mind. Changed the person she was.

"Tell me about your team."

"What do you want to know?"

"Their names."

Slowly, she spoke. With each word, with each syllable, with each sound, with each *breath*, she felt as if she was dying. With pain beating at her skull, she told him the names of her team because, hell, he already knew them. He'd been part of the team. He'd known the men and women involved. Of course he did. They must have told him a thousand tiny secrets over the year he'd infiltrated Impurity. They must have let slip a million miscellaneous facts that they'd thought boring and harmless and useless, and yet together could be woven into a tapestry of the *person*. And so, yes, she knew he knew, and she knew he knew that by getting her speaking he might set her going, loosen her tongue, begin her at the top of a slippery slide and then *push* and whoosh, down she goes in an attempt to stave off more pain.

And he was right. Sort of. She was buying herself time, buying herself courage. She did not think she would survive this place. This torture hole of Greenstar. *Oh, you motherfucking scum, you parade around the Four Galaxies, you claim to be cleaning up the place, ethical recycling of all toxic matter, making the Quad-Gal and Manna a Cleaner Place to Live and creating lirridium for the benefit of all. When all the time, you're taking back-handers, big cash advances to bury the shit and cover the shit and hide the toxicity. It went right to the top, and the top were corrupt, from Director Renazzi Lode, Assistant Director Sowerby Trent, Chief Recycling Manager Aaul Thon Lupy, Helle Mic, Sanne Krimez, gods, even down to Randy Zaglax... the bastard puppets who appeared on TV, nodding and bobbing and grinning and pontificating and spilling their vile dishonest vomit down their designer suits. Most of their faces and voices went out to trillions of souls in Manna, talking about the future of recycling, of saving the planet, of respecting the planet and its denizens and cultures...* what *fucking respect?* She wanted to scream it. *WHAT FUCKING RESPECT?* But instead, she told Randy what he wanted to hear, what she knew he knew, because that way... A tear ran down her cheek. *That way*, she might survive.

And then Randy was close. Close as a lover.

"Tell me about McGowan," he whispered, and kissed her ear.

Jenny chewed her lip, but was silent.

"I said, tell me about McGowan."

"I know nothing of McGowan."

"Liar!"

"I swear it. It is true."

"You were his lover."

Jenny froze then, a needle of ice driving straight through her heart. *How could he know that? How could he POSSIBLY know that? Nobody knew that. None of the squad. None of her friends. It was truly personal, truly private. Randy could not be party to that information...*

She gave a cold laugh. "What a load of shit. I've never even *met* McGowan."

"You were his lover."

"Why on earth would you think that?" She kept her voice perfectly neutral, but inside she was flapping. Flapping like a gaggle of flapping geese. Because... *because* if he knew about McGowan, he had to know a hell of a lot more... which meant somebody else had talked. Somebody else who knew about her; and knew intimately. *Shit, shit, shit. Which back-stabbing motherfucker had broken down and blabbed like a nine-year-old girl?*

And with a cold clarity Jenny realised she could not blame them. How could she blame them? This wasn't an exercise in strength or bravado or manhood. And as she watched Randy Zaglax appear, carrying a long, thin hypodermic needle, her mouth dry and stale with the taste of old blood, her skull throbbing from forced teeth extraction, Jenny Xi *knew* it was simply an exercise in survival.

"This is going to hurt," said Randy, brutally, his destroyed face flapping.

The needle pushed into her throat, sinking deep, and she gritted her teeth and forced herself not to cry out. Then the stars fluttered like escaping butterflies and the world went dark.

NINE

"HELLO THERE, HORACE," said Juliette JohNagle, the man-i-woman creature, an entity of merged flesh, of two human beings forced and squeezed and crow-barred genetically into one frame. Horace groaned, tongue lolling, sight not yet returned, and yet his instinct kicked in and a natural violence, a need to kill and to survive, was in his heart. He lurched forward, but tight bands of steel around his ankles and wrists held him to the wall. Cruel laughter mocked him.

"Go on, son, do your best. You're the fucking Dentist, aren't you? Sent here by God-only-knows-who to take me out. Well, sunshine, we've been watching you. Watching you enter the hotel, anyway. We have files on you, y'know? We're not as stupid as you think. Are we? No, we're not."

Horace frowned. Pain beat his head like a hammer. He could taste blood.

Horace opened his eyes. The world was blurred at first, but swam slowly into focus. They were in an extensive hotel suite. It was daytime, now, and green sunlight blazed beyond high smoked windows. In the distance, the Biohazard Ocean gleamed like mercury.

"Worm got your tongue?"

"The worms," spat Horace, focussing on his captors. There were two stocky men, typical bruiser types, heavy on neck muscle, steroid suppositories and mental napalm. They bulged in suits too small for them, presumably to make them look larger and more intimidating. To Horace, it just meant a larger surface area.

Silka? questioned his mind, but he bit his tongue before he said her name.

Dead, probably. But... maybe not.

"The worms?" said JohNagle, and grinned through a face like a breeze block. "Yeah, we froze the worms. But they're still inside you. Move away from this controller" – a stubby fist showed Horace a small red globe – "and they'll warm up, continue their little journey to feast on your heart and lungs and kidney and liver and spleen. They like a bit of spleen, do our little wormies. Ain't that right, guys?"

There came some grunts.

"So... *you're* Juliette?"

"Yeah, Juliette JohNagle. What of it?" grunted the politician. Horace confessed to having never seen a picture of this particular director of Greenstar. He had imagined a creature of feminine persuasion, but if anything, JohNagle was more masculine than masculine. Like a big fat bricklayer pumped up on steroids and fed nothing but meat pies for a decade.

"I just imagined you'd be... shorter," said Horace.

"Very fucking funny," snapped JohNagle, levering hisher bulk to hisher feet, and stomping across the carpet towards Horace. "Just because I have the finesse of a builder doesn't mean I have the brain of one. So shove that up your arse and squirt it."

"Charming," said Horace.

"Who sent you?" said JohNagle.

Horace's mouth clamped shut. It was *That Time* again. And That Time was a Bad Time. Horace readied himself, because it would hurt, but he had the ability not just to shut down from pain, but to shut down his body entirely. In effect, he could play dead, although he would have to suffer a pretty hefty beating first in order to make the "death" plausible. It was a trick shot, built into all Anarchy Androids...

He looked up into JohNagle's grinning eyes. "Yeah, that's right," mouthed the pudgy face. All it was missing were forehead tattoos and stubble. Heshe certainly looked quite *wrong* in the bright red shade of lipstick heshe wore. And the blue dress over the hairy legs and big, fat hairy feet in red high-heels took some beating, to Horace's imagination. It wasn't even the effect of a badly orchestrated drag queen; no. Horace quite liked drag queens. Drag queens were fun. No, this creature, this unnatural merging of two different entities was just plain wrong – wrong, because it wasn't truly one thing or the other. Not that Horace cared, because he was about to have his skull caved in by a political lunatic.

JohNagle continued, eyes alight with good humour and a glint of superiority. "I *know what you are*, Anarchy man. And I know you play dead. Which is why, the minute you shut down that pretty little body of yours, we're going to cut off your hands and feet." Heshe produced a long, narrow, serrated black blade. "I used to be a butcher, so it really don't bother me overmuch."

"That's quite a work history you have," said Horace, smiling.

"Don't try and be fucking smart. Now talk. Who sent you?"

Horace closed his mouth, and stared at JohNagle, and then he closed his eyes. He heard a *swish*, a gesture, and felt the two hefty beefcakes closing in on him. When the first punch connected it was a shock. It's always a shock. But after a while he rolled with the punches and felt himself swimming in an ocean not quite of pain, but of disappointment and frustration.

Brought down by his own fucking arrogance.

Never lose your temper...

The blows rained in. A pounding, like the Biohazard Ocean against a beach of insane improbability... and Horace felt himself slipping, falling, drifting, until he heard the laughter, and anger flared a bright rage that burned from the pit of his stomach all the way up his oesophagus and into the centre of his burning fucking brain. *How dare you laugh at me,* thought Horace, and information flooded into him from a different source, a different world, a different realm – and he felt, bizarrely, as if he was being *fed* information, because it was certainly not information he'd acquired on his own, and it came in a stream, like sausages of data from a sausage machine... *and the man-i-woman known as JohNagle is not what you think it is, it's an alien construct and as such cannot be killed in the normal way of most human beings, and the worms inside you have been frozen, yes, and you must cut into your flesh in the proximity of the freeze globe and remove them or they'll shred your heart and shred your life, and we are waiting for you because we have seen you, and we have waited these long, cold years, can you see us? can you hear us? can you feel us? for our flesh is your flesh and in the great cycle of things, we are all truly one being...*

Horace opened his eyes. Blinked. He spat out blood and, ironically, a tooth.

"Lucky they call you *The Dentist*," crowed Juliette JohNagle, hopping from one fat high-heel to the other and back again in an almost tribal dance, fists punching the air, face filled with glee at his pain and suffering...

"Anyway, why *do* they call you The Dentist?"

The sound came from beyond the spectrum of human hearing, a high-pitched *shreeeeeeeee* that seemed to go on and on and on, in a slowly descending spiral, and as it reached human hearing the two grunts went, "Huh?" and there was a blur, and something landed on one of the beefcakes' shoulders, ran around the back of his head, and drilled through the back of his cranium with teeth gnashing and spinning like drill bits and thrashing gears. All Horace saw was Silka emerge from the man's suddenly destroyed face like a mini tornado, all teeth and claws and fur in a blood slick, grinning like a lunatic having a good ol' time. Then she leapt and chewed through the bands on Horace's wrists, teeth moving like a diamond-tipped blade and rattling through the steel in an instant.

With hands free, Horace clenched and unclenched his fists, staring hard at JohNagle as if weighing up the man-i-woman; weighing up the odds. Silka had dropped to his ankles and gnawed through the bonds, and Horace stepped forward.

"Kill him!" screamed JohNagle, taking several staggered, panicked steps back.

The remaining beefcake launched at The Dentist, who delivered a powerful right straight – fist slamming through teeth, opening, grabbing the man's lower jaw, and wrenching it out through the hole in the front of his face.

Horace stared at the slick, bloody, broken jaw for a moment. So did the beefcake. Then his eyes rolled up, and he hit the thick hotel carpet on his face.

"No!" screamed JohNagle, "No, no, no!" as Horace dropped the jaw on top of the corpse.

"To answer your question, MrMrs JohNagle, they call me *The Dentist* because... well." He smiled. "I like to show my teeth."

He leapt forward, but JohNagle was screaming into the small red globe. "Activate, activate, activate!" heshe got out, before a punch caught himher and sent himher spinning backwards.

"Silka!" yelled Horace, as JohNagle suddenly switched tactics and, heaving hisher huge bulbous bulk around, attacked with more speed than any man-i-woman had a right to possess.

Silka leapt on Horace's back, and burrowed under his clothing, teeth gnashing, sending strings of fibre spitting outwards. As JohNagle launched at Horace, huge thick hairy arms encircling the Anarchy Android, Silka cut and bit into his flesh with long incisors, burrowing down into him as blood flowed down his skin, and chewed through muscle and burrowed deep and found the first worm, biting it in half. JohNagle spun Horace around, far stronger than Horace had anticipated, and launched him across the hotel suite. And even as he flew through the air, Silka ran across his belly and launched down into his abdomen. He grunted in pain then. It hurt. It *really* fucking hurt. Hurt more than the table he crashed through, sending spears of glass rearing up around him, jagged porcupine spikes erupting upwards. JohNagle ran at him, as Silka found the second worm and shredded it. She was deep in his bowel now. Her teeth felt like acid. Horace grabbed a glass shard and threw it, and it stuck in JohNagle's eye, squelching into hisher skull by six or seven inches and almost penetrating all the way through. JohNagle did not cry out. Did not falter. Just came straight on, a huge hulking bear. Horace rolled left, grabbing two more table shards and slashing them in front of him. JohNagle came up sharp and grinned at Horace through rivulets of blood.

"I guess the cat is out of the bag," heshe said.

"I'm going to enjoy killing you," said Horace.

"Save it for the fucking peasants," snarled JohNagle, and lunged. Horace slashed with the glass, cutting a long stripe across JohNagle's hand, but at the apex of the strike hisher hand suddenly closed and wrenched sideways, tearing the shard from Horace's grip. Hisher arm came back, and heshe launched the glass like a spear. Horace shifted, but not quite fast enough, and it cut across his shoulder even as Silka burrowed towards his liver and kidneys and he gasped, breathless for a second, disorientated by the feeling of his friend inside him, eating through him in search of the worms that would tear his organs apart...

JohNagle crashed into Horace, and they both slammed backward, staggering past the crushed table and into the bar. There was a *crump* under the impact, and the whole structure wobbled. Horace ducked a punch, and drove his own punch into JohNagle's groin. JohNagle grinned at him.

"Sorry man. No balls."

The head-butt caught Horace off-guard, and the punch to his windpipe felt like a sledgehammer blow. He hit the ground on his back, choking, as JohNagle disappeared for a moment and then loomed above him. Heshe heaved a safe, a huge block of steel, over hisher head.

"I'm going to crush you like a bug," growled JohNagle, and the safe came crashing down. Horace grunted as Silka found the last of the worm parasites and chewed it into oblivion, then turned – he felt her turn around *inside* his body – and followed her own chewed tunnel for the exit. Horace rolled fast, and the safe left a deep dent in the floor. JohNagle cursed, and bent to lift the safe again. Horace coughed blood, and rolled onto his hands and knees. Then Silka emerged from his mouth on a shower of blood droplets, landing sedately on the floor. She turned her head, grinned at

JohNagle in hisher act of lifting the safe, and launched at hisher throat...

JohNagle screamed, staggering back. The weight of the safe caught himher off-guard and Silka launched, biting into hisher belly, chewing through flesh and muscle, *burrowing* into the gestalt creature. Heshe screamed again, and the stagger became a fall, and the heavy safe intended to crush Horace's head instead crushed JohNagle.

Almost.

Heshe turned as heshe fell, the safe glancing from hisher head and compacting maybe a quarter of hisher skull into crushed brain paste. JohNagle gasped, legs kicking as heshe lay pinned to the floor by hisher squashed head. If hisher head had been smaller, heshe'd have been dead. However, JohNagle's head was such a heavy, blocky thing, the man-i-woman's (or as the stand-up comedians called them, *momens*, or *wen* – a-har-har-har) skull saved himher.

Horace lay for a while, panting, his insides feeling odd. He was churned up. Internally ruptured. Blood leaked from several orifices. He felt sick; he rolled over, and *was* sick.

Horace pushed himself to his hands and knees and squatted for a while, panting, drooling saliva and blood. Then he coughed, and spat, and when he rocked back on his heels his eyes were gleaming.

Horace eased himself upright, and with one hand flat against his belly, moved painfully to stand over Juliette JohNagle. He spat down into the Greenstar politician's face.

JohNagle had lost hisher cocky assurance. Hisher eyes were darting left and right, and the creature had lost the use of one arm, and the remaining limb had not the strength to shift the safe.

Horace stared at JohNagle. It was fair to say that his sense of humour had gone by this point.

"What are you doing?" snapped JohNagle. "How are you even alive?"

Horace grinned, blood and saliva stringing on his teeth. But man, he felt like shit. That was the hardest fight of his career. Of his *life*. What the hell *was* JohNagle? "It's time," he said, sitting down cross-legged in front of JohNagle's pinned body, "for us to have a little chat."

Horace fished inside his suit, and pulled out a velvet tool roll.

"What's that? What are you doing? What's that, you fucker?"

"These," said Horace, licking his lips slowly, "are the tools of my trade. And as you said, they call me The Dentist. Now it's time I showed you why."

"No," said JohNagle. "I have money. More money than you could ever dream possible! I can pay you! I can promote you! Power! Women! Boys! Cash! A high position in Greenstar! Anything, all this, I can do." Hisher eyes were twitching spasmodically. Hisher lips worked ceaselessly, as if recanting some religious doctrine that had condemned himher.

"None of that matters," said Horace, unrolling the black velvet. Tools gleamed. The tools of The Dentist.

"I'll tell you everything," said JohNagle, voice thick, words slurring.

Horace fixed JohNagle with a vulture's glare. "Yes. You will," he said.

AND THERE HE had it. His answers. Well, *some* answers. Laid out in neat little rows like fine food on a silver platter. JohNagle had sung. Heshe'd talked. Heshe'd chatted. Heshe'd begged, whined, screamed, drooled. Heshe'd cried, threatened, cajoled, wept. But ultimately, heshe'd talked. Given answers.

Because Horace was The Dentist and The Dentist always got answers.

They're tired of you.

They've had enough of you.

You are a threat.

Why am I a threat?

You are.

Says who?

Says The Children.

What fucking children?

Not any children. The Children. The psi-children from the sludge, from the puke, from the fucking toxicity, all right?

In what way am I a threat?

To Greenstar. To The Company.

I don't see how that's possible. How is that possible? I am employed by Greenstar. Fat Man gives me missions; assassination missions. I fucking WORK FOR YOU! I do your dirty laundry. I kill the terrorists who threaten you, I wipe out those who oppose you, I terminate those who backstab The Company.

They still want you dead.

Who?

I don't know.

Who?

I don't know! Aiiiiiiiiiieeeeeeeeeeeee. No, please, don't do that again. Please. No. I'll tell you. Everything. Anything you want to know. I'll tell you how to access my credits. I'm a fucking wealthy man-i-woman. Fucking wealthy. You're an assassin. You work for money. I can outbid those who sent you. Don't kill me. Please don't kill me.

How far does it go?

I don't know!

How far?

Vasta. She'll know.

Vasta?

Head of The Company's Security. She, like you, is a torturer.

Android?

Not sure. She's certainly a fucking bitch.

So. Then.

Don't do that. Not again. Please...

One more answer. Where do I find this Vasta?

The Hub. Greenstar Factory. Base HQ. East of the River Tox, west of Ebola Palace. Can't miss it. Ten fucking klicks wide...

Horace sighed.

Thank you, he'd said.

HORACE CLEANED HIS tools and stowed them away in the velvet roll. Silka, who had been cleaning herself during the torture and execution, ruffled up her fur and stared brightly at Horace.

"Are you okay?"

"I think I might have to repair myself."

"There's a medical kit in the bathroom. It's basic..."

"Can it repair a Silka-sized hole in my abdomen?"

"I'm sure it can," she said, sweetly.

Ten minutes later, with the biggest holes stapled shut but still feeling like a perforated sack of shit, Horace checked his T5 and then opened the door, peering out into the corridor.

"Do you think they know?"

"I guarantee it," said Silka, padding out into the corridor and standing by the skirting.

They moved down the corridor, as a chambermaid rounded the corner with a trolley.

"Oh!" she said in surprise, one hand to her mouth, eyes wide in shock at Horace's battered, torn and bloody appearance. She pushed a little wheeled alloy trolley containing towels and toilet rolls and soap. Her other hand came up with... a Makarov 11mm.

Horace's T5 cracked, and a hole appeared in the maid's head. She toppled back, dead.

"I told you," said Silka.

"Hmm," said Horace.

After that, there was no pretence. They took the back stairs, and five porters appeared with machine guns. Bullets screamed on trails of fire, spitting sparks from metal rails and thudding with puffs of disintegrating plaster into the walls. Horace returned fire, his T5 *blamming* down the stairwell. Two porters went down with bullets in their throats, fingers scrabbling at the wounds as if they might claw out the metal parasites. Then Silka jumped to the rail, paused for a second, bright eyes surveying the scene below, and dived, landing atop one of the porters. Her claws slashed left and right, ripping out one man's throat, and the other man's eyes. They dropped, screaming, and Silka glanced up, and Horace could see her face, triumphant and feral...

The explosion seemed to rock the very foundation stones of the hotel. Horace was picked up and thrown back through the door – actually *through* the door – by the pressure of the blast. Fire roared in the stairwell, which filled with thick black smoke in an instant. A Babe Grenade. Designed to really *fuck you up*.

Horace lay on his back, all wind knocked from him, brain swirling in a blast of confusion. Stunned, he slowly realised Silka was dead, and a heavy bitterness fell on him like funeral ash. Horace's eyes went hard. The bastards had detonated their own in order to take him out. The porters with guns had been a come-on, a prick-tease, urging him into a fight... a few more steps down that stairwell and he would have been minced dog food. Instead, Silka had dropped into the abyss – and had been detonated for her trouble.

"You bastards," said Horace, lips trembling.

Don't lose your temper...

Don't ever lose your temper...

Horace lost his temper. Not in an explosion of anger and rage; no. When Horace lost his temper it was a dangerous, internalised pressure. All rules of engagement were lost. Everyone would die: friends, enemies, babies in prams, dogs trotting down the sidewalk. All flesh to be annihilated.

Horace rolled to his knees, then his feet. Every bone in his body hurt from the blast, but he ignored the many agonies that assailed him. He was focused on the task.

A human would have died from the pressure of the explosion. Horace was hurting. But he channelled the pain to fuel his rage. He changed tactics: returned to the stairwell, stared down into the still-billowing thick smoke. Good cover. He headed upwards, noting that quite a few steel bars were twisted out of shape, and the whole staircase had lost its integrity. The building had been damaged, been *twisted* by the bomb.

Horace sprinted up the slightly skewed steps, noting cracks in the alloy and concrete.

A man appeared ahead of him, and Horace shot him in the face. He knew not whether he was an enemy or simply a member of the public. The gloves were off. All would die.

Fuck them, thought Horace.

Fuck the world.

He burst out onto the roof. A wind ripe with toxic stench slammed him, stealing his breath. Towering stormclouds rose overhead in great billows of iron-coloured bruises, offering naught but threat. Sunlight burst between the columns, radiating beams of freedom.

Horace stared around. The roof was large and flat, punctuated by thick pipes and blocks of fans.

Machine-gun fire rattled behind him. He squeezed off five shots down the stairwell and ejected the mag, replacing it with a *clack*. He limped across the roof and leant against the low wall. Below him, streets spread away, filled with queuing groundcars and ribbons of tourists buying tat and crap from tat and crap shops. There was no obvious place to jump; Horace was going to have to climb.

From over the Biohazard Ocean came the clatter of rotors. Horace's head snapped up. A chopper. Shit. Coincidence? He doubted it.

A hotel receptionist appeared at the stairway, carrying an SMKK. Horace shot him through the eye. He'd always wanted to do that. Fucking snooty hotel receptionists.

The chopper came close, making a bee-line for the hotel. Horace heard the spin and whine of charging miniguns and cowered behind the low parapet as bullets howled around him, chewing brickwork and rendering, sending huge chunks spinning off into the toxic tourist haven below. People started to scream and run, scattering for cover. Groundcar horns screeched. The thump of the chopper's rotors grew louder.

More people appeared at the stairwell and started to fire, SMKKs bucking in hands like live wild creatures. Horace returned fire, T5 slamming his hand, his mind bleak, memories a wasteland. One, two, three heads exploded, and Horace turned his attention to the chopper sweeping overhead, a line of bullets chewing the concrete by Horace's boots and skidding off across the hotel roof. Horace sprinted for a huge section of pipes, but had to dive low and long as more hotel staff appeared, all shooting at him. His mouth was a grim line.

I'm going to execute every last motherfucking one of you.

He smiled at that, tasting dust from the roof, and rolled onto his back. The chopper swept overhead once more, and Horace began to fire the T5. Bullets glanced from the flanks and whizzed and pinged through the rotors. Horace had been hunted by choppers before. And he knew he could bring one down with a T5 with just the *right* shot...

There came a strange whining sound, and Horace frowned. It was out of context; unusual. He'd never heard that sound before. What was it? He spun onto his knees, shot more hotel staff, who seemed to be pouring like an unending stream from the building beneath his feet. Bullets whizzed and flickered past him, but he seemed suddenly immortal, untouchable, as if God had blessed The Dentist and sent him forth onto Amaranth to do His Bidding...

Horace laughed out loud.

Shit. This was living! This was joy!

There came a hiss and *thump,* and Horace coughed. He coughed blood. A bright red splatter hit the concrete.

Horace looked down at the barbed hook protruding from his chest, then turned, slowly, following the swaying cable back up to the chopper. The whining sound. Now he understood. A tensioned harpoon gun. *The fuckers.*

He looked over to the hotel staff. There must have been twenty of them now, all heavily armed. Horace counted their dead. Thirteen. Nearly every single one had been taken out by a head shot. Damn, he was good. The rest of the staff had lowered their weapons and were staring at him. Their faces were grim.

The cable gave a small tug, and the barbed hook before him settled into his flesh. He heard steel cable grate against his breast bone as the barbs dug in tight and he gasped, coughing up more blood. The chopper engines increased in pitch, the rotors whining fast, and then suddenly he was yanked off his feet and up into the sky like a fish on a hook.

The pain was incredible, tearing through him like fire. But worse was the total helplessness...

The hotel dropped and Meltflesh City spun away like a toy, the streets, the groundcars, the cowering tourists, the bright Hawaiian shirts, the candy floss, the anti-tox chewy bars, the beach loungers and umbrellas to protect against the sun, the little coloured windmills for children, the foam surfboards with an anti-melt guarantee and a thousand other bits of trinket and tat endemic to any seaside resort... It all fell away, and Horace dropped his T5 weapon, his hands coming up to grasp the barbed steel fixed in his flesh, in his breastbone, barbs biting like steel teeth. His fingers prised at the barbs with inhuman strength, with android strength. But they were fixed tight, pinned in place by his own body weight. To get it free he'd have to carve himself a new chest cavity.

Horace spun like a child's action figure on a string. The chopper headed up, high, and then turned and powered across the Biohazard Ocean. Within moments, Meltflesh City was gone; within moments, all that surrounded Horace was the ocean, yellow and purple and red, sloshing and churning, an unhappy toxic mix of God-only-knew-what deadly chemicals and savage pollution.

Horace started to laugh.

He roared with laughter, as pain rioted through his punctured frame.

He was fucked. He knew that.

He was dead meat on a hook.

Greenstar had *won*.

Eventually, the chopper stopped and hovered in the sky against clouds of iron and lead. Horace hung, suspended, swaying in a sea breeze that cooled the dome of his skull and ruffled his disintegrated, bloodstained suit. That hurt him more than the pain. He was going to die looking scruffy. Damn.

Horace grinned, and his teeth were stained with blood.

"Hey!" came a voice. "Hey, Horace!"

Slowly, Horace looked up. There was a woman there, but he could not make out any features; everything was going blurred. Weakness crept through his limbs like a slow poison. Suddenly, his feet felt cold. That was bad, he knew. It meant he was dying.

"Who are you?" he slurred, voice barely audible over the sounds of the chopper.

The thump of the chopper's blades was giving him a headache. It reminded him of a bad hangover. A *real* bad hangover.

"I'm Vasta, Head of Security for The Company," she shouted. She seemed to be smiling. It was hard for Horace to tell.

"I... was coming for you," he said, and his head hung low. He could feel strength and life ebbing from him.

This was it, he knew.

This was it.

"I know," she shouted, and the chopper swayed. The storm was coming; Horace could see it sweeping across the ocean, a great wall of violent rain. He swung on his steel cable. His arms fell to his sides, limp and useless. He felt his eyes closing.

"We couldn't let you live," shouted Vasta.

"I know," whispered Horace.

"I'm sorry it has to be this way," yelled Vasta. There was true regret in her voice. After all, Horace had been a valuable asset. A perfect tool in the extermination of – well, whatever Greenstar needed exterminating.

Another face appeared beside Vasta. It was the Fat Man.

"Drop him," he said.

"No last words?" said Vasta, looking into the Fat Man's dark eyes.

"No. Fuck him," he said. "He's just a tool. An organic machine." He smiled. "He's just an android."

Vasta's muscles clenched along her jaw, but she said nothing. She signalled to the pilot, and the man hit a button. There came a click beside them in the winch gear, then a sudden violent whizzing sound.

Beneath, Horace plunged to the Biohazard Ocean, the cable flapping and plummeting with him. He hit the water with a great splash, and sank beneath the waves, turning slowly, unconsciously winding himself up in the steel cable and further sealing his fate.

The Fat Man spat after Horace. His face was a snarl. "Good fucking riddance to a bad android."

Vasta said nothing. She signalled for the pilot to take them back to the The Greenstar Factory Hub.

The Biohazard Ocean surged, and boomed, and rolled. And if Vasta hadn't known better, she would have sworn it was sighing.

TEN

"YEAH, SON. WHEN the music stops, then draw and fire. I'll do the same. Whoever's left standing gets the little lady." General Bronson said the words in a deadpan voice. A voice that had spoken the same words to a hundred condemned idiots down through the years. General Bronson never lost. He was the fastest gun in the West. Well, the South. You know what he meant.

"Er, Mr Bronson?"

"Yes, son?"

The watch tinkled away, the tune getting slower, and slower, and slower...

"I have a question?"

"Yes, son?"

"About this music, about when it stops..."

But it was too late.

The music stopped.

For Svoolzard Koolimax XXIV, Third Earl of Apobos, that splinter of time lasted an eternity. He remembered his childhood, sat under huge palm trees, writing poetry with his crayon. All the other toddlers toddled over to him and drew scrawls on his poetry, but for Svool, the poem was perfection, and he batted

away their crayons, then batted away their heads. They
tended to hit the ground hard, being only toddlers, and
sometimes Svool kicked them in the face for spoiling
his poems. Times were hard, and toddlers were rough,
and Svool knew how to deal with them.

Then he was in school and he remembered meeting
his two first playmates, Darren and Kevin. Darren
and Kevin were nice, and they also liked poetry, and
so began years and years of "poetry raps" and "fuck
yo bitch poetry comps," where they'd have stand-up
rows about poetry, and compete with alliteration,
personification, and battles of enjamment. It was truly
exhilarating! And in the under-11s, Svool ruled the
poetry in the playground. Nobody fucked with his
poems. Because Svool was Poet King.

The transition to high school – Raptor, as it was
known to the high fee payers and snub-nosed posh
parents – was difficult. Svool came, despite his grand
title of Third Earl of Apobos, from a relatively poor
family that struggled to feed its thirteen children. The
Estates of Apobos took every single dollarpound for
upkeep, and Svool's parents had such massive financial
headaches that even the basics of Svool's upbringing
were sporadic at best. Still, he had his poetry to care
for him, and spent hours and days – and weeks and
months – doodling away in his ever-fattening notebook,
convinced that one day his poetry would become the
saviour of the family. He would write his poems, and
become a zillionaire, and save the family fortune! In
the end, though, his mother ran off with what few
dollarpounds remained, and thus precipitated the crash
and sale of the Apobos Estates and Svool's ignoble
ejection from Raptor School. He remembered the day
with shame burning his cheeks red. The booing and
hissing as he dragged his huge trunk down the massive
gravelled drive, without help, its little wheels sticking in

every rut, its rectangular bulk bouncing and wobbling like a drunk fat lady on a hen night. All along the avenue, the other students booed and hissed at Svool, pelting him with wholemeal bread rolls and bananas (Raptor liked its students to be regular), and tears streamed down his reddened embarrassed face at the shame and the horror. Reaching the end of the drive, he turned back to face his thousand or so tormentors, and he screamed, screamed until he was blue, and spat as he screamed, "I'll show you! I will immortalise you all in my poetry!" And he did. He penned *The Horrors of Raptor,* which sold three billion copies before he was twenty years old.

Fitting into a normal state high school, Bolltton School for Dweebs, came with great hardship. He knew nobody, and found it hard to fit into any kind of established friendship group. Instead, he ended up siding with the idiots, the geeks, the muppets, the greebos and the... poets. Poetry became the outlet for his angst, for all his teenage fears, for the way he'd been treated by his old school chums after the complete reversal of their friendship. The back-stabbing bastards.

Poetry, and more importantly, quickfire poetry competitions where speed of mind and tongue were the Masters of the Competition, had helped sculpt and build Svool's life; but more, helped sculpt and build his *control.*

Now, as he faced General Bronson and his gunfighter brethren – dirty, stinking, kidnapping horrors to a man – as the tinkling of the music haunted him down through a billion years of primeval horror, he saw his terrible plight simply as a quickfire poetry contest. He deconstructed it back, stripped it way down from life and death to an exchange of words. And one thing Svool was superb at was exchanging words...

The music stopped.

"And although I walk in the valley of the shadow of death, I will not fear evil..."

"What?" snapped General Bronson, gun in hand and rising fast.

"'Cause you are a weevil," rhymed Svool, as he drew and fired.

A single bullet slammed across the space and took General Bronson between the eyes.

There was a hushed, shocked silence as Bronson stood, swaying, staring with disbelief at Svool and his smoking pistol.

"You goddamn killed me there, son," he said, sitting back down on his rump with a thump. Dust rose around him. Svool stared at the end of his pistol as if he was holding a tarantula.

With the other gunslingers distracted by the sight of their illustrious leader being gunned down by the Sheriff – not something they had expected in a million years and, truth be told, not the outcome *Lumar* had expected in her wildest dreams – Lumar knelt up and carefully slid a long knife from the boot of the gunslinger charged with keeping her down on the boards. By the time General Bronson hit the dust, Lumar had a knife in her hands and had cut the bonds which held her. By the time the gunslinger realised she had a knife in her hands, he had a knife through his heart and was coughing up blood as he collapsed to the boards.

What followed was a cinematic chaos.

Herbert reared up, neighing wildly, and charged at the other gunslingers, who leapt to their feet, drawing pistols, and Svool fired with maniac abandon, his arms like wild pistons, his mouth opening in a silent scream of prayer and insanity. Unfortunately, his one-in-a-million headshot on Bronson was not replicated, Svool's usual uselessness kicking in with a savage ferocity.

It took a few moments for Bronson's men to realise that Svool was charging towards them, firing his gun but without the actual ability to *aim*. They snarled and growled, showing yellow teeth and ugly faces, but by then Lumar had found her feet, and was in the middle of the group, with a knife and a serious axe to grind.

Lumar stabbed left, then right, ducked a pistol shot which filled the porch with gunsmoke, drove the knife through one throat and then back-handed it across another. Men screamed around her, suddenly scrambling to get away, their pistols firing wildly. Two gunslingers shot two of their friends. And in the middle was a cool, calm, collected Lumar, her tongue flickering, her knife cutting and gouging. There was no compassion there, no kindness, no empathy. Just hate and vengeance. They had abused her and promised further violence to come. Well, she'd show them. And she did.

Within a minute it was all over, and bodies lay strewn about the wooden boards, either dead or wishing they were. Herbert galloped to a halt, legs flying in all sorts of directions, and there was a *click* as the steel brackets released Svool. He leapt from the metal horse, scowling and rubbing at his cramping legs. His pistol was empty; he threw it on the ground in disgust.

Lumar strode from the wreckage of corpses and stopped, hands on hips.

"Well," she said.

"I came back for you!" beamed Svool.

Lumar stared at him, then at the horse, then off down the street. "So you did," she said. "Eventually." She considered her words, then sighed, and recognised that without Svool's help she would, in fact, be having a worse time that she currently was. "Okay, I concede, you did indeed come back for me. It was... a brave thing to do."

"I had some help," said Svool, sheepishly.

"Neigh!" said Herbert, Svool's Special Friend. "But you've got to admit, old Svool boy, that was one incredible piece of shooting! Never have I seen somebody so brazenly take down an evil gunslinger like General Bronson before. You know, I myself saw him stand in over two hundred gunfights and walk away without a scratch. It's almost like it was destiny!"

"Destiny," said Lumar, looking sideways at Svool. "You hear that?"

Svool was staring at Bronson's body. He sighed, and held out both hands, palms outwards. "I confess, it was an absolute fluke. If you notice I fired off all the other shots and hit *nothing*. It was a one-in-a-million lucky shot."

"Yes," said Lumar, "but it was the one that counted." She coughed, forced the words through tight, compressed lips. "Well done, Svoolzard Koolimax XXIV, Third Earl of Apobos."

Svool went bright red, which was ironic, for only a few short days before he would have accepted oral sex from five strangers without breaking stride. He was used to praise and adoration in his position as poet, musician, sexual athlete and academic. Not so much in the world of rugged adventuring gunslinger hero.

"We better get moving," said Herbert.

"Oh, yeah?" swaggered Svool, putting on his best tough-guy voice. "Well, we did indeed kill them all dead, we did indeed."

Herbert flapped his metal lips. "*Yee-es*, but Bronson's brother might be here real soon. They probably heard all the gunshots. And he won't be happy."

Svool paled. "Bronson's brother?"

"Yeah. Black Jake, they calls him. He's even *meaner* than General Bronson. Known to stake out men, women and children and let rattlesnakes eat their eyes."

"I'm sure we can handle one more unwashed cowboy," smiled Lumar, twirling the bloodstained knife.

"It's more his forty or fifty desperate wanted men I was worried about," said Herbert, grinning with his curiously intelligent metal horse lips. He flapped them theatrically, showering Svool with a shower of oily spittle.

"How do we get into this shit?" frowned Svool, staring at Lumar and opening his hands in confusion. "How did our lives go from a comfortable wealthy ease of constant drugs and sex to one of such incredible madness and pain in such a short time frame?"

"Speak for yourself," muttered Lumar, and rubbed her eyes. "Okay, let's round up some weapons and ammunition, find another metal horse and get the hell away from here. Herbert, we really need to make contact with the rulers of this planet – this is a disastrous diplomatic incident just *waiting* to happen. Svoolzard here, well" – she coughed, and clenched her teeth as she said it, eyes narrowing, tongue flickering – "he's a very important poet and film star. Very famous. We need to get to the capital city. Dare I say it? Take us to your leaders."

"You need Bacillus Port. No. No, wait! Even better, we could head for the Greenstar Factory Hub. That's where all the top dogs and nobby nobs and politicians and lawyers and bureaucrats hang out. All the important folk on Amaranth. You know. The buggers who poison it."

"What's the quickest route?"

"From here, buster, I'd say north, then northeast. But there are a thousand obstacles to overcome, from packs of radioactive hunting dogs to strange diseased creatures that have evolved from the mud. You think Bronson and his boys were bad? There's much more bad than that out in the Wild Wastes! Oh, yes!"

Lumar sighed. "What about the nearest city? Maybe renting some kind of high speed air vehicle?"

"All banned," said Herbert smugly. "At least within a thousand miles of where you're standing. Would *you* want someone like Bronson getting his hands on a military chopper?"

"So we're out in the shit, and we'll have to walk to safety?" snapped Svool.

"Yes. No. Well, there *are* the Mines of Mercury..." He allowed the words to hang in the air like an embarrassing metal horse fart.

"That doesn't sound safe," said Lumar, narrowing her eyes.

"Well, they're a *massive* old network of tunnels that run under the Mercury Peaks. That's a big wide mountain range that cuts this half of the land in two. If we go through the Mines of Mercury, we'll miss the Lungpuke Forest, the Faeces Teeth, the Strychnine Plains, the Anthrax Forest... oooh, it'd be my top vote for crossing this mad, bad country without getting a spear through the ear." His horse tongue lolled out and touched the ground, and with a mechanical clicking sound, he wound it back in again.

"You're sure these mines are safe?" said Lumar, eyes narrowing again.

"Oh, yes!" brayed Herbert. "They were cleared out by Greenstar *years ago*. There's nothing more dangerous than a luminescent mushroom. Trust me, I know whereof I speak."

"What do you think?" said Lumar.

Svool nodded. "Sounds like a plan. I seriously need to get off this shithole. It's ruining my karma, my clothing, my ego, my vanity, and my street cred. Let's get going!" He gestured to one of the hitched metal horses that stood, with heads lowered, looking forlornly at the ground now that their masters were all dead.

Lumar strode towards the metal beasts, and Svool rubbed his hands together, cackling inwardly. *Aha! Now you, too, can get your own Special DumbMutt Special Friend with a nine-hundred-and-ninety-nine-year lease and the ability to lock your ankles to its body whenever it sees fit! Try it on for size! See! I'm not the only dumb smack idiot around here, y'know?*

Lumar leapt nimbly into the saddle. The metal horse lifted its head and seemed to perk up considerably. Its head turned around. "Hello," said the metal horse. "My name is Angelina. Welcome aboard."

Svool capered forward. "Go on! Go on! Say it!" He flapped his hands frantically. "The special friend dumb mutt stuff! Say it!"

"Oh, no, no, no," said Herbert, coming up behind Svool and nuzzling him. "Angelina is a freehold model. Anybody can ride her without ownership protection clauses and deed of ownership. It's only *you*, buddy, that has that special relationship with your special friend round here! It's only *you* with that special honour and special friend trust."

"Hmm," said Svool, scowling. "I can't say that I asked for it."

Herbert's head rotated and fixed him with a beady stare. "A Special Horse Friend is for life, not just for [Insert Applicable Religious Festival Here], buster."

Svool frowned even deeper.

At that moment, Zoot the PopBot came zipping down the street and stopped, hovering equidistant between Svool and Lumar. He spun, slowly, lights flickering on his matt-black shell.

"Hi guys! Is everything okay?"

"No thanks to you, fuckwit!"

"Hey, I was zapped! A PopBot can't help it when he's zapped!"

"I thought you were supposed to be my bodyguard?" snapped Svool. "What use is a bodyguard that's taken down in the first three seconds of a fight, leaving me – *me!* – to fight my own battle and face certain death? Eh?"

Zoot grew haughty at this accusation. "Hey, how was I supposed to know he'd be carrying an anti-PB actualising necroliser? Eh? I might be your bodyguard-slash-PR-slash-management unit, but I can't read the mind of every psycho we come across!"

"Well, you're a useless shit," said Svool, and turned to Lumar. "Shall we get going, before Black Jake and his gang come looking for the man who killed his brother? I'm pretty sure he won't want to shake my hand and spank my bottom and buy me a pint of Japachinese lager!"

"I think that would be a good idea," said Lumar, softly. She nudged Angelina, turning the robot horse, and leading the way, trotted north out of the town. Svool followed on Herbert, who seemed to be watching Angelina's rump with a curious tilt to his rusty metal head.

A disgruntled and shame-filled Zoot brought up the rear, using his short-range scanners to check for any signs of pursuit.

THE LANDSCAPE CHANGED in sudden leaps and bounds and folds of rock and hills; first, from jungle to rolling grasslands: bang! they crossed a ridgeline and the whole world seemed to change in an instant, without the graduated change normally associated with real-world geographical topography. Lumar sat her horse atop a grassy hill and stared back at the distant jungle, then up at the sky with its streaks of black and violet and green, then ahead, past the grasslands and rolling hills to where mountains speared the horizon.

"This place is weird," she said.

"I'm not an expert on geography," said Svool, steadying Herbert with a twitch of the reins, "but I'd have to agree. I confess I'm not the sort of trendy cool dude who has travelled many a hill on the back of a metal horse, but I'd concur that I have never seen anything quite like this, not from the decks of a Pleasure Hover Cruiser, nor on the screen of my favourite filmy."

Lumar stared at him. Then looked back to the mountains. "Ho! Herbert. So those are the Mercury Peaks?" She pointed yonder, where titanic mountains of silver and white touched the clouds.

"That would be them, buster," said Herbert, pulling a face that should never belong on a horse. There were tiny sliding sounds as metal plates grated together. A few flakes of rust tumbled down to merge with the swaying grass on the hill.

"Er, guys," said Zoot, whizzing up to them.

"Yes, Zoot, trusty useless non-protection pile of shit PopBot?"

"I think we have company."

They all turned, and they all looked. Against the distant horizon behind them was a dust cloud. It was rather a large dust cloud, presumably spat up by the stampeding hooves of fifty or so metal horses galloping at full speed across the plain.

Lumar and Svool exchanged a quick, worried glance.

"They could be friendly," suggested Zoot, voice weak yet hopeful.

"Wanna bet, buster?" Herbert grinned.

"I'm assuming they can keep up that gallop all day, what with them being metal horses?"

"Oh, yes," said Herbert.

"But then, so can we," pointed out Svool.

"No, no," said Herbert, "I'm a *Special Model*. I have an inhibitor. That sort of behaviour can burn out circuit boards!" He made a *huh* sound, and tossed his head, as if to say those people who ran their metal horses all day should be ashamed of themselves.

"So they can, in fact, catch us, then," growled Svool.

"Er. Yes." Herbert looked suddenly sheepish.

"Let's get moving," snapped Lumar, kicking Angelina into a trot, then a gallop. Herbert followed, legs flying all over the place but by some miracle managing to lumber up to a gallop.

For Svool, this was a new nightmare to rival all the other nightmares of his recent existence. He tried to imagine what it would be like travelling on a high speed tractor with square wheels and no tyres and five legs attached to each wheel – that pretty much summed up how he was now being bounced around. His bottom went up and down, slammed and bashed and battered, each slam transferring a painful jar to the base of his spine, which elicited a pained yelp from his chattering chipping teeth. Svool was tossed about like a marble in a washing machine during a spin cycle, and he looked over longingly at Lumar, who seemed to be suffering no such problems. Her Angelina seemed to purr along on plush suspension as she sat upright, spine straight, face serene, enjoying a comfortable, cushioned ride.

They galloped down a range of long grassy hills. Green sunlight glowered overhead.

"Oy!" shouted Svool.

"Yes?"

"Is it comfy?"

"The horse?"

"YES!"

"Yes, she is. Why?"

Svool's answer was lost as they came to a ditch, and bunching his metal muscles, Herbert leapt the small ravine. He landed, legs thumping and churning, and started the long gallop up the sweep of a fresh hill.

Svool spat out a mouthful of blood. "There's something wrong with this heap of junk!"

"Hey buster, I can hear you, you know?" said Herbert, his head turning with a sound of metal ratchets. "It's the suspension, guv'nor. Sorry about that. It's all shot to shit. It's all the humidity from the jungle, like. You know how it is."

"I am sure that I do not," said Svool, frowning, then biting his tongue as they leapt and hit the ground once more. His mouth filled with blood. He scowled, and realised Herbert had trapped his ankles again. Svool pictured a prone Herbert tied to a workbench, and him holding a hacksaw.

Across rolling grass plains they galloped, Zoot scooting along behind them. Slowly, they wound towards the Mercury Peaks, which became ever larger, ever more massive as they came to the end of the foothills. There, the rolling grassland hills ended suddenly, as if some mad terraformer had just turned off his machine and wandered off for a long holiday.

They drew rein on their mechanical mounts, and Herbert cocked his leg and urinated black engine oil against a rock.

"Sorry," he said. "Sorry!"

Svool looked across their back trail, but could not see their pursuers. He was just about to open his mouth, when they galloped into view. They were closer. Much closer. They were gaining *fast*.

"Er, I think we should go," said Svool. Lumar glanced back and gave a nod, and the horses skidded down a scree slope and into a jagged, stone-walled canyon. Ahead of them, the valley led off and was joined by more steep-sided rocky valleys, presumably carved by running water; or maybe even sulphuric acid.

"This the right way?" said Svool.

"I will guide thee," crooned Herbert, and gave a heavy metal *clonk*.

The horses started forward across the broad valley floor. It was made from dark sand and heavily littered with rocks. Svool found himself looking up at the steep sides of the valley walls, which were rugged and jagged, and covered in all manner of hardy clinging bushes and loose-looking boulders.

"This is starting to feel dangerous," said Svool.

"As dangerous as fifty enraged bandits coming up fast behind us?" said Lumar.

"Point taken."

They moved further into the canyon. The walls got steeper, craggier, more violent. The canyon floor got narrower and more heavily littered with boulders. It slowed their speed, but would presumably also slow down their pursuers.

"How far do we have to travel to the tunnel entrance?" yelled Lumar.

"It's up ahead. Maybe a kilometre or two."

"Through canyons?"

"Oh, aye," said Herbert, and gave an acidic metal fart. There was a tinkling sound as several washers ejected from his metal bottom and spun on the rocky ground.

"Are you feeling all right?" said Svool, frowning. Last thing he needed was his metal horse to break down. That would mean – the horror – having to travel on foot once more.

"Just nerves," said Herbert, grinning sheepishly. There were more clonking sounds from within. "I've met Black Jake. I've seen the horrors he subjects Special Friend metal horses to!"

"And what about humans?"

Herbert made a large gulping sound, and issued another sour oil fart. "I think that sums it up."

"Great," muttered Svool.

They continued through the long afternoon, the heat of the sun baking them, the stench of something sulphuric and eggy coming to their nostrils with increased regularity. The canyon through which they journeyed crossed other canyons, and several times Herbert chose a new and different route, zig-zagging slightly but always heading north and northeast.

As the sun started to sink in the heavens and the Mercury Peaks reared above the travellers like some insane oil painting against the canvas of the world, the mountains filling the sky – *blocking* the sky – a harsh cold wind blew suddenly in down the canyon. Lumar, up ahead, dragged Angelina to a halt, and the metal horse gave a strangled metal *"Neigh!"*

There, ahead of them, was a tunnel entrance. Rubble rockfalls to either side had obviously been cleared in the past, and the entrance was about the size of a normal doorway. It looked cold and dark and very uninviting.

"Smells funny," said Svool, wrinkling his nose.

"Like something died in there," agreed Lumar, jumping down off Angelina and stretching her back. She patted the horse's rump, and Angelina nuzzled Lumar's green fingers.

Groaning, Svool climbed down from Herbert like a geriatric going backwards down a cliff. He hit the ground and stood for a while, like a sailor after a long voyage trying to find his land legs.

"Gods, I feel sick," said Svool.

Zoot zipped along the canyon and stopped, bobbing before him. "They're close," he said. "And there's seventy of them. All heavily armed."

"Seventy!"

"We should get into the tunnel," said Lumar. "At least it's easier to defend in there. Despite the smell." She moved closer, not just her nose but her whole face wrinkling. "Gods, that's a fuckawful smell. Is it like that all the way through? And what is it, anyway?"

"Well, the Asbestos Joy Mines are, despite the name, *not* a place for joy."

Svool and Lumar turned and stared at Herbert. The metal horse grinned sheepishly.

"Asbestos?" said Lumar. "Isn't that incredibly dangerous?"

"Yes. But not as dangerous as the other things down there!" Herbert gave a metal shudder, and his eyes went wide in a face like a rusted skip.

"Other things?" said Svool, carefully.

"You know, the toxic deformed creatures, the lakes of bubbling acid, the pits of nuclear waste, the pipes of rancid starship fuel – that sort of thing."

Svool stared at Lumar, then back to Herbert.

"*You* fucking said it was safe!"

"No I didn't."

"*Yes,* you fucking *did.*"

"Hold on," said Lumar, holding a finger in front of Herbert's nose. "*You* said the Mines of Mercury were a massive network of old tunnels, *you* said they'd be your top vote for crossing this mad bad country, *you said* they were cleared out by Greenstar years ago and there was nothing more dangerous than a fucking luminescent mushroom." She feigned a metal horse voice that was pretty close to the original. "*Trust me. I know whereof I speak.*"

"Yes?" beamed Herbert.

"So you mentioned nothing about deformed toxic creatures, bubbling acid lakes and pits of nuclear waste. Did you? Dickhead?"

"Ahh, well, you see, what I was actually talking about was the *Mines of Mercury*, you see, that Greenstar did indeed clear out and are friendly and safe and good, old-fashioned family fun."

"So these are not the Mines of Mercury?" laboured Svool.

"Oh, no! First, we have to travel the Asbestos Joy Mines, the Pit of Nuclear Despair, and then the Caverns of Certain Doom." He beamed. "Only then do you reach the sanctuary and relative safety of the Mines of Mercury." He gave a little laugh, and shook his rusted head, as if talking down to the mentally challenged.

"We have to go back," said Lumar. She thumbed a gesture at Herbert. "This rusty fucking idiot will kill us in there."

"Too late," said Zoot.

"Meaning?" snapped Svool.

"Meaning they're here."

"Who's here?"

"Er. Black Jake," said Zoot, and whizzed along, disappearing into the tunnel opening.

Svool looked back, and saw the huge crowd of gunslinger-type desperadoes advancing down the canyon towards them. There were indeed about seventy of the deranged-looking individuals, who had left behind their metal horses and were creeping along, pistols in hand, moustaches gleaming under the dying green sun.

"Er," said Svool.

There came a slither of steel on leather as Lumar drew two pistols taken from General Bronson's men.

"Get in the tunnel," she said.

"We'll die in there," whimpered Svool.

"We'll die out here," said Lumar.

"And there's another thing," said Herbert – happily oblivious, it would seem, to his impending doom at the hands of Black Jake. "That smell you're smelling. It's explosive. So don't be firing them there pistols, or you'll be bringing not just the roof down, but the whole dang and blast mountain." He brayed, spittle flying from rubber lips, as if chuckling at some incredibly funny joke.

Slowly, Svool and Lumar backed towards the tunnel mouth. Angelina and Zoot had already entered, and Herbert clipped and clopped his way round, metal legs working in all different directions, and headed towards the tunnel...

Black Jake loomed to the forefront of the group. He was a big man, broad-shouldered, stocky, heavily-built, and fearsome. His head was shaved close to the skull and his black beard bristled fiercely. He was dark-skinned, his eyes black, his teeth black with the occasional glint of gold. He was grinning as he eyed up Lumar.

"Are you the people who killed ma brother?" he said, and spat a long plume of brown phlegm to the rocky canyon floor.

"Er," said Svool.

"He did," said Lumar, gesturing with her head towards Svool.

"Oh, thanks a lot for that stab in the back," snapped Svool.

"Well, you did, didn't you? Shot him a good one between the eyes. BAM! Like that."

"Is that so?" Black Jake was scowling now, and his grin had gone, and a dangerous animal ferocity was on his face, in the hunch of his shoulders, in the clutching of his black pistols.

"*Get ready to run...*" hissed Lumar.

"Oh, dear! Oh, deary dear!" The voice was Herbert. He'd made his way to the tunnel entrance and pushed himself inside, but his metal hips seemed to have jammed in the opening. His back legs thrashed pointlessly and he clanked and clunked and made wheezing, unhealthy ratcheting sounds.

Svool risked a glance back. Lumar kept her eyes – and guns – on Black Jake. Around him, his many bandit compadres were grinning and licking foul, black, rotting teeth. Some of them rubbed their hands together; Lumar fancied she even heard a cackle.

"I'm stuck!" wailed Herbert suddenly. "Help! Oh, help! I have my arse wedged in the tunnel opening! I do implore you all to cease this aggravation and help a poor old wounded Special Friend. I'm your friend. A friend for life." His legs kicked some more. There came more buzzes and clanks and clonks.

Lumar watched as Black Jake raised his pistols. All around him, the seventy or so banditos also lifted their guns, a rippling of steel like spikes on a porcupine's back. He spat on the rocks. "Anyways. Hardly matters who killed ma brother," said Black Jake. He grinned wider. "Because I'm going to fuck you both."

"What do we do now?" hissed Svool, flapping in panic.

"Looks like we die," said Lumar, taking a deep cool breath, and firing both her pistols.

ELEVEN

JENNY XI AWOKE, upright, facing herself in a mirror. It was a strange awakening, from deep sleep to sudden total awareness. She was in a white stone room. There were arched windows looking out over a vast city – the capital city, Bacillus Port. Greenstar had a massive presence there, with a complex which itself could have been deemed a city; she remembered, as a child, visiting Bacillus Port and seeing the high white stone towers. Well, it would appear she was now inside one. And who would have thought, back when she was a child, that they were used for torture? She had always imagined something *noble* went on in there. Now, she was learning different.

She was naked, and tied to some kind of extremely solid upright slab. Her tall athletic body was bruised and lacerated in many places, as she could see in her sad pale reflection. She did not recall getting the wounds, but they'd probably come from the bomb blast at the factory. She sagged against her bonds and looked into her eyes, into those reflected portals to the soul, and saw that she had aged. She no longer looked like a proud, strong warrior – no. She looked beaten, and battered, and bettered. Her face was gaunt, hollowed almost, and with a start she realised the effect Randy Zaglax ripping free her back teeth had achieved. He'd hollowed out her face. Hollowed out her soul. The bastard.

She narrowed her eyes and scowled at her own weak, naked reflection. She was tied tightly to the slab, only her head allowed freedom of movement. She turned, looking out over the city she remembered so well from her childhood. A trip with her father, Old Tom. One of the good memories. They'd bought ice cream in the streets. Marvelled at the wonders of Greenstar's newly created magnificence; right at the start, before the corruption and – ha, yeah – the *toxicity* took hold at the heart of the company. Well, at first it had seemed it could be good. A chance for the planet of Amaranth to *shine*. How wrong they had been. How wrong they had *all* been.

Sunlight gleamed across the city.

Tears ran down Jenny's face.

"That's right, bitch. Cry it out. Because it's only going to get worse."

"Fuck you."

"I'm pretty sure, in your unconscious state, you already have."

Jenny started to laugh as Randy came into view, and she took a good hard stare at his ruined face. "And I'm sure that's how you have to take all the girls, isn't it? Or it certainly is now. Your face looks like an explosion in a distorted chicken factory. And, oh, look, there I can see part of a frog's arse. No matter how bad it gets for me, *Randy*, it'll never be as bad as it is now for you, you fucking deformo. They call you Randy, but no woman on this fucking planet – not even the *mutants* – would want to fuck a fuck-up like you."

Randy leapt forward, a knife in his hand, murder in his pain-filled eyes. "I'll cut off your fucking face, bitch, see how *you like that*..."

"Randy." The voice was female, and stern. With it came command, and Jenny was sure there couldn't be that many people who had any form of control over Randy Zaglax.

"Yes," he said, and his eyes focused, but when Jenny looked at him she saw a new-found core of hatred for her, nestling in his eyes and face and hands. He'd kill her as soon as he could, she realised. In fact, his insanity was probably only held in rein by iron-hard bands of authority. Who? Which bitch sat behind her, out of view, watching like the ultimate voyeur?

It had to be the Big Boss.

Renazzi Lode.

Small, perfectly formed, but with a tongue of acid, a brain of poison, and the military might of the entire Greenstar Recycling Company behind her. Jenny had a limited knowledge of the way the organisation worked – except, perhaps, for how to best destroy its factories with bombs – but one person she knew held the monopoly and the casting vote was Renazzi Lode. And the woman was, perhaps, in the room with her. If Jenny could get to her... reach the unreachable... and slit the bitch's throat. That would be a result, surely? Not exactly a direct command from Mr Candle, but hell, to assassinate the head of Greenstar? Surely it was every ECO terrorist's wet dream?

But how?

Randy was staggering in front of her, and he drew back her attention. He waved the long slender blade under her nose, and he was grinning, a lop-sided, hanging-flesh look Jenny had come to know and understand.

"You know something, Randy? I've known beautiful people with the insides of a fucking sewer. And I've known ugly, deformed, twisted toxic mutants – yes, worse even than you – with the hearts and minds of angels. Looks do not define a person. I know that. I *understand* that. But you, my happy little torturing rapist, you have it all. A face like the inside of a pig's rectum, and an inner poison worse than any pollutant Greenstar could ever pump into the soil. Truly, it would be a service to the Quad-Gal to put five bullets in your skull. And I say that without hatred or malice." She looked up then. "I say it out of love."

Randy made a strangled noise in the back of his throat, and looked off over Jenny's left shoulder. So. To the left. Good. She had a position.

"You think you're so perfect, hey, Jenny Xi? Well look at this. Look at what you've done..."

"What I've..."

The mirror before her suddenly gleamed, and then oozed into transparency. It was a screen, looking into a small, dark, damp cell. There was a figure chained tight and upright against a wall. It was the naked figure of Sick Note, his skinny arms and legs covered in bruises and blood, his hacking cough unmistakable. His face was filled with anger and defiance. "I'll never fucking talk," he was muttering, even as the three men waded into him with baseball bats. His arms and legs jiggled under the impacts. His head was batted left, then right, like a balloon on a string. They hammered him and Jenny felt her own mouth go slack in disbelief, for this was not just a beating, it was fucking murder, the murder of a man, one of her squad, whom she knew and loved...

"No," she hissed.

"Yes," said Randy, close to her, his stink, the stench of iodine and painkillers and antiseptic filling her nostrils. "Watch this bit. I think it's going to be good. And, you understand, we're not torturing him to make him talk... oh, no! What would be the point of that?" Randy grinned at her through destruction. "We're just fucking him up to show you what *you* are doing to your friends. You lost your last squad, right? Lost them to a man. The only survivor was Jenny Xi. Well, let's see if history can't repeat itself..."

"Stop," said Jenny, suddenly weak, voice husky. "Stop it, now!"

"Oh, stop, stop, stop!" exclaimed Randy effetely, placing his palms against his raw stitched cheeks, against his torn ragged face which made the effeminate voice and play-acting seem even more ridiculous; even more surreal. But what happened next was in no way a dream. What happened next forced ice acid into Jenny's brain and held it there; like her head was on a spike.

A chainsaw's roar broke the squelching and cracking in the chamber, and the men with baseball bats backed away. Sick Note sagged against his chains, weak, battered, but still defiant. He spat out blood and broken teeth. "Fuck you all!" he growled, and Jenny's heart went out to him then, went out to his strength and courage and fearlessness. The chainsaw was buzzing, and blue smoke filled the chamber. The blade came into view, and Sick Note was watching it uneasily, his face still strong but his eyes betraying a shard of fear for the first time.

"What's first?" came a woman's voice. "Fingers, toes or cock?"

"No," growled Sick Note, "not like this, not here, not with a chainsaw. Make it clean! A bullet! Give me a soldier's death."

"No soldier's death for you, you hacking, coughing piece of human offal." The woman – Vasta – advanced. She was dressed, bizarrely, in black PVC. Almost a sex suit. Jenny's mind was spinning.

"Make them stop," she snapped at Randy. "Make them stop! I'll talk. I'll tell you everything!"

Randy reached up with a tiny spray can, and sprayed it in her mouth. Something grew fast, like expanding foam, filling her mouth and bubbling out, forming immediately into a solid ball. It almost blocked the back of her throat. She wheezed, struggling to breathe.

"Shhh," said Randy, sharply, a finger to his lips. "I think he has something to say."

Tears were streaming down Jenny's face.

Ahead, Sick Note was trying to strain away from the tiny spinning blades of the chainsaw. It buzzed, revving again and again, each time accompanied by a squirt of blue smoke.

"No!" said Sick Note, head thrashing from side to side. "No, I'll talk, I'll tell you everything you want to know..."

"Too late," hissed the woman, and the chainsaw descended, buzzing and bucking, cutting through Sick Note's arm. Blood and flesh spat out and back towards the mirror, and Jenny found she was thrashing also, tears streaming down her face. Sick Note was screaming, screaming, screaming, and an ocean of blood flushed onto the floor. As the chainsaw cut through and came free, his body slumped to one side and his severed arm flopped about uselessly on its chain, drooling gore. Sick Note was, miraculously, still conscious. He was babbling inanely. "I'll do... do... do it. Anything. What you want? You want to know about Jenny? Jenny Xi? Please. No more. No more. Please. I'll talk. Anything you want. I'll tell you anything. Just keep back. Keep away. I can't... can't think."

The woman revved the chainsaw. "Who cares anymore?" she said, advancing on Sick Note's other arm. In a feeble display of desperation, he tried to beat at her with his stump. Jenny watched, face flooded with tears, unable to believe what she was seeing. It was a sick charade. A freakshow tortureshow. Designer-fucking-entertainment for the sick, slick masses. She was amazed they didn't have the cameras rolling with a billion fat fucks slouched in couches stuffing popcorn and pies into slack jowls whilst slack brains observed slack entertainment on the Dead Eye...

The chainsaw rattled and buzzed and cut into Sick Note's remaining arm. Flesh and blood spat. The chainsaw jigged. Sick Note thrashed, dancing, a marionette with cut strings.

There came a sudden *whap* and the chainsaw got stuck. The woman started to tug at the machine, and Sick Note was making a low moaning noise. She tugged and pulled and wrenched, but the damn thing was stuck halfway through his arm. She turned to the camera/screen in her ridiculous PVC outfit, and gave a kind of half shrug. *Sorry, guys,* that half shrug said. *Damn bloody chainsaw got stuck in a human being again!*

The scene faded, the long mirror returning to its state as a mirror and fading Sick Note from view.

"You see?" Randy was close again. "You see what you did? You fucking people, you fucking *terrorists.* You think you can go around destroying what is ours, what belongs to Greenstar Recycling, and you think that's fucking acceptable? We own the fucking police. We own the fucking politicians. And we own *you,* little bitch. So you will tell us what we want to hear. Or else..." He laughed then. "Or else fuck it, I'll kill somebody else just for fun. Just to watch your eyes widen. Just to watch the colour drain from your pretty little cheeks."

"Mmmnnnn," said Jenny, thrashing her head from side to side. *Don't! Please don't do it! Please don't kill my people! I'll talk! I'll tell you everything you want to hear. Anything and everything, and even shit I didn't know existed in the bottomless pit of my fevered brain.*

I'll do anything you want. Anything. You have won. I can't see my friends die like this... But of course she could not speak, and could not plead. She could not enunciate her message.

All she could do was watch. And suffer. Like her squad suffered.

FLIZZ WAS WHAT could only be described as glamorous. She was tall, voluptuous, with shining golden hair, perfect healthy skin, white teeth, blue eyes – but more than all these things, things that went up to make a glamorous woman, they all *connected* in the right way, every part of Flizz complementing every other part of her to create a platter of damn near perfection. She somehow was more than the sum of her parts. The day Jenny met Flizz, in a downtown toxpark at a wayward stubborn no-leave village at the foot of the Mercury Peaks, she had been quite literally *blown away.*

They sat together, on a bench, watching toxi-scarred children playing on the swings. The kids didn't seem to mind their horrific injuries, inflicted by Greenstar's ever-loosening safety procedures and an army of corrupt lawyers willing to sell their souls to whatever devils inhabited their own personal hells in order to win the case. So, much as it had always been.

Jenny took occasional sideways glances at Flizz, finding her at once beautiful and thrilling. There was disbelief there as well, because the squad slip she'd been sent by McGowan said that Flizz was the best sniper from their mountain training camps, high up in the peaks where the snow and rocks were streaked silver by mercury poisoning.

"You're our top ranking sniper?"

"Yes." Her voice was low and husky. Sultry. She gave a half-shy smile to Jenny, then looked away.

They talked for an hour, Flizz explaining how her father had been a hunter, out in the remotest parts of the mountains and out on the lagoons at their base. From an early age, he had taken her on week-long hunts, teaching her how to conceal herself in her environment; teaching her how to use all manner of different rifles. Flizz had been a natural. Not just a natural shot, but a natural born killer.

All that came to an end in the '68 Acid Tanker Crash in the city of Faex, where four hundred and seventy-eight thousand people died when the tanker pilot lost control, and the mammoth vessel fell on the city, breaking in two, spilling its fifty-billion-gallon load. Fifty billion gallons of sentacyclic acid. Flizz's mother and father had been amongst those thousands left writhing on the streets, skin burned off, eyes smoking in sockets, lips scalded from mouths, fingers and toes melting into the road like some bad cartoon on toxic comedy...

Of course, Greenstar had paid out some minimal compensation via its insurance policies; their smallprint was legendary. And the crash site at the core of Faex was turned into a shrine blessed by fifteen different religions. It was only when news leaked to the independent Quad-Gal media about both pilots of the Acid Tanker that things really started to kick off; a lax attitude to medicals on the part of Greenstar, a refusal to drug-test its pilots even though its pilots were controlling ships capable of mass destruction; well, it could only go one way.

After the story broke, and Greenstar Recycling Company were found culpable, Flizz had left her house and made it known around the shady quarters of the city that she was seeking gainful employment with the Impurity Movement. Her beauty stood her in no good favour, and it took several knives between ribs, and the burning down of a casino, to persuade the gangster syndicates that she meant serious business. Eventually, word did get around. Flizz was beauty *and* the beast. Bad news. Deadly trouble. And eventually she was picked up and monitored by Cell Commander McGowan.

In many ways, Jenny had fallen in love with Flizz the moment she met her.

She remembered their first intimate moment. It was like a dream. It was a dream when it happened, for even though Jenny knew she loved Flizz from the moment she saw her, Flizz was a hard woman to crack, and never gave any indication that she returned her feelings.

They been training out in the Shattered Uranium Jungle, building shelters, surviving off what they could find on the harsh toxic beaches, avoiding the wild deviated beasts and cannibals. A severe toxstorm had come in, smashing a bloody red string of bruises across the sky, followed by the blood rain. Huge red droplets pounded the jungle canopy in a torrential onslaught, and Jenny and Flizz had pushed into their narrow shelter in a panic of drenched hair, soaked clothing and giggling.

For the first time in her life Jenny regressed, felt like a happy schoolgirl again. This wasn't training for war and violence; it lost its sombre mood and purpose. In this slice of time, she was young and carefree, enjoying life, enjoying love. They were pushed in tight together, blood rain drumming on the broadleaf roof and running in rivulets along the ridges, dripping in long spumes of red. The sky darkened more, and thunder ripped in from across the ocean. Machine-gun lightning crackled, smacking into the jungle in ten, fifteen, twenty violent strikes that made the women hold their breath, anticipation shining in their eyes, fists clenched tight. They'd heard about the lightning before, but never experienced it first hand... until now.

Crack-crack-crack went the wild machine-gun lightning, random sparkles of electric violence through the blood-red rain. Aftereffects snapped across the sky. At any moment they could be pulverised, and they lay there, looking into one another's shining eyes, breath held, waiting for random destruction and death to visit them, to strike them, to merge them into one being...

Flizz leant forward. Her breath was sweet, tender, perfect. Their lips met, and they kissed as the lightning continued to crackle above them, striking the forest in random bouts of intense violence. And Jenny knew. To die now, that would be perfect. But they didn't die, and they kissed, and fell into one another, and as the machine-gun lightning passed it left behind the tropical rain, pounding against the shelter, and they kissed, and held one another, and slowly undressed one another until they were naked and pressed tight in that narrow space. Everything dissolved into nothing, into a microcosm of time and the universe. Time had no meaning. The old clichés are the best, thought Jenny, as time spiralled off into a maelstrom of eternity. They kissed and touched and eventually made love, moving together, wet, sliding together, tongues entwined, a languorous long eternal fucking.

Afterwards, they lay together and slept and the storm eventually passed.

JENNY HAD NEVER thought of herself as gay, and she'd had many lovers – all but one of them men. But that time, that day, that moment in the storm, focussed and distilled by the promise of lightning death – that had been the most intense and beautiful moment of her life. She'd always been slightly dubious of girl-on-girl relationships, wondering how you could possibly be satisfied without the right equipment; but in that tiny shelter she had been satisfied, and more than satisfied, not just by meeting a physical need but by love.

The morning after, they had walked through the jungle in easy silence, stopping by various blasted trunks to examine the damage. The storm had caused a riot, and the pools of standing water were just beginning to steam as the green sun rose and cast an eerie glow through the high jungle canopy.

"Why do they call it the Shattered Uranium Jungle?" asked Flizz, at last.

"It goes back to the early days, when Greenstar invaded Amaranth," said Jenny, leaping lightly onto a fallen tree and staring off through the jungle. "There were various indigenous local tribes, quite simple in their beliefs; they refused Greenstar's generous offer to relocate them to another universe, and instead waged war on the tankers and shitships that rumbled low overhead. So Greenstar sent in a series of mercenary units to remove them; but the shitbag dirtbox mercenaries were not regulated by Quad-Gal Military. They flew over the jungle using skimmers, located villages, and exploded depleted uranium shrapnel charges over the tribespeople. Men, women, children. Not military targets at all. Not *combat*, but extermination. Well, there were a lot of fucking tribes, and nobody to intervene; not police, not army, nothing. Greenstar were unregulated back then, and anyway, they claimed to have no knowledge of the mercenary army causing havoc in the southern jungles of the planet. It went on for months, and the bastards left an army of corpses and pollution in their wake. Pollution that causes severe birth defects. By the time Quad-Gal Military got involved and wiped out the mercs, it was too late. The tribespeople who survived – well, let's just say they were made very ill and very antisocial. Such is the way with corporate takeovers."

They continued on through the jungle, until Flizz gave a low gasp of wonder. Jenny moved to her and they stood at the edge of a concealed cenote. It was about a hundred metres across, with crumbling rock edges, a wide shaft that dropped perhaps two or three hundred metres straight down, a cylinder punched vertically through Amaranth's crust by the fist of God. It was almost perfectly circular, the rock a sandy colour, and deep down below them a turquoise lake sat, perfectly still.

"That's beautiful," said Flizz.

"Incredible," agreed Jenny.

"God's own private lake," said Flizz.

Their hands found one another's, fingers entwining, and they stood for long moments soaking up the atmosphere, the beauty, and listening to the tinkle of a narrow gentle waterfall that sprayed white foam into one edge of the distant lake. Birds chattered in the trees. And for the first time in her adult life, Jenny found peace. And joy.

Flizz turned to her, eyes sparkling. "Let's do it."

"It?"

"Jump."

Jenny peered down. "We might break our backs."

"We might die," agreed Flizz.

Fingers still entwined, they took several steps back. Their breaths caught in their throats, and laughing with pure adrenaline, with pure abandon, with absolute anarchy, a disintegration of convention and social expectation and normality and training and common sense, Jenny and Flizz ran, and leapt out into the wide expanse, and fell, fell, fell into the still turquoise waters of the deep, perfect cenote.

*   *   *

Now, JENNY WATCHED her ex-lover, ex-partner, ex-girlfriend, ex-God in the mirror. Flizz was tied up tight, head upright and proud, eyes harsh and narrow. She was naked, just like Jenny, and this fake reflection was a parody of their once beautiful relationship. Jenny still loved Flizz, and she knew Flizz still loved her; but they had chosen Impurity and their work of bringing down The Company over their love. To both women, Amaranth and its freedom was more important than their own desires. But now, as Jenny, strapped to her slab, mouth filled with injected foam, watched her true love through the transparent mirror, she wanted to scream – *no, oh, no, you cannot do this, not to my love, not to my Flizz, not to the perfect woman in my life; because that would be beyond comprehension, that would be a torture so great I might not arrive out of the other side...*

If you want to visit the realms of insanity; this is how to do so.

If you want to break me like a stick; this is the way forward.

Jenny watched, in horror, her mind ticking faster than any supercomputer. She struggled against her bonds, steel straps around wrist and ankle, but they were too tight, too strong, too permanent. She caught Randy from the corner of her eye and he was watching the peepshow-fuckshow-tortureshow about to begin, and he was grinning, and Jenny's brow darkened because she wanted him dead. She fought her bonds with renewed violence. They were too strong, too tight. Bastards. Bastards! Her eyes flickered to Flizz – Vasta, Head of Security, had appeared on the other side of the mirror. *Was it a direct portal to the place? Or just a TV screen projecting an image?* Vasta carried a long, gleaming cut-throat razor. They were speaking, but the sound had been muted. Jenny could see the muscles working in Vasta's jaws, saw Flizz, angry, eyes bright, talking to Vasta but watching the blade hung low, a curve of dangerous, sharpened steel.

"She won't be dissuaded, you know," said Randy, almost conversationally.

Jenny watched them talking, Vasta edging closer and closer, the blade coming up, a threatening, terrifying, simple sliver of steel. In her mouth, the ball of foam had started to loosen. Only a little, but spit had finally worked between her cheek walls and the compacted foam. Jenny started to probe and push with her tongue, working it around, pushing at the ball of foam.

"Flizz is talking now. Pleading. Telling Vasta everything. But it's too late." He turned and stared and moved close to Jenny. "Too late for you cunts. Tell me about McGowan. And Mr Candle. Especially Mr Candle. And then we'll stop..." – he glanced over his shoulder, where the cut-throat razor was resting against Flizz's perfect white breast – "peeling your friend like a ripe fruit."

Jenny nodded her head vigorously, eyes frightened, head bowing low, and Randy brought up another spray and pushed it into her mouth. He squeezed the trigger as, over his shoulder, the blade moved swiftly down, slicing off Flizz's right breast to leave an oval of raw flesh. Blood ran down her belly. Her muscles strained at her bonds, like vibrating tendons of steel. Flizz's mouth was open in a silent scream at the ceiling, as the cut-throat razor began to slash, carving up the flesh of her chest and belly into bloody ribbons. She danced and jerked against her bonds. She screamed and screamed and screamed...

The ball of foam was gone from Jenny's mouth, and she spat out the shrivelling phlegm lump, moaning, her eyes fixed on Flizz's dance of blood and torture, and Randy came close and his eyes were bright and the scars on his face were weeping. "Tell me, tell me where we can find Mr Candle..."

"My throat," wheezed Jenny. "Can't... speak..."

Randy was close, his tattered rebuilt ear close to Jenny's mouth. It was a simple duck and turn to place her teeth against his throat, and then she bit, and she bit deep and hard, her teeth sinking through flesh and oesophagus, taking in his entire Adam's apple and holding him there as blood ran down her chin and down her throat and Randy shrieked and gurgled, fists lashing at her, not punches but a panic-fuelled battering. And the more he struck her, the harder she bit, blood gushing into her mouth and throat, and all the time she could see Flizz being striped by the razor and dancing a jig like a puppet of death.

Suddenly, Randy stopped hitting and Jenny released her grip a little. He was panting, his throat held in her jaws; stalemate.

"Rweese mwe," said Jenny through her mouthful of flesh and windpipe.

Randy himself could not speak, but he got the idea real fast. Jenny heard a jangle of Minotaur keys, felt Randy's shaking, shuddering hands rising towards her bonds, and they melted away and her hands were free. For a moment, her muscles spasmed with cramp and nothing worked, but then she grabbed Randy's head and they both fell to the floor, and she relaxed her bite and spat blood in his face. He was vibrating like an epileptic having a seizure. She took the long digital keys from his grip and released her ankles, and gazed down at Randy, his eyes fixed on her, his mouth working soundlessly. She'd damn near bit out his throat.

Smoothly, she took a pistol from a holster at Randy's hip and, looking around, placed the gun at his head.

"Time to die," she snarled.

"Freeze, motherfucker!" screamed a voice and there came a cocking of guns, of SMKKs. Jenny rolled fast and leapt at the mirror/TV screen, arms up to protect her face, leapt towards the tortured, thrashing figure of Flizz in all her ribbon-torn tagliatelle-skinned agony, dancing like a marionette on rubber strings. There came a scream of shattering glass and sparking electronics as Jenny struck the portal, and she felt it fold around her, break around her, shards slicing into her arms and flanks, and she was through, sailing through cool air and she expected to land on the floor and see Flizz, poor tortured Flizz, and she'd put a round through Vasta's skull and rescue her true love, her one love, her *only* love...

Shards tinkled all around her. She landed on sharp broken pieces of glass in a tiny square room. All around, black holes filled with cables fed off into blackness. There was no Flizz. The image was a projection. Somewhere, Flizz was still being cut to ribbons. Jenny heard boots behind her, and reversed the pistol and fired off ten shots, the gun booming in this narrow confined place. Then she picked a tube at random and squeezed her slim, naked body into it, squeezing in amongst the cables and pushing herself forward as fast as possible. It was hot in the tube, and wires sizzled the hairs on her arms. She could smell hot oil and grease and hear a thousand different pitches of buzzing sound. Behind her, SMKK rounds screamed and clattered, but they faded as she shuffled quickly forward, onwards, not thinking about where she was going, or about rescue, or even about what she was going to do. One bright primal spark sizzled hot in the centre of her brain. It was a spark of existence; the need to survive. Jenny squeezed her way onwards into the darkness, tears leaving streaks in the dirt and blood on her face.

*   *   *

RENAZZI LODE STOOD, hands on her hips, as Randy was helped to his feet, one hand clamped protectively around his gashed throat. It took him a long time to look up and stare at the fury in Renazzi's eyes.

"You let her go," she said, voice soft.

When Randy spoke, it was as a low croak and caused him considerable, obvious agony. "She tried to bite out my throat."

"You fucking let her *go!*" snapped Renazzi, punching Randy on the nose. He fell back, and she strode over him and stared down and her eyes were narrowed and evil. "She went into the *tube,* fuckwit. There are ten thousand miles of fucking tubes in fucking Bacillus Port, linking every single fucking factory and unit we own. I want you to get in there and find her..."

"But... I need medical..."

"Now!"

Randy struggled to his knees, and patted where his pistol had gone, and looked up weakly.

Renazzi was pointing a gun. For a moment he thought she was going to shoot him, there on his knees. A basic execution. But she reversed the weapon and handed it to him.

Grimly, silent, Randy climbed to his feet, and – with one hand still clamped to the teeth gouges in his throat – shuffled through the smashed TV portal and towards the many tubes. He felt the dark brooding presence of Renazzi Lode behind him, like a toad on his shoulder; like a cancer in his soul.

"You'll need this," she said, and punched him in the back. He gasped, and felt the gem from her ring burrow through his clothing and flesh and bone, and settle in his heart, monitoring him.

Okay, said Renazzi in his mind, words buzzing like

insects. *Now I see what you see, hear what you hear. There's no fucking it up this time, Randy Zaglax. If she gets out of here in that state, tells the fucking media what she has seen, it could be extremely damaging for Greenstar.*

"You want me to kill her?"

Yes.

"But what about Mr Candle?"

Flizz spoke. Sang like a tortured chicken. Even now she's being fed through a mincer and will be en route to a recycling food plant within the hour. Now... kill Jenny Xi. Don't fuck it up, Randy, or you'll be in the mincer, too.

Randy moved to the central four tubes and examined them closely. One had a scuffed edge. He hoisted himself up and forced himself into the narrow space. It was hot and claustrophobic, cables digging into his arms and body and legs. He was forced to move his hand from his wounded throat, which wept blood into the cabling innards.

Randy vomited, then wiped his mouth with the back of his hand, and crawled through his own mess

Kill her, said Renazzi. *I'll be with you every step of the way.*

TWELVE

HORACE, THE DENTIST, Anarchy Android, one of the most revered and feared hunter, torture and killing models ever created by Anarchy Inc., tumbled under the ocean, turning slowly, beat left and right by currents but turning, turning, winding himself in a cocoon of the heavy steel cable which pinned his arms to his sides and weighed him down. Blackness filled his mind, poured into him like oil, and the Biohazard Ocean poured into his mouth, into his throat, was sucked in and down into his lungs and belly, filling him up with its poison; with its hatred. With its toxicity.

You are going to die.

Yes.

You are dying.

I know.

Fight it!

Fuck you.

Fight it, damn you! You're an Anarchy Android! Show some... RAGE!

No.

It was a simple word. The simplest of them all. *No.* But it carried such weight and such awesome power.

Horace was satisfied to impose his will over that inner voice which had haunted him for so long. His tormentor, his brother, his controller, his subversive, mocking inner demon. His KillChip. His fucking KillChip.

Yes. He knew about his KillChip. A Quantell Systems Sanity Module designed to keep him sane, ha-ha, how the fuck was that supposed to work? By giving him voices in his head?

With the first two generations of android, there had been a predisposition to go off the rails: crazy, postal, call it what you will. But Anarchy Inc., a wholly-owned subsidiary of Earth's Oblivion Government, had felt the need to fit a controlling module straight to the brain. Androids were never told about the implementation, and each one was massively different, a discrete AI personality but with a sole functionality – to keep the android sane, and by keeping the android sane, to make him a more efficient killer.

It worked. Some of the time. Most of the time.

By fitting a device that almost made the android feel like he was hearing voices in his head, a dark brother (or sister) who would mock and cajole and question his actions; well, instead of making an android crazier than a jilted paramedic who finds his wife being fucked in the woods by his best mate, it somehow made him more sane.

Dying, he thought.

I am dying.

But then... so be it, because I am an android and I'm an Anarchy Model; a torture and murder unit, a device that hunts down humans (and other androids, hush) and slowly takes them apart until I discover whatever insipid information I have been charged with finding. And then I kill. And I don't always make it sweet. This is no dying in your sleep. This is no sudden heart attack or being hit by a truck. No, I make it fucking personal, and I make it fucking personal on purpose because – well, death is a serious business. It should hurt. Should be remembered. Like the old Viking warriors dying in battle; if you didn't die with your sword in your hand, if it didn't hurt in life, then you're weren't getting into the fucking afterlife, that was for sure.

So death had to be special.

And the more it hurt, the more special it was. Right?

And so, yes, now I die. I am ready to meet my maker. Ha-ha. But I already met him, a sterile scientist in a lab of white Formica and cheap stainless steel. Glass test tubes. White lab coats. Oh, daddy, why did you forsake me?

So... you mean there's no Heaven? No android Heaven?

Do you not believe?

I believe, all right. I believe in the sanctity of the organism, I believe in replication and separation and multiplication. I believe every organism is an island and we're born alone, created alone, and fucking die alone...

But what of love? And honour? Friendship? Truth?

No such thing, my little KillChip compadre. Just social webs put in place to make us try to care; when, in reality, empathy is a learned thing. Look how cruel a human child is? Pulling the legs off spiders. Standing on slugs. Swatting wasps. Battering little brothers and sisters. Smacking other children in the playground over petty shit. There's no empathy there, no in-built natural need to look after fellow humans. Children are a distillation of the human condition – before social conventions are forced into place, like a behaviour brace instilling fear. You will behave like this, or God will punish you. You will behave like this, or you'll spend your life locked in prison. Or worse, hang from a loop of rope until your neck is broken. Humans don't protect other humans because they care about them – they protect them out of fear. Social etiquette is simply a framework for self-preservation.

Horace sank. His mind was a fluttering of black and blood red.

No oxygen, he thought.

He laughed at that.

Greenstar had fucked him up good. Killed him.

But that didn't matter. Nothing mattered. His death had simply been a matter of time, and Horace, The Dentist – well, he knew that his passing would make the world a better place.

What good deeds did you do?

I never executed a very young child.

That's good!

I simply crippled them.

That's not good.

Who are you to judge? That's the way I was programmed. The way I was made. I was a distillation of the human fucking condition. I never learned to fear the system. I wasn't force-fed alien religions in the hope of making me a better person. No. I was android. I was pure. A pure killing machine.

And that's the way you'll die...

Yeah. An eye for an eye, a tooth for a tooth... just like the Bible II Remix jokes about.

It's sad.

Why? Live by the sword, die by the sword. And I've lived so very strongly, Killer.

The water pressure of the Biohazard Ocean was growing now, not that Horace could feel or endure any more pain. He had reached his limit, as much pain as is physically possible to feel, and in reaction his body was shutting down; his brain was cutting off his pain synapses, severing nerves, halting vital functions.

Preserving itself. Until it, too died. And then it would be game over.

And yet...

Something was happening.

The murk, the undersea gloom, was growing brighter.

Horace saw rocks, huge mountain ranges under the ocean. And they glowed, glowed with toxic waste and toxic sludge, a radioactive, bacteriological nightmare of polluted seaweed and heavy metal detritus. Horace came to rest on a mountaintop, gently bumping along until he wedged between two rocks. He struggled for a moment against the steel winch cable that bound him, but then the last of the fire left his system and he lay there waiting for his brain to die, and for all thoughts to cease...

All around lay glowing weeds, shifting gently left and right in ocean currents. Tiny fish darted in front of Horace's eyes, deformed, many with beaks and legs and massive flippers, and then disappeared, flitting between the rocks on the ocean-floor mountain-top.

I've been on the mountain, thought Horace, and nearly died laughing.

He sat there for what seemed an age. It was certainly long enough to drown. Long enough to drown fifty times over.

I am not dead.

And then the voice came to him, and it was not the bitter, sardonic, mocking laughter of his inbuilt KillChip; this was something vastly different. The voice was soft, almost female, and it didn't come to his mind via his ears, but felt more to be absorbed from everything around him. Confusion was suddenly his master. Everything he had known and trusted and believed in turned out to be a lie. He should be dead. He should be fucking fish food...

Welcome.

Horace considered this.

I should be dead, he said, although he did not speak with his mouth.

Yes.

But I am not.

No.

Why?

Who knows?

Who are you?

I am... and a flicker of images that transcended verbal language. It showed the rocks of the ocean, the waters filled with pollution, the deformed fishes in the sea, the distorted seaweed on the rocks. It was all of these and yet more.

Horace felt suddenly very small, and very hollow.

Like an android speaking to God.

As he considered what next to say, he watched some glowing seaweed fronds detach, and float towards him. They hovered in front of his mouth, as if waiting to gain entry through an iron gate. Horace blinked, still incredibly weak and squatting on the razorblade of death.

May I?

What?

I wish to search your... again, images. But there was no doubt what the voice meant. It did not mean his mind or his feelings or his memories. It meant his *soul*. His *android soul*.

You may, he said, filled with sudden bitterness and regret. *But you will not like what you find.*

Horace opened his mouth and the seaweed drifted inside. He felt it slither down his throat, along with more gallons of toxic pollutant. Horace waited, suddenly tense, wondering if, when the floating voice discovered what a bad person – he corrected himself, a bad *android* – he had been, it would rip him apart from the inside out.

He waited. Waited to die.

Again.

He laughed at that, and bubbles escaped from his mouth in the underwater gloom.

Eventually, there came a sound. Like a sigh.

I see, said the voice.

So you hate me?

And he got a sudden image of an all consuming rage, like molten mountains rearing from the oceans across an entire planet and laying waste to a billion people who had destroyed the world...

Not unless you can match what Greenstar has done to me.

You're the planet, aren't you? Amaranth?

No.

You're the ocean? The waters of the world?

No.

Then what, by the Mother of Manna, are you?

I am the Toxicity, said the voice.

Horace considered this, and he considered it for a long time.

I do not understand.

For decades, toxic waste has been pumped into the oceans, under the mountains, into the air, into the very seams of the planet. Across the entirety of the world known as Amaranth, every manner of biological hazard, poisonous heavy metal, toxic pollutant, radioactive material and general purpose waste has been pumped and dumped and tipped and buried and strewn without regard for what was done; what, really, was being created.

You're the waste? said Horace, in awe.

I am the toxic scourge on this bedrock, said the voice.

How can you be alive? That's... impossible...

What is life but a chemical accident? Your race, your human race, began as a random chemical soup powered

*by proteins and nutrients and sunlight. Cells grew and
mutated and developed and split and mutated. Well, I
have proteins and nutrients and sunlight. I have radiation
and metals and carbons and every single element that
could form a human – and more. I have living cells. And
I have spread. And I have mutated. And I live.*

Greenstar created you?

Unknowingly, yes.

And... do they know of you?

*They suspect, I believe. They are suspicious that
something not indigenous to Amaranth exists, but they
can find no evidence. And that is because they examine
single samples without stepping back and looking at
the bigger picture. The Whole, as it were.*

So you're keeping me alive?

Yes.

Why?

*You are a killer, Horace The Dentist. A human-created
android killer. I find that incredibly sweet and ironic.
Amusing, even, to use an approximation of the concept
of humour as deployed by humans. I fear, however, they
would not think of my intentions as amusing.*

You have not answered my question.

Every organism that lives desires life, is that not so?

*Every man or woman I've assassinated has tried their
utmost to survive, so yes, on the whole, you are correct.
You have obviously kept me alive for a reason, and I can
only assume it is something to do with Greenstar...*

Yes. I have two tasks.

Horace laughed then. *I am a wreck. I am on the
verge of death. Look, I am bound by a steel winch
rope, wound about me so tight I can't even move my
fingers...* but even as he spoke, fronds of seaweed floated
towards the cable, and Horace sensed heat and watched
as the steel turned to jelly, and slowly disintegrated, and
floated away.

My toxicity is strong, said the voice.

Horace flexed his hands, but he was weak. He peered down at the gaping wound in his chest. The barbed spear which had skewered him like a fish had also disintegrated and melted away. But now there was a fist-sized hole through his chest.

He laughed.

If you can repair that, I'll do whatever you ask.

Don't you want to know first?

I am an assassin. An Anarchy Android torture kill model. I work for money. Horace's eyes went hard. *If you save my life, I'll do whatever you require of me. Whatever it takes.*

So be it. But it will hurt. And to survive, you will have to... absorb me.

Absorb the toxicity?

You will become as one with the toxic waste of my being.

Do it, said Horace.

HE FLOATED FOR what seemed an eternity. Every atom in his body burned as if with fever, as if with fire, as if with acid, as if with radiation. Horace felt himself bubbling away into nothing. Horace felt himself vomit every molecule of his body out into the ocean. Horace felt like he floated in a warm bath, his eyes closed, everything perfect around him as slowly his strength returned and his wounds healed and he became one with the tox. Mankind had created a toxic nightmare. Now, the tox was creating a man.

AS HORACE FLOATED, he saw the beginning of the Quad-Gal, for he shared atoms with that bright fiery explosion of matter. He witnessed the birth of humanity.

He witnessed the birth of the android. He witnessed the birth of toxicity. He witnessed their joining. And he heard singing, and it was a beautiful singing, the singing of children, and he realised they had been born of the toxic waste and he was not alone, he would have a hundred thousand brothers and sisters....

They are the children of the deep, said Toxicity.

They are the product of waste given life again.

Maybe there is a God. Maybe He saw fit to bring us back. To introduce Balance. To reintroduce Order.

What do you want me to do? asked Horace.

You will help bring down Greenstar. The Company. And then you will help to destroy me.

Why?

Because Amaranth needs to be free again. It needs to be clean again. The ECO terrorists are right, but they cannot do it alone. They seek to purify the planet – and I, the toxic waste they seek to remove – I will help them do this.

And your children? The singing children?

We shall see... said the voice.

STRENGTH FLOODED HORACE. He felt every cell being rebuilt from the inside out. All wounds were healed. His heart stopped beating because he no longer needed a heart. He found his skin changing colour, shifting through a million different hues until it almost returned to his natural state. Like toxic waste, he no longer needed oxygen to breathe, no longer needed food to eat or water to drink – he could just use the fuel that was the energy of his own existence.

Horace walked under the Biohazard Ocean on the tops of mountains, and revelled in his newfound body. In his brain, the KillChip was burned free and sent screaming into a silicon abyss.

What humans do not realise, said Toxicity, *is that every computer chip is a slice of life. Many elements may sustain life, and as you know, carbon and silicon are two of the major building blocks. Computer chips live, only in a different way from how humans imagine. The KillChip had to go. It would have stopped you doing that which you must do. It would have acted as inhibitor.*

As Horace grew strong, he felt a great weight lift from his mind. No longer did he feel anger or hatred or pettiness or greed. Money had no value. Life, he realised, in a total reversal of what he had been; *life* was what mattered more than anything. Life, not death. Saving, not killing. Rescue, not annihilation.

But sometimes you must kill in order to save.

Sometimes, you must murder in order to rescue.

Sometimes, you must annihilate in order to bring about birth...

Let me show you my children, said the voice.

Horace swam deep down under the Biohazard Ocean, powering down, revelling in his new strength. Every muscle felt ready to burst with energy and power. *This is what superheroes must feel like,* he reasoned. *Except none of them are made from... crap. Poison. Waste. Superradiation Man! The Biohazard Avenger! The Recycling Waste Machine Warrior!*

He swam down the mountain, through rocky crags and down rounded chimneys. Bubbles rose from here and there, and through the poorly-lit gloom, Horace started to make out other mountains... there, a massive stack of tyres, millions and millions of abandoned tyres dumped and left to rot and slowly disintegrate. Through slick pools of oil he swam, to see towers of fused glass – smashed and melded *bottles* – each tower bigger than a hundred-storey skyscraper. There were mountains of toxic chemical barrels under the ocean, their yellow TOXIC symbols still just visible through glowing green seaweed and parasitic barnacles.

The gods only know what shellfish have developed down here. Lobsters with high IQs? Mussels with muscles? Cockles with cocks? He would have laughed, except he realised he should in all reality be dead. *Maybe this is just a dream? A nightmare? Maybe this is the last dying remnants of my brain discharging, shutting down, sending me spinning into the abyss, the void... all I need now is darkness and oblivion.*

But darkness and oblivion did not come.

There. My children.

And Horace looked down on glowing pods made from toxic, living, deviated seaweed, tiny lifebubbles folded over to form egg-shaped capsules. And within each capsule Horace could see a child, a glowing child of great beauty, and they sang and their songs had no words, only sorrowful, mournful notes that conjured images of a great planet, a great world brought low by the scourge of humanity...

They are beautiful.

My psi-children. They can see the different paths of the future.

Incredible!

They have read you, Horace. Seen your paths. In one path, you bring about the destruction of Greenstar. You send the Giant Company wailing and screaming into the Void. This, they have seen, Horace. And when Greenstar scientists captured one of my children and tortured out her thoughts, they, too, knew of this future. That's why they decided to retire you, Horace. That's why Vasta had you speared and dumped here...

Horace swam through endless mountains of junk, powering ahead, staring around him in wonder. *How can this be? I thought Greenstar were a recycling company?* And yet he laughed, for he knew they were a sham. He'd been a part of the process to cover up their evil.

It's all about money, and it's all about lirridium. They recycle those products that are profitable to recycle; that can be turned into fuel and sold on. But if it's useless, then it gets dumped. Greenstar make political noises about the good they're doing for the planet of Amaranth, but everybody knows they are liars. Everybody on Amaranth. Everybody in Manna. Everybody in Quad-Gal. Everybody knows, but nobody does anything. It's the same as it's always been... money talks, and everyone turns a blind eye. People and aliens from other planets don't care as long as it isn't outside their own front door. They make the right cooing noises, but don't truly do anything; because it isn't their problem. As long as the lirridium is flowing freely and Shuttles can zip across Manna, then everybody is happy and Greenstar can do what the hell they like.

You said you want me to destroy you?

Yes.

How?

You destroy both me and Greenstar with one vicious blow. At the Greenstar Factory Hub, they have not just the fuel processing plants for lirridium; they also have the Central Manna Depot. Nobody really, truly understands how large it is. In the past thirty years it has grown and grown and grown, burrowing down into the bedrock of the planet, deeper than any ocean. Greenstar's lirridium output makes up one entire third of Manna's space travel fuel requirements. What they've also done, very cleverly, is merge their lirridium output with the seas and oceans of this world... already polluted, they have fed pipes under every kilometre of sea, the Biohazard Ocean, the Lake of Corrosion, The Sea of Heavy Metal; the Faeces Sea... all are loaded *with a water-lirridium blend. Right now, Horace, you are swimming through this lirridium blend. It means if times are tough and there is a sudden demand – for example, in times of war – then Greenstar can call on their hidden surplus within moments.*

You want me to ignite it, thought Horace in a moment of primal instinct.

Yes.

That will ignite the whole planet?

A cleansing by fire. You will destroy Greenstar totally. You will remove my toxic deviation. And yes, you will kill many; but many will survive to rebuild again. Horace, it will be a Biblical Fire. A Holy Fire. To wipe away the poison. To kill the toxicity.

How will I do this?

Travel to the Greenstar Factory Hub. The Core of the Processing Plant. Others will have been integral in the planting of explosives.

What then?

They cannot do this without you. You are a cog in the machine. You are a part of the Whole. I can explain it no more...

And then it dawned on Horace. This was the ultimate assassination. The ultimate mission. The final kill.

The final kill to bring about... freedom.

I will use myself, he thought, his understanding complete. *I will be the trigger.*

Will you do this? For Amaranth?

I do not wish to kill your psi-children.

We are willing to die. For our planet. To save the world. To purify Amaranth of its pestilence...

Horace considered.

"I will do it," he said.

THIRTEEN

LUMAR DROPPED TO one knee to steady her aim, whilst Svoolzard Koolimax XXIV stumbled backwards, flapping his arms above his head and making a noise like a little girl attacked by school bullies. Return fire boomed from Black Jake and his bandits, but as soon as the gunfight had started, it ended. And it ended because the mountains began to scream. Thunder rumbled overhead, only it wasn't thunder, but the mountain itself, shaking and growling, and the very rocks vibrating, stones pattering down the steep sides of the canyon where the antagonists stood... Lumar and Svool stumbled backwards, towards the tunnel entrance and Herbert's fat metal behind, whilst Black Jake and his cronies, superstitious to a man, looked around in wonder and awe and fear as the mountains shouted at them...

"The Gods are shouting your name!" cried one bandito.

"So they are!" shouted Black Jake, beaming, staring up at the sheer eight-thousand-foot wall of rock that towered above him, all the way above the clouds, all the way up to the ice and snow.

"Rockfall!" screamed Lumar, turning at last and charging at Herbert. She hit him with all her strength, all her weight, all her speed, and with an "Oof!" and a sound like a rock dropped into meshing gears, they burst through into the tunnel in a tangle. Svool strolled in after them, grinning for a moment and presumably about to make some quip about metal animal sex, when a wall of rock went *whoosh* directly behind him in the blink of an eye, scant inches from removing the back of his skull.

BLACK JAKE RAISED his arms to the Gods and beamed and prayed. The mountains were talking to him! His God was talking to him! The rocks and snow and ice came tumbling down from thousands of feet up. A wall of it. Black Jake frowned as his vision filled with an unspeakable horror. There was a name for this sort of thing. The name was *avalanche*...

Black Jake and sixty-nine of his bandit henchmen were crushed in an instant. Compressed under a hundred thousand tonnes of rock and ice, dislodged by the foolish ignition of discharged pistols...

One bandit survived, standing at the back of the group and scratching his chin. He blinked, and instead of seeing a huddled group of his colleagues squeezed into the canyon neck, pistols at the ready, plumes of brown sputum erupting from rotten mouths like sewage from a holiday beach overflow, suddenly he stared at a thirty-foot-high pile of rock. Several stones trickled down and bounced off his nose.

He took a step back, looked up at the wall, and decided that perhaps, on this day, the Gods were possibly against them...

IN THE TUNNEL, dust was thick in the air. Svool turned and stared at the wall of rock not one inch from his face. One inch, one second, and he'd be dead. Bent in half like a rubber toy. He gulped, choking a little on the thick dust, and staggered forward towards Lumar, who was busy untangling herself from Herbert's metal body.

"Why've you got so many *fucking legs?*" she was snarling, and finally found her feet, and gave Herbert a hearty kick with a *clong*. Then she turned to Svool, and saw the shock and horror in his pasty white face. "You nearly get squashed, buddy?"

"Yes."

"Dogmeat."

"Yes."

"Fishpaste."

"A-huh."

"Are you *okay?*"

"Yes, yes. Shit, yes. I'm great. I'm fine. Shit, I'm *alive*, baby, I'm alive! I wasn't squashed! It's a miracle, lo! We have much to rejoice about!"

"We do?"

"We certainly *do*. Weren't you listening, bitch? *I, the Great Svoolzard Koolimax XXIV, Third Earl of Apobos, am alive!*"

Lumar snorted a laugh. "Fuckwit. We're trapped in these psychopathic mines under the Mercury Peaks, led here by a metal robot horse who's stripped his thread, snapped his bolt, and popped his cogs."

"Hey, there's nowt wrong with me," said Herbert. It was tight for him in the tunnel, but he managed, hunkering down and sucking in his arse. Behind him, they saw the robot figure of Angelina, and suddenly realised she was *why* they could see. Light radiated from her robot nostrils.

"Can you do that?" said Svool, kicking Herbert on the leg with a *clang*.

"A cheap party trick," snorted Herbert in derision. "A *real* Robotic Special Friend doesn't lower himself to such trinkets of performance. Next, you'll be bringing on the dancing bears."

"Look," said Zoot, buzzing over to them in the gloom where long shadows sent spiders scampering up the walls. "I've been monitoring the atmosphere down here, and it's, er, dangerous. Our metal muppet over there wasn't kidding when he talked about poisons and toxins and nuclear waste. My scanners are showing huge caverns down here – no doubt through which we have to pass. And each one is full of... something."

"Something?"

"Yes."

"What kind of something?" said Lumar.

"Dangerous something," said Zoot.

"Let's get moving. The sooner we get out of this shithole, the sooner we can go home."

"Home!" wailed Svool, wiping away a tear from the corner of his eye. "Alas, a place I wish..." He stared down at the end of Lumar's pistol. He saw she had the primitive weapon cocked. The safety catch was off. And she had her finger on the delicate trigger.

"Don't fucking push it," she growled, forked tongue flickering. She turned to Zoot, and the PopBot glowed at her. "You're able to map out the internals to this place?"

"Yes. It is a labyrinth indeed. Herbert has certainly led us to the most dangerous craphole on the planet, by my reckoning. But I can scan no life. These toxic creatures he was babbling about, I cannot locate them."

"Maybe he was mistaken?" said Lumar, eyes narrowed again. "Zoot. You fly up ahead and navigate. I'll follow, and Svool can come behind me because... well, he's a useless moron..."

"I saved you!"

"Okay, I'll grant you a lucky shot and the balls to give it a go; but I wouldn't put my trust in you if I had to. You're flakier than a chocolate flake. Right, then Angelina can follow, and finally we have Herbert bringing up the rear."

"Why am I at the back?" snorted the horse. "It's those at the back who get picked off first by deranged toxic beasties! I've seen it, in the filmys at the Bacillus Port Filmy Showhouse."

"Yeah, well it's your fault we're in here. So you can take the greatest risk."

"Charming."

"And besides," smiled Lumar. "You obviously have the widest arse. I wouldn't like to get trapped behind you again during an impending rockfall, would I? So *you* go at the back. That way, your bulbous arse condemns nobody but yourself."

THEY WALKED FOR hours. Lumar padded along, alert, using Zoot's weak but effective travel lights and the projected glow from Angelina's nostril headlamps to light the way. The narrow tunnel ran through miles of rock, all rough-hewn and seemingly hacked by hand using primitive tools. The place had the air of long abandonment. Lumar couldn't decide if that was good or bad.

Before long the tunnel split into seven other tunnels. Zoot guided them, and they padded off into the darkness, heading down. Before long, one wall fell away in a jagged diagonal, and they walked alongside an underground river. It was wide and flat and dark, and flowed swiftly and without sound; without the light of Angelina's headlamps, they could have quite easily toppled in. The smell was much stronger here as well, and the group eventually halted on a natural stone platform overlooking what appeared to be a lake. Angelina shone her lights across the vast still water, but they could not make out any far shore.

"It's real creepy," said Svool, who seemed subdued now. The reality of the situation was encroaching past his ego and manic self-belief. He was starting to feel claustrophobic, and the smell did nothing to help him. His head hurt, and he was sure he could see modest fumes rising from the surface of the lake.

"I wouldn't like to fall in," murmured Lumar, nodding across the expanse.

"Rubbish!" beamed Herbert. "It's totally safe! I'd wager you could fall in, swim around, and get out just as happy as a punter on a fairground rollercoaster with a big stack of sticky candyfloss."

Svool looked at his horse. "You really are an annoying gimp," he said.

Herbert winked. "Better get used to it, buster. You've got me for the next thousand years."

Svool stared at the horse, then at the lake. An idea occurred to him. "I tell you what. Why don't *you* jump in and prove your theory correct? Go on. If you do it, I'll buy you a banana."

"An apple."

"What?"

"Horses like apples."

"Whatever," said Svool. "Go on, pal. *Jump in*. Let's see how long it takes you to melt..."

"Actually," said Zoot, whizzing over, "that's no over-exaggeration. I've just completed a toxic analysis of the lake, and of course the river that feeds it. It is highly dangerous. Lethal. Deadly. A killer. It would kill both you and Lumar instantly. And yes, it would melt Herbert – within about three minutes."

"What is it, then?" snorted Herbert.

"It's unrefined lirridium," said Zoot quietly.

"Unrefined... you mean *spaceship* fuel?" said Svool.

"Yes."

"Isn't that flammable?"

"It has its moments. In this state, it's more stable, but trust me, if you give it enough heat, or enough spark... *VOOM!* Goodbye Grandma." Zoot turned on Lumar. "So you need to put the pistols away. For good. If you fire them down here, you could ignite..."

"Yes?"

"Well, the whole damn mountain."

Carefully, Lumar packed away the pistols. She stared at Herbert, shaking her head.

"What?" he said. "*What?*"

They followed the edge of the lirridium lake for a while, and Svool jogged up to stand beside Lumar. "Hey," he said. "Why do you think all this is down here, then? An accident?"

"This is no accident."

"What is it, then?"

"This is something to do with Greenstar. Some massive underground reserve. Why? I don't know. But what I *do* know is it shouldn't fucking *be here*. It's just another example of their pollution, their control, and their open lack of respect for the land, the earth, the world."

"Heavy shit," said Svool, nodding.

"Like you'd ever understand, *poet.*"

They followed dank, low-roofed tunnels for hours. At one point, Svool touched the damp wall and then sniffed his fingers, frowning. "Zoot?"

"Yes, boss?"

"What's this? Can you give me an analysis?"

Zoot blipped and blopped, several blue lights flickered in his casing, and then he said, "That would be lirridium."

"Seeping through the walls?"

"It would appear that way."

"Is that dangerous?"

"Most certainly so."

"A chance of it exploding?"

"There is that distinct possibility."

"So the tunnels would flood with lirridium?"

"Yep."

"And we'd all die and bubble away into a melt-pot of organic smush?"

"I think that would be the end result."

"Shall we speed up?"

"I'd recommend that."

"*Now.*"

"Most certainly!"

They accelerated their pace, and as the path started to climb, a tiny flame of hope sprang into their hearts. But just as the tunnel reached a high point, they breached a rise, the walls closed in, and they plummeted back down into the depths of the mountain.

Once again they emerged onto a platform overlooking a mammoth lirridium lake. It shimmered softly in the light of the metal horse headlights, and filled them with a slow-growing terror. If all these billions of gallons of lirridium were to ignite... it'd be a fast game over. And a hot one.

Lumar padded up beside Svool and leaned close, her breath sweet, her scent suddenly making Svool snap round and stare into her deep green eyes. He smiled, but she said, "We're being watched."

"By who?"

"I don't know, dickhead."

Svool's ardour wavered, but he frowned, and looked into her eyes only inches from his own, and said, "This trip has really brought us together, hasn't it, Lu?" He saw her frown, tongue flickering, and hurriedly said, "What I mean is, I know you think I was pretty horrible to you back on *The Literati*. You think I'm a spoilt rich-but-talented bastard who always gets his own way; and I suppose I am and I did. Although it has to be said, my poetry was rather grand and I *was* welcomed as a genius in all four corners of the Quad-Galaxy..."

"Get to the point."

"Well, our feet really haven't touched the ground since we landed here, have they? It's been a mad, bad dash, an adventure of insane proportions. And now we're here, stuck in an underground mine or whatever it is, and I have to say – I notice you. I notice the way you move, the way you turn your head, the way you hold your body; I notice the sway of your hips when you walk – and what a fabulous sight that is to behold! I notice the shine in your eyes and the smile on your lips, the cute little flicker of your tongue and the way you twitch your little finger when you're thinking. I admire your bravery and your strength, and the fact that you never back down, no matter how big or tough the enemy seems to be." He stopped, and looked at her, embarrassed. Then he gave a little cough and realised it was probably better to be silent than to continue on his present course.

"So, you're perving on me?"

"No! I'm not perving on you. I'm trying to say..."

"Yes?" It was a wide, friendly smile, and Svool looked into her eyes, then quickly looked away.

"Er. I'm trying to say I... like you."

"I knew that. I suffered *hours* with your tongue down my ear back on the ship."

"No, no! I like you as *you*, as a person, as a beautiful person..."

"Is this going to take all day?" hissed Zoot. "Only there's somebody watching us."

"I know," said Lumar, rolling her eyes. "I've been trying to tell lover-boy here."

"Is he still trying to spit out his undying love for you?"

"Yeah, it looks that way."

"Hey!" snapped Svool. "I am bloody stood here, you know? I can hear everything you're saying."

"We know." Lumar grinned. "Look. Important things first. There's a far off ledge – *no don't look* – with a sort of cave on top of it. Huddled towards the back of the cave there's a person. At least, I think it's a person."

"Scans human to me," said Zoot.

"I suggest we keep on moving; maybe they're hiding..."

"Maybe it's a spy!" said Svool, eyes wide.

"Or a monster!" said Lumar, her own eyes widening.

"Now you're taking the piss."

"You're giving it away," said Lumar, smiling to take the sting out of her words. "We need to move on, Svool. There are more pressing matters at hand than your urgent need to get your end away."

"What? *What?*"

"Your urges, you know, like back on *The Literati*."

"Give me some *credit!*" he snapped.

"Why?"

"*Why?*"

"Yeah, why would I give you some credit? A man is defined by his actions. Your actions are, shall we say, less than heroic."

"I rescued you."

"After running away."

"There's no pleasing some people."

"Okay, okay, you came back for me," said Lumar, "and for that I am indeed thankful. However. Prior to that it has to be said, you were not exactly hero material. In fact, you were more of an academic pervert with an ego bigger than a Titan-Class Cargo Cruiser."

Svool looked glumly at the ground. "This isn't about

sex. It's about me waking up. About me growing as a person."

"If that *is* a monster in that cave, there'll be plenty of chances to show me how much of a man you are."

"No, what it is – I've faced death, now. When General Bronson was pointing that gun at me, and that tinkly music was playing, I *knew* I was going to die. There was no way I could win that battle. And, and, and, I kind of woke up; I was going to die, without achieving everything I'd wanted to achieve, without saying everything I'd wanted to say; and what I wanted to say the most, Lumar, was that I have feelings for you."

They were silent for a while, and she put her hand on his arm. "This is neither the time nor the place."

"Is there ever a right time or place?"

"Come on." She gave him a dazzling smile. "If we get out of these mines alive, then we can talk some more."

She set off up the narrow rocky trail, the still lirridium waters black in the underground cavern. Svool trudged along at the back, hands in the pockets of his sheriff costume, face forlorn and glum. Herbert the metal horse slowed his pace, dropping back to walk alongside Svool.

"You okay, buster?"

"No. Get lost."

"Awww, come on, buster. I'm only trying to help! I know how you feel. I know *exactly* how you feel. I know how you feel so bad it hurts! I know how you feel so bad it makes me want to shit nuts and bolts!"

Svool stopped, and stared at the robotic horse. "You're not helping," he said, through gritted teeth.

"I, too, have been in love," said the horse.

"How? How the hell has a rusted robotic heap of shit been in love? You're a fucking machine, mate. You're a collection of steel plates and cables. You have a battery, a sump, and a fuel pump. How, by all that's holy in Manna, can you have ever experienced my human emotions?"

Herbert leant close, and Svool could smell old engine oil. He winked. "I just have, buster." There came a whining, whirring noise as a leg jerked upwards in a succession of jarring, snapping jerks, and a hoof the size of a dinner plate slapped Svool on the back – in what Herbert probably thought was an act of camaraderie, but in practice almost sent Svool face-first into the lake of lirridium and certain death in the depths. "Come on! There's work to be done!"

During the course of the day-long trek, they stopped four or five times, and each time Lumar pointed out the figure watching them.

"How can it be the same person?" said Svool, looking down into his noodles.

They'd stopped for a rest, weary from incessant walking and the constant on-edge feeling of trekking alongside the world's greatest fuel tank. Rooting through Angelina's saddlebags, Lumar had found tins of beans and packets of noodles. Tipping noodles into a small pan, Herbert had opened a door in his flank and warmed the pan for them. The upside was they now had warm refreshing noodles to fill their empty grumbling bellies. The *downside* was they tasted of rotting sump oil.

"All I can think," said Lumar, "is that there's a complex of parallel tunnels that our spy is using to keep pace with us. Either that, or there's more than one person."

"You mean, like a tribe of fish-eyed monsters living down here?"

Lumar looked strangely at Svool. "Your mind works funny. You know that?"

Andy Remic 327

"Hey, that's why I'm such a fabulous poet! Us creative types, we're completely zany, you know." He said it with a straight face.

"Hmm."

"Zoot?" said Lumar.

"Yes?"

"Head back there. See if you can find a secondary tunnel network. Try and flush out our little spy up ahead. Let's see who's so interested in watching us."

"Is that such a wise idea?" said Svool.

"You'd prefer a bullet in the back of the skull?"

"Good point."

Zoot zipped off, and was swallowed by the darkness.

In silence, Lumar packed away the pan in her saddlebags and, with weary sighs, they moved on through the jagged tunnels.

It was a large square chamber, stacked high with metal slabs. Svool trotted forward and poked one, then frowned. "It's soft," he said.

"It looks like processed ore," said Lumar, checking behind and then looking ahead, her pistol up near her cheek. The chamber was perhaps a kilometre square, and stacked high with these metal slabs – each one about the size of a groundcar, and probably running to tens of thousands in number. They were set out in a grid, so that corridors ran off at regular intervals from what Lumar considered to be the main passage through.

"I don't like this," she said.

"A good place for an ambush?"

"Yeah. That's right." She took a good look at Svool. "I am astonished at your acumen."

"I'm not just a pretty face," he said.

"Yeah. Right."

They moved on, Herbert's plate-hooves clipping and clopping. Eventually, Lumar whirled on him. "Oy! Useless bastard who's going to get us all killed! Haven't you got a stealth mode or something?"

"I could, neigh, perhaps walk on my tippy toes?"

Lumar stared at him, then rubbed at her forehead. It was getting too much: everything, just creeping up on her a bit at a time. She wasn't built for this; this wasn't her goal. To be surrounded by idiots! All the time!

"Okay," she said, voice a low growl. "You walk on your tippy toes. That'll be great."

They drifted down silent, ghostly corridors. For Lumar, rather than the corridors adding to a sense of normality – compared with the rough-hewn rocky walls of the mines – instead, it seemed to add to her tension.

Lumar stopped. Her nostrils twitched. Something felt wrong. Her eyes narrowed, and up ahead, from the towering stacks of raw metal, stepped a child. She was small, and huddled under the rags that served as clothing. Her hair was long and matted, and her face was simply a mass of sores and open, weeping wounds.

"Urgh," said Svool.

Lumar turned, and kicked him in the balls. As Svool hit the ground and lay foetal, Lumar holstered her pistol and moved forward with hands spread out, a loving smile on her face, hoping to instil some kind of trust in the desolate little girl...

"It's okay," said the child.

"You're not frightened?" said Lumar.

"No. I've been following you. Watching you."

"Yes." Lumar nodded, and smiled again. "Are you okay? Do you need help?"

"No. This is where I live. This is where *we* all live."

Svool, grunting on the ground, rolled over and tapped Lumar on the calf muscle.

"Not now," she snapped, then back to the girl. "What's your name, child?"

"I am Chorzaranalista. Welcome to my home."

"Is she diseased?" wheezed Svool, managing to crawl to his knees. "Ask her, ask her if she's diseased. We don't want to" – he stared at her disfigured face with a shudder – "catch anything."

Chorzaranalista smiled. "No. I am not diseased," she said, and her great large eyes looked incredibly sad. "Come with me. I'll show you our home. Maybe then you'll understand."

She moved away, almost drifting, a tattered shawl around her shoulders. She moved like a ghost.

Svool got to his feet, hanging on to Herbert for support. He grimaced at Lumar. "What you fucking go and do that for?"

Lumar stared at him, and a tear rolled down her cheek. "Have you no soul?" she said, then whirled about and followed the girl down the corridor of metal slabs.

Svool stared after her, then back at Herbert. "Huh?"

"Don't look at me, buster. I just work here."

He spread his hands. "What did I do wrong? That deserved a kick in the balls?"

Herbert looked down his rusted equine nose at Svool, then shook his head. "I thought you had an imagination?"

"I do!"

"Well, use it," said Herbert, and clattered off after Lumar. Angelina sauntered over, offered her buttocks in Svool's direction, and emitted a long dribbling shit of black oil filled with metal shavings. Then she, too, followed the disfigured little girl.

Svool made a clucking noise, and fell in behind, trying to work out what he'd done wrong. He walked fast, and soon caught up with Angelina, but her huge swaying horse buttocks stopped him from passing in the relatively narrow confines of the corridor. He tried – unsuccessfully – to squeeze past her a few times, but always, strangely, she would sway one way or the other, and her great metal arse would whack him into the wall.

The journey lasted perhaps half an hour, through endless corridors of metal slabs and always heading gently downwards. Eventually they emerged by the banks of the lirridium river, only here there seemed to be some kind of mesh gate, a filtration pool of some kind; and rather than the still waters they'd seen before, it was a quagmire of crap, a giant lake of almost solid effluence, detritus, junk and garbage, which here went through some kind of filtration process and then carried on, beyond the gate, beyond the mesh, as pure, unsullied, de-chunked lirridium. Or its unrefined form.

Svool held his nose as he stumbled into the group once more, and holding his nose, he said, "By the Gods of Fuck, this surely stinks like a ten-week-dead whore after the rats have built nests inside her."

Chorzaranalista looked down at the ground; at her holed shoes, scuffed and battered and colourless. "This is my home," she said.

"You might have tidied up a bit, girl!" said Svool, looking around once more. "I mean, look at the mess!"

Chorzaranalista shrugged. "This is where I live. This is where I was born." Then she stared at Svool and his mouth clacked shut. She pointed, out over the gently bubbling lake of – *whatever it was*. Decades of filth had been filtered here, clogging back for God only knew how far inside the mountain. "I was born in there."

"Where?" said Svool, shading his eyes to take a closer look.

"In there."

"In that?"

"Yes."

"In that shit pit?"

"If that's what you want to call it."

"But it's a shit pit! How could you be born there?"

Zoot appeared, slamming from the darkness and braking with a hiss of superheated air. He spun, seemingly agitated. "Ah!" he said. "So. You found her. The girl, I mean. She's not human! Watch out! She's very, er, dangerous."

"Thanks for the early warning," said Lumar, pushing past the spinning PopBot. "Some defence mechanism *you* turned out to be!"

Chorzaranalista grinned suddenly, and ran her hands through her tangled, matted hair. The closer Lumar got to the child, the more she realised it wasn't actually hair. It looked more like metal strands. Wires. Cables. Copper and iron.

Chorzaranalista looked at Svool. "To answer your question, I was born in the tox. *Of* the tox."

"I don't get it."

"Let me show you."

Chorzaranalista moved to the edge of the lake. She lifted her hands and chanted, and spoke, her words floating back to Lumar and Svool, to Zoot, Herbert and Angelina. "All life is an accident. Throughout the Quad-Gal Bubble, this has been demonstrated time and time and time again. You, Svool, are of human descent; and yet all humans evolved from a chemical soup. A soup of proteins and toxins and shit. Yes, that's right, Svool. You were born from shit."

"Tush!" he said. Lumar presumed he was disagreeing.

"And so were we," she said, as out of the toxic waste rose what appeared to be huts, tiny igloos of waste, green and brown and putrid, a rotting organic slurry; slowly, the huts came to rest on the surface of the waste pool and Lumar, standing by the edge, knelt down.

She reached forward, and her hand sank into the thick soupy substance. It wasn't solid, and yet the children who emerged from the small huts walked across the surface as if by magic. There were about thirty of them, some male, some female, each seemingly modelled on a human child and yet with subtle differences; some had long tentacles drooping down from their faces, as if a human face had merged with an octopus. Some had teeth made of glass, or an elephant's trunk for a nose, or ears like butterfly wings. And each one appeared to be an open, festering toxic sore, a platter of pus and disease and gangrenous, rotting matter.

"I think we should run," muttered Svool to Lumar.

"Shh!"

"Where would you run to?" said Chorzaranalista. She was smiling, and it was a friendly smile, but Svool didn't trust anything that had more teeth than him. In fact, he didn't trust anything with less teeth than him. He basically trusted nobody but himself.

More toxic children – children born of the toxicity – emerged from the corridors surrounding Svool, Lumar, Zoot, Angelina and Herbert. Herbert started to issue a strange, fear-filled braying.

And from the huge bubbling lake, yet more pods began to rise. Ten at first, then twenty, then fifty. Then more than Lumar could count. The entirety of the lake was filled with toxic huts, and from them came a flood of diseased and deformed creatures that looked like human children, but who smiled with black rubber teeth, and had old pieces of car tyre welded into their skulls. Lumar and Svool saw fingers made from pencils, faces inset with shards of glass, broken bottles, old alarm clocks; bones from different creatures poking out at odd angles from their own flesh – and they knew, knew that what walked and ambled before them was an army not of human children, but of creatures, evolved beings made from the very toxic waste itself...

The figures moved in tight, non-aggressive but threatening them with their very natures. And Svool, Lumar, Herbert and Angelina shuffled backwards in a rapidly shrinking circle. In an act of great heroism, Zoot slammed off high into the air and disappeared amongst the columns and corridors of slab metal.

"That's right!" screamed Svool suddenly, waving his fist. "You run away, you bloody PopBot coward! You're fired! You hear me? Bloody fired!"

"Shut up," said Lumar through clenched teeth. She held her pistol, but held it low, pointing at the ground. After all, how many could she shoot before they overwhelmed her? Before they put out her eyes, bit off her cheeks and ate her brains?

Suddenly, the advance seemed to bubble to a halt. There were thousands of them. *Thousands* of the children of the slime.

Chorzaranalista smiled as she moved close to Lumar. So close, they could have kissed.

"We have seen you, Lumar. And you, Svoolzard Koolimax XXIV. We have seen you in our dreams. We are the psi-children of the Waste. We know your every thought and feeling, every dream and emotion and memory. We have seen you. We have dreamed you. You have been in our prayers."

"You want us to do something?" said Lumar.

"We need your help."

"To do what?" whispered Svool, face filled with fear.

"We want the Greenstar Factory Hub. We're going to drag it all the way down into our toxic world..."

FOURTEEN

JENNY XI – NAKED, battered, torn, wounded, exhausted, frightened – crawled for hours, and hours, and hours. The tubes were narrow and uncomfortable and sharp, and kept nipping at her flesh, slicing her here, cutting her there, until she screamed her frustration at their constant biting and fell onto her arms, onto her stolen pistol, and slept.

RANDY CRAWLED, BITTERNESS and hate in his mind. But that was not the only thing.

You're slacking, said Renazzi Lode, the Greenstar Director. He had her with him. In his head. She could see what he saw, hear what he heard, feel what he felt. It was a total mindfuck. An mRape, they called it in the barracks. When he'd been a soldier. Before he became a spy. Before he became the Governor of Internal Affairs. Back then, it had been a simpler time. Before he had his *boss* in his head.

Yeah. Back then had been a much *better time.*

What are you thinking about? came the suspicious voice of Renazzi Lode.

Nothing.

You sure?

Oh, yes.

Shit. Great. Bastard. Bitch! Just what he needed. It was one thing to go on a terrible mission; another to go on a terrible mission with your throat half-ripped out. But to have your boss in your head as you did it? It was the ultimate in managerial observation tools, and to be fair to Renazzi Lode, it was used in many a "profession" where a boss might want to keep *a very close eye* on an employee. LET US FUCK WITH YOUR EMPLOYEES, went the marketing slogan for iSPY, the "spying solution for all managerial needs." LET'S WATCH THEM TOGETHER! LET'S SEE WHAT THEY GET UP TO! LET'S CHECK THEY DO THEIR JOB PROPERLY! LET'S REMOVE THEIR MOTIVATION, CREATIVITY, AND INDIVIDUALITY AND SHOW THEM THE LACK OF RESPECT THEY DESERVE. THE FUCKERS.

Randy had added that last bit himself.

Randy had a friend who'd been a teacher. Damn good at his job, teaching at the New Space Academy in London, Earth. The kids loved him, and he loved his job. And one day some engineers had arrived, just as he was teaching *Astro Macbeth*, and installed video surveillance equipment in his classroom, much to the amusement of his pupils – until he pointed out to them that they wouldn't be able to get up to any mischief either.

After the lesson, he visited the Head. This was how the conversation went:

"What's with the video surveillance equipment?"

"That would be for your own protection."

"How so?"

"In case anything happens in the classroom."

"Such as?"

"A pupil attacking you." Mr Bob, for 'twas his name, looked down at himself. He was six foot five inches, and used to play quarter back for the London Olympic Stags.

"I've never been attacked."

"You might."

"What you mean to say is, 'it's there to protect the kids.' Go on. What have I done that you don't trust me any longer?"

"Nothing. It's just a surveillance measure."

"*But I don't like it.*"

"Why not?"

It was actually a valid question, and Mr Bob had to search inside himself for a long, long time to find the answer. "It's about freedom," he said. "It's about trust. It's about professionalism. It's about stress. It's about permission." He shrugged. "You've read Orwell, right?"

"Wasn't he that corrupt politician?"

"*No.* Look, I just want it noting that I don't like it, okay?"

"Your comments have been duly registered, Mr Bob."

Mr Bob left, muttering, and spent the next month being watched 24/7. And he proved that he was indeed trustworthy, and professional, and honourable, and that his lessons were great fun and his relationship with the kids provided for lots of learning. But iSPY had just developed *their new managerial monitoring system,* the FU-ckU/ v1.2. Mr Bob had it installed in his head. And for two weeks, all day, every day, Mr Bob had his boss in his head *with him* during every single lesson, offering a constant stream of advice, tweaking his performance and offering constant and permanent happy appraisal! It was a manager's wet dream. And better than reality TV.

After two weeks, Mr Bob walked in the Head's office, fired up a set of petrol hedge-clippers on the third pull of the starter-cord, and, amidst accelerating shouts of panic and alarm, proceeded to trim the head's hair. From the neck up.

Randy had visited him in the clink. "They pushed me too far," moaned Mr Bob, head in his hands. And Randy had made soothing noises, but now, finally, he knew how Mr Bob had felt. *You don't get the best results from fucking over your staff! You don't get superior performance by shitting on those below you! Just... leave them alone to do their fucking jobs!*

And now. Oh, the irony.

Did you hear that?

What?

The scream? Frustration?

Randy narrowed his eyes, and he *wanted* to think to himself – I'll show you frustration when I see you again, bitch. I'll shove this pistol sideways up your arse! But he knew he could not. She was crawling inside his head like an electric ant, poking into every tiny place, into every orifice. He could feel her scratching across the outer surface of his brain. He could feel her raping through his memories. It hurt him. Hurt him more than the hole in his throat. Hurt him more than his lost–then-badly-rebuilt face.

Dammit!

Go on, up ahead. Move fast, now...

Renazzi... please... give me some mental space! You're sending me mad!

Meaning? He could not believe how frosty the words were as they tumbled over themselves in his skull. And now her anger came. Now, her rage. It pounded the inside of his brain like an enraged tomcat trying to escape from inside a dustbin.

I need you out! Out of my fucking skull! What do you hope to achieve? What do you get out of giving me this little bit more torture? Do you think I'll thank you for it? Do you think I'll buy you chocolates and an expensive fizzy wine?

No. But I will give you this...

The mental blast slammed Randy, and now it was his turn to scream. He could not lift his arms up to grasp his head, such were the confines of his entrapment, but if he could have, he would.

Panting, and drooling, his throat a raw agony, head pounding, face a constant burning field of napalm, Randy Zaglax struggled on through the narrow tube, struggled on, squirming and fighting his way forward in search of Jenny...

Good boy, chuckled Renazzi.

WHY DO YOU hate your father?

Oh, well, that's a long story. A complicated story.

Well, why do you hate your brother?

Longer. More complicated. More savage.

And your mother?

Poor dead mother. Don't cry for me, darling.

And... your sister.

Nixa? Poor sweet dead Nixa. I'll cry for you, honey. We'll all cry for you.

AND AGAIN.

Why do you hate your father?

Oh, well, that's a long story. A complicated story.

Why do you hate him?

I hate him because...

Go on. Explain it to me. Was it because of the drink? The womanising? More drink? The whiskey bottle, constantly stuck to his lips like a baby bottle? He'd glug it down, couldn't get enough, stagger down the middle of the road with groundcars swerving around him, then fall over outside his own house, piss in his pants, sleep on the concrete. Isn't that right? ISN'T THAT RIGHT?

Nixa. You came back.

Why do you hate him, Jenny?

I hate him because he died. I hate him because he left me. I hate him because... I love him so much.

JENNY HELD HIS hand. It was warm. Too warm. Warm with the fever. She looked down into his eyes. They were watering, and weak, so unlike the strength he had once shown. Strength, and a love for his country. His world. Amaranth. Beautiful Amaranth...

"I want... to say. Something."

She looked down with pity, and her own tears fell into his eyes. They shared an intimacy that only incoming death can bring. A total intimacy that made a mockery of words.

"Of course," she whispered, her lips trembling with fear; because it was Old Tom, her father, her dad, the man who held her in his arms when she was frightened, the man whom she snuggled up to, smelling of tobacco and whiskey, his whiskers rasping against her skin and making her squeal. And he was as big as a giant, bigger than God; bigger than the world. Swimming in the sea, he supported her weight and stopped her sinking under the waves. In the woods, he pushed branches out of her way and lifted her over fallen trunks. When riding her bike he was there, holding the saddle and laughing as she weaved a random track, learning her balance. But he was always there. To stop the fall.

How could he die?

How?

"I love you, Jenny. You know that, don't you? I've always loved you. Ever since I held you as a babe. I couldn't cut the cord – you know that? The midwives laughed at me. I said I was frightened of hurting you." He started to cough, and endured a savage coughing fit. She held a handkerchief to his mouth. It came away with spots of blood.

She held his hand. It was huge. How could a man with such huge, strong hands die? It was impossible. They were wrong. The doctors had to be wrong. After all, what did they know?

"I want you to promise me something," he said. His eyes were distant. Milky. Dreaming.

"Anything. Anything at all."

"I want you to save Amaranth. Save our world. Make it green again."

"I will. I promise."

Old Tom smiled then. And his eyes closed. And he died.

"I WILL. I promise."

Jenny opened her eyes. She was shivering. Freezing cold, fingers and toes frozen and stiff. Something smelled funny. Something smelled... *bad*. And then she realised. She knew the scent. Knew that scent more than her own. It was Randy Zaglax, the pampered poodle without a face. She should have known. He'd spent enough hours trying to smooch up to her with the sole intention of getting her into bed. Now, the only bed she'd be willing to share would be a coffin.

She started forward again, and then froze as fingers closed around her ankle.

"Gotcha," he said.

She lifted her knee, and drove her free foot as hard as she could into his patchwork face. There came a breaking sound, and Randy screamed, long and loud. She stomped him again. He screamed again. It gave her some small satisfaction.

Jenny scrambled forward as fast as she could, pistol still gripped tight in one chilled hand, claustrophobia a cold dark mistress in her chest. Her mouth was full of her panicked heart.

"I'm going to kill you, whore!" shrieked Randy. He fired his own pistol, and a bullet whined and whizzed up the tube. It hissed past Jenny so close she felt the spin and heat of the bullet. This sent another burst of panic firing through her. How many shots would it take in such a confined space to hit her?

Another shot whined past, bouncing from the inside of the tube and sending sparks shrieking.

Jenny was sobbing now, and she stopped, and tried to focus. She rolled onto her back, opened her legs in a most undignified posture, and pointed the gun, like a black metal dick, and fired from her own crotch into the darkness of the tunnel.

There was a pause, and a *slap*, and Randy started screaming, screaming so long and hard that Jenny thought her ears would bleed. She scrambled along again, arms and legs, elbows and knees raw and scraped and bruised and battered – and suddenly the ground seemed to give way, and Jenny was falling amidst a tumble of what felt like polystyrene planks.

She hit hard tiles with a slap and lay there, stunned. Like a fish on a block.

Slowly, she rolled onto her back and stared up at the hole through which she'd tumbled. Shivering, aching, fear raw in her mind and stomach, she lifted her gun and aimed and focussed and waited.

Randy appeared, slick with blood, his twisted rebuilt face manic and inhuman. Jenny fired, one-two-*three-four-five* shots, and gunsmoke drifted, and Randy had gone.

Jenny climbed to her feet and looked around. She was in some kind of kitchen. The floor was made of hard white tiles, small squares which stretched off to walls of polished stainless steel. Steel benches lined the walls, littered with pans. Everything gleamed as if some maniac with a love of polish had been at work. The kitchen wasn't in use; no pans bubbled, no happy chefs tossed salads or pared meat from bone. It was deathly still, quiet as the grave, cold as a corpse.

Jenny walked, feet slapping, and found a door. It led to a corridor, and the corridor led to more rooms. She peered through glass squares in each door, and the third one down was some kind of locker room. She tried the handle, stepped inside, and started going through the lockers. There was a wide range of different outfits, mainly of the chef or kitchen orderly variety, and thankfully Jenny pulled on baggy white pants and a cotton smock. She found white pumps, which she gratefully pulled onto her freezing feet, and all of a sudden she felt less vulnerable. A little bit of her confidence returned.

"You've been through a lot, girl," she murmured, eyes narrowing. "Now it's time to finish this thing." But she could still hear Flizz's screams echoing in her ears. Still see Sick Note's face as the chainsaw came down on him, and his blood splattered the ground. Her face twisted into a nasty grimace and she looked up, looked around. "I'm going to bring you all down, motherfuckers. Going to give you a taste of your own sour medicine."

It took her three hours to find the cell block. Most of the blocks were automated, and Randy's magical set of keys unlocked *everything*. He was high-ranking, that was for sure. A regular ziggurat type of guy, no doubt with a CV as long and fictional as it was fancy and stencilled. In the end, sick of searching endless corridors and empty kitchens – *What was this place? It felt like a complex waiting to be filled with an army!* – she found a terminal in an empty office, which smelt of polish and wax and air freshener, and she sat and booted up the computer and, using the codes on Randy's keys, managed to find herself a map of the complex. It was big. No. BIG. Her eyes scanned the images, and noted the underground private train system which linked most of the major cities on Amaranth with the Greenstar Factory Hub.

"Bingo," she said, without any form of smile or self-congratulation. But she *had* found it. The base of operations.

The Factory Hub.

But first?

She needed backup.

Now, however, she'd come across a problem. Three guards, seated around a steel table, reading. She really didn't want to kill them, but... hell. They'd put a bullet in her skull first chance they got.

Luck was on her side. A comm buzzed and one of the guards had a heated conversation. Cursing, he scraped back his chair and disappeared into the depths of the prison block complex. A few minutes later, one of the remaining guards stood and stretched, complaining about his back. "I'm going for a piss. Hold the fort."

Jenny followed him at a discreet distance, sneaking into the restroom thirty seconds behind him and thanking her lucky stars that he'd locked himself in a cubicle. She decided to work on the shock principle.

The shot blasted a hole in the steel door and punched a hole in the tiles six inches from the man's head. When Jenny kicked the door open, it smacked him in the face and he sat back down on the toilet, pants still round his ankles, blood pouring from a broken nose.

"Don't kill me," he said, clamping the bridge of his nose between thumb and fingers.

Jenny advanced. She smiled. "All I need is information," she said.

Five minutes later, the guard with the broken nose, relieved of his weapon – which sat in Jenny's belt – stopped outside a blank steel door. It was heavy duty, reinforced with bars, and Jenny smiled nicely at the guard. His comrade was unconscious back at the desk, a copy of a pulp paperback covering his face, his hands and feet tied tight with wire.

As the door opened, the man within rose like a ponderous mountain. He had dark skin and wore simple prison clothes. He'd been beaten badly, his nose was still bent, but his eyes were bright and filled with fire.

"Jenny!"

"Zanzibar. Come on. I'm breaking you out."

"I knew you'd come."

He grinned at her, and in that face, in that smile, in that *connection,* Jenny realised she was back; back with her family. Zanzibar stepped out of the cell, and stretched, and glared at the guard. He grinned, and it was the grin of a shark. The guard visibly flinched.

"You okay, girl?"

Jenny nodded, and burst into tears.

JENNY STOOD HOLDING her pistol, and stared at her squad. What *remained* of her squad. Her *friends.* There was Meat Cleaver, stocky, his eyes narrow and slanted, looking almost naked without his trademark knives and sharpened *meat cleaver.* Nanny was there, face wrinkled, hair hacked into a crew cut, haggard, shoulders square, almost a *cube* of muscle, but looking even more fearsome in the harsh glare of the prison. Bull was there, a short stocky man with angry eyes, an angry face and a horde of facial tattoos.

And then there was Zanzibar. Her old comrade. Her old friend. They'd been in it together; from the start. Through training, field ops, bombing raids; they'd saved each other's arses a hundred times. He was a dark-skinned man-mountain, hair short-cropped and brown, eyes so deep they were pools of velvet.

"Flizz?" he said.

Jenny shook her head, looking at the ground.

"What about Sick Note?" asked Nanny, her voice a soft rumble. There'd always been rumours about her and Sick Note, which they'd both vehemently denied. And not just because it was against squad protocol; they both seemed embarrassed at the *notion* of love, as if it would destroy their "hard man" image.

"I'm sorry," said Jenny, looking at the ground again.

Nanny made a strangled sound. "How did he die?"

"It wasn't... good."

"*How did he die?*" There was a furious light, like the eternal fires of Hell, in Nanny's eyes.

"With a chainsaw. At the hands of a woman called Vasta. She's the Head of Security."

"I will kill her."

Jenny nodded, and took a deep breath, and looked up at Zanzibar. He was staring at her, head tilted to one side.

"You have a plan?" he said.

"This place is linked to the Greenstar Factory Hub by an underground train network. All the major Greenstar places are slotted into this crazy spider's web they've built. But what I also saw, in the schematics, was a network of pipes running from the Hub to every damn Greenstar base, carrying lirridium fuel to large tanks – I mean *large* tanks – which resupply Shuttles and Dumpers. You see where I'm going with this?"

"Detonate the Hub, a chain reaction should feed through the pipes and take out every Greenstar base on the planet." Zanzibar's eyes were shining. "Sounds dangerous, though."

"Certainly," said Jenny.

"Suicidal, in fact."

"Without a shadow of a doubt."

"But we cleanse the planet of Greenstar."

"Guys?" Jenny Xi looked around at what remained of her squad. "We've been through some shit together. Through some pain. I am going to the Greenstar Factory Hub. And I'm going to blow it, or die trying. I don't expect any of you to follow; you have your own lives to lead. In three minutes, I leave this room, and I won't think anything less of those who choose to walk away."

"I'm with you," growled Nanny. "I want some fucking payback."

"Me as well," rumbled Meat Cleaver.

Bull gave a grunt, which Jenny knew from experience was an affirmative. Once again tears sprang to her eyes; but these were tears of love, and a feeling that she was part of a union, a joyous need to do the right thing and get the right thing done.

She looked to Zanzibar. He was grinning, despite the torture on his face. "We're all with you, little lady. Just lead the way."

Jenny gave a nod, approached the guard and put a pistol to his head. "First, we need the armoury. If you'd be so good as to give us directions."

"We have no armoury here," said the guard.

Jenny lowered the pistol and put a bullet in his shoulder. Blood exploded. Shards of shoulder blade hung from the wound. The guard gasped, dropping to one knee, but Zanzibar grabbed him and hoisted him up.

"I think you should take us to it," said Jenny, little more than a whisper.

"Okay," said the guard, lips trembling, blood leaking between his fingers.

"Let's move," said Jenny.

BOOTS THUDDED DOWN the polished steel corridors. Jenny, Zanzibar, Meat Cleaver, Bull and Nanny were now dressed in black combat fatigues, courtesy of Greenstar's secret armoury, and carried a range of D4 shoguns, SMKK machine guns and Techrim 11mm pistols. They had packs full of HighJ explosives, and Nanny had treated herself to Kekra Quad Barrel Machine Pistols. It had been a particularly well-equipped armoury.

"How did you know they'd have such a stash of hardware?" rumbled Bull, as they stopped at a corridor intersection and crouched, weapons bristling and covering arcs of fire.

"Greenstar sort out their own problems. Each and every factory has a stash that makes the Amaranth Regular Army look like chicken farmers. It's almost as if... they're preparing for a war."

"Maybe it's a precaution in case the other planets of Manna decide they no longer want to allow Greenstar to abuse the ecology of this world?"

Jenny nodded. "If politics fail, then they will resort to violence. Yes. I can see the logic in that; after all, it's the way it's always been with politicians, down the ages. Fucking scumbags. All in it for the power, the glory... and the money. Especially the money."

"Let's move."

They sprinted down another corridor and stopped, peering down a stationary escalator. Below them, they could just see the edge of a platform – like any underground train station. Only this was for the internal use of Greenstar staff only.

Jenny made several hand gestures, and led the way down the escalator, treading softly, SMKK in her hands. The schematics had shown that the trains were automated; but that didn't mean they weren't guarded. But then, this place was hardly a hive of bustling activity. Jenny felt suddenly uncertain about what would happen when they reached the Greenstar Hub – after all, it was central. The core of all Greenstar's Amaranth activities. They'd have to leave the train early, do the last few hundred metres on foot. See if there were access tunnels they could use to bypass what was surely a "central" station.

Reaching the bottom of the escalator, Jenny stopped, Zanzibar by her shoulder. Something felt wrong. It was just too easy. Too quiet. Did they know the escaped ECO terrorists were on a new warpath to destroy Greenstar in totality? Or were they tied up with some other problem?

Jenny motioned to Zanzibar, and she veered left down the cold, deserted – but sparkling clean – platform. Zanzibar went right. Meat Cleaver followed Jenny, and Nanny followed Zanzibar. Bull turned and covered the escalators with his SMKK, his face set and hard, eyes focused.

Jenny reached the end of the platform, but it was deserted. She signalled back to Zanzibar, who also confirmed no activity; they jogged back to the centre of the platform and peered into the dark hole of the tunnel.

"So we wait," said Zanzibar.

"They know we're coming."

"I, also, have this feeling." Zanzibar slapped her on the back. "Into the lion's den, little lady. Don't worry overmuch. We'll give them a taste of their own toxicity; that is a promise."

Jenny nodded, ran a hand through her hair, and checked her weapon. It was new, and stiff, still showing traces of manufacturer's grease and PASS testing stickers. *It's like they're waiting for a war... preparing for a day when each and every factory or base will have to defend itself with an army.* There'd been enough weapons in the armoury to indeed equip an army; five armies, if the truth be told. Certainly many, many battalions.

Within minutes, they heard the train rattling down the tracks. It roared from the tunnel, decelerating with incredible force and noise. It was a single carriage, and it was empty. The doors slid open with a hiss.

"Too easy," muttered Jenny.

"Like stepping into the jaws of a beast," said Zanzibar. "And yet we must do it."

"I know. Let's go..."

"You're not going anywhere," said a strangled, pain-filled voice, and Jenny's head swung up fast. There was a clatter of a grille, and Randy Zaglax crawled from the narrow pipe with his pistol trained on Jenny's face. He was soaked in blood, presumably his own. One arm hung limp by his side, the other held the pistol. However, despite his ragged, battered, torn appearance, the whistle and hiss of air moving through his torn throat as well as his lipless mouth, and the sodden footfalls on the platform from his blood-soaked feet, his one good arm, holding the gun, was straight and true and steady.

Jenny felt Zanzibar tense by her side, but raised a hand. "No!" snapped her command, and everything fell into languid, honeyed slow motion. Jenny lowered her own weapon, which had snapped up the moment she heard Randy's voice, and her eyes narrowed, fixed on Randy.

"You can't stop us," she said.

"Oh, but I can."

"If you shoot me, my squad will drill you full of bullets. You'll be dead, Randy. Dead and gone and wasted."

Randy's rebuilt face twisted in pain, and he twitched, the fingers of his limp arm clawing his leg spasmodically. "No!" he hissed. "Stop it! Stop telling me what to do! Get out of my fucking head!"

"We still clear on the escalator?" said Zanzibar from the corner of his mouth.

"Yeah," growled Bull.

"You have two minutes before the train departs," came a mellow female voice over the speaker system. The train sat on its tracks, humming gently to itself. It seemed almost to vibrate, as if in eagerness to be off on its journey.

Randy's gun wavered now, and then sharply rose, the heel of his palm rubbing against his own forehead. His pistol was pointing at the ceiling. Zanzibar made a gesture to kill, but Jenny waved him down. She approached Randy.

"Hey. Randy?"

His gaze snapped back to her. His eyes were rolling and crazy. Saliva pooled from his lips, falling down his bloodied chest.

"No! No, I won't do it, I don't care, you can only push a fucking man so much and *you've gone beyond a fucking joke, bitch!*"

The gun was waving around manically, and Jenny lifted her own weapon. Randy had passed beyond sanity and she could see he was a danger to everybody. Even himself. She made a grim decision. It was with no joy she would have to kill him... maybe once, when he'd been sane and evil; but not now. Not like this. This would be like putting down a rabid dog. Simply a necessary act that had to be done. Complete. Finished. A necessary kill...

"Wait!"

Randy's hand slammed up, gun still pointing at the ceiling, and his lips were twisting silently as if speaking impossible words. And then he fixed Jenny with a look that she would never forget until her dying day. It was like a man looking out from behind a mask. Utter, total, cold sanity stared out through those bloodshot, watering eyes. Randy looked out at her from the cage of his own mind; from a torture cell of his own making.

"I'm sorry," he said, through the blood and the spittle.

Jenny stared, unsure of what to say.

"I'm truly sorry I did those things to you. I'm sorry about everything that happened. I had a madness upon me." Then he seemed to relax. He was breathing deeply, the hole in his throat whistling. "It all got fucked up. Can't you see? I went beyond the mortal realm. Into Hell." He laughed. "Go, Jenny. Detonate the lirridium pumps at the Hub!" His gun turned on himself, and a single shot rang out. There came a *chink* as the shell casing bounced on the hard tiled floor of the station. Randy's body crumpled straight down in a heap, and blood leaked from the bullet hole as his pulped brains dribbled like a streamer of jellied mush.

"Shit," breathed out Jenny, and turned to Zanzibar.

"Jenny?" whispered Randy.

Slowly, very slowly, she turned back to the corpse. The eyes were lifeless. Gone to another realm. But the mouth was moving, tongue flickering, teeth chewing spasmodically.

"Yes?"

"Come to us, girl. Come to us at the Greenstar Hub... we want to watch you die!" Randy's lips and voice made a high-pitched cackling sound, and then were still.

"Holy Mother of Manna," said Zanzibar, and made the sign of the protective horn. "She possessed the dead!"

"Who did?"

"Renazzi Lode. The Director. I recognised her voice!"

"Thirty seconds until departure," came the mellow voice of the train's simple AI brain.

"INCOMING!" yelled Bull suddenly from the foot of the escalators. Machine guns screamed. Bull's SMKK rattled, return fire ejecting from the barrel, bullets yammering up the incline and punching three guards from their feet. Bullets kicked shattered tiles from the tunnel wall, punching dust into the air, sending shards flying outwards.

Then there came a dull bass *WHUMP*. Bull was picked up, folded into a ball, and tossed across the space. He hit the back wall of the tunnel with a slap. There was a rattle like machine-gun fire, but it was Bull's bones snapping within the pulped skin ball of his body. He fell onto the tracks, instantly dead.

"Onto the train!" screamed Jenny, and the remaining members of the squad backed onto the train, guns blazing. Zanzibar shot out the windows and they hunkered down between benches, guns yowling across the platform. Guards came sprinting down the escalator, wearing body armour and helmets. Their own guns were roaring. Bullets screamed like jungle insects.

And there was Vasta, cool, calm, walking between the guards and holding... an E3 Accelerator.

Jenny's gun trained on Vasta, but her bullets seemed to worm around the woman, failing to puncture her flesh.

"Time for departure." The door shuddered shut, peppered with bullet holes.

The train gave a sudden jerk, then a lurch, and accelerated rapidly into the tunnel opening. Jenny turned, breath caught in her throat, and saw Vasta run, leaping down onto the tracks. The Head of Security turned the E3 Accelerator into the darkness... and the remainder of Jenny's squad ducked down, heard the painful dull WHUMP... and for a second, nothing seemed to happen. Then the rear of the train screamed and steel compressed and the train bunched up into an alloy-and-steel fist, slamming towards Jenny, whose mouth was open in an O of shock and surprise...

I never thought I'd die this way...

I never thought it would end this way...

And the darkness of the tunnel seemed to last forever.

FIFTEEN

SVOOL WAS EXHAUSTED. Never had he felt so tired. Not even when he'd slept with the Sixteen Sluts from the Wheels of Hell, drunk a full three litres of Jataxa Spirit and taken enough drugs to drop a platoon, before going on to pen (what was widely agreed to be) one of the greatest Saga Poems of the millennium, in a fit of alcohol and drug-fuelled debauchery which left his sexual health in tatters, but garnered him considerable respect from his peers. No, not even that *blip* on his chart of insanity could match the utter, total, complete sense of emptiness, hollowness and despair that now filled him from crown to crotch with the direst exhaustion. He stumbled along, often held up by Lumar who was there for him, strong for him, mopping his brow and helping his legs motivate.

They had marched for days. Through caverns and tunnels, through mines and stairs and portals and up and down sheer rock chimneys. After a day, Herbert and Angelina had been left behind, for the under-mountain terrain had become narrow and impassable for them, breaking down into crawl-tunnels through which only Svool and Lumar could squeeze. So they had parted – but not before Herbert had blown Svool a big, oily, sloppy kiss, winked, and said he'd catch up with him *real* soon. After all, they had a nine-hundred-and-ninety-nine-year relationship to look forward to. Svool had scowled and looked less than impressed, and even as they left in a steel boat across a deep lake of lirridium, Herbert had blown yet another kiss and waved a sheet of metallic, hole-punched paper at him.

"What was that?" said Lumar, eyes narrowed.

"My deed of ownership," said Svool miserably.

"Meaning what?"

"Meaning he'll find me, no matter where I go. Curse Metal Mongrels, Inc. Curse their mad robotic creations of Hell!"

That had been two days previously. Now, Svool was ready to weep. No. It was worse than that, and he never thought he'd be willing to voluntarily shuffle off his own mortal coil; but dammit. He was ready to chuck it all in and die.

Svool staggered on, lost in a private world of pain and suffering and misery. The cool breeze helped soothe his skin, but it really was a disgrace, really was asking *too much* of a poet and future awesome film star of the Quad-Gal. His cowboy boots clattered on the metal walkway, but he felt weak at the knees and almost collapsed. He grabbed at a metal rail and again Lumar was there, bless her little cotton lizard socks, there to help him along as he murmured on the edge of reason and understanding. And then bright lights dazzled him, and he dropped to his knees, and vomited again, and no matter how much Lumar urged him on he just lay there and sank, swiftly and with welcoming arms, into a state of deep unconsciousness.

WHEN HE OPENED his eyes, Svool was in a bed. He stared at the ceiling for a while, luxuriating in what he could only describe as the most unbelievable comfort he had ever experienced. No more walking. No more crawling. No more starving. No more pain... and then the pain *did* hit him, and it was a pain of chafed skin, of blisters, of tiny cuts and scratches and bruises that seemed to run up and down his entire body.

"Urgh. Where am I?"

"Hello, Svool!" It was Zoot, hovering at the foot of the bed. Zoot seemed to be glowing pink, which was the colour he always used when extremely happy about the entire Manna Galaxy and everything happening within it.

"What's going on, PopBot?"

"We've been found! Rescued! By a crack military team of military crack specialists! After your horrible terrible crash, the Shamans sent out search parties, and all these bulky heroic soldier types have been scanning the waves and sands and mountains for you, beloved Svoolzard, the greatest of poets."

"So... they found us?"

"Yes! Isn't it wonderful!"

"So... our adventure is... over?"

"YES!"

"So, no more, y'know, adventures with Lumar?"

"Correctamundo!"

Svool's head was buzzing. It felt familiar and yet alien at the same time. He forced out several words, but they slurred into a slurry of oblivion. His vision started to waver uncontrollably. "What's wrong with me?" he managed, through thick rubber lips.

"Oh, the soldiers brought you lots of pampering, Turkey Whiskey – which they've fed to you intravenously – and 10mg of SLAP, a snort of TWAT and a hefty dollop of SPUNK. All delivered straight to your no-doubt pining and drained drug-fuelled metabolism!"

"No, oh, no!" groaned Svool, sinking back on his bed with his head spinning. And that was the feeling, and it felt bad, and he realised – suddenly – that during his time on Amaranth, on *Toxicity*, in a massive ironic reversal, he had thrown off the shackles of his internal toxicity – his drug dependency. He'd gone cold turkey and survived. And now the bastards had force-fed him another circulatory system full of shite.

Claws tried to drag him back down to sleep, but instead he forced his legs out of bed and stood up, swaying. He was naked, but that didn't matter. Giggling, a horde of young hellakunga girls came stumbling in, long breasts wobbling like streams of jelly.

"Ooh, Svool, remember us?"

"The times we had!"

"The suckling we did!"

"Your tongue is so horny!"

"Your hands are so thorny!"

"Come and sit on my face!"

"Can I sit on your face?"

"Oooh, Svool, recite us some poetry!"

"Want to feel this? Touch this? Squeeze this?"

"Gah," said Svool, and pushed his way through the quivering jelly-flesh, a selection of nubbins and lots of nuzzling warm noses. Outside, in a sterile alloy corridor, where it was so cold Svool's breath emerged as smoke, Lumar L'anarr was waiting, her green eyes focused on him. She was dressed in fresh combat fatigues and looked... incredible.

Svool blinked and took a deep breath. He felt the drugs thundering around his veins like a freight train. *Make it stop, make it stop, make it stop!* But of course, it wouldn't stop, because it was inside him, in his flesh, in his blood, taking over his *control*. "Shit," he said, and leant against the wall, and vomited.

"You okay?" Lumar crossed to him, and patted him on the back.

"They force-fed me SLAP, TWAT and SPUNK!"

"That's what they thought you wanted. Sergeant Hardspore, well, I tried to reason with him, but he had his instructions." She slapped a fake salute at her head and wobbled her lips. "You know what these bureaucratic army types are like."

"Instructions?" snapped Svool, standing up and wiping his lips with the back of his hand. Suddenly he smelled perfume, and in disgust realised it was his own golden curls, which had been oiled and combed with rancid scent. "What docile dumb son-of-a-bitch muppet gave the stupid dumb docile bastard instruction to perfume my hair, fill me full of drugs and let a platoon of naked jelly-tit hellakunga girls loose on me? Eh?"

"You did," said Lumar, smoothly.

"Er. Eh?"

"Here. Look." And she handed him a document on a metal leaf, and it said in big bold letters: IN THE EVENT OF ME BECOMING LOST, OR DETACHED, OR OTHERWISE KIDNAPPED OR SOME SUCH NONSENSE... and went on to specify exactly *what* the Quad-Gal Authorities and the Shamans of Manna should do in order to have their favourite poet returned to them...

"Ahh," said Svool as he read down the sheet. "Ahh. Oh. Ahh. Yes, I see. Oh, dear. Oh, bugger."

When he finished, he met Lumar's steady green reptilian gaze. "I bet you think I'm an idiot."

"Oh, no..." she said.

"Oh, yes." He held up one hand, and tried to look regal.

"No. Let me finish. I don't *think* you're an idiot. I *know* it. However, I am willing to look past your failings, because Chorzaranalista brought us here for a reason. She has a plan. All the children of Toxicity have a plan. And we are to be involved... if you can get the skag out of your brain for a moment."

"Hey! I was force-fed this shit..."

"Under your own instruction."

"*Admittedly* under my own instruction, however, I have changed, my time on this planet has changed me; my time here *with you* has changed me!"

"How so?"

"Well, once I would have tumbled into bed with all those jelly girls!"

"So why don't you go back to them? Svool? Hey? After all, you are... the *Poet Master*. Behold, Svoolzard Koolimax XXIV, Third Earl of Apobos, poet, swashbuckler and bon *viveur*, a legend in the hallowed halls of poetic creation, in the art of verse and alliteration, in the dazzling creation of metaphor and pun, sexual athlete, comedy chef, genius extraordinaire, Svoolzard Koolimax XXIV!"

"You've got a good memory," coughed Svool, averting his gaze.

"Yes, I have."

"Er. Listen. We've come this far together. I have a proposition."

"Oh, yeah? Go on, fucker, make my day."

"First, we will do whatever Chorzaranalista requires of us. And I mean *whatever*. What I've seen on this world, well, nobody should have to live like that. Such levels of pollution and disregard; it should never have happened. Greenstar are evil, and they need to stop their polluting right now. They need to be stopped!" He stared hard at Lumar. "*We* need to stop them!"

"Good. At last. Now you're talking. Outside, there's a military film crew. Chorzaranalista wants us to make a... documentary. A film. About Greenstar. About the pollution they have wrought. She wants us to head for the Greenstar Factory Hub – and film it."

"We can do that."

"And Chorzaranalista wants you to write a poem about it."

Svool stared at her, eyes narrowing. "Are you taking the piss?"

"Noo-*oo*," she said, softly. "If you write a poem, and recite it in front of the Greenstar Factory, you'll hit the news big time. *You* will get us more coverage across Manna than if somebody nuked a planet. It will make everybody take notice. *Your fame* will make the Shamans take notice. Then, everybody will have to sit up and watch and fucking *do something* to halt this aberration! Don't you see, Svool? In the past, you've always used your skills for the purposes of *entertainment*. This time, you can actually do something to *help*. Something worthwhile. Something that will change people's lives. Change the galaxy. Something that will make a difference, my friend."

Svool considered this. *If you do it, and it doesn't work, then your reputation will be ruined. You will have sold out, used your wonderful God-given poetry, your genius, for something that flopped. And as any entertainer knows, with a big flop resting across your shoulders like some huge and terrible turd, well, that's the kiss of death for any poet of perfection.* Svool started to imagine a million scenarios where he lost his ability to be a poet; to perform; to change the world using personification. *Hot-damn-and-bloody-buggery! What can I do? What shall I do?* He eyed Lumar, and licked his lips. *What must I do? For the good of the planet, the people, and the whole Galaxy of Manna?*

Svool coughed. Quietly, he forced out the word, "Okay."

"You'll do it?"

"Yes."

"Well done that man! So the guilt of Amaranth's terrible predicament finally got to you, eh? To put your entire career on the line, your entire reputation as the Poet Master, your entire *world and history!* Wow. That's some sacrifice, Svoolzard Koolimax." She kept a perfectly straight face.

"I'm not doing it for Amaranth," said Svool. His gaze had become intense.

Lumar was looking down, checking her pistols. "What?"

And then he spoke, and it all came out fast, all came in a rush as if the TWAT and SPUNK had taken hold of his brain and riddled his mind with mental diarrhoea. "I didn't do it for Amaranth, Lumar, because all I can ever think about is *you,* and all I ever dream about is *you,* and all I ever want is *you*, and you can laugh and mock me but I don't care, because I'm in love with you, Lumar, in love with every little smile and gesture and movement, and I know what you think, you think I'm a sexual athlete, but that isn't anything to do with this, it's not about sex, it's about wanting to be with you, and spend the rest of my life with you, and when we get out of this shit, I'm going to use all my wealth, and all my contacts and all my personal mercenary warriors, to head to your homeworld and find these dastardly kroon ganga gangs, and we'll find and rescue your sister, and kill all the bad kroona mafia, and you'll never have to worry about anything ever again."

He stopped abruptly, and realised he was staring at his feet. His feet were naked and cold. Svool realised he was shivering, quite violently, but it had nothing to do with the cold.

He looked up, a quick movement.

Lumar was staring at him, her mouth open, tongue flickering.

He looked down again.

There came a long, long pause.

Outside, heavy military engines were revving. Sergeant Hardspore probably wanted to be on his way. After all, there were heroic things to do and machine guns to fire and bad guys to blast.

Lumar gave a little cough. "You mean that?"

"Yes. *All of it*."

"And... about rescuing my sister?"

"Yes. We'll find her. We'll snatch her from the claws of those nasty mafia gangster people."

Lumar stepped closer. Svool could smell her scent, and it was an intoxicant cutting through his own rancid perfume. She looked deep into his eyes, and he felt himself lost to her, lost to her magic. It was like she had cast a spell on him, and the magic ripped out his brain and spinal column and beat him savagely over the head with them.

"I love you," he said, speaking the words he once used to mock, as he left award ceremony parties with five girls on each arm, laughing and saying he would never, ever utter such a platitude...

Lumar kissed him. It was a good kiss. Like no kiss Svool had ever experienced.

"Come on," she said, finally. "We have a lot to do, and time is running out."

"Time until what?"

"Until Chorzaranalista tries to destroy the Greenstar Factory Hub."

JENNY FOUND HERSELF ducking involuntarily, although to be caught in the direct blast of an E3 Accelerator would compress a person to the size of a bucket. Instead, Jenny, along with Zanzibar, Meat Cleaver and Nanny, were all picked up and *accelerated* down the single train carriage, where they connected with the forward bulkhead, leaving dents in the alloy, and all landed in a crumpled heap.

The rear of the train bent and twisted and screamed, a huge section disintegrating as flowers of sharpened alloy splinters twisted and folded around themselves, chasing the ECO terrorists for half the length of the carriage...

But the train was powered from the front, and despite losing three sets of rear wheels and a twenty-foot stretch of compartment, the train carried on, pushed and *accelerated* down the tunnel by the force of the E3 blast. It was the train's momentum which saved it. If it hadn't already been in motion when the weapon struck it, it would have been slammed and crushed into oblivion...

Vasta disappeared in the wreckage and noise.

Jenny groaned, opened her eyes, and patted herself down in a sudden panic, checking for lost limbs or massive wounds. She rolled herself off a groaning Zanzibar, who opened one dark eye and regarded her balefully.

"Yeah, you're okay, lady. Because you used old Zanzibar, here, as a bloody cushion!"

"Sorry, Zanz." She helped the large man up. He stretched himself, and checked all his joints were working. Then he rolled his neck, with a rattling succession of *cracks*.

"Ouch. That hurt."

He peered suddenly out of the rear of the train, and then strode forward as Jenny helped up a complaining Meat Cleaver and a curiously focussed, narrow-eyed, teeth-clenched Nanny. She cocked her D4 shotgun and scowled out of the open, wind-whistling rear of the train.

"What a mess," said Zanzibar, holding onto a sharp edge of torn, tortured alloy and leaning slightly into the train's vacated exhaust. He glanced back at what remained of the train. "We were lucky not to get pulped!"

"Yeah," grinned Jenny, uneasily. "I think Vasta wanted us turned into sushi!"

"Well, the bitch missed."

The remainder of the group spent several minutes composing themselves, and made a point of not mentioning Bull's sudden demise. There was no way he had survived the blast from Vasta. He was dead as a butchered pig on a chopping block.

Zanzibar returned to the front of the train, and using bolt-cutters from his backpack, broke into the pilot cabin. It was unmanned, but Zanz checked the controls, his eyes roving over the digital map.

"Found anything?" said Jenny, peering over his shoulder.

Zanzibar shifted out of the way. "Yeah. Check the map. You'll see there's about twenty stops between here and the Factory Hub; and what we *really don't want* is other people trying to get on the train. And possibly alerting Greenstar that we're on our way. What I suggest is..." – and his finger traced another network, in faded brown, on the scanner – "there."

"What is it?"

"Emergency tunnels. We jump our wounded ship, here, and head in on foot. That way, there's no easy way for them to see us coming. Last thing we need is arriving with all our guns bristling to find a battalion of Greenstar bastards waiting for us. Capiche?"

"Okay. You suggest getting a bit closer? Then we can pull the emergency stop..."

"No. No emergency stop." Zanzibar's eyes were hooded and serious. "We'll have to jump this one."

Jenny nodded, and the remainder of her squad stood at the back of the damaged train as Zanzibar went back to the cockpit and, with a squeal of tearing steel, wrenched the train's underground map from its bracket. He jogged back to Jenny, swaying in rhythm with the jostling train, and grinned at her.

She stood, hair whipping around her face, and pushed

her SMKK onto her back. This was going to hurt, she knew it. But then, everything of worth in life required one to suffer just a little bit of pain. Right?

"We good?" said Zanzibar, and Nanny, Meat Cleaver and Jenny all nodded.

"Let's do it," said Jenny, and she leapt...

The world spun in a chaos. Surprisingly, it did not hurt. Not at the beginning, anyway. Curled in a ball, the whole world became a spinning, bouncing craziness, filled with black and red and bright flashes. Jenny had leapt at an angle, missing the rails, but just as she came to a halt, her boots thumped the wall of the tunnel and she lay for a moment, her body shocked into immobility, her brain rushing to catch up with the fact she'd jumped from the blasted rear of a fast-moving train...

The sudden deafening noise retreated in corrugated echoes, and Jenny could only hear her own fast breathing. Then the pain hit her, and despite her body-armour, it felt like she'd done ten rounds with a supercruiser heavyweight. Pain drummed down on her body, beat her from every angle. The world was suddenly a cold, dark place that smelled of burnt steel and old engine oil. She lay for a while, wondering what the fuck hit her, and then she remembered – and remembered Vasta with that damn E3 Accelerator. She rolled onto her side, and heard the sounds of Zanzibar and the others coming back to life. She reached out, touched the old blackened wall, and slowly dragged herself to her feet. She ached in places she didn't know existed. She gritted her teeth, thought about her father, thought about his vision, and decided it was time to man up.

"Okay. Zanzibar, Meat, Nanny. You all okay?"

Coughing and muttered curses met her query. Zanz flicked on the light on his SMKK, and a narrow beam illuminated the track. It was old, filled with dirt, but the rails were polished bright silver. Often used.

"You got that scanner?" snapped Jenny.

"This way." And Zanzibar led the way, all four ECO terrorists jogging, weapons at the ready, alone with their private thoughts. Thoughts of Sick Note, Flizz and Bull all meeting a nasty, violent end. Thoughts that this, in all reality, was their last mission. But if they could help bring down the Greenstar Factory Hub; well, that was a fitting note on which to leave this mortal realm.

They ran. Jenny's bruised and battered muscles groaned at her. Meat Cleaver ran beside her, panting, a little out of shape.

"You need to lay off the beer, my friend."

"I don't think that'll be a problem in the future, do you?" he said, grinning in the darkness.

"Maybe not," she conceded.

"Up here. Another klick, then we can get off this main track before another train comes along and crushes us into fish paste."

"Such a way with words," said Nanny, voice more of a growl, shotgun in her hairy fists.

Zanzibar shrugged, and winced in pain. The jump from the battered train had hurt him, Jenny could see. Hurt him bad.

They ran on, through gloom which smelled of oil and metal and a seeping, invading stench. Like sewers; like toxic waste.

After a kilometre, Zanzibar signalled, and they found a narrow vertical space in the tunnel wall through which to crawl. It was perhaps thirty feet thick, narrow, and filled with cobwebs and bugs. They squeezed through, moaning, and standing on the other side, they found themselves in a disused tunnel. Zanzibar's flashlight illuminated ancient rusting track, and up ahead, several huge pieces of old timber lying across the rails.

"What is this place?" said Meat Cleaver.

Jenny shrugged. "Probably their original underground line. Then, in the name of progress and updating, they built a new, dirtier, shittier one for larger, dirtier, shittier trains." She smiled. "Whatever. At least this track is unused."

As if on cue, a train flashed past the gap through which they'd just squeezed. A hot wind rushed across the squad, and Jenny closed her eyes for a moment, breathing in hot stinking air. It was like somebody rushing across her grave. It was a digital haunting, a vision of the future. A vision of a private Hell.

"Come on."

"We're going to die down here," muttered Zanzibar, his eyes still staring at the gap, even though the train had gone. They'd been a minute from being crushed and pulped. It wasn't a pleasant thought.

"I can live with that, as long as we take those Greenstar bastards with us," said Jenny, and set off, her own SMKK flashlight leading the way.

THEY'D BEEN TRAVELLING for a couple of hours, and time itself had lost its meaning. But they heard voices. Shouting. A muffled stomping of boots. Zanzibar held up a fist and they halted, killing their lights. They stood there, amidst broken lumps of wood and concrete, amongst rat droppings and cobwebs and old pools of oil, and listened...

More voices. All muffled. They sounded harsh and alien. Then, gradually, the voices faded and were gone.

"Trouble, you think?" said Zanzibar.

"Yes. I reckon that was our friend Vasta, attempting to hunt us down. Probably jumped up a few stops, found the empty train, then back-tracked down the tunnels, searching for us."

"Do you think they'll realise what we're doing?" said Zanz.

Jenny gave a curt nod. "Just a matter of time. So let's get on. Let's get this done."

They travelled for another hour, jogging on, faces streaked with dirt and sweat. Again Zanzibar called a halt. Flashlights bounced around the walls. Again, they heard a distant shout. This time, there was no muffling.

"They're behind us," said Jenny, softly.

Zanzibar nodded, and the squad increased their efforts, following the old line on the scanner in Zanzibar's hands.

"We're getting close," he said, after a few minutes. "This track emerges into what I presume is a deserted station; it's built pretty close to the new Greenstar Factory station, as far as I can see. There must be some form of access. If not, we'll have to create one. We've got enough damn bombs."

Jenny gave a nod, and they carried on, labouring now, limbs weary, minds growing sour. Jenny could see so many flaws in their plan, so many opportunities for them to be discovered, for them to be killed, she could no longer bring herself to turn them over in her head. What if Vasta had simply called ahead? What if Renazzi Lode and a thousand soldiers were waiting? Of course, they would be. Lode had said it herself. *Come to the Greenstar Hub. We want to watch you die.* But a part of Jenny still hoped they'd found a backdoor – then all they needed was some central control centre, or support struts, or access to fuel dumps – and BANG! Goodbye Greenstar Factory. After all, Zanzibar carried enough HighJ in his "special pack" to send a city skywards.

"Shit. Shit, shit, shit and shit."

"What is it, Jen?"

"This fucking place. Our fucking plan. We're just too dumb to be doing this. What are our chances of success? Fucking minimal, is what. We've steamed ahead with an arsenal of weapons and not really thought this through. Even if we approach through the station, they'll know we're coming from that direction. Come on. Follow me."

She led the way, and in a few minutes they emerged into the old, deserted underground station. They halted, waving their weapons about the station, then hoisted themselves up onto a fire-blackened, dusty platform. They searched the three small buildings they found there, each one empty except for overturned, rusting chairs, a smashed desk and some old cabinets full of mouldy paperwork.

They stepped back out, onto the platform, boots thudding hollowly. "What now?" said Zanzibar.

Jenny pointed with her SMKK. Above one of the buildings was a ventilation shaft. "Get me up on that roof," she said, and Zanzibar hoisted her up. Her fingers found a grip, and she hauled her legs over the edge; then, she reached down and pulled her three squad members up behind her.

Using her combat knife, Jenny prised off the grille. Behind it lay a dark shaft, containing piping and optic cables. She grinned back at Zanzibar. "Let's do some exploring."

One by one they climbed into the shaft, and Zanz pulled the grille back into place behind them. Then, stowing away weapons and moving on all fours as quietly as they could, they headed – east, by Jenny's reckoning – into the heart of the Greenstar Factory.

It didn't take them long to find the station from which they should have emerged on their Accelerator-blasted train. In fact, the carriage stood there to one side, surrounded by soldiers with machine guns and disintegrators, huge weapons that buzzed softly, nozzles glowing blue.

Jenny felt herself turn cold, and through a tiny air grille could count... maybe a hundred armed men and women in olive-green uniforms, with the gold emblem of the Greenstar Company.

If they *had* ridden the train to its termination, *they* would have been the ones terminated.

The soldiers were on edge, wary, constantly looking about them. Several groups had taken positions on opposite platforms. Anything coming out of that tunnel would be cut to bloody ribbons within the blink of an eye.

She turned back to Zanzibar. "You were right to seek an alternative."

"Yes."

"We need to find some kind of control centre."

"Yes."

"Then bring this motherfucking place to the ground."

"Let's do it."

HORACE SWAM, AND he felt more powerful than he had ever felt in his android life. He had killed hundreds of people... killed *thousands* of people using his superior strength, and agility, and intellect... but never had he felt like he felt now, infused with the organic toxic sludge of an evolved sentient decadence. He was filled to overflowing with toxic waste. It brimmed in him, like a jug filled with water, to the point of overflowing. And he welcomed the feeling, revelled in the power, and swam under the water, under the Biohazard Ocean, until he found the inlet which met with the fast-moving waters from the Yellow Virus Peaks: the River Tox. Horace flexed his muscles and drank in toxic waste, breathing on the pulp of radiation and heavy metals and chemical slurry... and with each gulp it made him stronger, made him more powerful, until he felt like he would burst...

He swam, powering upriver, skimming the river bed with its vast collection of dumped waste. And as he swam in great lazy strokes, so he felt others join him, psi-children who emerged from the underwater rocks and dumped, battered cars and old oil drums. They emerged, and smiled, and swam behind him and he did not mind, welcomed their company, for it meant he would not go into battle alone...

He swam for a day and a night, never tiring, his toxic intake and excretion working in perfect harmony. It was only when he reached the first set of vast waste pipes, leaving the Greenstar Factory Hub and dumping straight under the wide, swirling, deep waters of the River Tox, that he began to feel strange. First it came in his forearms; a gradual swelling of the muscles, a tightening of his new body all over, but mainly in his forearms. The uncomfortable feeling spread through him and he paused, under the sludge, grasping hold of the thick metal grate guarding the exit from the massive pipe into the river. With one hand curled around the huge bars, Horace looked down at himself, at his naked toxic form, his flesh now a puke-green colour, his skin covered with warts and sores and bubbles and lumps, open wounds bubbling with pus and toxic venom, and *something*, a sudden uncertainty, rippled through him. *Is this right? Or am I bubbling away, disintegrating before I can complete my mission? Have my genetics rebelled? Has the toxic overload destroyed me?*

And then a hand, on his shoulder. It was one of the psi-children. He looked back at her, down at her, and realised she had shrunk. No. *He* had grown. He had become filled with toxicity. Filled with waste. A carrier of filth and hardcore poison.

It's okay. Do not be frightened.

I will not die?

We all die.

I will not die... yet?

Not yet. Be strong. Fulfil your destiny.

With a roar, Horace grasped the heavy grille protecting the outlet pipe, and his toxic muscles bunched and warped and the steel screamed and bent, and bubbles shot up to the surface of the river. Horace clamped himself to the grille, and fought the steel, and slowly it bent out of all shape and recognition, and in disgust, Horace tossed it onto the river bed, where ancient sludge awoke, arose, and engulfed the iron, sucking it down into its toxic embrace.

You are inside, said the girl. And she smiled.

Yes. I will go now.

We will accompany you.

Thank you.

They swam, a phalanx of toxic creatures, inside the massive pipe, through which a juggernaut could easily pass. Horace led the way, and now a hundred or so psi-children swam in his wake, like an army of mermaids, only these had no pretty faces or pretty fins or tails, for these psi-children were made from chemical effluvia and disease and sludge and waste and poison.

I am the trigger, he thought.

And then, *Don't ever lose your temper.*

And he smiled. And he remembered. And he found regret.

On they swam. Through the pipes.

Into the Heart of Greenstar.

SVOOL STOOD ON the blasted, bleached moorland. It was dark, and a cold, sour wind blew from the south, chilling him to his very core and filling him with bitter thoughts. To one side, Sergeant Hardspore and his men, Quad-Gal Military in all but name and sent on this insane rescue mission by the Shamans of Manna, had set up a base camp. Three sets of cameras had been arranged in banks, with the Greenstar Factory Hub in the far distant background. Between here and there was a bog, a bubbling waste of fetid, sulphur-stinking marshes. They made Svool feel sick.

He was about to head for his tent – in the hopes it hadn't melted – when the army AD arrived, waving a sheaf of notes. "Oh, Mr Koolimax, Mr Koolimax, I need to go over a few things before you retire to your trailer..."

"I haven't got a trailer."

The AD looked at him, head to one side, as if to say, *oh, how unprofessional of you to point out such a basic lack of film-maker luxury for our main star!* but he didn't actually say it. Just drilled it into Svool's head with the drill-bit of his stare.

"We need to go over a few directions..."

"Wait! Wait!" Svool held up a hand. "You want me to create a poem, right? The most incredible piece of anti-Greenstar poetry ever, yes? Well, I need to *finish the damn thing.*"

Svool stalked off across the barren wasteground, and ducked as he entered his military green tent. Lumar was lying back on a small canvas bed, reading a manual. Svool slumped down onto his own bed, which creaked in warning.

"Are you okay, Svool?"

"Yes. Let me work."

And he picked up his pad, which he had named *The Pad of Doom*, and he opened it and stared down at this, the most incredible poem he had ever written, filled with mourning for an entire planet, laid waste by the decadence and stupidity of the creatures who abused Her...

Only he didn't.

Because, for the first time in his life, Svool had writer's block.

SIXTEEN

JENNY HALTED, AND held up her fist. Behind her, Zanzibar, Nanny and Meat Cleaver readied their weapons as quietly as they could. They had agreed it was time to leave the ventilation shafts, find a core location, and put down some heavy destruction before they were found and killed. But this had proved trickier than any of them had anticipated. A few hundred metres back, they had passed some kind of control room – vast in size, and containing massive black tubs, short and squat and fat, and numbering perhaps a thousand in total. Some of them bubbled, and some were still. Around the entire vast laboratory were banks and rows of computers and delicate machinery, and many benches set up with apparatus for obvious experimentation. And yet they were still stuck in this shaft...

"What is it?"

"I think I've found something."

Jenny crawled forward, her gloved fingers describing the shape of the inspection hatch beneath her. She listened for a while, then eased her fingers under the rim and lifted the hatch. She popped her head down, then lowered herself, dropping into a crouch in the corridor. She braced her SMKK and covered both ends of the corridor whilst Nanny and Meat Cleaver dropped down behind her. Zanzibar came last, slotting the hatch back into place as he fell. It wasn't perfect, but at least it didn't leave a gaping hole in the ceiling to attract immediate attention.

"We going to check out the lab?" said Zanz.

"Yeah. Looks like an important centre for operations. What concerns me is the lack of lab rats."

"Lunch break?"

"Too convenient. You got the HighJ? I would suggest this is a good place to start."

Zanzibar rattled the canvas sack. "Let's leave them a present they won't ever forget," he grinned.

They moved warily into the vast laboratory. The black tubs bubbled, and the bright lighting soon gave Jenny a headache. Zanz tossed her a few cubes of HighJ, and more to the rest of the squad, and they moved across the laboratory to the centre. Everything was pristine, immaculate. Almost as if...

"It's unused," said Jenny, the penny finally dropping. "The staff aren't away on a lunch break; they're just *not here*. It's new. Clean. Perfect." The others looked around the room, and had to agree.

"I don't get it," said Zanzibar.

"Well it's quite simple, really," said Vasta. She had stepped from a half-concealed side-door. The E3 Accelerator that had killed Bull was in her hands, and she had a tight, cruel smile on her face.

"You bitch," snarled Jenny.

"So we meet again," smiled Vasta, and ran a hand through her hair, as if preening before a new boyfriend. "It's interesting, tracking you – for believe me, you leave a trail so wide a new college boy could follow you blindfolded – how totally incompetent you really are. Is this *really* the best ECO terrorist outfit that Mr Candle could summon to do his dirty work?" She laughed, a cold, cruel laugh. "Well. You won't be carrying out any more of your little plots and schemes. Flizz is dead. Sick Note is, shall we say, very, very sick. Or at least, in separate pieces. And Bull... poor old Bull." She pulled out a sulky lower lip, like a child who'd had a lollipop confiscated. "You all ran off in such a hurry, you didn't hear him begging and squealing on that underground train track." Her face went hard. "An 11mm Techrim bullet soon put an end to that."

Zanzibar growled and reached for his gun, but Jenny's hand shot out, halting him.

At that moment, from both ends of the laboratory, came the rattle of guns being readied and cocked. The olive-green-uniformed soldiers came stampeding through the lab, boots stomping, guns trained on the four ECO terrorists. Guns trained on Jenny and her squad. She felt a cold fear settle in her belly.

They weren't getting out of this one alive, that was for sure.

Jenny felt the cube of HighJ in her hand. If she could just arm it... then if they shot her, BAM! They'd all be cat food. She twisted her hand, attempting to shield the small black cube, but Vasta caught the movement and gestured. Three Greenstar soldiers strode forward and relieved her first of the HighJ, then of her SMKK.

"Such a shame it had to end like this. Mr Candle will be *so* disappointed..."

Jenny tensed. She could feel the killing moment speeding towards her. She tensed. And heard a tub go *gloop*. She frowned. Another tub went *gloop*. Vasta didn't notice; she was too busy self-eulogising.

"And so we followed your little squad – you thought you were so clever, so covert, using those back-door disused tunnels, but that was a sadly obvious tactic. If you'd actually taken the time to really think things through..."

There came another... *gloop*.

This time, a large one.

Vasta stopped talking, and moved her focus from Jenny to the tub. She gestured to a soldier with a short beard, who walked across the polished lab tiles, boots clacking. The black tub came up to the man's waist; he halted at its edge, looking down into what appeared to be a thick, black tar.

It gave another *gloop*.

The man looked to Vasta, half-smiled, and shrugged... as an explosion from the tar showered him. *Something*, a figure, a small, lithe figure with long wild hair and flashing bright eyes, leapt from the tub, attached itself to the soldier using hands and feet, and bit into his face. The man suddenly screamed, staggering back, and his SMKK stuttered and coughed, bullets cutting a line across the ceiling in an explosion of shattered tiles and popping lights and sparks. The *creature* growled and bit and wrestled with the man's flesh, tugging and chewing him, pulling his beard and lips away in a long string of skin. The man, screaming, punched at the figure, to no obvious effect.

"Get it off him!" snapped Vasta, attention focused on the sudden fight.

Three soldiers moved to the man's aid, grasping the childlike figure and attempting to drag it off. All they did was tear their comrade's face further from his skull, and he hit the ground with a bustle around him, still fighting and thrashing and moaning as the child bit and chewed and absorbed the blows of the three large soldiers. One finally hit the figure in the head with the butt of his SMKK. The *crack* sang across the lab – and had *no* effect.

Vasta levelled her E3 Accelerator. All the soldiers in the vicinity suddenly ducked, hands covering heads. As...

More figures leapt from the tubs, an explosion of action and activity all across the labs. They landed on the soldiers, on the ceiling, on the floor, crouched on all fours like cats, backs arched, choosing targets and leaping again in a single spring. Fingers flexed like claws, slashing throats and tearing out eyes. Teeth snarled and bit. Blood pattered across the floor. The world of serenity in the lab went from calm to insanity in a few quick heartbeats. Jenny charged Vasta, whose E3 was still levelled at the first victim and his chewing attacker; she slammed into the Head of Greenstar Security, one hand grabbing the controlling arm and pushing it *up*. There came a *whump* and a diagonal shaft was sliced up through the ceiling, up through vents and pipework and flooring to the room above. It started to rain desks and computer equipment, screens and keyboards bouncing down into the tubs of black goo, stationery clattering from the scuffling forms of the panicked soldiers.

Jenny, grasping Vasta's arms, drove an elbow back into the woman's face. There came a *crack*, but Vasta was already moving, rolling with the blow. She drove a low punch into Jenny's ribs, but Jenny whirled about, releasing Vasta's arms and slamming the palms of both hands into Vasta's face. Vasta let go of the weapon and staggered back, clawing her own eyes. The E3 clattered to the ground. Jenny leapt forward, almost serene, eyes calm, breathing regulated, and pounded her fist into Vasta's retreating form, three times. Vasta fell back, but her boot slammed out, kicking Jenny in the stomach. Air exploded from her, but she came on and Vasta grabbed her, tossing her backwards over her head and scrambling to her feet.

Jenny rolled and leapt up. She turned on Vasta, fists raised, but Vasta drew a knife. Zanzibar turned his SMKK on Vasta but Jenny waved him away. "This bitch is mine."

"You reckon?" snapped Vasta. "I've heard puppies yakking just like you. Come on, cunt, let's see how well you bleed."

Jenny drew her own combat knife and advanced, as all around them the lithe figures with the wild hair covered in tar leapt and cavorted, biting and swiping, chewing and dancing. Occasionally an SMKK rattled or a pistol fired, and everybody ducked. None of the children – the *girls* – seemed to die. But soldiers died. Plenty of soldiers.

Knives hissed through the air, and Jenny parried a blow. Sparks glittered. She stepped back as a soldier staggered between the two, a child on his face vomiting toxic puke that burnt out his eyes. He fell, screaming, head steaming, hair in flames.

Vasta leapt over his squirming body, her knife tearing at Jenny's eyes. Jenny twitched, focused on the knife, and brought her own weapon up suddenly. Vasta took it in the belly and gagged, then staggered back, hissing and spitting. The knife was dragged from Jenny's hands. Blood soaked through Vasta's uniform and she looked down in disbelief. Slowly, she took hold of the dagger and withdrew it from her flesh. She stood and allowed the weapon to clatter to the ground in a pool of gore.

"I'm gonna kill you for that."

She leapt, and the punch lifted Jenny, slamming her back against a bench. Delicate glass equipment shivered and toppled, clattering and chiming and smashing all around Jenny. The blow had been too quick, too sudden; especially for a woman with a mortal knife wound to the abdomen.

Vasta was on her, and another blow rocked Jenny. She felt a tooth come out, and blood flooded her mouth. Her arms slammed up, catching Vasta under the chin, but the Head of Security rode the blow and grinned down at Jenny. She'd dropped her knife, and they wrestled for a moment, until Vasta pinned Jenny's arms above her head and leaned down, her mouth opening, so close her words almost tickled.

"I'm going to enjoy killing you," she said.

The blow hit Vasta in the side of the head, catapulting her from Jenny's prone form and into an incredible tumble. She landed on her feet, atop a lab bench, uncurling gracefully. A few droplets of blood had trailed across the bench surface. She glanced down at Zanzibar with a frown. He was holding a length of iron. A crowbar. She tutted, and touched the long red welt on the side of her head.

"I'll deal with you later," she said.

"What are you?" said Zanzibar. "Class JJ? Or android?"

Vasta tilted her head. Then relaxed, and smiled. "Android."

"What class?"

"You don't ask a girl a question like that," said Vasta, clenching her fists. "Now, who wants to die first?"

"That'd be you," said Nanny, a cigar in her grizzled old mouth, as she pulled the trigger on the E3 Accelerator. The E3 gave a *whine* and energy exploded outwards. Vasta moved damn fast, but not fast enough. Her leap carried her torso, head and arms above the blast – but her legs were torn and *accelerated* free in a sudden slurry of blood and bone and winding, stretching, *snapping* tendon.

There came a long, long pause.

Most of the violence had finished, and the soldiers were dead or dying. The tar-coated figures were arranged around the laboratory, heads hung low, eyes averted, almost as if they were ashamed. Or... had completed their mission?

Jenny shuddered, and breathed deeply. She climbed to her feet and walked over to the bench where Vasta's corpse lay. Only it wasn't a corpse. She was still alive, her eyes bright and feverish, her lips working soundlessly. She suddenly focused on Jenny and smiled.

"Come. Here. My. Child."

Jenny moved close. Vasta was twitching, and blood surged out of her mouth. "Yeah, motherfucker?"

"You were... tougher. Tougher. Than you. Look." She smiled, and looked away, almost in regret. Her hands were quivering. More blood and drool ran down her chin. She looked back up.

"Better believe it," grimaced Jenny.

"I'm an android. Anarchy Android. Waiting. Here for. Horace."

"Horace?"

Vasta's eyes were glazed. Her whole body, or the remains of it, was twitching now; twitching on the bench, like a side of quartered beef.

"It doesn't matter. I killed him. Killed my... own kind."

Her eyes lowered. Jenny shuffled closer. Suddenly, Vasta's hands shot out and closed round Jenny's throat. The strength was incredible, as if all the lost energy and power from Vasta's legs had transferred into her arms. Jenny's hands slammed up, trying to relieve the grip, but they were iron. Vasta pulled Jenny close. Real close. Her eyes were bloodshot and burning, burning bright. Her mouth opened and she was grinning, blood on her teeth, a maniacal snarl hijacking her face.

"I should have tortured you..." she said... as Zanzibar slammed Jenny's combat knife straight between her eyes with a *crack* of puncturing skull. Vasta went rigid, then relaxed, and Jenny fought her way from under the android's grip.

Zanzibar grabbed her shoulders. "You okay?"

Jenny nodded. "Yes. Yes! Shit. What a bitch. A torturing android bitch."

"Look," said Zanzibar, and Jenny gazed around. The child-like figures had lifted their heads after the mass slaughter of the hundred or so soldiers. Now, they were watching Jenny. One came forward, a slim girl, and she smiled up at Jenny, who was still rubbing at the savage bruises on her throat.

"It's time," she said.

"Time?" said Jenny.

"Time to plant your HighJ charges. I'm Chorzaranalista. Me and the other psi-children have come to help."

"But..."

"We saw you. In a dream. A prophecy. For us, the future is written. The toxicity has given us that gift... at the expense of many other things."

"I don't understand. Where have you come from?"

"The waste. The shit. The Toxicity. But you need to move quick. You need to focus *now*. More soldiers come. Thousands more! And... *one* who is hidden from me." She touched her temples then, as if in great pain. When she opened her eyes, they were bright as falling stars. "This chamber is a connecting Fuel Port. Blow this with enough force, and the chain reaction will spread like you could never believe possible... destroy this Fuel Port and you destroy the Greenstar Factory. You destroy Greenstar."

Jenny nodded, and signalled to Nanny and Meat Cleaver, as Zanzibar hoisted his pack of HighJ explosives.

"Come on, guys. Let's blow this fucking place to the stars."

*   *   *

"Wait."

It was almost a whisper. Almost.

He stood there, in his armour and carrying his weapon, and he looked out of place, alien, but it was him. It was him, all right.

"Saul," said Jenny, and stared at her brother.

Her brother.

After so much, after so much time and so many millions of miles and years. He was here. He was now. He was part of this. He was part of Greenstar. A betrayer. A back-stabber. Acting a part to get Jenny to confess. Tortured? Ha. He wasn't just an actor. He was a base, gutter-Greenstar pawn.

"What the fuck do you want?" Her SMKK was already in sweaty fingers. She wanted to kill him. Kill him *now*. He hadn't just betrayed Amaranth. He had betrayed her. He had betrayed their father. He had betrayed their fucking *species*.

"Don't do it. Don't plant the HighJ." He was looking around, at all the dead soldiers. Tentatively, he picked his way through the corpses. The psi-children let him be. *Why?* screamed Jenny's brain. *He's alien evil a fucking piece of shit who should be on a noose kicking. Why?*

"I want you to stop. I want you to walk away from Greenstar. This is not your fight. This is not your war."

"Fuck you."

"Jenny, trust me..."

The bubble burst. The tears came. A riot of rage engulfed her brain. She opened her mouth and the words poured out, spilled out, puked out, and she said, "I've got to say, Saul, and this is a long time in coming, but you are a sorry fucking excuse for a human being. Yeah. You and your back-stabbing, cock-sucking wife. Look around, Saul – you have NO friends, cunt. Maybe you should ask yourself the fucking question – why? I remember you, remember your drug paranoia, remember you driving like a wedge straight through the heart and soul of our family... You say we behaved appallingly. What? *WHAT THE FUCK?* This just underlines your dual stupidity, and your dual ignorance. The truth is, Saul – you were stressed about all your stupid life decisions... no doubt TWATTED and PUKED up to fuck, on your needles and drugs, and with a few brandies chucked in there, eh, mate? And I *dared* to question you? About money? About responsibility? About our father? About your twisted fucking bitch of a wife? So you attacked me, and demanded the things you knew I could never deliver... Oh, you fucking cunt. You threw away your sister and our friendship – forever. And because of what? Because of your cheating wife, fucking her army of secret lovers. And I found out. And that made *ME* the bad fucking person. You asked my advice, and tracked her with the tracker in her car, and you bought that PI, and you caught her, Saul. You fucking caught the bitch. Yet you chose to take her back and forgive her, even though you told anybody who would listen what she did to you. You told me you would slit her throat and dump her in the canal. I truly believed you meant it. My advice to you was *don't do it*, you're my brother, I love you, don't do it, don't go to prison for that scum white trash. You told me how she fucked all those men, including the one in the wheelchair, sucking his cock and saying your name as he came down her slick, eager throat. You told me how she was fucking you financially, and what did you expect me to think? What did you expect me to *do*? Well, fuck you. Fuck you real bad, motherfucker. Your lack of humanity in the past always disturbed me. I saw it when no other cunt did. You're not just immoral and illegal; you're just *bad*. Bad to the bone. A bad fucking egg. Bad blood, through and through. So. We have two ways forward, fuckwit. We can agree to disagree – and you never, ever come near me again. You walk away now and that's the end of it." She cocked her SMKK. "Or I'll give you a present you'll never forget."

Saul stared at her. His eyes were burning. But there was no love there. No sense of family. No joy. No kindred.

Just hate. Pure hate.

Saul leant forward, slowly, and spat on the ground. Then he looked back at Jenny and his eyes were masked; his face was a mask. He smiled then, a slow evil smile, and she knew she'd lost him –

This was no longer her brother.

This was some other thing...

They raised their guns at the same time, but Jenny fired the first round. Bullets screamed from her SMKK and hit Saul in the face. His own bullets cut into Jenny's shoulder and then off up the wall, chewing tiles and spitting plaster and sparking from steel joists. But Jenny struck *first* and her bullets chewed a hole in his face so big she could put her fist through it.

Saul hit the ground dead, his face destroyed. Smoke rose from the charred rim of the hole.

Zanzibar put his hand on Jenny's shoulder, and she jumped.

"I'm sorry," he said.

"Fuck him," she said, but she did not mean it. For, once, they *had* been best friends. Once, they *had* been brother and sister. But he'd destroyed it. Now it was gone and done and over.

IN GRIM SILENCE they planted the charges, the psi-children watching and standing guard against further attack. Jenny, Zanzibar, Nanny and Meat Cleaver moved methodically around the laboratory, planting the small black cubes that looked so harmless in gloved hands, and yet could deliver a punch big enough to destroy cities.

Jenny placed a cube next to a tub of tox, which, Chorzaranalista had informed her, contained a skein of lirridium fuel that would spread across the entire Greenstar Factory network and beyond...

Jenny's mouth was dry as she planted the final cube of HighJ. Slowly, carefully, she slid in the charge relay, and it blinked with a tiny green light. On. Active. Ready to blow...

As Jenny stood, mind whirling, Chorzaranalista approached her and stood, looking up, head tilted to one side. Jenny had the horrible feeling her mind was being rifled with the same precision as a professional burglar going through a jewellery box. She blinked, and felt... *something* withdraw.

"Now you must get as far away from this place as possible."

"We must detonate," said Jenny.

"No," said Chorzaranalista, and her finger lifted and touched Jenny's lips. "You cannot detonate *here*. It will not work. Your conventional detonators and charges have been neutralised by focused EMP blasts. Greenstar has protected itself – and protected itself well."

"So how do we blow this shithole?" snarled Jenny, feeling suddenly cold and empty inside. All this way for – for nothing? So many dead to fail at the last hurdle? *What use a bomb without a detonator?*

"We will take care of it," said Chorzaranalista, and her toxic, ravaged face smiled. She winked, then turned and leapt, splashing into the toxic tub, a pipe leading *down, down, down* to the bowels of the Factory.

The rest of the psi-children left, clambering into the black waste. One by one, with a splash and a kick of their legs, they disappeared from view. Jenny stood there, arms limp by her sides, wondering what to do.

"Come on, let's get the fuck out of here," growled Zanzibar.

"We've failed," said Jenny, crestfallen.

Zanzibar grabbed her chin, and lifted her eyes to meet his own. His dark brown orbs were triumphant. "No. We've won. It'll happen, Jen. Trust me. I promise you. I can feel it, here, in my breast." He thumped his own heart, then ran a hand through Jenny's hair affectionately. He growled, "Meat, check our exit. And Nanny, cover the rear with that beautifully devastating E3 Accelerator. Let's go."

They ran across the laboratory, HighJ planted but... *dormant.* Jenny hated herself, hated herself for leaving the job unfinished. And she realised – she no longer trusted *anybody.* Except, maybe, the tattered remains of her ECO terrorist squad. They had become closer than family. They were her *friends...* in life, and death, and oblivion beyond.

Meat Cleaver reached the lab exit, slid to the edge, peered around the corner – and was blown across the room by a shotgun blast. He hit the ground hard, face a bloody pulp, sliding across tiles to slam into a bank of steel cupboards, denting their fascias. He twitched, then lay still.

Jenny and Zanzibar sprinted forward, SMKKs screaming, bullets howling out into the corridor. Nanny, behind them, fired a random blast with the Accelerator across the lab. Cupboards and computers and equipment were picked up in a maelstrom of swirling violence and with a huge *WHOOSH* slammed across the space, disintegrating everything in the blast zone. Jenny and Zanzibar reached the doorway, and Jen fired off random rounds as Zanz crawled over to Meat Cleaver. He rolled the big man onto his back and checked for a pulse. He shook his head, once.

Growling, Jenny fired off another ten rounds and then slammed her back to the door. She glanced to Nanny; they were too open, in too big a space. They needed cover. They needed a new escape route!

A red dot appeared on Nanny's skull, and a silenced round hit her forehead, drilled through her skull and brain, and exploded the back of her head in a mushroom shower of pulp. She was still chewing her cigar.

"No!" screamed Jenny, searching for the sniper, disbelief ringing in her skull.

"Get down!" yelled Zanzibar, and crawled back towards Jenny, slamming his back to the wall alongside her. Their SMKKs shifted and weaved gentle patterns, searching for the enemy. They were on edge, fingers on hairline triggers.

Suddenly, Zanzibar turned his head and stared at Jen. She could read his eyes. Read his face.

We're going to die, said that expression. *There's no getting out of this shit alive!*

She opened her mouth to speak, and Zanzibar smiled; an *it's been great knowing you, working with you, fighting with you* smile.

Suddenly, bullets yammered down the corridor outside, and there were crumpling noises, then silence. Zanz and Jenny stared at one another. Jenny licked her bone-dry lips.

Shoes clicked on tiles, and a figure appeared in the doorway. He was tall, physically big, brown hair greying at the temples, and with a broad, strong face and neat moustache. He lit a thin, evil-looking cigarette and took a long drag. In one hand he carried a small 9mm pistol. He wore an expensive black suit, long overcoat, and brown polished shoes. He looked more like the director of a company than a killer or assassin. He was smiling.

Jenny looked up, and he was gazing down at her. "Hello, Jenny," he said, and the voice clicked immediately and Jenny found herself unable to speak. The voice was instantly recognisable because, *because* she'd been dealing with this man and his orders for a decade. This was Mr Candle. He organised the Impurity Movement terrorist cells. Hell, he *was* the Impurity Movement, handing out contracts to McGowan and all the other Cell Commanders. Candle organised funds, guns and explosives, and decided which targets to hit.

"Mr Candle," she said, blinking rapidly.

He held out his hand to her, but she glanced about nervously. "Get down, sir! There are still enemy in the vicinity!"

"No," he said, gently, smoking his cigarette. "I have neutralised all enemies in the area. You are safe, now. You can stand up, Jenny Xi."

Still Jenny did not move, her eyes fixed on Candle's strong, open, honest face. Then she glanced sideways at Zanzibar, who was also looking at Candle, but wearing a different expression. His eyes were narrowed, his expression one of confusion. As if to say: *Why are you here? How are you here? What the fuck is going on?* Didn't Zanz recognise their illustrious terrorist leader?

Suddenly, Mr Candle levelled the pistol at Zanzibar and shot him through the head. Zanzibar slid slowly sideways, leaning against Jenny, blood tricking down from the gunshot wound just above the bridge of his nose. His hands went slack, and the SMKK shifted slowly down his crouched body to *clack* on the floor. And Jenny was staring at him, watching, and she could not believe this, could not understand what was happening, and what had just happened. Zanzibar's eyes were open, but she watched the light die in them, slowly, going out like a starved (Candle, hush)...

"No," she sighed, and took Zanzibar's head in her hands, and stared at him, then stared up at Candle with tears streaming down her face. That was the last of it. This was the end of it. They were all dead. All dead and gone. And she was alone. Alone in a cold, cruel world, and without the job done.

Greenstar were laughing at her.

She looked up at Mr Candle, who was still smiling, still holding his smoking pistol. He took another drag on his cigarette, and Jenny sat there, waiting for the bullet. But it did not come.

"Stand up, Jenny. We have a lot to discuss."

"Why?" she said, looking down meaningfully at Zanzibar, who still rested against her, as if the big man was asleep. "Why did you kill him?"

Candle's face went hard, then. "He turned against us, Jenny. They all turned against us. You were a pawn. Part of a bigger game. A bigger tapestry. But you will see. I will show you. You will understand. Come with me."

He held out his hand. It was a large hand, powerful, and Jenny found herself staring at it.

Who did she trust?

Did she have any option?

Slowly, she eased Zanzibar down to the ground with as much respect as she could muster, then climbed to her feet. Her head hung low, her SMKK dangling on its strap. Every limb felt lead-weighted, useless. All the fight had gone out of her. All the life had poured from her.

They stepped into the corridor, and there was a squad of twenty soldiers. They wore the olive-green of Greenstar, their gold logos emblazoned proudly on military jackets and berets. Their weapons were held smartly. To attention.

Jenny went for her SMKK in a rush, but Candle reached out, steadying her with his strong hands. She looked into his face. He reminded her of her father. He smiled at her, and shook his head.

"You are Greenstar," she said, understanding dawning.

"Yes."

"But why? *Why* betray us?"

"I have not betrayed you. I have always been Greenstar."

Jenny wrestled with this. "Greenstar, the very fuckers who we hunt down and kill and bomb and exterminate – they employ us to do this? Greenstar own and organise and run and supply the Impurity Movement?" She started to laugh, and the laugh was touched with hysteria. "Greenstar use ECO terrorists to bomb their own factories?" She was laughing openly now, tears tumbling down her face.

"Yes."

"But why? Why, you bastards? I don't understand!"

And Jenny was in his arms, a small child again, a small child needing protection from the world of the grown-ups. Because this was a different place, a different game. Jenny no longer understood the rules, if indeed there were any. Jenny was divorced from reality, cut out from the equation of life. Everything she knew and trusted and believed and fought for – all of it was built on a foundation of quicksand.

Candle squeezed her, hugged her, murmured soothing noises into her hair.

"Come on," he said, whispering in her ear. "We must go to the Director's Office. There, everything will become clear to you. There, everything will be explained. Do you trust me?"

Jenny looked up through her tears. "I trust nobody," she said.

"That's okay. Come on, come with me. I'll answer all of your questions there. We won't hurt you. Nobody will hurt you again."

And weeping, Jenny allowed herself to be led. Like a lamb on a leash.

HORACE, ANARCHY ANDROID, otherwise known as The Dentist, swam through the toxic sludge. Slowly, he could feel his body failing him. His new, incredibly powerful toxic body – it was failing. The lirridium in the sludge, filtered through in channels, in skeins, was burning him. It was decaying his toxicity. It was neutralising the acids and alkalis, reducing the pollutants, halving the half-lives. And yet he fought on, pushing through the tox, swimming through the miles and miles of vast pipes that ran under the ground and under the rock, under villages and towns and cities, taking in their crap, taking in their toxicity and pumping it *somewhere else*.

Horace pushed on, only one thought in his mind now. And he realised they were lining his route, the psi-children, hundreds of them, thousands of them, products of evolved toxic waste, products of the world of Amaranth that had been abused and crushed and dumped on, a living breathing toxic *Hell,* and he had to push on, *had* to make a difference...

Had to be the Trigger.

Now his body was soaking up lirridium, it was flowing into his mouth and ears and nostrils, flowing into his lungs, his bloodstream, his lymphatic system, and he became infused with the fuel, infused with the liquid gold so important to space travel, so important to Greenstar, so important to Amaranth, so important to Manna...

And realisation hit him like a hammer.

To become the trigger, the spark, the ignition, the detonator.

He knew how it would be done.

And all around him, the psi-children began to sing... they sang a long, low, crooning song, a song of lamentation, a song of desolation, for their lost world, for their dying world, for their dead world.

THE DIRECTOR'S OFFICE was the top floor of the Greenstar Factory Hub, at the pinnacle of the central tower. It was a vast space, incredibly opulent, with thick glass carpets, marble windows and mercury furniture, which rippled gently on contact.

The lift doors hissed shut, leaving behind the squad of Greenstar military.

Silence greeted Jenny, and she looked up, looked around, absorbed her new surroundings.

Mr Candle left Jenny at the door, still with her weapons, and walked forward to a massive boardroom desk. By the wall, decorated with original paintings by some of Amaranth's most famous and unique "Toxic Painters," renowned across Manna for their work using toxic materials to create *art*, Mr Candle poured himself a drink from a crystal decanter and lifted the small glass in his huge hand. He turned and looked back at Jenny.

"Why don't you come in, Miss Xi?"

Jenny stared at him, then shifted her gaze. Several figures were seated around the mercury boardroom table. There was Renazzi Lode, the Director of The Greenstar Recycling Company. Small and powerful, she sat upright, hands clasped before her, a forced smile on her face. Jenny could tell it was a forced smile; she could smell insincerity from a thousand yards.

Jenny padded forward across the carpet and stopped, staring at the people before her. Mr Candle made introductions. "Renazzi Lode, I am sure you are aware, is our Director. She handles every facet of the company from the top down, and makes all our truly important decisions – as any thoroughbred director should." He gave a small laugh. Jenny's keen eyes moved from Renazzi Lode to the others seated around the table.

"This is the Assistant Director, Sowerby Trent." Jenny looked her up and down, the barbed-wire hair, the face like a puckered cat's arse, small and shrivelled as if worn down by decades of bowing and scraping and fighting, fighting, fighting to get to the top, top, top and beyond... but never succeeding. "She aids Renazzi Lode with some of our more complex ethical problems."

Jenny switched her gaze to a small man, small and squat and looking uncomfortable in his expensive suit, as if he really shouldn't be wearing one. He had a massive explosion of boils across his neck and the side of his head, which Jenny attributed to some kind of contact with a toxic substance, perhaps. She smiled inside at this, but not very hard.

"Aaul Thon Lupy, Chief of Recycling Management. We have a joke in The Company. We call him *The Toxic Poisoner*. Obviously, the joke being that he doesn't so much *recycle* waste, rather he poisons every single thing around him." A ripple of brittle crystal laughter went round the head of the table.

Jenny did not smile.

"Now, quickly moving around the rest of our management team, we have Helle Mic, Head of Communication Services" – Jenny stared at the slim, acerbic-looking woman, hair back in a tight ponytail, overbite sturdy enough to crack the caps off a bottle of beer; indeed, the wheels off a JCB – "this is Head of Public Relations Management, Sanne Krimez, the woman responsible for smoothing over, shall we say, some of our *biggest* social networking disasters" – he gave a little chuckle – "and lastly our Foreign Affairs

Director and keen pink leather motorbiker, Arroon Lupar, the man responsible for making sure we don't get a Halo Strike up our arse for upsetting the Shamans." He laughed again, only this time with less enthusiasm.

Jenny looked around at the group, in their neat suits and fake smiles, and they all seemed to be watching her expectantly. She was also painfully aware of the SMKK hanging slack by her hip with a pretty much full clip. One twitch, one spray of bullets, and she could wipe out the bastards who had done this to Amaranth. The fuckers who had crucified her world. But first, some answers...

"Explain it to me," said Jenny.

"Which part?" said Mr Candle.

"Start with the Impurity Movement. Why the fuck would a company intent on poisoning a world then employ its own terrorists to bomb its own factories? It doesn't make sense."

Mr Candle had moved to stand before the window, which took up the entire wall and looked out over Amaranth. He gestured for Jenny to join him, and warily she padded across the rich carpets. It was late, and the green sun hung low in the heavens, casting beautiful rays over the planet below. The scene was... stunning. And yet the beauty was marred by distant factories and towers belching smoke, scarred by the dumps and slag heaps and teetering towers of waste – all waiting to be "recycled."

"Jenny, Jenny, Jenny," he said, and placed a hand on her shoulder. She was sorely tempted to draw her combat knife and smack it through the back of his hand, but she resisted. Just.

"Don't keep saying my name, you'll wear it out," she said.

Mr Candle looked down at her. "What Old Tom used to say, right?"

Jenny stared at Candle for a long, cool time. "How could you know that?" she said, eventually.

Mr Candle grinned at her. "Don't you see the family resemblance? Of course you do, you just won't admit it to yourself. I'm your uncle, Jenny. I am Old Tom's *brother*. I am Kaylo Xi. They call me 'The Candle' because I stand alone, a solitary flame against the dark."

And it clicked into place. *Everything* clicked into place, like a videogame of falling bricks which suddenly aligned in a rush and a blink of an eye, aligned and popped and buzzed and progressed you to the next level *of understanding*. Mr Candle was Old Tom's brother. Jenny's uncle. And she remembered: distant memories, toddling around when her huge kind Uncle Canny used to come and visit, always bringing her wonderful gifts, sitting her on his lap and bouncing her. She would pull at his neat moustache and he would roar with laughter...

"No," she said.

"Yes," said Candle, eyes sparkling. "Greenstar Recycling Company is *my company*. But more, it was also Old Tom's. We had a 50/50 share. That other fifty percent – well, now that's yours. On your thirtieth birthday... which is..."

"Tomorrow," said Jenny, mouth dry, eyes watering.

"Now. To answer your previous question. Greenstar are aware, of course, that our actions are not favourable to a very large part of the Amaranth population. Fucking do-gooders always getting in the way. Well, it was your father's idea. If we began an ECO terrorist group, made them high profile in the media, give them some redundant or useless targets to destroy – then..."

"Then they'd attract every like-minded individual to their cause," said Jenny, her voice like gravel, a voice of the tomb, a voice of the dead. "You would assemble a massive army of terrorists – whom you would control.

No rogue bastards destroying Greenstar stuff, oh, no; you'd pull the strings. If there were going to be rebels, going to be terrorists, then you might as well control them, right?"

"Of course," smiled Mr Candle. "It always helps to know what the ruffians are going to do next. The power of information, my dear. Never, ever underestimate its worth. It's worth more than gold, diamonds, and even lirridium."

Jenny put her face in her hands and shook her head. She groaned. "I have been such a fool," she said.

"Nonsense, my dear! You have been doing your father's work!"

"No, no, that's not how it was. He wanted me to destroy Greenstar! He wanted me to bring it down. It was the last thing he told me before he died."

"That doesn't make sense," said Mr Candle, and there was a crack in his voice; a fracture in the crystal. He quickly recovered. "Old Tom liked his drink, did he not?" He laughed. "Yes, prone to saying some wild things on occasion. But the fact of the matter is, and we have paperwork and filmys to show you to back this all up – Old Tom *wanted* his half of the business to go to you. You would become *Ruling* Director on the Board of the Greenstar Recycling Company. You would help us grow the business, expand to take over other worlds. For as you must have noticed, Amaranth is nearing the end of its Pollutant Cycle..."

"Pollutant Cycle?"

"We can only abuse a world for so long," said Mr Candle, smiling kindly. "Every planet can only take so much before it reaches capacity. You met the psi-children, did you not? Down in the laboratory, where you planted your little HighJ devices? They emerged from the toxic pipes, killed a few of my soldiers – those naughty little children." He was laughing. "Oh, yes.

That reminds me. This so-called *Trigger* of the psi-
children is coming up the lirridium pipe network, in
the firm belief he can set the detonators on the HighJ.
The idiot. Doesn't he realise we have disarmed all the
det and ignition systems? You there, Helle. Go give the
order to have this *creature* flushed and fired from the
system..."

The small, nasty-looking woman rose to her feet.

Suddenly, Jenny lifted her SMKK and pointed it
at Helle Mic. "Don't move, bitch, or I'll blow your
fucking head off."

"What do you think you're doing?" said Mr Candle,
his voice neutral.

Helle moved, and Jenny fired five bullets, exploding
her skull. Blood rained down over the other shocked
managers, and the woman's body slapped the carpet.
An awed hush descended on the room.

"That was a *very* foolish move, child," said Mr
Candle. Now his eyes blazed with anger.

"I am no fucking *child*," snarled Jenny, "and you, all
you people, you are the fucking *enemy!*"

"How can we be the enemy?" snapped Mr Candle.
"We own you. Your terrorist outfit *belongs to us*. You
are our *employee*. And..." – his voice softened, and he
took several deep breaths – "this is not the outcome
your father wanted. Think about it, Jenny. Think hard.
Your old father, Old Tom; me and him, we built a
world of toxicity! For *you*! And now it's yours, girl, all
you have to do is *believe*, believe in me, believe in your
father, come to us, lay down the weapon! You will be
the richest woman in Manna!"

"I don't want your fucking money!" she screamed,
and the SMKK rounded on Mr Candle. Her eyes were
on fire, and lit from behind by the dying green sun, she
appeared like some demon-eyed blazing angel of death.
Calmer this time: "I don't want your money. Or your

position. Or your job. Maybe what you say about my father is true; maybe he did help build this company. This dark *Empire*. But at the end, on his deathbed, he saw what he had done. He understood. He hated Greenstar. He wanted it annihilating. And now, yes, I can do this. I SAID, DON'T FUCKING MOVE!"

Renazzi Lode had stood and was sidling towards a comm. She froze, eyes locking on Jenny and the SMKK, which had swung to point at her. Renazzi looked at Mr Candle, who gave a small hand gesture, as if to say, *sit down, I'll handle this, it'll be okay in a few moments*.

Jenny turned the SMKK back on Candle. "So, uncle. We find ourselves in a little bit of a stalemate."

"You are talking about the HighJ?" He gave a brittle laugh. "You have no method of detonating the explosives. It needs the right frequency electronic trigger. Even if this so-called messenger of the psi-children arrived, he could do nothing..."

"I believe you are wrong," said Jenny, softly. "Now, sit down. Sit down, all of you. Or I'll fill you full of bullets and spit on your graves."

"What do you propose?" said Mr Candle, stiffly. He, too, was eyeing the comm.

Jenny smiled, and moved to the high-backed Director's chair. She sat down, and surveyed the Board. "Well, Uncle. I propose that we simply sit here and wait awhile..."

HORACE SURGED THROUGH the tox, feeling the lirridium pushing into him, pushing through him, filling him up with its fire and holy purity... every muscle ached, expanded, contracted, expanded, every molecule buzzed with the raw hot energy of Horace's converting physiology... and every atom vibrated and screamed and screeched like a banshee in a tight cage clawing to be free...

The tox parted before Horace's onslaught.

And he felt the proximity...

Felt the pressure building....

This is it, thought The Dentist.

This is it.

"You won't get away with this," said Mr Candle. He was sat, body tensed, as Jenny's SMKK swept over him, past him, covering the other members of the Greenstar Board.

Jenny laughed. "Get away with it? Hell, I'm just happy to live to see the destruction of this shit-hole."

"Think about what you're doing," said Renazzi Lode. She stood up, and Jenny waved the SMKK with scowl, so she sat down again. "This is a great and honourable organisation; we turn the Manna Galaxy's waste into *lirridium starship fuel!* Without our input, the whole galaxy would grind to a halt. The Shamans will not allow you to get away with such atrocity."

"I seem to be getting away with it so far," said Jenny. She gave a tight smile.

"If you destroy this facility, hundreds more will spring up to take its place."

Jenny gave a mocking laugh. "Well, if that's the case, why are you sitting there like your pants are full of ants? No. This place is special, and you fucking know it. I don't know what you and the Shamans have been up to – *never trust a fucking machine* is my motto – but you're not doing it on my watch. Not whilst there's still breath in my twitching, bullet-riddled body."

"Think about it." Mr Candle's voice was soft. "Think about what your father created. What he built up, with me as his right hand man. This is Old Tom's dream, child. Don't you see that? And half of it is *yours*. Come, stop this nonsense, take my hand, we can do this thing together – we can make Greenstar Recycling Company truly *great!*"

"But you don't recycle," snarled Jenny, "you fucking pollute, you take the waste, remove what you need and dump the rest of the shit, and everybody on the planet suffers. The world suffers! Can't you see the destruction you've wrought? Can't you see the nightmare you've created?"

"Nightmare?" Mr Candle looked genuinely hurt. "We have created an Eden, child. We have created a world where, once we vacate, and move on to the next planet in the Chain, everybody can begin again... they will start with a fresh palette, a blank canvas on which to paint the broad strokes of a new civilisation..."

"You are dreaming," said Jenny, shaking her head. "How can you be so twisted? So fucking deviant?"

Her head snapped right. "Where is she? The bitch?"

Renazzi Lode hit her around the midriff, one hand punching Jenny in the cunt, the other slamming the SMKK skywards. Bullets screamed, tearing a new arsehole in the ceiling. Jenny gasped, staggering from the chair and back, and Renazzi followed her, her squat, powerful form pushing down and raining down punches onto Jenny's face. The blows came so fast that Jenny didn't know what hit her, and when Renazzi Lode finally stood, knuckles dripping blood, Jenny's face was unrecognisable. Her nose and one cheekbone was broken, her lips smashed, her teeth shattered.

But Jenny was laughing. Laughing through the snot and the blood.

"What's so fucking funny, *bitch?*" said the Director.

"You." Jenny's words were garbled, forced through swollen lips. "You're not human, are you? You're a fucking android... no human moves that fast. No soldier I ever met."

Mr Candle gave a great sigh, and Jenny's eyes turned on him.

"And you! You as well!"

"All of Greenstar," said Mr Candle, giving a narrow smile. "No empathy, you see? We don't care how many shitty worthless humans we abuse. Put down. *Exterminate*. You're just rancid, raw meat. Something rotten to be put out with the garbage."

Jenny and Mr Candle stared at one another for a long time. "That's why father turned against you. You didn't see it. He was human. He cared."

"No," said Mr Candle, shaking his head briefly. "He was an Anarchy Android – just like the rest of us. And you, my sweet little child, are an anomaly."

The words sank in. Jenny frowned, and leaning to one side, spat out a mouthful of blood and broken teeth.

"Androids can't have children."

"This is so."

"So if Old Tom was an android..."

"He did the impossible."

"He learned to care."

"Maybe."

"So what now?"

Mr Candle shrugged. "You had every opportunity, Jenny. Every opportunity." He made a gesture to Renazzi Lode, and turned away.

"No!" hissed Jenny, and rolled fast. Renazzi's knee landed, slamming the floor, cracking the boards. Her hand slapped out, hitting Jenny in the throat, and she scrabbled back, choking, her own hands squeezing her throat which, had she been an inch closer, would have been crushed.

Renazzi Lode stood, as Jenny shuffled backwards until her back hit the wall. Jenny rubbed at her windpipe, making choking sounds, her eyes crazy with pain, and watched Renazzi Lode approach her. The android knelt, grabbed her jacket, and picked her up, kicking and struggling, and pulled her close, and stared directly into her eyes.

"Now you die, half-breed," she said.

Her finger came back, aimed directly at Jenny's eye, and the soft mortal brain within.

Outside, just as the sun sank – and Jenny turned thirty – there came a heavy, bass *boom*.

Fire flared up, igniting the darkness.

Mr Candle stared through the tinted glass.

"No," he whispered, eyes growing wide.

"Yes," snarled Jenny through her broken face.

"It's... impossible," said Candle.

"Nothing is impossible," said Jenny.

"Kill her," he said.

HORACE FELT THE proximity of the lirridium centre, the core, the HighJ, and it all came together in the heart of his mind, the centre of his being, in a beautiful Whole. The pressure built, built, built, and it wasn't just the lirridium starship fuel – although there were many billions of gallons of it, stored in the tunnels and lakes and cities and pipes circling the cities and continents of Amaranth... it was the toxic pollutants, it was the psi-children, it was the liquidised forms of the children's souls, for they were a connection to the planet, they were part of the world, an extension of a consciousness that went beyond human comprehension. Horace felt himself *become* a part of something Huge. Something Galactic. And the Something could see the Shamans of Manna, see their machine logic and machine planning and machine focus. They were not organic. They were not human. They were not alien. They were... *machine*. And as such, they could never understand the great Cycle of Life.

Horace was an android. Created. Engineered.

He had learned the true meaning of understanding. Of empathy. Of learning. Of caring. Of love.

Are you ready? said Amaranth.

I am ready.

You are willing to die?

To set you free? Of course. I would do anything.

Thank you.

HORACE SWELLED TO the point of explosion. And ignited. And as he burned, he screamed, but it was not a scream of pain or angst, but a scream of joy. He launched into the laboratory and the shockwave of his toxic explosion pressured the HighJ into detonation... the laboratory was vaporised in the blink of an eye. But more. The entire level of the Greenstar Factory was vaporised. Then... more. The ground floors, their supporting struts and the lower fifteen subterranean levels were vaporised, then ripped upwards, taking out the rest of the factory. Fire screamed and moaned, spat and roared, and the detonation shook the entire planet and ignited the lirridium streams down, down, down through and under the River Tox. Under the land. Under the oceans. Under the mountains.

THE GREENSTAR FACTORY HUB, core of the Greenstar Recycling Company's operations in the entire Manna Galaxy Bubble, burned. Green fire roared five kilometres into the sky. A cloud of black smoke poured into a mushroom the size of the continent. More explosions were triggered along the lirridium streams as, one by one by one, the lakes and rivers detonated, ignited, screamed with bright green fire, and from a vantage point in the dark deep reaches of space, the planet of Amaranth seemed to glow – at least for a moment – as brightly as the star which gave it life.

No part of Amaranth went untouched.

From the holiday resorts of Meltflesh City, from the jungles by the Sea of Heavy Metal, from the Mercury Peaks, the Cholera Mountains and the Yellow Virus Peaks, all the way to the Lake of Corrosion, the Faeces Teeth, Strychnine Nine, the Cobalt Funmines, the city of Bilirubin, the Asbestos Forest and the Nuke Peaks... all were ravaged by fire; all consumed in a lirridium furnace; all cleansed by the purity of the intense, raging flames.

The Greenstar Factory Hub toppled, exploded, and burned, and slowly sank – sank into the pit of its own devising, sank down, down, down into the soil and mud and rock of Amaranth, which reclaimed the deviation, reclaimed the aberration as a lost child of its own; welcomed, back into a bosom of slaughter and murder and desolation, the Greenstar Factory Hub, which sank for an eternity beneath the Land.

Down.

To where Amaranth waited patiently.

The inferno raged for a thousand days.

And when it was done, it was done.

EPILOGUE

"WE'RE GOING TO die!" screamed Svoolzard Koolimax XXIV, Third Earl of Apobos, Genius, Sexual Athlete, Bon Viveur, and now *bona fide Action Hero*. The chopper whined, powering high above the raging inferno that spread across the vast tectonic plates of Amaranth.

Explosions roared. The air was filled with gas and toxins *more dangerous* than the gas and toxins that plagued the surface. Thick black mushroom clouds filled the skies. Explosions rioted across the globe. Below, the landscape was a tormented, writhing inferno. Below, Amaranth had descended into Chaos and *Hell*...

Lumar leaned close, and with gritted teeth, said, "Look at it this way. Better up here than on the ground, mate."

Svool nodded dumbly. Down there were the camera crew. Or what remained of them. They hadn't seen the wall of fire coming. Svool and Lumar had, and screamed and ran for it, leaping aboard the spinning, whining, accelerating chopper which had leapt into the air, avoiding the hundred-foot wall of charging green fire by scant inches. Everything down there had been vaporised.

"Still. We can look on the bright side now," said Lumar, wearily.

"Which was?"

"The broadcast went out. To the whole of Manna. They saw what Greenstar had done. They heard your poem on the eco-horrors of this abused, tortured and massacred world."

There was a long pause, against a backdrop of hammering rotors and further, distant explosions. Outside, night had turned into day.

The pilot leaned back. "We have a base over the mountains to the east, just outside Pukebelly City. Underground bunkers, that sort of thing. Lots of military hardware. It's the safest place I can think of. They'll probably send a Shuttle for you. Probably." He didn't sound very convinced, or convincing.

Svool shuffled close to Lumar, on the bench in the back of the chopper. She looked at him. He looked at her. Slowly, he put his arm around her shoulder. She carried on looking at him.

"Can I ask you something?"

"Sure."

"My poem."

"Which one?"

"This one. The new one. The eco one. The eco one that's just gone out to the whole of Manna; indeed, no doubt, the whole of the Quad-Galaxy, by the time the news and the filmys get hold of the footage."

"You want the honest truth?"

"Yes."

"It was crap."

"Oh."

"In a nice way."

"Oh."

"You got the message across. Suitably aided and abetted by the Greenstar Factory blowing up in the background during the final stanza. That was quite an amazing feat of timing. Incredible."

"Well." Svool puffed out his chest. "I... thank you for your honesty."

"My pleasure."

"And I want to ask you something."

"Go on, Svoolzard." She tilted her head. He loved it when she did that.

"Will you marry me?"

Lumar turned and stared out at the raging fires below. More military choppers had joined them, perhaps twenty in all, and their squadron, carrying dirt- and smoke-smeared refugees, thumped through the poisonous, toxic skies of a burning Amaranth.

"Yes," she said, turning back. "On one condition."

"Anything!"

"We get married... here."

"*Here?*" choked Svool.

"Yes. They're going to need a lot of help. Rebuilding. Purifying. Detoxifying."

"And you..." he shuddered as he considered the implications, "you want us to become aid workers?"

"Yes. For the Greater Good. And all that."

"For the Greater Good," echoed Svool, through gritted teeth.

"You could write a poem about it."

"No."

"Why not?"

"I'm done with poetry."

"Really?" Her voice was just a little *too* bright.

"Yes. I think I'll... yes. I'll write a *novel* about our experiences here, instead!"

Lumar fixed him with a steady stare. Then she smiled, and took his hand, squeezing it gently. "Do you think anybody would believe you?"

Svool shrugged. "It no longer matters. We did our

part in bringing down the Greenstar Corporation. And looking at that inferno, I'll be amazed if anybody survived. Amazed beyond comprehension!"

"Yeah. Well." Lumar turned away again, gazing out into the smoke and the chaos. "Sometimes, you'd be surprised what a cockroach can survive."

"I have some good news!" shouted the pilot, turning back to them again. "You have some friends. Some survivors! They made it back to Base Camp. They're waiting for you there."

"Friends?" said Svool, frowning.

"Yes. A... a Mr Zoot, a Miss Angelina, and a... a Mr Herbert. Does that mean anything to you?"

"Aww, shit," groaned Svool.

And Lumar's pretty laughter pealed out across the raging, toxic fire.

NEWS ITEM KX33657824# 65678ggg

It was a moving and eloquent speech and poetry recital by the missing, and now presumed dead, Master Poet Svoolzard Koolimax XXIV, Third Earl of Apobos. Against a backdrop of chaos and fire and mayhem, Svoolzard told us of the world of Amaranth – commonly known as *Toxicity* throughout Manna – a world used, abused and polluted by the Greenstar Recycling Company in their quest for accelerated wealth. It is indeed a beautiful planet, destroyed by greed and lust and power. Svoolzard, who was recently married to Lumar L'anarr of the alien *kroona* species, despite death threats, had vowed to stop Greenstar continuing trade after what the *still operating* recycling giant has called "an industrial accident on a planetary scale." Lumar L'anarr's Bride of Honour was her sister, Dajenga L'anarr, who wore a quite fetching outfit of green silk and lace, and carried a bouquet of tanga tanga greena flowers...

*   *   *

MR CANDLE TURNED to Renazzi Lode. His face was carved from granite, and his eyes were dark and unreadable. His face was a terrible mask, still bearing the irreparable burn scars from the genetic milk tank in which he'd spent the best part of the last three months.

Outside, fusion motors hummed, and the orbital shifted slightly, keeping in line with the remains of the Greenstar Factory Hub far, far below on the planet of Amaranth. The aircon hissed. After the fire, Mr Candle liked it cool. They *all* liked it cool.

"Report?"

"80% of all surplus lirridium stock destroyed. All factories destroyed. The share prices plummeted, obviously, but we had various canny brokers who almost seemed to sense the crash coming and sold billions of shares. When we cash in the surviving lirridium supplies, we will still have massive cash reserves. And the Manna Core Bank has guaranteed us a practically unlimited line of credit. After all" – she smiled – "we were their best ever customer."

"Good. Sowerby? Give me some good news. Tell me you've found a suitable destination where we can put in a successful bid. I am sick of wasting time. I am ready for the launch. *Greenstar II Recycling Company! Recycling Your Crap into the Starship Fuel of the Future! LirridiumII: A New Fuel for a New Space Age!*" He gave a long, low chuckle.

Sowerby Trent nodded, barbed wire hair bobbing. "My team have located a suitably disused and already 50% toxic world. It has a breathable atmosphere – just – but I am sure we can get it at a fair price."

"Good. Are there inhabitants?"

"Just a few hundred billion, but we'll offer them the usual relocation packages. And if they don't vacate?"

Her eyes went hard. "Well. Fuck 'em. We'll do what we always do. You know we always win."

"Any other foreseeable problems?"

"Just one. This planet has great historical context. Apparently, it is, and I quote from the History Guild: '*The Cradle of Humanity*.'"

Mr Candle started laughing. "You mean the *Earth?*"

Sowerby Trent nodded. "Can you think of a better world to shit on?"

"No," said Mr Candle, lighting a fresh cigarette. "No, I suppose I cannot."

THE END

ACKNOWLEDGEMENTS

This novel was a joy to write, mainly because the characters had their own minds and did their own thing (well, *I* certainly had nothing to do with their awkwardness and obstinacy! Damn... don't railgun me, I'm just the messenger!).

Still, every author writes by abusing the goodwill of those around him, either by demanding endless cups of coffee and sandwiches at their keyboard, being distant and vacant whilst being addressed regarding *very* important issues ("yes my love, I totally agree, the pink and magenta curtains *would* look fabularse in the lounge"), or basically by presenting that consistent obdurate front that their work *must always come first*. And thus I feel it would be most rude not to thank those who receive the brunt of my weird working ways: thank you to Sonia, Joseph and Oliver, for putting up with me. Hot damn! I suppose somebody has to!

ABOUT THE AUTHOR

ANDY REMIC is a larger-than-life action man, sexual athlete, chainsaw warrior and chef. He has written a variety of SF, thriller and fantasy novels, and sometimes delves into the murky underworld of teaching. When kicked to describe himself, Remic claims to have a love of extreme sports, kickass bikes and happy nurses, and is a cross between an alcoholic Indiana Jones and a bubbly Lara Croft, only without the breasts (although he'd probably like some). Remic lives in Lincolnshire, is married with two raggle-taggle little boys, and enjoys listening to Ronan Keating whilst thinking lewdly about zombies.

Find out more about Andy Remic at www.andyremic. com.